GOD'S LIONS

GOD'S LIONS

THE SECRET CHAPEL

John Lyman

ISBN: 1463738439
ISBN-13: 9781463738433

Quote from "Bible Code Bombshell" by R. Edwin Sherman with Nathan Jacobi, PH.D, and Dave Swaney, second printing: May 2006, page 74. Used with the permission of the publisher – New Leaf Press, Green Forest, AR; Copyright 2005 by R. Edwin Sherman.

Cover art by Travis Schmidt

For Leigh Jane … who illuminated my path.

"What we are talking about here is nothing short of a proof of the miraculous that directly challenges the wisdom of our scientific age, a 'wisdom' that denies all miracles."

From "Bible Code Bombshell"
By R. Edwin Sherman
With Nathan Jocobi, PH.D, and Dave Swaney

"After exhaustive analysis, I have reached the conclusion that the only information that can be derived from the codes discovered in Genesis is that they exist, and the probability that they are mere coincidences is vanishingly small."

Harold Gans, June 3, 1997
Senior Cryptologic Mathematician
U.S. Department of Defense, Retired

"Thou Daniel, seal up these prophecies and shut up the words of this book, until the time of the end, when travel and knowledge have greatly increased."

Book of Daniel 12:4

FACT

In mathematical research, a "p-value" of one in twenty usually indicates that something is "true". In 1989, a senior cryptologic mathematician with the Department of Defense—working in the offices of the National Security Agency—made a startling discovery. He was awaiting word from his wife on the solution to a nineteen-day-long calculation running on his home computer. As a skeptic, he had set out to disprove the claim that a team of Israeli scientists had found a code in the Torah—a code that would prove to the world that the Bible was divinely inspired by God. When his wife called, he was astonished to hear that the "p-value" was one in sixty-two-thousand five hundred, meaning that there was a 99.998 percent certainty that the code was real. Mathematicians around the world have yet to disprove this finding.

PROLOGUE

ISRAEL—THE NEGEV DESERT
MAY 15, 1948

On the last day of their lives, the British troops were breaking camp. For the past year, the soldiers had been living in an isolated region of the desert—one that appeared devoid of any visible life, making the men's daily patrols seem pointless. Their only contact with the outside world had been the monthly visits from the army supply trucks and a few brief encounters with the Bedouin tribes who passed through the area.

Faced with the prospect of fighting and dying in a land far from home, the time spent in monotonous anticipation of combat that never came had taken its toll on the weary band of men who had been consigned to a bleak existence for way too long. On this day, however, the somber mood in camp had changed. The men were celebrating the news that their tour of duty was finally coming to an end, and that soon, they would all be home with their families in England.

High overhead, the relentless thermal presence of the midmorning sun reflected off the desert sand, creating a shimmering effect over the heated landscape as a tall, thin sergeant drove his open jeep through the camp. Peering through the dusty orange haze, he spotted a group of tanned soldiers loading the last of their equipment into a line of waiting trucks. He pulled up beside them and stopped.

"Let's keep moving, lads. The captain wants us out of here before noon."

A shirtless private grabbed an empty water container and turned toward the jeep with a grin. "Not to worry, Sergeant. Every minute we spend here is one minute less we'll have at the bar tonight."

They all laughed as the sergeant threw the jeep into gear and headed for the last tent that remained standing. His blue eyes gazed out across the desert at the blurred images of desolate gray mountains and saffron colored cliffs surrounding their position. He smiled to himself with the knowledge that, after today, these images would be nothing more than a distant memory.

Sliding to a stop in a cloud of dust, the sergeant jumped from the jeep and ducked into the captain's tent. In the relative darkness, he saw the young, blond captain sitting quietly on a folding wooden chair, his once-cheerful face masked by a look of quiet resolution. He was holding a letter from his wife, a letter that he had read at least twice a day for the past month. Enclosed with the letter was a picture of a dark-haired young woman holding an infant—a girl barely six months old. The child had never laid eyes on her father, but that would change, the captain had promised himself, as soon as they were out of this hellish place.

"What time is it, Sergeant?"

"It's almost ten o'clock, sir. We're ready to move out."

"Just throw everything in the back of my jeep. I'd like to be out of here before the sun gets any higher."

Reaching into the pocket of his faded khaki shorts, the sergeant produced a handkerchief and ran it over his forehead and through his hair. "Yes, sir, most of our gear is already loaded in the trucks. This is the last tent standing. These Arabs can have this bloody desert. I never want to see sand again unless it's at the beach."

A rare smile brightened the captain's features as he tenderly folded the letter and placed it in the pocket of his sweat-stained shirt. "I have to admit, lying on the sand under the sun doesn't have quite the appeal it used to."

Flicking a small brown scorpion from his boot, the sergeant motioned for two privates standing outside the tent to enter. The soldiers moved quickly, and within minutes, the captain's home for the past twelve months was nothing more than a rumpled mound of canvas lying on the sand.

The soldiers tossed it into the back of one of the large sand-colored military trucks, while a British flag flying from a makeshift pole was lowered for the last time, becoming the final thing to be packed away before the convoy set out for Jerusalem.

Climbing into the passenger side of the lead jeep, the captain turned to make a final visual inspection of the deserted campsite. The men had done a good job. It appeared as though no one had ever been there. *No one ever should have been.* He glanced over his shoulder at the line of vehicles behind him and motioned for the column of trucks and jeeps to begin their final patrol out of the desert.

Straining motors and grinding gears echoed off of the encircling mountains as the sergeant squinted ahead from under the brow of his cap and worked the steering wheel to avoid the occasional large rock or deep rut that lay in their path. Puzzled by the absence of wildlife, the captain adjusted his sunglasses and gazed out over the barren landscape. "Tonight I'll be having a scotch on the rocks in the bar at the King David Hotel in Jerusalem."

"That sounds like a bit of heaven, sir. Some of the men will be downtown hoisting a pint or two themselves this evening. Have you heard anything from headquarters?"

"About what, Sergeant?"

"Did they say when our ship would be leaving for England, sir?"

"I imagine that will be in a few days from now, after the government formally announces our intention to pull out of Palestine. I was saving it as a surprise, but you and the men have earned a well-deserved leave. Headquarters is rewarding all of you with some long overdue rest on the coast in Haifa before we board the ship for home."

"A dip in the Mediterranean sounds mighty good right now. You could use a nice cool swim yourself, Captain."

"I plan to."

"Any ideas about what will happen to this country after we leave, sir?"

"Unfortunately, I'm afraid the Jews and Arabs will have a go at each other like cats and dogs after we're gone. Britain is through policing these people, and I for one am glad."

"Yes, sir. No more patrols out in the desert with the sun boiling our brains and nothing green to look at."

"At least the patrols at night were cooler. My only regret is that we never found the source of that odd red glow out there by the canyon ... or that awful howling that came from the same area. Every time one of our patrols got close to that light, it just faded away. I thought it was interesting, but the look on the general's face when I mentioned it made it obvious my discussion on the subject would be a bad career move."

"Kind of like looking for a pot of gold at the end of a rainbow, eh, Captain?"

"We never found a single track in the area, human or animal. It's a real mystery. The blokes at headquarters even flew a bomber over the area and took pictures. Nothing. Not a bloody thing on the film. All of the pictures came out as black as night when they were developed. I stopped logging it in my daily reports before they started to think we'd all gone loony out here."

As the jeep rumbled across the hard-packed sand, the men watched the wavering mirages rising from the heated ground in the distance. Looking ahead, the sergeant thought he saw something appear on the horizon, then disappear just as quickly. He continued to stare over the steering wheel until a blurred image reappeared and stabilized into a definite shape. "Well, would you look at that, sir?"

The captain cupped his hands over his sunglasses and peered through the dusty windshield. Alone in the flat expanse before them, an old woman was standing directly in the path of the convoy. She was covered from head to toe in black, the only opening a thin slit at the level of her eyes.

"There's no one around here for fifty miles. What the bloody hell is she doing way out here all alone?"

"Must be one of them Bedouins, sir. Maybe she's lost or hurt."

"She's not lost, Sergeant. These people know this desert better than you know your own living room back home. Pull over so we can give her a look ... and give the medic a shout on the radio just in case."

The jeep stopped twenty feet away from the solitary figure—a lone sentinel standing in the middle of the desert with no one else in sight. Except for the crackle of the radios in the trucks, the eerie silence of the scene was unnerving. The two men exchanged glances and paused to look back over their shoulders at the line of trucks behind them before walking slowly toward what was obviously a lone Bedouin woman.

"Say there, Miss," the sergeant called out.

Nothing. The figure remained silent.

"I say, Miss … are you alright?"

Nothing. Even with the slight breeze, the long robes hung motionless. The captain and sergeant traded looks once again just as a faint whiff of rotting flesh passed through their nostrils, prompting the two men to stop as the hair on the back of their necks stood straight out.

The captain held his hand over his face. "What's that smell?"

"It smells like something *dead*, sir!" The sergeant's pulse was beginning to rise.

The men took a few hesitant steps toward the woman, getting to within a few feet of her, when suddenly they stopped and began to back away, almost stumbling over each other in their haste to retreat.

The thing seemed to flicker for a moment.

"What the hell is that?" the sergeant shouted.

The figure began to change shape. It wavered like a broken hologram, dimming and then becoming brighter. Inside the slit in the black robes, where the men should have seen a pair of human eyes staring back at them, only a dull red glow burned within. The two men turned and began running toward the jeep, frantically waving at the troops to get back into their trucks.

Terror replaced the look of confidence on the face of the captain. "The eyes … it's just … there's just red light coming out of them!"

The two men reached the perceived safety of their jeep just as a strong wind began to blow over the convoy. High overhead, dark tornado-like clouds were forming—blotting out the sun and turning day into night. An unearthly scream, like the garbled howl of a primeval beast from another dimension, shot from within the black-robed creature standing frozen before them.

Behind the figure, an endless swarm of strange and hideous-looking red insects materialized from the base of the dark clouds and headed for the men. The soldiers looked on in horror before diving to the ground clutching their rifles in their hands. They lay there with their faces inches from the dirt, breathing in the dust of the parched soil. They had trained and equipped themselves to do combat with other men, but nothing had prepared them for this.

The tiny winged creatures drew closer and circled the trucks in a solid mass before spreading out and tearing through the troops, shredding their clothing and going for their exposed flesh. The insects seemed particularly interested in the eyes of the men, blinding the soldiers who were now screaming in agony, blood running from hundreds of bites on their bodies.

Firing their weapons aimlessly into the air and out into the desert, the men inadvertently struck many of their own in the ensuing panic, but their weapons were useless. The repulsive insects practically devoured the outer layer of their skin before flying away as suddenly as they had appeared.

The menacing black clouds continued to descend until they reached ground level and blanketed the entire convoy, while a demonic wind began to rage, gaining strength and swirling in a circular motion as it blew sand into the men's now sightless eyes. The smell of sulfur infused the air before a searing heat blasted from out of nowhere, building in intensity until everything was ablaze, as if the sun had touched the earth at that very spot. Fire roared about the soldiers in the last moments of their earthly lives before their blackened bodies fell to the ground. Then silence.

Order began to replace chaos. The black clouds and swirling wind vanished, along with the black-robed figure that had stood in the path of the approaching convoy. Shining from above, the sun now revealed the newly scorched landscape. The only sound that could be heard, if someone had been alive to hear it, was the crackle of the flames as they slowly burned themselves out within the hulks of the vehicles and the bodies of the men. The acrid smell of sulfur slowly evaporated into the atmosphere, and thick, black smoke from the burning tires rose high above the grisly sight, the only sign to the rest of the world of what had just occurred in the middle of a barren desert far from prying eyes.

On the smoldering ground, the young captain's body was curled next to the burning jeep. A few feet away, beyond the reach of his outstretched, blackened hand, lay a singed picture of a young mother holding a baby girl. The hot desert wind began to blow ever so slightly again, stirring the landscape and slowly covering the picture in the sand, where it would remain for years to come.

CHAPTER 1

PRESENT DAY

The taxi swerved into a space between two others in front of the international terminal at New York's JFK Airport. A tall, dark-suited figure emerged and hurried into the building, clutching a small carry-on bag and brown leather briefcase. Embossed in gold on the briefcase were the words "Leopold Amodeo, S.J." To the casual passerby who noticed the Roman collar, he was just another Catholic priest one sees in all busy international airports. To the initiated who noted the letters S.J. after his name, he was a Jesuit, a member of the Society of Jesus. In times past, they were known as the soldiers of the church, a genus of sanctified commandos.

Hearing the last call for his flight to Rome, he jogged up a curved ramp that led to the departure gates. Darkness enveloped the windows outside the empty waiting area as he noticed the solo gate agent glance up at him from behind a small counter at the entrance to the Jetway. "You'd better hurry, Father. They're getting ready to close the cabin door."

The priest quickened his pace. "Thank you. I've got to make this flight."

The agent grabbed the boarding pass and watched as the priest ran down the worn blue carpet of the Jetway. "Have a nice trip. It's beautiful this time of year in Rome."

The priest waved over his head without looking back before stepping into the plane and brushing past a young flight attendant who was already swinging the heavy aircraft door shut. "You just made it, Father." She glanced at his ticket and motioned him toward the front of the big jet.

The Alitalia 747 smelled strongly of coffee and jet fuel as a senior member of the flight crew caught his attention and ushered the breathless priest forward. He surveyed the plush surroundings. "Are you sure this is where I'm supposed to sit?"

"Yes, Father. You have a first-class ticket. Can I help you with your bags?"

"No … thank you. I can manage." He sighed as he double-checked the seat number on the ticket and hefted the small carry-on bag into the overhead compartment. Clasping his worn leather briefcase tightly in one hand, he slid across the empty aisle seat into the one next to the window.

The plane appeared half empty as he looked around the cabin at all the well-dressed people seated nearby, engrossed in their books and cell phone conversations. It seemed to him that fewer people were flying to Europe now since the global economy had taken a nosedive.

Through his window, he watched the baggage handlers below in the glare of the terminal lights, wiping the sweat from their brows while tossing an endless parade of bags onto a moving conveyer belt. He felt self-conscious sitting in this section of the aircraft and was mystified at why the Vatican had paid for the extravagant luxury of a first-class ticket.

"Can I get you anything?" the flight attendant asked in fluent Italian, testing his knowledge of the language.

"Yes, a small glass of wine. Red please," he replied, also in fluent Italian.

She smiled back at him. "I'll bring it to you as soon as we're in the air." She turned and walked back down the aisle, stirring memories within the priest of a time before he had become one.

Settling into the cushioned leather, he fastened his seatbelt and listened to the engines begin to whine, one after another, until the quiet pulse of power had transformed the aircraft into a living thing.

For the past twenty years, Father Leopold, or Father Leo as he was affectionately known to his friends and students, had been a professor of history at Boston College. He had arrived in New York the week before to give a series of lectures at Columbia University on ancient Christian doctrine and its effect on modern life. Seven hours earlier, the priest had returned to his hotel to find a bored-looking courier standing outside his room holding a sealed folder along with an airline ticket and a letter from the Vatican ordering him to Rome.

The sudden urgent request for him to leave New York on the midnight flight had caught the priest by surprise. Along with the letter, the courier had also handed Father Leo a puzzling note telling him not to open the folder until he was on the plane. Exhausted from a long day at the university, Leo had been left with little time to collect his thoughts or wonder about the contents of the folder before catching a few hours sleep and rushing to the airport.

The takeoff was quick and uneventful, and soon he had his glass of wine before him. He adjusted his reading glasses and opened the well-worn brief-case, removing a burgundy-colored folder with a dark red ribbon tied around it. His eyes scarcely blinked as he untied the ribbon and began to read the document inside.

Although this was obviously an official Vatican document dispatched from the office of the pope, Leo recognized the name of the author. His name was Anthony Morelli, a fellow theologian and long-time friend. Leo had known this priest since they first met in Jesuit seminary thirty years earlier. In addition to being a Jesuit priest, Father Morelli was also a well-known and respected church archaeologist who lived and worked in Vatican City. He was one of those veridical scholars who were always researching something, haunting the Vatican archives in an effort to uncover some small and seemingly insignificant piece of information that would lead him to his next archaeological discovery.

Morelli had spent most of his career exploring archaeological sites around the world, especially the ancient tunnels and Christian ruins under the Vatican. The emotion Father Morelli experienced while down in the consecrated world beneath the Basilica was mystical. He had once told Leo that he sensed he was in the presence of a divine being when he was digging in the sacred earth beneath the church.

The two priests had spent many a late night together in the small cafes of Rome, locked in a wine-induced debate about the value of their individual research and the historical relevance it had in today's world. Leo remembered that the last time the two had talked, Morelli had just returned from Jerusalem where he had been collaborating with a multi-disciplinary team of researchers on a project he felt would offer the world proof that the Old Testament was divinely inspired.

Father Leo was something of a scholar himself. A renowned and much sought-after church historian, he relished studying the past but disliked archaeological field work. "I don't share your enthusiasm for digging up old pottery shards," he had once told Father Morelli, indicating his preference for researching ancient manuscripts in an effort to bring church history into the light of the twenty-first century. He loved presenting his students with tangible written evidence of the times he so dearly wanted to demystify. Three decades earlier, before he had become a history professor, he had spent nearly five years at the Vatican, working on his doctoral thesis about early Christian sects, specifically, how they came together to form the Catholic Church.

Father Leo continued to read as the airliner reached its assigned cruising altitude and adopted the distant muted roar that would envelop the cabin for the duration of the trip across the Atlantic. The flight attendants had barely begun to pass out snacks when the jet entered a line of dark clouds, blotting out the bright stars shining from above. Within seconds, everyone felt the first in a series of bumps as the aircraft began to shake in the sudden turbulence.

In the darkened interior of the plane, Leo reached up and focused the beam from his overhead light onto the folder. His eyes narrowed at the papers in his hands as the turbulence outside increased and the "fasten seatbelt" signs blinked on throughout the cabin. As the shaking became more violent, the flight attendants groped for their seats and tried to reassure the passengers who were caught up in the wave of fear that grew with each new shudder and thump created by the push of dark air rising outside their windows.

Under the glare of the tiny light above his head, the priest's eyes grew wide and he let the burgundy file drop into his lap. He stared straight ahead while the color drained from his face and a bead of sweat trickled from his hairline.

Anyone watching would have interpreted his reaction to be in tune with the fear those around him were experiencing, but in truth, Father Leo had barely noticed the turbulence enveloping the aircraft. He was reacting to what he had just read on the last page of the file.

As quickly as it appeared, the turbulence vanished, and soon the flight attendants were up passing through the cabin and offering drinks to their shaken passengers.

Gazing out through the window at the darkness covering the ocean below, the priest's thoughts were interrupted by the voice of the flight attendant standing in the aisle. "Can I get you another glass of wine, Father?"

"I'm sorry. Did you say something, Miss?"

"I asked if you would like another glass of wine."

"Yes, please ... make it a large glass."

A quizzical expression crossed her face as she looked down at the official-looking burgundy folder and the papers lying in his lap. "That paperwork looks serious. What are you reading about?"

Removing his glasses, the priest looked up at her with kind eyes and managed a weak smile. "Oh, just the usual end-of-the-world kind of thing."

She laughed and turned to fetch his wine. *If only she knew he wasn't joking.*

CHAPTER 2

Father Morelli was late. He knew that his good friend, if his flight had arrived on time, had already been on the ground for twenty minutes, but even Moses could not part the sea of Italian traffic in Rome at this hour. For the past seven months, Morelli had been absorbed in a new project, and time had become abstract, as it sometimes does to scholars who think of little else but their research. The priest's latest obsession was not something to be stored in a warehouse, waiting to be cataloged and placed in a museum.

Swerving to avoid one of the ever-present motor scooters, Father Morelli brought his car to an abrupt stop in front of the Alitalia Airlines baggage-claim area just in time to glimpse Leo emerging from the terminal. He knew his friend was not expecting him.

"Leo, over here."

Leo turned to see Morelli jump from the car. "Anthony! What …?"

Morelli grinned as he grabbed Leo's bag and threw it into the trunk. "I knew you were coming, so I decided to spare you a ride into town on the train."

"Why am I so surprised? You always seem to know who's coming and going at the Vatican." Leo stopped to admire the bright red sports car with the top down. "Driving a new BMW now, eh, Anthony?"

"It's a small luxury to make up for my years of celibacy, Leo. The way I look at it, this car is helping the Lord to keep me from breaking my vows. A man must have a little excitement in this mortal life."

"I doubt the Lord needs any help from BMW to keep you from breaking any vows during your priestly midlife crisis. Not to mention the red color, Father, a color no doubt the cardinals would appreciate."

"Can't you let an old friend indulge himself just a little?" Morelli said, adopting a mock look of despair.

"Well, since I just flew first-class, I guess I can't fault you for the car. I don't see why the Vatican spent so much money on my ticket when I would have arrived at the same time flying coach. How did you know I was coming to Rome?"

"I'm the one who sent for you."

Leo stopped on the sidewalk and faced his friend. The content of the file he had just read on the plane was still weighing heavily on his mind. "But I ... I received an urgent papal summons ordering me to report immediately to the Vatican. The documents contained material written by you, but they were in a sealed communication from the pope."

"And did the communiqué also specifically advise you not to open the folder until you were on the plane and in the air?"

"Yes, but how did you ...?"

"As I said, dear friend, I sent it. I knew I had to utilize the power of the Holy Father himself to get you here. I was afraid that, if you read my paper before you boarded the plane, it would arouse your curiosity, to say the least. I couldn't risk having you call the Vatican."

"I guess that explains the first-class ticket. What in God's name is going on, Anthony?"

"We'll talk more this evening, Leo. You must have patience, my friend. This is a homecoming worthy of fine Italian food and wine."

Looking beyond the terminal at the darkening clouds of the late-April sky, Father Morelli noticed the misty signature of a spring rainstorm in the distance and began raising the top on the car.

"Looks like a storm coming," Leo said.

Morelli winked. "Yes, indeed, Father. There is a storm coming."

They squeezed into the small car parked behind an idling tour bus spewing diesel fumes into the air. Safe for now from the approaching storm, Morelli threw the sports car into gear, and the two priests sped off into the late-afternoon Roman traffic.

CHAPTER 3

Morelli stopped the car in front of the steps to the hotel. "I'll call before I pick you up for dinner, Leo. Tell Arnolfo I said hello."

"I'll give him your regards," Leo swung his legs out of the low sports car and retrieved his suitcase from the trunk before walking around to the driver's side of the vehicle. "Take your time, Anthony. I need a little time to rest up from my trip."

Morelli looked up at Leo and frowned. "You can rest later, after dinner. Tonight we celebrate your return to Rome. You have a lot to absorb over the next few days. We'll go to *Civitas* and drink their marvelous *Brunello*."

Leo heaved a sigh of resignation and watched the car speed off toward the main gate of the Vatican. He turned and mounted the ornate stairway to the hotel just as the warm, moisture-laden skies finally succumbed and a light rain began to fall.

The Hotel Amalfi was only steps away from the walls of Vatican City on the Via Germanico. Located in a nineteenth-century building, the intimate hotel had been tastefully remodeled since his last visit. Arnolfo Bignoti spotted Leo through the tall etched-glass panels of the dark wooden Victorian doors as he topped the stairs and entered the lobby. "Father Amodeo! *Buon giorno!*" The small-framed man rushed from behind the front desk to embrace Leo. "*Come sta*? How are you?"

Leo returned the embrace. "*Molto bene,* Arnolfo. How is your family?"

"Fine, fine, Father. How long will you be staying with us this time?"

"Probably just a few days. Is my usual room available?"

"Of course. Father Morelli called ahead. Give me your suitcase. Go right up and take a nice hot shower and get some rest. Here's the key."

"Thank you, Arnolfo. It's been a long day, and I still have to go out to dinner with Father Morelli."

"I am so happy to see you, Father Leo. It has been such a long time."

"Yes, too long, my friend, too long."

"You must come and have dinner with my family while you are here. We have much to tell you."

Because of the hotel's proximity to the Vatican, Arnolfo was a great source of local gossip and delighted in telling Leo funny and lurid stories during his stays.

Leo gave him a sly wink. "I'm looking forward to it." Carrying the well-worn briefcase, he crossed the lobby and took the ancient wrought iron elevator to the third floor. The priest walked down the familiar red-carpeted hallway and used a large brass key to enter his room. He knew that, within minutes of his arrival, a bottle of red Tuscan wine would appear mysteriously outside the door. It was a tradition begun by Arnolfo when a young Father Leo began staying at the hotel in the seventies.

Leo loved the Amalfi. It was the only hotel he stayed at when visiting Rome. Run by the Bignoti family since 1939, Arnolfo and his wife had been the sole owners since his parents had passed away a decade earlier. The rooms were painted a pale yellow with blue and white carpeting. Below the high ceilings lined with ornate crown molding were tall, white-shuttered windows framed by thin white draperies. There was a large mahogany-colored armoire facing a king-sized bed, and the bathrooms, Leo noted, had been redone in a beautiful green marble, a luxurious touch for such a small boutique hotel. He heard the clink of glass outside his door and quickly opened it to find a silver tray on the floor of the hallway, holding the Tuscan wine and two glasses. No one was in sight.

Leo poured a small glass and walked out onto the covered balcony. It was late afternoon, and the rain continued to fall while the sky turned golden over the Eternal City. Across the way was the Vatican, a country unto itself. The towering dome of Saint Peter's Basilica, the largest church in the world, marked it as the very epicenter of power for the Catholic Church. Leo always smiled when he heard people refer to the church as a cathedral, for contrary to popular belief, Saint Peter's is not a cathedral, as it is not the seat of a bishop. Instead, it is a papal basilica. The Basilica of Saint John Lateran is the cathedral church of Rome.

Caught up in the majesty of the setting, Leo slowly began to feel his body relax. He had been coming here for the past thirty years, yet he never failed to be completely awed by the beauty of this special place. He watched the pedestrians hurry by on the street below and wondered if they had become immune to the ancient grandeur and baroque art that surrounded them.

Father Leo looked anything but a priest. An amateur boxer in high school, his scarred left eyelid and blunted nose gave him the appearance of a longshoreman after too many alcohol-fueled, rowdy Saturday nights. Raised in a large Catholic family with five brothers and two sisters, Leo had worked in the coal mines of Pennsylvania with his father and uncles before being accepted to Georgetown University. He was tall, six feet two inches, and at the age of fifty-eight, he still retained a muscular build and a full head of dark, gray-streaked hair worn long over the ears and in the back. In spite of his jagged looks, the fire behind the green eyes divulged the quick mind and academic enlightenment he had attained through years of study and teaching.

The phone rang on the bedside table. "Leo, are you ready?" It was the voice of Father Morelli.

"Give me an hour, Anthony."

"OK, my friend, but no longer. I'm starving." Leo hung up and smiled as he thought of his free-spirited friend speeding around Rome in his new sports car. He could afford it, of course. The man had a knack for the stock market, and although it was rumored that Father Morelli had accumulated a small fortune, Leo knew that most of his money went to charity. In addition to the BMW, the priest owned a beautiful seventeenth-century country estate south of Rome, where he planned to retire someday and save the church the expense of supporting him in his old age.

As the head of the Vatican's department of archaeology, Morelli spent the majority of his time on official church business, so despite the fact that he owned a large house in the country, his main residence was a spartan apartment inside Vatican City. Since all priests within the Jesuit clan took vows of poverty, a Jesuit who drove an expensive car and possessed a magnificent house might have been looked upon with disapproving eyes, but since Morelli was also a source of so much money for the Church, these two luxuries were overlooked.

The product of an Italian American father and an Irish-born mother from the Bronx, most people thought Morelli looked more Irish than Italian. Dark red hair framed his brown eyes and ruddy cheeks, and a slight paunch gave substance to his medium frame. Leo was always amused by the surprised looks on the local's faces when the Anglo-looking priest spoke Italian.

Leo showered and changed into a light-blue polo shirt and gray slacks. They would be going to a favorite restaurant this evening, catching up on old news and probably drinking a little too much. He didn't want to wear "the uniform."

Even though the wine and beauty of Rome had softened his mood, he felt a vague twinge of apprehension. The contents of Father Morelli's file continued to fill his mind with disturbing images. *Why did this information, as frightening and controversial as it was, need to be kept from official prying eyes?* The priest looked down on the street below as Father Anthony's bright red car pulled up to the hotel entrance. Leo would have his answers tonight. No more stalling from the good Father Morelli.

* * *

It was still drizzling outside when Leo bounded down the steps of the hotel and squeezed into the passenger seat. "Why didn't you buy the large sedan?"

"Not as much fun. Anyway, I'm usually by myself, and this car is perfect for those narrow, twisting roads when I drive to my house in the country." Father Morelli stepped on the gas and spun the tires as he left the hotel and raced through the narrow streets, missing parked cars by inches.

Leo tightened his seatbelt. "You should have been a Grand Prix driver."

"I used to daydream about being a racecar driver when we were in seminary. I do some of my best praying when I drive this car to the Italian Grand Prix near Milan every year."

"What a coincidence," Leo said. "I also pray when you drive."

The sight of an Italian police motorcycle in the rearview mirror prompted Morelli to drop his speed for the remainder of their drive to the center of the city.

Civitas was a small restaurant located across the river Tiber on a side street close to the Spanish Steps. The rain had ceased, so the two priests had decided to take a table outside, where they were finishing off their first course of *crostini di polenta con pure di fungi porcini e tarufo*, polenta squares with a puree of porcini and truffles. This would be followed by rabbit roasted with tomatoes, onions, and garlic and accompanied by a dark, rich *Morellino di Scansano* wine.

A warm breeze ruffled the white tablecloth as Leo looked across at Morelli and decided that his friend had stalled enough. "So, Anthony, care to let me in on what all this is about? The subject matter in that folder you sent me was a tad disturbing, especially coming from someone as pragmatic as you.

"Got your attention, didn't it, Father."

"That's an understatement. A hidden code in the Bible ... a secret chapel connected to the end of days as prophesized in the Book of Revelation. Do you seriously believe any of this?"

"I'm now convinced of it, Leo." Morelli passed the glass of wine beneath his nose, inhaling the aroma as he tried to think of where to begin with this fellow Jesuit he had known for most of his adult life. "Do you know of my work with Professor Lev Wasserman?"

Leo had to think for a moment. "The famous mathematician in Jerusalem?"

"Yes. He's also one of the world's leading experts in group theory, a field of mathematics that underlies quantum physics. A few years ago, he was reading about the Genius of Vilna, an eighteenth-century Jewish sage in Lithuania who predicted 9/11 to the day and spoke about the possibility of a code being embedded within the Torah. Lev became fascinated with the idea and learned that, throughout history, many Bible scholars had been trying to prove that there was a secret code in the Old Testament. He convinced a group of scientists at the university in Jerusalem that they could find it using modern code breaking methods, and to their surprise, they did. Their work has been replicated by the code breakers at the National Security Administration in the United States, using their most powerful computers, and Lev Wasserman's paper on the subject has passed academic peer review and has been published in leading scientific journals."

"He's Jewish, isn't he? I mean, how did a Catholic priest become involved in all of this? Why not a rabbi?"

"He was born Jewish but converted to Christianity several years ago, before his American wife died. Believe it or not, Lev's also an archaeologist, and our paths have crossed many times over the years on various projects. He invited me to spend all of last summer with his team in Israel as their resident expert on biblical prophecy."

"Biblical prophecy? Is that what all of this is about? You think this code in the Bible has the power to predict the future?"

"It's complicated," Morelli said. He poured some more wine into Leo's glass. "Lev said the first evidence of the encoding was discovered in the *Pentateuch*, the original five books of the Old Testament, otherwise known as the Torah. The code only exists in Hebrew, because that was the original language of the Bible as it was first written. Evidently, sixty years ago, a rabbi from Eastern Europe noticed that, if he skipped fifty letters and then another fifty and then another fifty, the word Torah was spelled out at the beginning of the Book of Genesis. He then used that same skip sequence again and spelled out the word Torah in the Book of Exodus. To his amazement, the word Torah was also embedded at the beginning of the books of Leviticus, Numbers, and Deuteronomy."

"That's interesting, Anthony, but even in biblical times it would have been relatively easy to embed a word in the text of any written work, and it doesn't predict the future."

"That's what most people thought until modern technology came along. Lev and his team found additional hidden messages by using computers to alter the sequencing and then scanning the pages both horizontally and vertically, like a crossword puzzle. That's when they found words grouped together on the same page that mentioned historical events that occurred after the Bible was written. For instance, words like *airplane* and *Wright brothers* would appear together with sentences like *they will fly* and *first flight at Kitty Hawk*."

Leo stared across the table at Morelli and breathed in the fresh air washed clean by the recent rain. *As a college professor, why hadn't he heard about any of this before?* The whole subject smacked of pop religion.

Morelli took a piece of crusty bread and broke it in half. "Did you know Sir Isaac Newton believed there was a hidden code in the Bible that would reveal the future?"

"You're kidding! I never knew that about him."

"When Newton's biographer went through his papers at Cambridge, he was amazed to find that the father of modern physics was obsessed with the subject. Newton even learned Hebrew and spent most of his life trying to find it. For centuries, many have suspected there was some kind of code in the Bible, but now, Leo, with the advent of computers, we can finally see what many have suspected was there all along."

Leo pushed his plate away. "Now that I think back on it, I remember hearing somewhere that the assassination of Yitzhak Rabin, the Israeli prime minister, was predicted by some kind of code recently discovered in the Bible."

"The encoded message not only foretold his assassination, but the year he would be murdered. The name of the assassin, Amir, was spelled out on the same page of the Bible above Rabin's name. The Prime Minister had been warned beforehand by the researchers who found the encoded message, but he shook them off when they presented the evidence to him. He refused to believe it. We also found the name of every American president and the years they were in office. Lev's team knew who was going to win the last presidential election before it was even held. Hundreds of other events are also encoded in the Bible. Both World Wars, the Holocaust, men landing on the moon, 9/11, the Gulf War, even the exact date of the collision of the Shoemaker-Levi comet with Jupiter. All are encoded in the Bible."

Both priests reclined in their chairs and sipped their wine as the waiter arrived with the second course. The perfectly cooked rabbit was swimming in a rich, dark sauce that Father Leo had been trying to duplicate for years with little success. Leo savored the tender meat along with the sauce he had coveted for so long. He had been thinking about this meal ever since he stepped off the plane.

"So," Leo said, "what about this mysterious chapel that you mentioned in the letter? Have you found any proof that it actually exists?"

"The first indication of the chapel's existence surfaced a year ago when we found a single reference in the code to a very holy Christian chapel buried for almost two thousand years. Then, the day before I sent for you, Lev's team discovered two additional encoded passages. The first passage placed the chapel right here in Rome, but the second passage had more chilling implications. It linked this secret chapel to the end of days as prophesized in Revelation."

"What's the Church's position in all of this?"

"I have no idea."

"Haven't you discussed it with anyone at the Vatican?"

"Only a few trusted friends know about my work, and I've asked them not to discuss it with anyone else for now."

"That sounds a little ominous. Why not?"

"Because there are powers, maybe even evil ones, that don't want us to know about the chapel's existence."

Father Leo stopped eating. "Did you really just say *evil powers*?"

"There is a section encoded in the Book of Genesis with the words *against mankind* written in Hebrew. It appears vertically on the page. The word *Satan* is spelled out horizontally over it two thirds of the way down, forming an upside-down cross in the middle of the page. You would not be able see this in the English version of the Bible. You can only see it in the original Hebrew. Lev Wasserman and I believe this finding is a clear indication that there are forces aligned against those of us who work in God's name. We also found another encoded message in a different section that clearly states this malevolent force is now embedded within our own church."

Leo sat back in his chair and tried to make sense of everything Morelli had just told him. The implications were frightening but tantalizing at the same time. *A code in the Bible that foretold the future could be considered secular proof of God's existence.*

Morelli looked around before leaning over the table so that only Leo could hear him. "Things are beginning to happen quickly now, Leo. A few hours ago, we found a reference to an ancient Christian seal that apparently points to the chapel's location under the Basilica."

"A seal? Where?"

"Not a clue, but according to what we read in the code, it's very special and we'll have no trouble recognizing it when we see it. The team in Israel has gone to a twenty-four hour schedule in their search for a description. Everyone on the team, including myself, has encrypted software installed in their computers that searches for coded words and sentences hidden within the Bible.

I've entered the words seal, chapel, seal under the Vatican, plus hundreds of other combinations, but nothing has surfaced yet. It can be an exhaustive process, Leo, but if you use the computer program and let it run through all the various sequences, the code soon reveals itself."

Leo took a sip of wine and gazed across the piazza over Morelli's shoulder. In the distance, he spotted a tall man dressed in a black cassock and wearing the crimson skull cap of a cardinal. It was Marcus Lundahl, and he was walking in their direction. The cardinal was accompanied by his ever-present assistant, Father Emilio, a short, quiet man with thinning hair that contrasted with heavy dark eyebrows.

Following Leo's gaze, Morelli swiveled in his chair and swore a silent oath before turning back toward Leo.

"What's wrong, Anthony?"

"No one's supposed to know you're here."

"What?"

Morelli shot Leo a cautionary look as they both dropped their napkins and stood to greet the cardinal. "I didn't tell anyone I sent for you. Just follow my lead and remember not to mention anything about the chapel."

The cardinal stopped in front of their table and, without a word, extended his hand. Ritual and etiquette required lower-ranking priests to kiss the ring of a cardinal out of respect for his rank as a Prince of the Church. He studied the two priests like a cat watching a doomed insect run across a carpet as they bent to kiss the large gold ring. "Good evening, Fathers. I apologize for interrupting your meal."

"Good evening, Your Eminence. Won't you join us?" Morelli cast a sideways glance at Leo. "You remember our old classmate, Father Leo, don't you, sir?"

"Yes, of course. It's nice to see you back in Rome, Father. I'm sorry, but I'm afraid I can't stay. I'm late for a meeting. Why don't you come by my office the day after tomorrow, Leopold? We can have lunch, and I can catch up on news from America."

"That is most kind, sir. I look forward to it."

The tension generated by the unexpected encounter with the cardinal and his assistant was as thick as the rain-induced humidity hanging in the warm air.

"A pleasure as always to see you too, Father Morelli. I hear you have been busy under my feet lately."

"I beg your pardon, Eminence?"

"I'm referring to your recent excavation under the Basilica. Father Emilio likes to keep me posted on your work." The cardinal smiled at Morelli. "See to it you don't knock anything loose that would cause the entire church to cave in."

Morelli glanced at Emilio before turning back toward Lundahl. "Oh, no, sir. I'm very careful in my digging, Eminence."

"I'm sure that you are, Father," Lundahl's expression was like a blank canvas.

The cardinal's usually stone-faced assistant was now glaring at Leo. "I didn't realize you had business in Rome, Father. You usually notify us before you come."

"He wanted to surprise me," Morelli said quickly.

The assistant's eyes narrowed. "Yes, it is a surprise."

"We're just happy to see you again, Leopold," the cardinal said, raising his hand in front of Emilio. "Call my secretary and put yourself on my schedule."

"I will, sir. It was good seeing you again."

With that, Lundahl was off, taking long steps as he crossed the cobble-stoned piazza while his assistant tried to keep up.

"What is it about that man that makes me so uncomfortable?" Morelli wondered aloud. "It's like he thinks he's better than us. Did you notice the way his eyes move?"

"You know how Marcus is, Anthony. Even in seminary, he seemed distant. I always thought it was just because he graduated at the top of our class. Now that he's a cardinal, we'll just have to adjust."

Morelli shook his head. "It wasn't Marcus I was referring to. I was talking about Emilio. He's the reason I didn't want you to say anything about the chapel. I have to get permission every time I want to do any archaeological work under the Vatican, and all my requests go through him. He's one of those small-minded men who believe we shouldn't be poking around under the Basilica, and he has the ear of the cardinal. Finding the chapel is too important to be stopped by some prejudicial bureaucratic nonsense, so for now he needs to be kept out of the loop."

Leo took another sip of wine and observed the people at nearby tables. It was good to be back in Rome, even though the politics at the Vatican never seemed to change. Father Anthony's frequent clashes with Lundahl and his staff were no secret around the Vatican. The competition between the cardinal and Morelli had been fierce throughout their arduous fourteen-year climb from novices to the day they took their final vows as Jesuit priests.

Norwegian by birth, Cardinal Marcus Lundahl usually received amused responses when he informed friends that his first name had actually been chosen by his parents from a list of acceptable Norwegian names. Norway's strict name law dates from the 1800s and was intended to protect Norwegian children from any name that sounded or looked strange to the government.

He was tall and blond with probing blue eyes and the stride and grace of an athlete. Marcus had been a track star in school. In fact, he had made it to the Olympic trials as a distance runner but failed to make the Norwegian team by seconds in his final race. In his late fifties now, his blond hair was turning white at the temples, highlighting his Nordic features.

At the age of eighteen, Lundahl left home for America to study theology at Georgetown University. There he met Leo and Morelli before all three moved on to Woodstock College in Woodstock, Maryland, the oldest Jesuit seminary in the United States before it closed its doors in 1974 due to decreasing candidates. Lundahl went on to become an expert on Canon Law and was a rising star at the Vatican, becoming one of the youngest cardinals in church history.

Father Leo was feeling the fatigue of the past twenty-four hours as they finished their wine and lifted themselves slowly from their chairs before heading for the parked car along a narrow street filled with brightly lit shops. Leo watched the Gelato-slurping tourists peering into the store windows and thumbing through their Italian-English translation handbooks while the local populace took advantage of the break in the rain to venture outside and visit with neighbors.

The BMW was surrounded by admiring teenagers who were startled to see a Roman Catholic priest hop behind the wheel. Morelli revved the engine for their benefit before driving away slowly through the pedestrian-filled streets. He wound his way back to the Amalfi as the rain again began to fall, causing the pavement to take on a shine that caught the reflection from the lighted dome of Saint Peter's Basilica across the way.

Pulling to a stop in front of Leo's hotel, Morelli glanced at his watch. "I'll meet you for Mass in the morning. Six o'clock in front of the Basilica."

"Sounds good," Leo said, crawling from the ground-hugging car.

"Welcome back to Rome, my friend." Morelli grinned at Leo and waved before roaring off down the wet street and sending a rooster-tail of spray in his wake.

Leo turned to see a fashionably dressed young couple locked in a passionate embrace inside the hotel's entranceway before they descended the aged stone steps. They smiled at the priest before walking hand-in-hand down the wet sidewalk, oblivious to the rain as they stared into each other's eyes. Father Leo watched them round the corner before looking up at the darkened window to his empty room. A familiar feeling of loneliness crept into his soul.

CHAPTER 4

In Vatican City, thick maroon drapes were drawn in front of a row of tall windows, blotting out the lights illuminating the Basilica. Inside the darkened room, a man dressed in the long black cassock of a priest paced in front of a gilded Italian desk and stared at the phone. He walked back and forth with his hands behind his back before finally coming to a decision and lowering himself into the chair behind the desk. He glanced at a heavy bronze clock next to the phone. It was time to make the call. His pulse quickened as his breath came in shallow gasps. With hands shaking in nervous anticipation, he dialed the number.

A deep voice with the slight hint of an accent answered. "Yes?"

"It appears that Morelli has enlisted the help of an old friend, sir."

"Who?"

"Father Leopold Amodeo. He arrived today from America." The priest shifted uneasily in his seat. He was talking to his master.

"Is he a part of this?"

"I don't believe so, but he could be. He and Morelli have been friends for years."

"Do you think Morelli knows where it is?"

"No, he doesn't even know where the chapel is."

The voice sounded distrustful, almost angry. "Are you certain?"

The priest felt a surge of panic rising in his throat. "Yes, sir. So far we've been able to prevent them from finding it without raising suspicion. There's no way they can get to it without our knowledge."

The voice seemed more relaxed. "Good."

The priest started to breathe normally again. "Thank you, sir. What would you like me to do next?"

"Now that they've discovered the code, it will only be a matter of time. We're going to have to take more aggressive steps to make sure their search stops now."

Panic again seized the priest. "What should I do if they discover the chapel?"

The voice became angry. "It's your job to keep that from happening. The possibility still exists that they may find some clue there that will lead them to it. You will do whatever has to be done to assure that it remains safe. Anything! Is that clear? Morelli must not be allowed to continue."

The priest's body trembled behind the desk. "Yes, sir. I understand." He heard breathing on the other end of the line. After a brief pause, the voice became soothing, almost fatherly. "Our work here is far from over, and you will have to find the strength to carry on."

"My life is devoted to you, sir."

"Your dedication has never been an issue. You've always been one of our most faithful servants, and your reward will come in time."

Excitement replaced fear within the priest. *His master loved him.* "Thank you, sir. I will call you tomorrow and let you know of my plan." The phone went dead in his hands as he leaned back in his chair and gazed up at the hand-painted ceiling covered with images of angels and saints. Below that, a crucifix hung on the wall over his bed. Soon he would paint over this ceiling and replace the crucifix with a symbol of his own. *One his master would approve of.*

CHAPTER 5

It was still dark outside Saint Peter's Basilica when Father Leo arrived the next morning and ascended the steps. In front of the enormous open doors, a brown-robed figure stood framed by bright yellow light streaming from inside the Basilica, making it difficult to see the face under the hood. "Father Leopold Amodeo?"

Leo looked up at the monk. "Yes."

"Hi. I'm John. John Lowe. I work with Father Morelli. He just called to say he's running late and asked me to meet you here for Mass."

The monk brushed the brown hood from his head to reveal a young man in his twenties with soulful eyes, long black hair, and a short, trimmed beard. They shook hands and turned to enter the massive church created by Michelangelo and Bernini.

"I see you are a Franciscan, John."

"My sense of fashion usually gives me away," John laughed. "Actually, the Franciscan Brothers in Assisi have allowed me to live in their community while I consider the priesthood. I'm currently on loan to Father Morelli as his assistant for the next few months. We met this past year while I was finishing some graduate work on an archaeological dig on the outskirts of Rome."

"Father Morelli seems to be involved in a lot of projects around here. Are you an archaeologist also?"

"I have a PhD in history, and I'm working on my master's in anthropology."

At least this new assistant had the right training to help Morelli, Leo thought.

Practically everyone who had ever entered the immense Renaissance church was overcome by its unparalleled beauty, and Leo and John were both awed as they passed through the mammoth doors and headed up the center aisle toward the main altar.

"What kind of history, John? I mean, what was your thesis work about?"

"Classical Rome ... the Roman Empire during the time of Christ. That's what drew me to Italy in the first place."

"Interesting. When did you first think of entering the religious life?"

"I've been thinking about it on and off since grade school. I was raised Catholic, went to Catholic schools all my life. You get pretty well indoctrinated by the time you reach high school. Two of my friends from school became priests."

Leo looked up at the ceiling as they walked along. "I went to Catholic school too, but a lot of my friends became police officers and firefighters. I came out of a working-class neighborhood, and we had a lot of kids from my graduating class who entered those fields. It's funny how we all gravitated to professions where we could help people."

They continued up the center aisle of the enormous basilica that contained eleven chapels and forty-five altars before seating themselves near the *baldacchino*, a monumental canopy that sheltered the papal altar and the holy relics of Saint Peter. Made of dark bronze accented with gold vine leaves, it was created by Lorenzo Bernini in 1624 under the direction of Pope Urban VIII. For centuries, Christians had built their churches in the shape of a cross, and Saint Peter's was no exception. The altar lay in the center under the colossal dome designed by Michelangelo; although sadly, he never lived to see it finished.

"I'm surprised the Jesuits didn't grab you, John. How did you end up in Assisi?"

"Actually, I applied to Jesuit seminary shortly after I met Father Morelli. He realized I needed time to make a decision about the priesthood, so he arranged for the brothers in Assisi to accept me as a novice for a year."

"What do you think of the monastic way of life so far?"

"It's definitely not my calling. I have a feeling the Church is going to need men of action in the years to come, so that's why I've chosen the Jesuits."

"You have a lot to decide, John. As you probably already know, the ranks of the Jesuits have begun to dwindle over the past several years. We're kind of like a peacetime army now. The priesthood is in trouble, and the Church is desperate for qualified candidates, especially men who are morally incorruptible in today's climate of hostility toward our religion. A few bad ones have destroyed the work of thousands of good ones, but I'm heartened by the words of Saint Paul when he said, 'Where sin has abounded, there grace will even more abound.'"

With the smell of incense permeating the air, an elderly bishop ascended the steps to the altar and raised his right hand in the sign of the cross. "*Te igitur, clementissime Pater …*" The High Mass spoken in Latin had begun. Leo was thinking of how much he had missed the Latin version of the Catholic Mass back in America when he glimpsed Morelli sliding across the wooden pew.

"Good morning, Leo. I see you've met John."

"Yes, and I see you've already been at work this morning, Father."

Morelli's eyes widened. "How did you …?"

Leo cast his eyes down at Morelli's mud-covered shoes.

"Oh. I wanted to take a look at something under the Basilica, but it appears that Emilio and a team of construction workers were there first. Evidently, he's had a wall constructed sometime in the past few days to block me from reaching my latest excavation. That little toad of a man has been spying on me again."

"Why don't you go over his head?" Leo asked.

"Now is not a good time to rattle any cages around here. Until I know who we can trust, I can't afford to bring any unwanted attention to my work."

Morelli looked across the aisle at a group of nuns burning holes through them with their eyes and lowered his voice. "Did you know that Emilio made the suggestion to the cardinal that we should have a subway station constructed right under the Vatican? Can you imagine that? The man thinks it would be a great way to control the crowds and eliminate bus traffic. We could let the faithful just pop up like ground squirrels for a quick look around and then duck back down again. His plan would destroy literally thousands of years of history and make it impossible to do any further archaeological exploration of the area."

"I agree, that's pretty appalling, Anthony, but I'm sure the archaeological committee of Rome would put a halt to any plan like that as soon as it was presented to them." Leo knew that the subway system in Rome would have been much more extensive if it weren't for all the historical treasures buried below.

"The Italian government doesn't have any say about what goes on inside Vatican City. I seem to be fighting a constant losing battle against those who want to destroy our past for some reason."

A final blessing from the altar brought the Mass to an end and the multitude streamed past the immense doors into Saint Peter's Square and through the colonnade created by Bernini. The three men loitered in the cool morning air before deciding to head across the street for breakfast in a small sidewalk café.

The waiter brought strong Italian coffee while the three men studied their menus and chose the Italian version of ham and eggs. Leo scanned the table for condiments and looked around at the different foods being served at other tables. "Too bad you can't get hash browns in Italy." He had a weakness for greasy American food.

Father Morelli reached into a napkin-covered basket and pulled out a peach muffin. "This café caters to Americans, but you can tell by the flavor of the meat that they serve only local ham that's been cured according to strict Italian law. Thankfully, hash browns haven't found their way here yet. I highly recommend their pastries."

The sun was rising across a pale blue sky, erasing the early morning shadows crisscrossing the narrow Roman streets and bringing warmth to their outside table as the men began to eat. John was still studying his ham, looking as if he had discovered a new life-form, while Morelli gobbled his eggs and smothered his muffin with butter.

"Are you familiar with the ancient area below the Basilica, Leo?" Morelli asked between sips of coffee.

"I've only heard stories about it, but I've never had the opportunity to go down there myself. It must be fascinating, especially for an archaeologist."

"It is. Directly below the Basilica, under the main altar, is the Vatican grotto, a sanctified crypt where many of our most venerated popes are buried. Then, below the grotto, is an ancient pagan and Christian necropolis that dates back to the second century. It was discovered by a team of archaeologists in the 1940s. That was the area I was looking around in this morning. About the same time they discovered the necropolis, they found a small tomb there dating to AD 160. That was the tomb that held the bones of Saint Peter. It's one of the most important archaeological finds to date in the Christian world."

"Saint Peter died years before that," Leo said. "How did they know that was really his tomb?"

"It's believed by many that the first few generations of Christians moved his body around for almost a century in an effort to hide it from the Romans. The archaeologists who made the discovery found an inscription that marked it as his final resting place."

John was sipping his coffee in silence as he listened to the two priests. "I noticed that you still use the term AD, Father Morelli. Haven't modern scholars decided to replace it with the new abbreviation CE?"

Morelli winced. "I absolutely hate the new abbreviation CE. As you both know, AD is Latin for *Anno Domini*, meaning 'in the year of our Lord'. CE stands for Common Era. What kind of garbage is that? We've been saying in the year of our Lord for two millennia, and now they want to take that away from us, calling it, instead, the Common Era. It's just another veiled way to slowly erase God from our everyday speech."

Leo had to smile. His old friend was very perceptive about a lot of things other people let pass without notice. "So, you were digging around below the Basilica before breakfast?"

"Oh … yes. I wanted to check that area one last time for evidence of the ancient seal mentioned in the code, and that's when I discovered the wall they had built to keep me out."

"Keep you out of where, Anthony?"

"There is another, even deeper and more ancient area beneath the one I was in this morning. One of the workers discovered it by accident about six months ago, and for the past few weeks, John and I have only been allowed to spend a few days down there exploring and mapping the region. From what we've seen, the area appears to be a section of the old Roman catacombs. The seal we're looking for is either in the Vatican grotto, which is above the level I was in this morning, or behind the newly constructed wall in the deeper area we haven't fully explored yet."

Leo took another sip of coffee. He loved the ambience of these small side-walk cafés in Rome. There was something about the light and the air, along with the history and pace of life that made thinking clearer, more in tune with living in the moment. Maybe that's why so many artists and writers were returning to Europe for inspiration like they did back in the 1920s.

Leo's reverie was interrupted by Father Morelli's voice. "I'm sure you know by now, Leo, that my fascination with archaeology has always had a higher purpose. I've never doubted that the Bible was inspired by God, but proving it has been something that has eluded scholars for over two thousand years. Do you know why, at this exact time in history, we've uncovered the hidden code in the Bible?"

Leo had to think back to their previous discussion of the night before. "I suppose it has something to do with the development of computers."

"Exactly. It also coincides with the timetable set in the Bible. The Jews returning to their homeland after two thousand years was the first prophecy to be fulfilled. The discovery of the embedded code within the Bible, and the ability to decipher it, was never meant to happen until now. We are on the verge of a whole new understanding of just what the Bible contains. It's like a tumbler has fallen on a cosmic time lock to a holy vault, opening a door to what was previously unobtainable."

"You're being a little too cryptic for me, Anthony."

"We're dealing with a cryptic subject, Father. That's why I believe the discovery of the seal and the ancient chapel mentioned in the code was always meant to happen now. Not one day sooner or one day later."

Leo ordered a second cup of coffee and reclined in his chair while Morelli finished the last of his eggs. "What are you going to do now that they've blocked your way into the deeper catacombs?"

"We'll just have to find another way in," John interjected. "We still need to check one more section in the grotto, but if we don't find the seal there, then we have no choice but go down into the area behind the newly constructed wall. Personally, I'm hoping that we do have to go into that deeper region. We were only allowed to explore a small section of it. Imagine what might be down there."

Leo liked this young man. He had a rebellious streak, and his youth was refreshing in this world of pious intellectuals, even though John was something of an intellectual himself. The enthusiasm generated by these two men gave Leo the feeling that they were all on the threshold of a great adventure. Conversely, it could very well be an adventure that contained a large degree of terror for himself, his friends, and maybe even the whole world.

It was a little after nine o'clock in the morning before they had finished their breakfast and departed the café. Leo returned to his hotel while Anthony and John walked to their individual apartments in the Vatican to gather the equipment they would need. Leo hadn't considered the fact that he would need work clothes for this trip and decided to do a little shopping before he met his friends at eleven for their descent into the tunnels under the Vatican.

Entering through the front doors of the hotel lobby, Leo spotted Arnolfo behind the desk. "*Buona la mattina*, Arnolfo." Good morning.

A large smile crossed Arnolfo's face. "*Buona la mattina*, Father. What can I do for you this glorious day?"

"I need some jeans and hiking boots. Do you know of a shop nearby that might have them?"

Arnolfo smiled. "So, you are going under the Basilica with Father Morelli."

Leo was always impressed at the hotel owner's knowledge of what went on in Vatican City. "Is there anything you don't know about that goes on across the street?"

"I only listen, Father, that's all. If people want to talk, I let them talk. Mostly, they see me as part of the room, like a piece of furniture. A chair or a table hears many things not meant for prying ears." Arnolfo's last statement had shown that he was much more than just a simple hotel keeper.

"At least I know who to come to if I want to find out what's going on around here," Leo said.

Arnolfo winked and wrote something down on a piece of paper before handing it to Leo. "Here, Father. Go to this address. I think this man might have something you will be interested in."

Leo's curiosity became aroused. "What does he know, Arnolfo?"

"He knows what kind of clothes you will need. He owns a sporting goods store, Father."

Leo turned crimson as Arnolfo burst out laughing.

"Nice," Leo said, smiling to himself at how Arnolfo had led him into that trap. "I'll have to think of a way to match you for that one my friend."

"I have no doubt, Father. I will be on the lookout for it."

Both men continued to chuckle as Leo walked out of the lobby into the bright Roman sunshine. The day was brilliantly clear, not at all like the rainy day before when he had arrived. He walked along the narrow streets before finding the sporting goods store sandwiched between a small, family-run bookstore, and a butcher shop with little strings of sausages and plucked poultry strung overhead in the window.

There was no hint of a mall or chain store here, although in truth, Rome had been home to the first shopping mall in history. Leo remembered the first time he had seen it. Named after its creator, Trajan's Markets was built in the second century AD by Emperor Trajan and his architect, Apollodorus of Damascus. Together they had built a visionary multistory complex of one hundred and fifty shops, the ancient Roman equivalent of a modern shopping mall. Everything an ancient Roman might want could be found there. The shops sold everything from silks and spices imported from the Middle East to fresh fruit, fish, and flowers. Considered among the wonders of the Classical world, this archeological treasure remains standing today in the Forum area of Rome.

Leo thought back to when America had been a country of small shopkeepers, and the change he had seen over the span of a single generation was not pleasant in his mind. The Italians had their small stores and neighborhoods, with extended generational families kept intact in the same town or village, while America's families had undergone an enormous change in the moral and corporate explosion that now forced them to endure a commercial landscape run by powerful conglomerates.

The unique charm that had once marked the boundaries of different cultural regions throughout America was being erased, and almost every city and town across the country now resembled every other city and town from one coast to the other. Due to corporate greed, huge box stores covered the land with no respect for individual communities, forcing small family-run businesses to fail and dispersing young people to seek work hundreds or thousands of miles away from their parents and grandparents.

The change had left a barren expanse of sameness and apathy across the nation. The distancing from past values, coupled with dwindling opportunity for working men and women spurred by globalization, unaffordable college tuition, and the widening gap between the very rich and everyone else, was creating a violent underclass that was spreading like a virus across a land previously occupied by a mostly peaceful and moral populace.

Who or what had ushered in this new age was a subject of much debate at the university where Leo taught. He had formed a theory that the Great

Depression had so victimized our "greatest generation" that they had unwittingly sowed the seeds for a selfish, winner-take-all postwar grab for material wealth. Their efforts to raise themselves out of poverty and give their children a better life had changed the very core values of an America they had worked so hard to create and left the generations that followed without a unifying sense of community.

In the wake of the country's newfound wealth, a religion of consumerism had spurred a mindless pursuit for greater corporate profits. This greed-fueled race eventually led to companies sending millions of manufacturing jobs overseas, resulting in the decline of the cherished middle class who made their living making things. For the first time, America's children were looking at a lower standard of living than their parents. Corporate profit and material possessions were the new idolatry, shoving God's message of 'love thy neighbor' into a dusty corner.

Many of Leo's fellow professors had begun to agree with him that Europe was also evolving toward the corporate model of profit at any cost. At least their governments provided free healthcare, but in the new Europe, religion was beginning to fade into the background as its small countries relinquished their individual identities and morphed into a giant union more intent on worshiping the Euro.

In America, Leo was seeing the Catholic Church and other religious denominations beginning to wither on the vine in the new culture of every man for himself. He had shocked other priests when he told them that, if it weren't for the evangelicals and nondenominational mega churches springing up over the land in response to what was happening to individuals and families across the country, he could see organized religion dying out completely over time. Leo knew that, someday soon, something big would have to happen to push the Church and God's message of love back into the forefront of people's minds before it was too late.

Father Leo opened the door to the small store and was greeted by a frail man with an innocent smile on his face. "*Buon giorno*, Father. How can I help you today?"

"*Buon giorno, signor.* I'm looking for some work clothes, maybe some jeans and a cotton shirt. Also, some boots, waterproof if you have them."

"Yes, Father, we have all of that. Arnolfo called me a few moments ago. We have a special discount for priests, especially priests who are friends of Arnolfo." The man began scurrying about the store, excitedly gathering up items for Leo to choose from. "Are you working in one of the Vatican gardens this beautiful day?"

Father Leo looked across the aged wooden counter at the animated shop-keeper. "I have a feeling I'll be doing a lot of digging today, signor." He tried on some boots and strolled the aisles, picking out a few more things before walking to the front and pulling a credit card from his wallet.

"I'm sorry, but we take only cash, Father."

"Do you take American money or only *lire*, signor?"

The store owner looked at Leo as if he had just stepped out of a time machine. "We're part of the European Union now. We take Euros." Leo peered into his empty wallet.

"I'm afraid I haven't had time to get any cash yet."

"Don't worry, Father. Take the receipt and give the cash to Arnolfo when you have it. He will see to it that I get the money."

Leo felt his face flush and thanked the man. These people were so trusting, but he was a priest after all, and that counted for something, especially here in Italy.

Leo stepped out into the sunshine with a bundle of clothes under his arm wrapped in brown paper and tied with a string. He followed an alley-like street back to his hotel, wishing he could just keep walking around the city all day. Maybe he would rent a small motor scooter while he was in Rome. Morelli's words on the subject echoed in his mind. "You wouldn't last a day in Rome's traffic on one of those!" Still, Leo had a fatalistic way of looking at things and was considering it anyway. It was a beautiful day, and Morelli's freewheeling lifestyle was beginning to rub off on him.

* * *

Within an hour, Leo had changed clothes at his hotel and had joined Morelli and John at the basilica. After all the trouble he had gone through to buy more suitable clothes for exploring underground, Leo noticed that, except for his hiking boots, Morelli was still wearing his priestly garb.

"I thought we would be digging around in the dirt," Leo said. "Why are you dressed like that?"

Morelli tugged at his stiff white collar. "I need to be dressed like this to avoid suspicion when we pass through certain areas of the Vatican. Don't worry, Father; you'll get your chance to get those new clothes dirty today."

As they passed through the doors and approached the altar, Morelli stopped for a moment. "You know, Leo, I'm always amazed whenever I stand here and look at that altar. I can't help but think back on what Jesus said when he spoke about Peter. He said, 'Upon this rock I will build my church'. Of course, Jesus wasn't talking about a building, but the man, Peter himself. Jesus wanted His chief disciple to carry on with His ministry, and I think it's more than just coincidence that Peter's bones are now encased just below that altar in a church that bears his name."

"I have to agree, Anthony. I've always thought there had to be a greater power at work here when you consider the fact that Peter's remains lay undiscovered for almost two thousand years until they found him buried under this very church."

"Did you know the expedition that discovered his bones was led by an old friend and mentor of mine?" Morelli said. "His name was Father Gilberto Bianchi, a Jesuit archaeologist who was in charge of the digging at the time. You met him once, Leo. He was one hundred years old when he died last year."

Leo remembered him. He had seemed more like a grizzled old caretaker than a priest. Morelli, however, had practically worshiped the man. Bianchi had not only introduced him to the area under the Vatican, but had tutored him for years in the fine art of biblical archaeology.

The three men continued to stare at the altar until Morelli finally motioned them forward. Leo and John followed behind until they angled off to the right and stopped in front of one of the four main pillars supporting Michelangelo's dome. Morelli then circled the pillar until he came to a small stairway that led below to a darkened bronze door.

"Beyond that door at the bottom of the stairs is the Vatican grotto, a huge crypt where the remains of many of the Catholic Church's royalty are located, including ninety-one popes."

"Are we allowed down there?" Leo asked.

"Yes, the main area is open to everyone. They have daily tours for the public, but they use a different entrance."

The trio descended the stairs and Morelli opened the door to reveal the grotto. Leo was surprised. He had imagined a dark, cave-like area, but instead, subdued lighting highlighted tall stucco arches that met a curved, white ceiling. Long hallways branched out from the area under the altar, where niches carved into the walls contained sarcophagus-like tombs of popes and others who would spend eternity beneath the largest church in the world.

Walking through the sanctified space, the men arrived at the entrance to a long hallway trailing off to their right. Morelli looked around to see if anyone was watching and stepped over a chain with a "do not enter" sign attached. Scanning the area once more, he gestured for the other two men to follow. Leo looked around nervously before jumping over the chain behind John and following Morelli down the unlit hallway to its end, where they encountered a thick wooden door with medieval-looking metal hinges.

Leo stared at the door. "What's behind there?"

"Another crypt, one not open to the public," Morelli answered.

The door was locked, as they all knew it would be. John looked around before reaching inside his robe and producing a small crowbar.

Leo was horrified. "You can't be serious. A crowbar? You're actually thinking of breaking into a locked area of the Vatican with a crowbar?"

Morelli chuckled to himself as he pulled a key from his pocket. "Of course not. That's for later." John grinned at Leo who was still staring in disbelief at the crowbar. Morelli unlocked the door, and the three stepped into the second crypt, closing the door behind them.

Morelli studied their surroundings. "It's down here to the right."

"Just what are we looking for, Anthony?" Leo asked.

"The tomb of a Swedish queen who converted to Catholicism over two hundred years ago. Lev called me from Israel this morning after we left the café and told me that he found her name encoded in the Bible. According to the code, the seal is beneath her tomb."

Leo was incredulous. "How can we possibly look beneath her tomb?"

"These tombs are really stone caskets similar to Egyptian sarcophagi, but luckily for us, they are much smaller and lighter. We only need to move one away from the wall to see the floor underneath."

Leo marveled at the sight of so many popes in their stone vaults lining the walls. "I never imagined this place was so extensive."

"Even people who have worked in the Vatican their entire lives have never seen this area. This crypt is open only to cardinals and researchers with special permission. I happen to be a researcher with special permission, hence the key."

"I wasn't even going to ask you about the key. I'm just thankful we aren't all going to jail."

"Well, I'm not going to jail, but you and John don't have special permission. I've heard the food in Italian jails is excellent though."

Before Leo had a chance to respond or bolt for the door, they reached the tomb Father Morelli was looking for. John sprang into action and placed the flat end of the crowbar between the wall and the stone tomb. He then began to inch it away from the wall, and with the help of the other two, the tomb began to move, slowly revealing the floor beneath.

"Careful you don't chip the marble, John," Morelli warned. He was starting to feel some guilt at disturbing the final resting place of a queen.

"I'll do my best, Father. This thing is heavier than it looks."

After about twenty minutes of slow work, the heavy marble tomb was far enough away from the wall to observe the surface of the floor that had been covered for over two hundred years.

"No seal," breathed John, wiping the sweat from his face.

All three men stared at the blank floor.

"Maybe the seal is on the bottom of the tomb, Anthony," Leo ventured.

"It's possible, but we can't just turn this thing on its side." Morelli had visions of the tomb breaking open and a two-hundred-year-old queen rolling out onto the floor.

Leo studied the tomb and floor around it. "Maybe we can get a block of wood or something to use as a pivot point and pry an edge up enough to shine a light underneath. That way we can visualize the bottom."

John emptied the contents of his backpack on the floor and let out a sigh. "I forgot to bring a flashlight."

Leo proudly withdrew the small flashlight he had purchased that morning at the sporting goods store.

Morelli looked surprised. "Well done, my friend. I forgot you once worked in a mine."

John was grinning from ear to ear. "Now, where are you going to find a block of wood, MacGyver?"

Laughing out loud at the MacGyver remark, Leo looked around. "There are two other types of people who have permission to be down here: janitors and maintenance people." Leo headed off down the line of tombs until he came to a small door. He turned the knob, and the unlocked door opened easily. It was a janitor's closet. Inspecting the contents inside, he found a large push broom with a thick wooden head. He unscrewed it from the handle and returned to the tomb.

"This should work."

Morelli winked at John. "Now you know why I like this man so much. He possesses a very practical mind."

Using the wooden broom head as a pivot point, Anthony and John placed all their weight on the opposite end of the crowbar, slowly lifting the edge of the tomb six inches off the floor. Leo then placed his head on the floor and peered underneath with the flashlight.

"Do you see anything?" Morelli grunted.

"Not that I can tell. I'm pretty sure there's no seal here."

"Are you sure? Not even a mark? Something?"

"Nothing," Leo replied. "The bottom is smooth polished marble, just like the top. There's nothing here."

Morelli and John strained as they lowered the tomb and sat on the floor. Their breathing was labored and their clothes were beginning to stick to them.

Now what?

Leo wiped the sweat from his brow. "Well, I don't know about you, but I don't want to try Italian jailhouse cuisine. Let's move this thing back against the wall and get out of here."

Morelli barely hid his disappointment as the three men moved the tomb back into position against the wall. They were just starting for the exit when they heard voices echoing in the distance.

"Are you sure you saw them come down here?" It was the voice of Cardinal Lundahl.

"Yes, Your Eminence," a different voice said.

The three men froze, not knowing what to do next.

"Quick," Leo whispered. "Into the janitor's closet."

The group raced down the hall and crowded into the cramped space. They had just managed to squeeze the door closed when Cardinal Lundahl rounded the corner with Emilio in tow.

Lundahl sounded irritated. "There's no one here."

"Maybe they left when I went to call you, Eminence."

"What do you think they were doing?"

"I don't know, sir. Father Morelli has a key and official permission to enter this area, but the two with him do not."

"I'll talk to him later today and find out exactly what he's up to. Leave a message for him at his residence and say that I would like to speak with him immediately."

The cardinal and his assistant continued to walk throughout the area, checking each tomb for signs of tampering, while the trio in the closet held their breath, praying they would not be discovered. After several tense minutes, all was quiet. They waited another few minutes, then opened the door slightly and peaked out into the crypt. No one was there. They slowly moved toward the exit and stopped.

Leo looked around at the walls and up toward the ceiling. "How did they know we were down here, Anthony?"

"They probably have hidden security cameras," John said.

"They do," Morelli answered, "but even in the areas without cameras, they always seem to know what I'm doing at any moment of the day." Morelli was growing impatient. "Anyway, I think they've gone. Open the door, and let's go before security shows up."

Passing through the medieval doorway into the grotto, the three made it to the end of the narrow hall where it joined the public area of the crypt. A hushed group of T-shirted and wide-eyed tourists wearing *de rigueur* baseball caps filed by on the grotto tour, seemingly oblivious to the three men standing in a darkened hall behind a security chain.

Morelli waited until the large group had passed and winked at Leo and John. "Care to join the tour?" The trio peered around the corner before they jumped across the chain and joined the camera-encrusted tourists, blending in with the crowd until they exited into the sunshine above.

As soon as they were clear of the basilica and walking through Vatican Square, they began to breathe a little easier.

Morelli pulled at his collar. "We have to get into that newly discovered area right away. I think the cardinal's assistant knows we're looking for something, and he'll be watching our every move. We've got to find another way in. Today."

"What's the hurry, Anthony? Maybe this would be a good time to rattle some cages. Why not enlist Marcus's help in getting Emilio off your back?"

"I don't want the cardinal directly involved for reasons I'll go into later."

"Why? Don't you think he would understand, especially if he knew about the code?"

"I've filed several requests with his office to do a complete archaeological excavation of the newly discovered area. My application was answered by having that wall constructed by Emilio over the entrance. The cardinal's assistant is intentionally blocking my research for some reason. If we don't find the seal soon, I fear we will never be allowed to go anywhere under the Basilica again."

John was deep in thought as he ran his fingers through his beard. "Father, do you remember the drawing of a tunnel entrance we saw in the old plans of the first Christian church … the one that once occupied the site of the present church?"

Morelli had to think for a moment. "You mean the ancient tunnel we thought might lead underground from the Vatican and end somewhere under the Forum?"

"Yes, that's the one. After we looked at those plans, I drew a line on a map from the tunnel entrance to the Forum. It led right to the church of *San Giuseppe dei Falegnami*."

"Saint Joseph of the Carpenters?" Leo asked.

"Yes," Morelli said. "That's the English translation. The church was built in the sixteenth century above Mamertine, the old Roman prison. According to Christian legend, that's where Saint Peter was imprisoned."

"What's that church got to do with finding the seal?" Leo asked.

Morelli was starting to get excited. "I think I see what our young friend is getting to. The old prison was once a cistern with access to the city's main sewer, the *Cloaca Maxima*. There had to be a tunnel there sometime in the past that ran under the Vatican at the same level of the ancient area that's been sealed off from us. If the tunnel still exists, it should take us directly beneath the Basilica. The seal has to be located in that area."

Bound together for the moment in a brotherhood of conspiracy and armed with the beginnings of a plan, they sprinted across the square to the BMW parked along a side street with its top down. Squeezing into the cockpit built for two, the three men raced across the city toward the ancient Roman prison.

CHAPTER 6

The overcrowded BMW came to a halt on the *Via Dei Fori Imperiali*, close to the Forum of Caesar. John and Leo hopped from the car in front of the church, while Morelli searched out a spot to park among the crowds and large tour buses that lined the streets around the most ancient part of the city.

Jogging back to the church from his distant parking space, Morelli was out of breath as he motioned for the other two to follow him. "My department got an e-mail the other day from Cardinal Lundahl's office. Apparently, the region below the church surrounding the ruins of Mamertine Prison has been closed temporarily due to structural concerns. That means the tourist entrance in the back of the church that leads down to the area will also be closed, but there's a hidden alcove behind the altar with an old circular stairway we can use to go below."

They paused at the main doorway to the sixteenth -century church, where Morelli left a hefty donation in a steel box mounted to the wall next to a hollowed-out piece of carved stone brimming with holy water. The three entered with a group of worshipers and fell back, stopping next to a small wooden door that led behind the altar. They waited impatiently, knowing they had to choose the right moment to pass unobserved through the doorway.

Multicolored light from a row of stained glass windows above painted an elderly woman leading a slow-moving dog in their direction. She inched by the trio and smiled as the aging dog stopped to sniff John's leg. This was the only church in Rome that welcomed animals, and people from all over the city brought their beloved pets here to be blessed. The woman and her dog rounded a pillar, and when it seemed like they were finally alone, the men opened the door and slipped into a dark hallway. Looking ahead in the faint light, they moved along through the tight space until they reached some circular metal stairs that descended below the church.

The three circled down into the darkness on the rusty iron stairs, passing a small, long-forgotten medieval Christian chapel that had been excavated between the church above and the old Roman prison below. Reaching the bottom, they stepped out into a dank-smelling, dimly-lit passageway constructed sometime around 640 BC by Ancus Marcius, the fourth king of Rome.

"Are we close to the area where Saint Peter was held, Father?" John asked.

Morelli pointed to the wall behind John. "It's on the other side of that wall. There's a small dungeon-like cell there that once held Saint Peter and possibly even Saint John. It was said that Peter received several angelic visitations while he was imprisoned in that cold stone room and that he baptized his guards from a spring that miraculously appeared one day."

John breathed in the musty aroma. "It's hard to believe actual miracles and angelic visions have occurred here, right where we're standing now." He touched the wall outside the cell and conjured images of what the scene inside must have been like then.

Morelli took out a map and looked up and down the empty passageway. "Speaking of miracles, it will be a miracle if we can find that tunnel. It's probably been sealed off somewhere behind the thick outside wall for hundreds of years, if not longer."

Many of Rome's buildings had ancient ruins for basements. Restaurants and private homes used them for wine cellars, and many still had original Roman frescos covering the walls. The whole city was honeycombed beneath with interconnecting tunnels, most of which had been blocked off for security reasons.

A voice punctuated the darkness behind them. "Can I help you, Fathers?"

The three men froze in place before slowly turning to face a weathered-looking man holding a broom. The man had a kind face with wide eyes and a perpetual smile.

"Yes," Leo said. "We're looking for a tunnel that runs west from here to the Vatican."

The other two turned and stared at Leo with their mouths gaping open. What was he thinking? He had just given away their plan, and it was only a matter of time before they would be escorted out of the building by security or, worse, arrested. Italian jailhouse cuisine was one step closer to becoming a reality.

"Oh, the tunnel," the man said. "Come with me, Fathers."

Morelli leaned over and whispered in Leo's ear as they followed behind. "You're either crazy, lucky, or brilliant. I haven't made up my mind yet."

"Neither," Leo whispered back. "I don't think that janitor is part of some grand conspiracy to keep us from discovering an ancient chapel. He's just a working class man who enjoys helping people, especially priests. Anyway, at this point, what have we got to lose?"

The man led them down the brick hallway to a freshly excavated area cordoned off with yellow construction tape. Beyond the barrier, a seemingly endless dark tunnel stretched out before them.

The man paused to light a cigarette. "The archaeologists who were here yesterday dug away this wall and found the tunnel."

A sudden chill ran down Morelli's spine.

The janitor took a deep puff and exhaled the smoke. "They didn't want to go any further until they had a map of the catacombs. The priest in charge told me that some other priests from the Vatican would be coming back with a map. Are you the ones with the map? We weren't expecting you until tomorrow."

"Did the archaeologists who found this tunnel mention who they were working for?" Morelli asked.

"Yes, they were priests, just like you, Father. They work at the Vatican. Don't you work for the Vatican?" The man's perpetual smile was beginning to fade.

Morelli took the man by the arm. "Yes, of course, my friend. We just have so many people working on so many projects, we can't keep them all straight. We had some extra time today and wanted to see the tunnel for ourselves." Morelli sighed with the knowledge that he would be admitting to these lies in his next confession.

The man's smile returned as Leo glanced in the direction of the tunnel and winked at Morelli. "We might as well check out the area while we're here, Father."

"Yes, we have to be at another project tomorrow. We'll just survey the tunnel right now to make sure it's the right one and report our findings back to the Vatican."

The man looked bored. "*Molto bene*, Fathers. *Mi scusi*, but I must finish with my duties." With his cigarette dangling from his lips, he hefted the broom across his shoulder and walked off down the hallway. As soon as he rounded the corner, the three began to breathe normally again.

Stepping over the yellow tape, they noticed several lanterns and large flashlights in boxes and shovels and pickaxes stacked against the wall. Gathering up flashlights, a lantern, and a pickax, the men made a last check of the empty hallway before entering the tunnel.

"What if he tells someone we're down here?" John said, turning his head to look back over his shoulder.

"I'm more worried about the people who uncovered this tunnel," Morelli said. "As the chief of Vatican archaeology, I think I would have known about a group of 'archaeologist priests' from the Vatican doing an excavation under Mamertine Prison. Whoever they are, they aren't from my department."

Morelli's fear of an evil conspiracy now seemed closer to reality as Leo peered ahead into the darkness of the tunnel. "This just keeps getting stranger by the minute. Do you think they're looking for the same thing we are, Anthony?"

"Yes, and that makes me even more anxious to get into that deeper area and find the seal. There's only one explanation for them using this tunnel to access the catacombs beneath the necropolis, and that's secrecy."

Leo felt a twinge of fear as they began moving cautiously into the maze of catacombs that snaked beneath the city. All three men were well aware of the stories of people actually getting lost and dying in these ancient subterranean graveyards.

The tunnel had obviously been sealed off for centuries. Debris littered the hard-packed earthen floor. It consisted mostly of plaster that had once been used to seal ancient tombs, rocks from minor cave-ins, and, disturbingly, human and animal bones. The animal bones were left over from feasts held long ago in the catacombs by family and friends who came to honor their dead, while the human bones were the result of grave robber activity over the years.

The tunnel was otherwise in surprisingly good shape for its age, probably dating to around AD 100.

"How far do you think it is to the area beneath the Basilica?" John asked.

Morelli shined his light ahead. "About a mile. Of course, it seems farther when you're underground."

The men trudged forward through the maze, coughing now and then in the fetid air saturated with carbon dioxide. For the next hour and a half, they trekked through the dark labyrinth, crossing intersecting tunnels and trying to stay on a straight course to the Vatican. Morelli produced a thick piece of yellow chalk and began to mark the walls with an arrow when they passed an intersecting tunnel. He wanted to provide them with a sign if they got lost or accidentally doubled back in the maze.

John had tried in the past to use GPS to locate positions under the Vatican, but the device never seemed to work this far underground. The only way they would know when they had arrived at the area below the Basilica was their knowledge of the site.

The men were becoming exhausted from the long walk in the stale air, but the prospect of discovery pushed them on. After climbing and descending a series of steps, they rounded a slight curve and entered a large open area that rose almost twenty feet above their heads.

Morelli shined his light on a sloping pile of rubble that tumbled down from a newly constructed wall above. "There. That's the wall Emilio had built to keep me out. We are now directly under the Basilica. This is the area we first entered a few months ago after a workman's shovel pushed through into this section of the catacombs by accident. This site is definitely Christian, not pagan. The ancient Christians probably inhabited it when they were still being persecuted by the Romans. They hid from their persecutors down here and prayed together. This area must have been dug out around the time of Nero, the mad emperor who burned down half of Rome."

Leaning on his pickax, John shined his light around at the crumbling red-and-white-colored plaster that still covered several of the intact tombs. "We've already checked out most of this area, Father. Where do you want to start?"

"Let's look in the last section we mapped. We didn't have a chance to examine the walls or all the little nooks and crannies. Pay careful attention to anything that looks like a tomb. Sometimes the ancients painted seals to indicate the location of something or someone of importance."

Leo craned his neck to gaze up at the ceiling. "Is there any way we can find out where the queen's tomb above us is located?"

Morelli and John looked like they had both been struck by lightning.

"Of course!" John said. "Under the tomb of the queen!"

"Brilliant, Leo." Morelli retrieved the map case he always carried with him on excavations and removed three diagrams. The first was a modern blueprint of the grotto under the Basilica, the second was an archaeological diagram of the fully explored necropolis below that, and the third was a crude and hastily drawn map of the section of the catacombs they were standing in now.

Placing the diagrams on top of each other and holding them over the light of the lantern to make the drawings transparent, Morelli could see exactly where the tomb of the queen was in relation to their present location. He circled the corresponding spot on the crude map of their current location, and voila, he knew exactly where to start looking.

"You're a genius, Leo," Morelli said.

"Not too shabby, sir," John added.

Morelli's mood changed. He was seized by the fever of discovery and took off down a side tunnel that he had explored only briefly before the area was blocked off. Holding the lantern above his head, he slowed his pace and began scanning the walls. The other two followed his lead and bathed the walls with their lights.

It took every ounce of the men's strength to carry on in the oxygen deprived atmosphere of the catacombs. The high concentration of carbon dioxide made them feel sleepy and slightly disoriented. John was trying to stifle a yawn when he suddenly stopped next to a plain section of tunnel wall and stared above his head. He rubbed his eyes and looked closer.

"Fathers, I think I found it!"

The two priests aimed their lights at the spot. Above them, faded with age and grime, was undoubtedly a seal of some kind. Despite the stain of time, the border of the seal was more colorful than the surrounding walls and appeared to glimmer in the light, while in the center, the trio could see what looked like a painting under a layer of dust.

"Did you bring a brush?" Morelli asked John.

"Yes." He reached into his backpack and pulled out a small house painter's brush. "Here you go, Father."

Morelli began to gently sweep away centuries of caked-on dirt. As the colorful painting was slowly revealed, the three men let out a collective gasp. Encircled by a shining golden ring, the painted surface displayed the representation of an event that could not have occurred in ancient times. They were all staring at the unmistakable portrayal of a city engulfed in flames with the mushroom cloud of an atomic bomb rising above the surface.

CHAPTER 7

The men were clearly astonished as they continued to stare openmouthed at the seal.

"Well, you were right about recognizing the seal when we found it, Anthony," Leo finally said.

John reached out and ran his hand over the raised surface. "Yeah. I don't think we need the code to tell us this is what we're looking for."

With eyes glistening like a father admiring his newborn baby, Morelli gazed up at the gold-ringed seal on the wall. "This is astounding. I believe Lev and his team will be able to verify it, but I'm almost certain this is the seal we've been searching for."

A blinding flash of light caused Father Morelli's heart to skip a beat. He spun around to see Leo taking pictures of the seal with a small digital camera.

"Good idea, Leo. We can e-mail those pictures to Lev in Israel tonight. Hand me that pickax, John."

"Why don't you let me do the honors, Father? Remember your bad back."

"Be very careful, John. Try to keep the entrance hole as small as possible."

"What are you doing, Anthony?"

"What we are doing, my dear Father Leo, is knocking loose those bricks beneath the seal. If I'm right, the ancient chapel is right behind that wall."

The two priests shined their lights on the spot as John began to swing the pickax. They noticed that the section of the tunnel wall they were looking at had a distinctly different look from any of the others they had seen in the catacombs. Unlike the rest of the tunnels, which were carved out of the soft, reddish, volcanic tufo rock that supported the city, this wall was constructed out of large, pinkish-colored limestone blocks. John brought the sharp end of the pickax against the stone, slowly chipping away at the mortar holding it in place until one of the solid blocks gave way and fell into an invisible space beyond. It was for moments like this that every archaeologist lived: the possibility of a sealed-off room, unseen for centuries, with untold treasures waiting on the other side.

Knocking out two more large stones, the hole was now large enough for a man to poke his head through. John laid the pickax aside and peered into the void. "There's definitely a hollow space here."

Father Morelli pushed in beside him and shined his light into the blackness. He backed away and let out a loud whoop while slapping John on the back.

"It's huge!" Morelli exclaimed. "It's the size of a ballroom ... it's bigger than anything I've ever seen in any of the other catacombs under Rome."

John lifted up the pickax again and continued knocking away the stone blocks until a small two-foot by two-foot opening stood in a cloud of dust before them. Without a word, Father Morelli squeezed through the opening. John grinned at Leo and motioned him forward. Leo felt a sudden rush of excitement. "Go ahead, John. I'll follow you."

Once inside, the men's voices echoed in the space as they began shining their lights around, looking for evidence that this was the ancient hidden chapel they had been searching for. The immense room was totally empty except for a large, rough-hewn stone structure built atop a raised area at the far end. Morelli and the others noticed right away that the eerie and unusual space was constructed of the same stone blocks they had seen outside in the tunnel.

"I'm beginning to wonder if the people who created this room transported their building material to Rome from somewhere else," Morelli said. "It appears that this area was excavated just for this room and lined with this pinkish-colored stone for some specific reason."

"Why would they do that?" John asked.

"That's what we're here to find out," Morelli said, eyeing the opposite end of the space. The scene had a dreamlike quality to it as he approached some steps leading to a raised area supporting a structure that resembled an altar. It consisted of a long, flat slab of gray stone supported by two massive four-foot-high carved blocks of stone, each several feet thick and placed six feet apart. Above the altar was the unmistakable image of a five-foot tall Christian cross carved into the wall.

There was no doubt among the three men that they had just discovered a very different and ancient Christian place of worship. They paused to look up at the beautifully carved cross before resuming their exploration in silence, slowly walking back and forth, illuminating the walls, floor, and ceiling with their lights.

"This is definitely not what I expected," Father Morelli said, finally able to bring himself to speak. The other two were just as dumbstruck by the discovery.

Looking for symbols or anything that looked like writing, Leo walked along one of the walls and shined his light up at the ceiling fifteen feet above their heads. "What do you think, Anthony? Is this the chapel?" The sound of his voice reverberated in the empty space.

Morelli grinned at his friend. "This has to be it. The same reference in the Bible code that refers to a seal also mentions an ancient chapel, and there's no doubt in my mind that the seal outside is the one we were looking for. Somewhere here, there's a message, a message from the past that was meant for us now, in the present."

Father Morelli was barely able to contain his excitement as he walked from one side of the space to the other in triumphant glee.

Stopping to catch his breath, Leo wiped the dusty sweat from his face. "You know, Anthony, I'm just as excited as you are about finding this chapel, but have you given any thought to the fact that, if the code is correct, this discovery means that there could be some very dark days ahead for the world?"

"We're only excited because finding this ancient chapel validates the code, Father. The future of mankind is in God's hands. Since the information we found in the code led us to this exact spot, does this not prove that the hidden code in the Old Testament is real? We may have received a message from God himself written thousands of years ago. Is this not reason enough to be excited? I would have thought you of all people would have understood the meaning of this."

Morelli seemed spent. He sat down on the stone floor and let the meaning of the moment soak in. An exhausted Father Leo sat down on the floor beside him.

"Anthony, I want to learn more about this code in the Bible. If what you say bares any truth at all, we can all rejoice at the implications. However, I have to admit, I'm very concerned at the thought of where all of this will take us."

"I promise you, Leo, that tomorrow we'll go over all the data we've collected up to this point. But I tell you now, there is no other explanation for our being led to this exact spot except for the hand of God himself."

Following his inspection of the chapel, John walked over and joined the two priests. "Except for the altar, there's nothing else here. It's just a bare room with no doorway."

Morelli began to sense that something wasn't quite right. "I think we've spent enough time down here for now. The carbon dioxide levels are too high for us to stay any longer. Let's move out into the tunnel and replace the bricks in the hole we made. Until we know the chapel's true purpose, we need to keep its location a secret."

The trio began to gather the stone bricks that had fallen inside the chapel and piled them in the tunnel by the entrance. They worked quickly to fit all the bricks back into the hole while using the water from their canteens to moisten the powder-like mortar that had fallen to the floor. Scooping up the mud-like substance, they smoothed it into the spaces between the stones.

When they were almost finished with their reconstruction, Leo's eyes fell on a lone brick lying on the earthen floor. In their haste to enter the chapel, they had forgotten to check the loose bricks for any marks or symbols. He stepped closer and shined his light on the stone. His breath began to come in shallow gasps as he reached down and brushed away some of the dust that covered part of the image he was staring at.

"Anthony ... John ... I think you two need to see this."

Father Morelli and John shined their lights down on the stone brick. On its painted surface, they saw the clear and unmistakable image of a modern jet plane hitting one of two very tall towers.

"Oh, my God," John said. "It's 9/11!"

All three looked at one another in disbelief. The ancient image depicting a modern event on a brick from inside a chapel sealed for nineteen centuries was too much to process at the moment.

"We need to take that brick with us," Morelli said.

John concentrated on composing himself before grabbing the brick and shoving it into his backpack. "We really have to go, Fathers."

The three men finished sealing off the chapel in silence. They used existing tunnel debris to fill in the hole left from the missing brick and began making their way out of the long-forgotten section of the ancient Christian catacombs.

Leo felt himself sway as the tunnel walls began to close in around him. "How much farther is it, Anthony?"

"I don't think we'll have to go all the way back to Mamertine Prison. On the way here, I noticed an older side tunnel that appeared to lead in the direction of *Castel Sant' Angelo*, and if we can find an exit there, we should be breathing fresh air in fifteen minutes."

The exhausted men made their way through a series of right and left turns until they came to a crumbling side tunnel. Trading looks, they entered the narrow passageway and followed it until they came across an old wooden ladder that led to a covered opening above their heads.

Leo climbed up and found the name of the castle engraved on a heavy metal cover sealing the exit. He pushed as hard as he could with little success before John climbed up beside him with the pickax. They placed one end of the axe under the edge, and after some levered pushes, the cover inched away from the opening. Breathing even more heavily now, they all climbed up into a basement room of the ancient castle and collapsed on the floor.

The massive fortress of *Castel Sant' Angelo* was named after the Archangel Michael. It was built in AD 139 as Emperor Hadrian's mausoleum. In the year 590, the Archangel Michael appeared above the mausoleum to Pope Gregory the Great. Returning his sword into its scabbard, the angel signaled the end of a plague. Since then, the castle has served as a medieval citadel, a prison, and as a residence to popes in times of political unrest.

The lower levels were composed of stone cells, which were used mainly for storage. It was into one of these cells that the three men had climbed before collapsing from exhaustion and lack of fresh air. After resting for several minutes, they slid the heavy cover back over the manhole and continued to breathe in the oxygen-rich air.

John raised himself to his feet and walked over to the only exit in the room. He lifted a heavy metal latch on the door and peered out into a brightly lit hallway. Backing into the other two, John held his finger up to his lips and quickly closed the door.

Two security guards in impeccable dark blue uniforms were coming directly at them from a stairway at the far end of the hall. Had the guards seen him open the door? Footsteps stopped in the hallway outside. The three men listened. They could hear voices, then laughter, as the footsteps trailed off in the distance. John inched the door open and looked out into the empty hallway before glancing over his shoulder. "If we have to join another tour to get out of this place, I'm buying a full-season tourist pass."

The nervous trio stepped into the hall and made their way unseen up the stairs to an outside door that opened onto a street teaming with tourists. Catching a few stares, the tired, dirt-covered men stumbled out into the bright sunshine and summoned the last of their strength to make their way back toward the Vatican.

Morelli stomped the sidewalk in an effort to shake the dirt from his shoes. "I've got to take a shower and go pick up my car. I'll meet you at your hotel in a few hours, Leo."

Almost too weary to speak, Leo nodded before stopping to gaze up at the statue of Saint Michael perched on the summit of the castle. He turned toward Morelli. "Did we really just use the Bible to find an ancient hidden chapel?"

Morelli smiled. "Amazing, isn't it."

CHAPTER 8

Following a hot shower, Father Leo dressed and opened a bottle of wine. After pouring a large glass, he walked out onto the balcony and breathed in the warm spring air containing a mixture of flowers, motorbike exhaust, and cooking smells heavy with garlic. It was pure Roman perfume that existed nowhere else on earth. He felt refreshed, and the events of the day had stirred him to feel more focused and alive with a kind of hyper-alertness guiding his thoughts.

A knock at the door startled him. Setting his wine on a small glass-topped table, he moved back inside the room with unreasoning apprehension. Leo pulled the door open slightly and felt a surge of relief to see the grinning faces of Morelli and John standing in the hallway.

"Well, can we come in?" Morelli asked, looking at his friend with a sense of amusement.

"Of course. Sorry. I, well, I …"

"You mean, you're still a little freaked out about today," John said.

"Well, yes, to be frank. I mean, this whole business has been so sudden and has such profound implications. Aren't you two at all fazed by what we've found?"

Morelli put his hand on Leo's shoulder. "Pour us some wine, Father. We have a lot to discuss."

John opened up his backpack and unceremoniously dropped the painted brick from the chapel onto the bed. There, before their eyes, was the image of a modern jet plane hitting the Twin Towers. It was unmistakable in its breadth and clarity.

"I think the first thing we should do is have it carbon dated," John said.

"Yes, naturally," Morelli agreed. "We also need to call Lev in Israel. He'll want to run an analysis with the Bible code software right away. I feel we are on a breakthrough of … "

"Of biblical proportions?" John laughed.

For the first time all day, Leo began to relax. These two tireless individuals were able to deal with what was probably one of the most astonishing historical discoveries of all time without losing their sense of perspective. With the thrill of discovery, the specter of unseen *evil forces* drifted off into the background.

Morelli sat on the edge of the bed and picked up the phone while Leo and John walked out onto the balcony. The glow from the wine, the sunset, and the day's events, had given Leo a feeling of total gratification to be at this place at this time in history as he listened to Morelli's animated discussion with Lev Wasserman in Israel. This discovery was most likely the highlight of both their careers and went a long way toward validating the code.

Leo handed John a glass of wine. "Where do you think we'll go from here?"

"Well, to tell you the truth, that's not entirely clear, Father. A lot depends on the two men talking on the phone right now. Those guys are probably the most knowledgeable people in the world on what is happening and where all this may lead. I mean, can you believe it? We are actually waiting for an encoded message in the Bible to tell us what to do next. It's like receiving a text message from God. If this doesn't convince people of the existence of our Heavenly Father, then I don't know what else will, besides an actual witnessed visitation."

"You seem pretty excited about all of this, John."

"Who wouldn't be? Aren't you?"

"Of course. This is definitely the most exciting thing that's ever happened in my life. I'm just glad to see someone from your generation so pumped up about history and the Bible."

"I've always loved history, Father. I grew up on a ranch in New Mexico, and we were surrounded by ancient Native American cliff dwellings. I used to ride my horse up into the mountains around the ranch house and sit among the ruins. The wind would blow through the canyons and you could almost hear the voices from the past. I would imagine the people who once lived there going about their daily lives in that very spot over a thousand years ago. I got the same feeling today when we were down in the catacombs. That's why I decided my life's work would be to learn all I could about history and the different civilizations that have evolved over time."

"Where did you go to school?"

"The University of Arizona in Tucson. They have one of the best history programs in the country. One of the professors there is an authority on the Holy Land, and he got me interested in the time the Romans occupied Israel in the first century."

"So why the priesthood, John?"

"I've always had the idea in the back of my mind, but I still don't know if I'm ready to take sacred vows that will affect the rest of my life. At least the time I've spent in Assisi has opened my eyes to a lot of what the religious life is all about."

"You're smart to give it some time. It's a lifetime commitment and not one to be taken lightly, but I'm encouraged that more men of your caliber are considering it. You know, since 1965, candidates for the priesthood have dropped by an astonishing ninety percent."

John swirled the wine in his glass. "That could change after today. In the space of time between breakfast and supper, we've discovered what could arguably be called one of the greatest biblical finds ever. Even though we don't yet know the meaning and purpose of the chapel, we do know that the Bible led us to it. That alone is proof of a higher power at work. I mean, think of it. Ancient man lacked the technology to embed such a sophisticated code in the Bible when it was written. If you ask me, divine intervention has to be the only logical explanation for the existence of a code so complex that it takes modern computers to reveal it. This could be the smoking gun in proving God's existence to those who lack faith, Father."

Leo looked across the street at the dome of Saint Peter's. He was totally spent from the day's activities. Doubt began to seep into his subconscious. It was not the kind of doubt one experiences from a lack of faith, but a hesitancy that may well accompany all great and unbelievable finds men have stumbled upon throughout history. Conceivably, every one of mankind's paramount discoveries, whether in math, astronomy, medicine, or archaeology, have all been greeted with similar doubt. *Have we truly found what we think we've found? Can this, indeed, be real?*

Father Morelli hung up the phone and walked out onto the balcony. "Lev was so excited to hear we found the chapel that he put me on speaker phone so that his team in Israel could listen to all the details. I could hear them shouting and singing in the background. When I told him about the brick with the image of the plane crashing into the two towers, he was speechless. He's well aware of the code's ability to predict things, but to find a two-thousand-year-old stone with an image of the 9/11 attack painted on it is beyond comprehension. If I know the good professor, and I do, he'll be awake all night studying the code trying to see how all of this fits."

"When do you think you'll be hearing from him again?" Leo asked.

"Oh, it might be in an hour or four in the morning or a month. One can never tell with the code. Even with computers, there is no limitation to the amount of information encoded in the Bible."

"I'm no mathematician here, but how is that possible?"

"Think of the Bible as a cryptogram sent to us by God himself," Morelli said, "a cryptogram with a series of time locks that could not be opened until certain events came to pass. Obviously, one of these events is the invention of the computer. This one leap in technology has enabled scientists and cryptographers who've been working on the code to discover hidden messages placed there by an intelligence greater than any that exists here on earth. There is another Bible within the Bible. It's like a massive puzzle in layers, similar to a three-dimensional hologram. Some believe that the Bible itself is a computer program left to us by the Almighty, and there are an infinite number of combinations and permutations yet to be discovered. Even with all our computers and code-breaking programs, no one could have encoded the Bible the way it was done thousands of years ago."

Leo became even more fascinated with the implications as he listened to Morelli speak. "Just how much information is there?"

"All of our past and all of our future. The name of every person who has lived before us, who is living now, and who is yet to be born. All of our greatest historical events, plagues, disasters, wars, and future wars. All are encoded in the Old Testament."

"But that's utterly impossible!"

"Well, Father, you'd better be prepared to argue with some pretty knowledgeable people who have done the research and proved its existence with a 99.998 percent probability. These guys were renowned scientists who set out to disprove the theory of the code, but instead, what they found sent chills up their spines. They saw the hand of God at work."

Leo refilled his glass. "Then if what you say is correct, we are looking at an intelligence that encoded our past, present, and future over three thousand years ago, using a mathematical model we can't even grasp today."

"Exactly," Morelli said. "And being a man of faith, I'm convinced that intelligence is God. He has given us proof with a modern twist that He exists and is sending us a message."

"Or opening up a dialogue," Leo added.

The three men gazed silently at the twinkling lights of Rome as darkness descended over the city, providing a backdrop to the brightly lit Basilica of Saint Peter's.

"I think we're missing something," John said, after a moment of uncharacteristic silence.

Morelli turned toward the young man. "Go on, John. I see those wheels turning inside your head."

"Well, for one thing, why is there an ancient seal in the catacombs depicting a nuclear attack? And of course, the big question is, who painted the image of the 9/11 attacks over two thousand years ago? Only someone with prophetic ability could have created pictures like that. Then there's the question of who built the chapel and why."

Morelli leaned against the balcony railing and took a sip from his glass. "Good points, John. I wish I could answer those questions right now, but I can't. We still have a lot of work ahead of us, so for now, that part of the puzzle will have to remain a mystery until we have time to sift through all the information."

"Do you think someone could have cracked the code that far back in time and constructed the chapel and painted the images as some kind of sign or warning to us now?" Leo asked.

"I doubt it," Morelli said. "Like I said earlier, without computers, the code would have been virtually invisible back then. Whoever built the chapel and painted the images may have had a little help in the form of divine intervention. Maybe it was constructed for a specific reason by ancient Christians led by a prophet who saw into the future. Who knows? We may never know who actually built it, but it's there just the same, and that's all we have to go on for now."

Morelli stretched with his arms above his head. "Well, my friends, the day is late, and I must rest."

John set his glass on the table. "Yeah, me too."

"Right. When we were your age, this discussion would have gone on until dawn," Morelli said. "Oh, I almost forgot." Morelli reached under his shirt and pulled out a large, gold pectoral cross. "This is for you, Leo."

"Where did you get that?"

Morelli kept a straight face. "The cardinal store."

Leo looked puzzled. "The what …?"

"I'm kidding, my friend. This cross once belonged to a pope when he was a cardinal. It's my gift to you."

"I can't possibly accept—"

Morelli shoved the cross into Leo's hand. "Yes, you can. I insist. Besides, I have a feeling it might come in handy someday, Father."

Leo turned the large cross over and admired the magnificent workmanship. "It … it's beautiful. I don't know what to say. Thank you, Anthony."

"Just be sure to wear it under your shirt, at least until you become a cardinal."

"Chances of that happening are slim to none, but thank you anyway. I've never owned anything like this in my life."

"Wow," John said. "That really belonged to a pope?"

"Yes," Morelli said, "a very special pope."

Walking toward the door, Morelli clasped Leo's shoulder in farewell. An expression of sadness clouded his face.

"You know, Leo, I've been waiting all my life for a discovery like the one we made today. I just never expected that it would make my faith even stronger. The more we learn, the more we realize that the code in the Bible is not as reliable as we first thought for making predictions. I believe the real purpose of the code is to authenticate the Bible as a book of divine and supernatural origin. The most beautiful thing about all of this is that it will announce to the whole world that, yes, God does exist, and He is still talking to us today using modern methods."

"Maybe that's His intention, Father."

"Get some rest, my friend," Morelli said. "You've got a lot ahead of you in the days to come."

"You mean *we* don't you, Anthony?"

Father Morelli paused as if he had misspoken. "Of course. *We* have a lot to do in the days ahead."

Leo closed the door and thought for a moment before walking back out onto the balcony. Looking down at the street, he saw Morelli and John descend the hotel stairs and climb into the BMW. In the quiet night air, he could hear their voices clearly before Morelli revved the car's engine in a prelude to his signature high-speed departure. Father Morelli glanced over his shoulder and spotted Leo standing on the balcony. His ever-present smile was absent as he waved and let his foot off the clutch before roaring off into the night.

Leo sat alone on the balcony for another hour, drinking his wine and looking across the street at the Vatican. He breathed in deeply before finally getting up and walking back into his room. The priest sat on the bed and grabbed the TV remote. He thought the distraction of a little Italian television would help to clear his mind, but it was no use. Father Leo Amodeo knew deep down inside that something was very, very wrong.

CHAPTER 9

The ringing phone jarred Leo awake.

"Hello?"

"Father Leo, *buon giorno. Mi dispiace* to awaken you. It is me, Arnolfo, at the front desk."

"*Buon giorno*, Arnolfo. *A che ora?*"

"*Sei*, Father. Six in the morning. You have a call from the Vatican. It is from a cardinal, and he wants most urgently to speak with you."

Leo could tell from Arnolfo's voice that he was close to being hysterical at having to put a cardinal on hold.

"That's fine, Arnolfo. *Grazie*. Put him through."

"Hello … Leopold?" Leo knew that only Lundahl called him Leopold.

"Yes. Good morning, Cardinal. How—"

"You need to come to the Vatican right away, Leopold. I have some bad news. Very bad, I'm afraid."

Leo felt a tightening in his stomach. "What is it, Your Eminence? What's happened?"

"It concerns Father Morelli. I hate to tell you like this on the phone, Leopold, but he passed away last night. I know how close you two were, and I thought you would like to know right away."

Leo felt the room sway. His mind went immediately to that place where it rested in a state of denial one experiences upon hearing the final, awful news that death has come to someone close. He crossed himself and began to pray.

"Leopold? Are you there?"

"Yes, sorry." Leo began to gather himself. All he could picture at the moment was Father Morelli driving away in his red sports car the night before.

"I realize this must be a terrible shock to you, Father. We will be gathering in his room to pray for his departed soul. Can you come to the residence hall as soon as possible?"

"I'm on my way, Eminence. Give me twenty minutes."

Leo was just reaching for his clothes when the phone rang again.

"Yes?"

"Leo, it's me, John. Have you heard the news about Father Morelli?"

"Yes, I just talked to Cardinal Lundahl."

"I still can't believe it. What a horrible time for this to happen. I know he is with God in heaven, but he had so much more he wanted to do here on earth. He told me just last night that we must be very cautious, especially now, at this time in history. Before he went upstairs to his room, he warned me again about dark forces at work that will try to keep us from learning the secret of the chapel. Now this. The timing is eerie."

Leo looked at the clock next to the bed. "I'm on my way to the residence hall now."

"Good," John said. "We need to talk. Something's not right. The cardinal's assistant has ordered a search of the residence hall, and the plain-clothes men from the Swiss Guard are all over the place."

"The entire building?"

"Every room. When you get here, be sure not to mention the chapel or yesterday's discovery. I'll explain everything to you later. Right now, I need to pray for Father Anthony. I know he's looking down on us now. He's undoubtedly getting used to his new wings and telling the angels some of his favorite jokes."

Leo had to pause for a moment. "Does anyone else know about our discovery yesterday?"

"As far as I know, only Lev Wasserman and his team in Israel."

"Well, that kind of narrows it down then. We need time to think."

"I know I'm probably overreacting, Leo. It's just the timing and the shock of losing Father Morelli."

"I'll see you in a few minutes. Anthony was fortunate to have a friend like you, John."

Leo hung up the phone and quickly dressed in the standard uniform of a Roman Catholic priest. Looking in the mirror, he brushed his teeth and combed his hair as the mental picture of Morelli's smiling face caused a lump to form in his throat. The sudden loss of his best friend was a shock, but he was comforted by the knowledge that Father Morelli had prepared all of his life for the journey he had just taken.

Leo stepped from the elevator into the hotel lobby just as Arnolfo rushed up and handed the priest a tiny porcelain cup filled with dark, steaming espresso.

"I know you are in a hurry, Father. My wife and I, we pray for Father Morelli."

"Thank you, Arnolfo. God bless you, my friend."

Leo gulped down the thick, dark coffee and handed the empty cup back to Arnolfo before running outside and crossing the street to the Vatican.

The residence hall was located inside the main gate to the right. It was basically a large five-story apartment building for priests living at the Vatican. The rooms were sparse but comfortable, with private baths and small kitchenettes. The building included over one hundred apartments, plus a library, computer room, meeting spaces, and a small but ornate chapel. The fact that Lundahl's assistant was having the whole building searched was raising all kinds of red flags to Leo, especially on the heels of the death of Father Morelli.

Arriving in front of the residence hall, Leo noticed a number of uniformed police officers milling about outside. Once inside the lobby area, he saw several Swiss Guard security men stationed in front of the staircase and talking on their radios.

The Swiss Guard dated back to the Renaissance when, in 1506, one hundred fifty fearless Swiss mercenaries under the leadership of the warrior-pope, Julius II, marched into Rome to protect the Vatican. For over five hundred years, the elite corps had protected the pope and had evolved into a force resembling the U.S. Secret Service.

Leo began walking toward the main stairway but found his path blocked by a large security man dressed in a suit.

"I'm sorry, Father, but the residence is temporarily closed. Do you live here?"

"No. I'm Father Leopold Amodeo. Father Morelli was a close friend of mine. Cardinal Lundahl called and requested that I come over here immediately."

With the mention of Cardinal Lundahl's name, the man stepped aside.

"One of my officers will escort you to Father Morelli's apartment on the third floor. We are all sorry to hear of his death. He was much loved by everyone."

A uniformed guard snapped to attention and led Leo up the marble staircase past several medieval paintings and statues to the third floor. They turned onto a wide hallway, where Leo noticed several men going in and out of the various rooms, apparently searching for something. A guard stationed at Morelli's partially open door held his hand out in front of Leo, blocking the entrance to his room. "Excuse me, sir, but the cardinal has given me strict orders not to let anyone inside. He said you would be allowed to watch the last rites from the doorway."

Leo was mystified. "But I was Father Morelli's best friend."

"Orders from the cardinal, Father. Please try to understand."

Leo was unable to summon any anger at this strange turn of events; the sorrow of losing his friend was forcing him to hold all his emotions in check.

He peered through the doorway into Morelli's tiny apartment. The curtains were pulled tightly over the closed windows, making the room especially dark and airless. Two priests, along with an older and very seasoned-looking security man, were also in attendance, while Emilo, the cardinal's assistant who seemed to follow him everywhere, was strangely absent. The security man inside the door blocked most of Leo's view, and he could barely see Father Morelli lying on his bed.

Cardinal Lundahl stood on the opposite side of the bed by the window, looking across the room and through the door at Leo with unblinking eyes. He was an imposing figure dressed in a black floor-length cassock with red piping and a scarlet watered silk fascia draped around his waist. The bright red skull cap of a cardinal crowned his short blond hair, while a large, gold pectoral cross hung from his neck at the level of his chest, hence the name, pectoral.

The room was clean and neat, reflecting Morelli's need for order in his life. Leo saw that he was lying on top of the bedspread with his shoes off, as if he had just stretched out for a quick nap. He was still clothed in the simple black shirt and trousers of a priest, with the Roman collar draped open for comfort. His red hair was still neatly combed, and from a distance, it appeared that he was just sleeping. Leo felt a sudden rush of relief as he realized that Father

Morelli had obviously died of what appeared to be a natural death in his sleep. With all the police presence, the thought had occurred to him that his friend had been the victim of some crime or act of violence. Unbelievable as it may seem, murders had occurred in the Vatican.

Without speaking, Cardinal Lundahl took a purple surplice from one of the priests and placed it around his neck, kissing each end before letting it fall to the front of his cassock. He then took a small bottle of holy water and poured it on a silver cross before using it to anoint the forehead and hands of Father Morelli. The last rites of the dead had begun.

In truth, there really are no so-called last rites in the Catholic Church. What most people refer to as the last rites is actually the sacrament of the Anointing of the Sick. This sacrament is used for healing, both spiritual and physical, and is performed by a priest when a person requests divine intervention. It is meant to save souls here on earth before they cross over, for once they are dead, the soul is no longer here but with God and beyond a priest's intervention. All that any priest can do at that point is offer prayers for the soul.

Following the ritual, the two priests covered the body in a white sheet and placed a plain wooden crucifix on his chest. Leo turned away from the door and gave a silent prayer for the gentle soul of his friend. Wiping the tears from his face, he stood in the hallway as Lundahl and the others exited the apartment. It was only then that Leo realized John was nowhere to be seen.

A strong hand clasped Leo's shoulder from behind. He turned to see the cardinal looking at him with a mixture of questioning and sympathy. "I'm glad you could be here for him, Leopold. Our dear brother is now in heaven. We are all deeply saddened by the loss of such a good and noble man. I'm sorry that we could not allow you into the room, but it was a request from Father Morelli himself. He gave instructions that, in the event of his death, he didn't want any of his friends to stand around and look down on his earthly body. I suppose he wanted to preserve your memory of him in life."

"Thank you, Eminence." Leo was touched by the apparent sincerity of the cardinal's words. Lundahl clasped his hands together and stood silently for a moment before continuing. "Father Morelli was one of a kind. Out of all our classmates at seminary, he was the most intriguing, a true Renaissance man. I only wish the Church had more soldiers of the cross like him. I know we had our disagreements, but he was a special and valuable member of a dwindling community."

Leo took a deep breath. "The Church is like a big family, Cardinal, and families sometimes disagree. I never felt that Father Morelli took your differing views personally."

"You're very wise, Leopold. I hope you will stay close to us in the days to come."

"I plan to stay until after the funeral, Eminence, longer if you need me."

The cardinal paused for a moment, looking down at the floor. He then lifted his gaze and fixed Leo with what could only be called a look of total exhaustion. "I fear I must cancel our lunch appointment today. I have something of a situation on my hands, and I'm sure you need some time for solitary reflection."

Leo's concern and curiosity was getting the best of him. "Can I be of any assistance, Eminence? I noticed all the security men around. Is everything alright?"

Lundahl's look of exhaustion disappeared. "Oh…yes…of course. Coincidentally, Father Emilio was notified that some valuable historical papers went missing from the Vatican library last night and our security people are looking for them. Sometimes scholars studying manuscripts take them to their apartments by mistake."

The stern-looking security man took the cardinal's statement as his cue to speak. "Yes, it has nothing to do with the death of Father Morelli."

Leo watched Lundahl stiffen noticeably. The cardinal was staring at the man with the expression one gives a child who is misbehaving in public. The security man immediately realized he had spoken out of turn and made a hasty retreat down the hall, where he began shouting orders to the guards searching the rooms.

Leo saw that the cardinal's gaze had shifted back to him.

"Please give my secretary a call tomorrow, Leopold. I'll instruct him to set up a lunch meeting for just the two of us. I need to talk with you about some matters of great importance. God bless you, and also Father Morelli." With that, Lundahl turned and strode down the hall, his black and scarlet cassock flowing out behind him.

CHAPTER 10

Father Leo exited the building into the din of early morning traffic. Crowds of tourists were streaming into the holy city. Most were heading toward the Sistine Chapel to view Michelangelo's magnificent ceiling, while others circled Saint Peter's Square, hoping for a glimpse of the pope. Distraught with the terrible news of Father Morelli's death, Leo had no appetite for breakfast. What he really needed now was a drink. As a priest, a man of faith, he should feel joy for a soul now in heaven. But he was also a mortal man and, as such, was grieving for a friend he had known most of his adult life. Yes, what he needed now more than anything was a drink.

Leo walked out of Vatican City, numb to the brilliant sunshine and rows of multicolored flowers springing to life in nearby flowerbeds. His ears were deaf to the birds singing from the rooftops. He kept his head down, not wanting to acknowledge a smile from anyone crossing his path. He crossed the *Ponte Vittorio Emanuele II* over the river Tiber and continued along the *Via Giulia*, one of the first Renaissance streets to cut through Rome's hodgepodge of medieval alleys. Turning left onto the *Via Del Pellegrino*, he walked slowly until he found himself in the *Piazza Campo de' Fiori*. He crossed the piazza, finally coming to rest under one of several green umbrella-covered tables located in front of a traditional family-owned *trattoria*. Father Morelli and Leo had come here often. Together, they would share a bottle of wine and eat pasta in the afternoon, talking and laughing with friends and students about the day's events.

Leo ordered a glass of wine and sat staring out into the piazza. The tables around him were full of customers bound together in the time-honored Roman tradition of people watching. This activity usually relaxed him when he was tense or stressed, but despite the pleasant surroundings, questions nagged at the periphery of his thoughts.

Why wasn't John at the residence hall this morning? Were there really "evil forces" at work against them? If this were true, had something happened to John? Who were the archaeological priests who had uncovered the tunnel at the Mamertine Prison? And finally, why did Anthony summon him to Rome? He was pummeled by questions, like the punches he received years ago when he fought in high school boxing matches under the gaze of his father and brothers. Morelli could have found the chapel without his help, but he had wanted Leo to come to Rome for a reason, even if Leo still had no clear idea what the true motive really was. One thing he knew for sure: Father Morelli's work was not finished, and time had run out for him. Whatever the rationale, Leo knew he was now committed to learning more about the code and the ancient chapel under the Vatican.

A waiter hustled around the table. "Another glass of wine, Father?"

"No, *grazie*."

Opening his wallet, Leo saw that it was still empty and remembered that he had again forgotten to get cash.

"*Accettate carte di credito?*" Leo asked.

"*Si*, Father, we take cards."

Leo began thumbing through his wallet when he felt a tap on the shoulder. Squinting up into the sunshine, he spied the unmistakable brown robe of a Franciscan brother.

"I've been looking all over for you," John said, exasperation showing on his face. He threw some Euros on the table and grabbed Leo by the arm, practically lifting him from the chair.

"We have to go. Now, Father."

Leo pushed back his chair. "What's the hurry, John?"

"Do you know what the security guys were looking for?"

"Not really. Some stolen church documents, according to Cardinal Lundahl."

"Wrong," John said. "They were looking for this." He shoved a small, blue plastic object in front of Leo's face. "This is what they are looking for, and we really must go."

Looking around the piazza, John slid the object under his robe and into his pants pocket. Whatever was going on, Leo instinctively knew that, at this moment, he should follow John and ask questions later.

Racing across the piazza, the two men entered a side street, where Leo saw Father Morelli's bright red car parked along the curb with the top down. John opened the trunk and threw his brown monk's robe inside next to the backpack holding the ancient stone brick. Wearing only jeans, a white T-shirt, and sandals, he jumped into the driver's seat and motioned for Leo to get in. Leo hesitated for a moment, feeling slightly uncomfortable about getting into Morelli's beloved sports car.

"Let's go, Father. We have to hurry."

Leo opened the door and slid into the passenger seat while John fumbled with the gear shift. After finding first gear, he gunned the engine and lurched the car into the maze of side streets.

John pulled an envelope from under his T-shirt and handed it to Leo. "I went to Father Morelli's room this morning before dawn. He didn't answer the door, so I went back to my room. Someone had slipped that envelope under my door with your name written on it. Then the phone rang, and a Vatican security officer told me that Father Morelli had died. At first, I didn't know what to do. Father Morelli told me that, if anything ever happened to him, I was to go to his office and mail his laptop to Lev Wasserman in Jerusalem. I express mailed it to Israel after I phoned you this morning. Here, take this." John pulled the blue plastic object from the pocket of his jeans. "I'm sure this is what they were searching for."

"What is it?" Leo asked.

"It's a computer flash drive. On it is all our research up to now on the hidden chapel. There are also some private records with details of Father Morelli's financial assets, including his bank pass codes. After I finished mailing the laptop, I went straight to his apartment to meet up with you. When I saw that the cardinal and all the security men were still around, I just kept walking down the hallway past his room. They were frantically searching the building for something, and I put two and two together."

Leo took the flash drive from John and studied it for a moment. "You think they were looking for this?"

"I'm pretty sure of it. Father Morelli was very suspicious of elements within the church that he felt were working against us. They would love to have the information on that flash drive."

Leo pulled a lever under his seat and pushed it back as far as it would go to straighten out his legs. "Where did you find this?"

"Father Morelli insisted that I keep it. He was always misplacing it and knew that, if anyone was looking for it, they wouldn't think to look in my apartment. I had it in my pocket when I walked past the security men and right out the front door. I saw you enter the building and decided to get Father Morelli's car and wait for you in front of your hotel. When you didn't return, I started looking for you in all the cafés close to the Vatican. I kind of figured you needed a drink at that point. That's when I remembered Father Morelli said you and he always went to that café back there when you were in Rome. It was one of his favorite places."

The BMW sped under the Farnese archway designed by Michelangelo on the *Via Giulia*. Leo noticed they were heading back toward the Vatican. "Where are we going?"

"We're on our way back to your hotel. You need to change clothes, pack your stuff, and check out. Don't forget your passport in the hotel safe. You need to ditch that Roman collar too, right now."

"What in the world are you talking about, John? Are you losing it? Maybe we should stop the car right now. I think I need to walk for a while and clear my head."

"You might want to read that letter from Father Morelli before you do."

Leo studied the expression on John's face. He knew that this young man had been extremely loyal and devoted to Father Morelli and that, at this moment, he was totally panicked by something. Leo removed the letter from the envelope and began to read.

To Leopold Amodeo, my dear brother in Christ,
I am writing to you tonight in the hope you will join with a special group of friends in Israel on a holy mission of critical importance. I have just spoken with Lev Wasserman about our discovery under the

Basilica today. He and his team have discovered more information about the chapel in a completely different section of the Bible from the one we had been looking in. The chapel we discovered is very special. Apparently, it was built to receive something. The code specifies only that, whatever this object is, it must be delivered by you to the chapel. You must work with Professor Wasserman and his team. They will guide you in your search. Your name was discovered encoded in the Bible in conjunction with the chapel and as an instrument in a battle between good and evil. You are part of God's plan to save humanity from Satan himself.

At this time, we have no idea exactly what we are looking for or its connection with the ancient chapel under the Vatican. All we know at this point is that the object is located in the Holy Land, and you are tasked by God to find it. You are mentioned by name as a leader in the quest. If you truly believe that the code is a message from God, you must devote yourself entirely to this search. I believe that you have seen for yourself the power of the code to reveal things that have been hidden for millennia. It led us to the hidden chapel and will continue to guide you.

This is a holy quest for the truth and for the salvation of all our brothers and sisters around the world, nothing less. I believe your name was spelled out in the code because you are incorruptible and possess a strong faith in God. Leo means lion, my friend, and you are now God's lion. He has a plan for you and you must follow it through to the end.

Sadly, my name does not appear in the code along with yours, so even though I want more than anything else to be a part of this great adventure, I have decided it is best for me to remain here in Rome.

Lev called me this evening and said that, according to the code, the object we now seek is very old. He placed the date of origin around the time Lucifer was cast from heaven by God. This will be the most important archaeological undertaking in Church history. It will also be the greatest holy task ever assigned to man by God himself.

Remember, the code also speaks of evil forces at work against us. Use caution and trust no one except those listed as "chosen" in the code. The "archaeological priests" who uncovered the tunnel under the Mamertine Prison were not from the Vatican. If they were priests, they are part of a rogue element in the Church and are the evil ones I spoke of who have infiltrated our faith and know our every move.

From this time forward, your life is in danger, my brother. I have been coaching John for this very moment. He and Lev will help you, but let God be your guide. Although its importance has not yet been revealed, the ancient stone brick we found in the chapel must remain with you and John at all times. If you have received this letter from John, it is because I am unable to give you this message in person. You must leave for Israel at once. Godspeed, my dear friend, and may God keep you and protect you always.

Yours in Christ,
Anthony Morelli, S.J.

Father Leo was shaken to his core. His question about the real reason Father Morelli had summoned him to Rome had been answered. Speeding through the streets, the slipstream blew the tears from the corners of his eyes as he and John looked at one another with expressions usually reserved for soldiers preparing for combat.

Leo pulled his cell phone from his pocket and began to dial.

"Who are you calling, Father?"

"My travel agent in Rome. I need to buy two airline tickets to Israel."

"Better to buy them at the airport with cash. We don't want to leave a credit card trail for anyone to follow."

"You're pretty good at this, John. How do you know all this?"

"Father Morelli and I had been having discussions about this scenario. The more we learned, the more paranoid we were becoming. We even ordered a book on the Internet about how to disappear without a trace. We learned a lot from that book about how easy it is for people to be followed using their credit cards and cell phones."

"I have to use my credit card to get cash, but I'm afraid I don't have much. I think my total worth is less than five thousand dollars."

John smiled. "I don't think money will be a problem. Father Morelli set up a special numbered account in Switzerland. The account number is on the flash drive. He wanted me to keep all of his important papers for him, and his will left everything to you, including this car."

"He left me his car?" Leo felt a lump in his throat. He still had trouble bringing himself to the realization that his friend was gone forever.

"Did he ever mention being ill, John?"

"No, at least not to me. I thought he was in perfect health, but he had grown more distant recently and kept double checking everything to make sure all his bases were covered. His work with the code was extremely important to him, almost to the point of an obsession. I think that's why he called you to Rome. He wanted to make certain that someone he could trust would continue his research. It was kind of like having life insurance, with his work as the beneficiary."

"Is there enough money in the account for plane tickets?"

"Is ten million enough?"

Leo took a deep breath. "Did you just say *ten million* dollars?"

"Actually, it's ten million Euros, Father. As far as I know, Lev Wasserman and I were the only ones he revealed his true wealth to. Father Morelli had money in various Swiss banks and offshore accounts that he used when he wanted to donate to worthy causes he believed in."

Leo was stunned by the figure. "I guess this qualifies as a worthy cause. I only wish I was better prepared for what I need to do."

"We're coming up to your hotel, Father. Just grab your passport and your clothes, and let's get away from here as soon as possible."

The car screeched to a halt in front of the hotel. Leo took the steps two at a time before he burst through the doors and entered the lobby. He looked around and spied Arnolfo exiting the old cage-like elevator.

"Arnolfo. *Buon giorno.*" Leo tried to slow his breathing. "Would you mind getting my passport from the safe while I go upstairs and pack? I have an important meeting out of town and I'm running late for my train."

"Yes, Father. I have it out on the desk. A man from the Vatican just called to say he was sending a security officer over to deliver it to you."

Leo froze. Forget the clothes. He had to think.

"Oh, yes, I forgot. When the officer gets here, please tell him that I picked it up myself. Tell him I'm already on my way to Assisi."

"Assisi is *molto bello* this time of year, Father. My sister—"

"I'm sorry, my friend, but I'm afraid I'll miss my train if I don't hurry. The passport, Arnolfo. Can I have it please?"

"*Si*, Father."

Arnolfo walked over to the desk and picked up two passports before handing one to Leo.

"Why do you have *two* passports, Arnolfo?"

"The one in your hand is yours, Father. The other is the one I was going to give to the security man. An innocent mistake, yes? Do you think I would give your passport to anyone else but you?"

Once again, Arnolfo had proven that he was much more than just a simple inn keeper. "Thank you, Arnolfo. You are a good friend."

"Father, what about your belongings?"

"Keep them for me. I'll call you."

Leo flew from the hotel and jumped into the waiting car. "Arnolfo told me that someone at the Vatican just called to say they were sending a security officer to the hotel for my passport."

Without a word, John put the car into gear and smoked the tires as he sped away on the *Via Germanico* toward Fiumicino Airport, leaving a very worried-looking Arnolfo standing in the hotel entrance.

CHAPTER 11

The breathless priest hurried down the worn brick staircase at the back of the Vatican library. Turning a corner, he passed between tall canyons of books before reaching a hidden alcove that contained a small table with an old-style dial telephone. He looked and listened for signs of anyone nearby. He was alone—giddy with excitement. His master would be pleased.

After an additional quick look around, he dialed a number. It rang only twice before the familiar deep voice answered. "Speak, priest."

"Morelli is dead, sir."

"Are you sure?"

"I saw them carry the body out with my own eyes."

"What about his papers and the computer? Did he leave anything behind?"

"Nothing, sir. We checked his room this morning … it was practically empty."

The voice breathed in deeply. "What about his young assistant? Do you think he told him anything?"

"Uh, we can't seem to locate him."

The voice rose almost to a scream. "You what? Find him! And find that other priest. They know something; I'm certain of it."

The priest felt the sweat begin to flow from the pores on his face and run down his neck. His Roman collar was stained with it. What else could he have done? His master was angry. *He was angry at him.*

"Please don't worry, sir. I have our people looking for them. They can't get far without us knowing about it, that I can promise you."

The voice descended to a whisper that sounded progressively more menacing. "Don't make promises you can't keep, priest. You must not allow them to find it. This task is too important to let incompetence keep us from obtaining that which belongs to him."

The line went dead. The priest stared at the phone for a few seconds before hanging up. He began to stand up but was dizzy with fear. *He doubts me. Have I not proved my devotion time and time again? Have I not sacrificed everything, even my immortal soul?*

Soon his master would know how devoted he was. He would do whatever it took to make him happy again. He reached once again for the phone and dialed a number.

A strong male voice answered, "Yes, sir?"

"Have your men locate them and see where they go."

"Yes, sir."

"We need the information on Morelli's computer. Keep looking for it and make sure they don't leave Rome."

CHAPTER 12

The traffic in Rome at this hour was beyond chaos. The weather had turned the sky dark as storm clouds began covering the city. The BMW inched through streets crammed with traffic in an effort to reach its destination as Leo and John scanned the environment, constantly looking in their rearview mirrors for any hint of a familiar car or face.

John was forced to deviate from a straight route to the airport by turning right and then left down the narrow side streets in an effort to see if they were being followed. No one turned in behind them. So far, so good. They snaked their way along the gridlocked streets until they reached the *Grande Raccordo Anulare*, also called the A90 or ring freeway, that circled Rome.

Leaving the old part of the city, they traded the ancient beauty of Rome for the typical industrial look alongside the six-lane expressway. The car exited the A90 and sped west on the A91 toward Fiumicino and Leonardo da Vinci Airport.

The sign for Terminal C and all international flights shot past the right side of the car as they turned up the ramp and came to a stop at the departure entrance of the Euro futuristic-looking structure. Outside the terminal, the human and motorized traffic was frenzied.

"I'll go inside and buy our tickets," Leo said. "You park the car and join me inside."

John was staring at the terminal. "I don't think that's a good idea."

"We can't just leave it here," Leo said, wondering why John was suddenly hesitant about parking the car.

"Look over there." John motioned to the main entrance. "You see those two guys in suits? They're Swiss Guard security men. I've seen them around before. We need to get out of here without being seen."

Leo scanned the crowd in front of the terminal and ran through a mental checklist of their options.

"Wait, John, I've got an idea. When I say go, put the car in low gear and smoke the tires. Make a real show of it and drive away as fast as you can."

"What are you thinking, Father?"

"Just do it. Once we're out of sight of the terminal, drive back toward town."

"Then what? Are we going to stay in Rome?"

"No, we're getting out of here tonight … get ready and wait for my signal."

The BMW inched forward as Leo watched the two Swiss Guard security men for any sign of recognition.

There. The shorter security man nudged the taller one next to him. Both fixed their gaze on the bright red car.

"Now! Go!" Leo shouted.

John pressed the gas pedal to the floor and lit up the tires, making a loud and smoky scene in front of the terminal. Pedestrians flew in all directions as the car rocketed forward, receiving the attention of not only the Vatican security men, but also the Italian police. In an instant, the car was speeding down the airport ramp away from the terminal.

John swerved the BMW to miss a slower car. "Care to tell me what you're up to, Father?"

"I want them to think they scared us off. We'll drive back to the city and park the car. Then we can take the train from the city back to the airport. I'm hoping our little show back there convinced those two men that we won't go back to the airport anytime soon."

"Where do you want to go first?"

"Head into the center of the city, John. I need some time to think right now. We'll have to buy some different clothes so we won't be spotted when we return to the airport. If we can make it through the terminal without being recognized, we can buy our tickets with cash, board the plane, and be out of Rome before they figure out we've left."

"Not bad, Father. What books have you been reading? James Bond?"

Weaving through the traffic, Leo suddenly realized that, in their haste to get to the airport, they had forgotten to get cash. It was a chronic problem for him since he rarely had any money. He pulled the flash drive from his pocket, turning it over in his hand.

"Where can we find a computer?"

"How about the library?" John said. "We're only about five blocks from one right now."

"Let's go."

John swerved to the right and exited the ring freeway. He drove along the *Via Galvani*, looking for one of his favorite places, the *Municipio Roma I Testaccio* public library. The nineteenth-century building was set back from the street by the *Parco Testaccio*, a beautiful city park where mothers usually strolled with their children, but was now empty because of the threatening sky.

John pulled to the side of the street under a huge tree full of birds seeking refuge just as a heavy rain started to fall. He flicked a switch to raise the top up on the car while Leo bolted across the park to the library and entered the massive stone building.

Leo ran his hands through his wet hair and glanced around before crossing the cavernous lobby to the main desk, where he stood dripping wet. Without a word, a young dark-haired woman behind the counter reached into a shelf below and produced a clean white towel, which she handed to the priest.

"*Grazie. Mi scusi signore*," Leo said. "Do you have public computers?"

The woman smiled and led him down a hallway to a large room as he rubbed the towel over his head. She was dressed in a simple black dress and kept turning to make sure Leo was still following, her long black hair swinging from side to side as she walked. *She's really gorgeous,* Leo thought. Ever since Leo had become a priest, he had struggled with the issue of celibacy. If he had a weakness, and he did, it was for beautiful women. This battle within him had raged for years, and only prayer and hard work had kept him from breaking his vows while many of his friends continued to leave the Church over this very issue.

Several computers were in use by the usual student-looking types along with several elderly Italians surfing the Internet. The woman showed him to a small computer kiosk before taking her towel and returning to her station at the main desk.

Looking over his shoulder, Leo inserted the flash drive into the computer. Scrolling through Morelli's simple menu, he quickly retrieved the bank account number and password. He looked over his shoulder once more and scanned the room for anyone watching him with more than a casual interest before logging off.

The dark-haired woman behind the counter stared in disbelief as Leo raced across the lobby and back into the storm outside. Black birds in the trees called out to the black-suited figure of the priest as he ran through the park in the downpour, as if they had spotted a kindred spirit looking for shelter. He grabbed the door handle and squeezed into the car as the rain drummed against the canvas top over his head.

The windshield wipers barely kept up with the cascading water as John turned on the headlights in an effort to see his way through the dark flooding streets. He turned onto the *Viale Aventino*, and after several blocks, Leo spotted a branch of the Bank of Rome.

Money services were not always quick in Rome. Transactions involved lots of paperwork and lots of waiting around. Leo wanted to withdraw enough cash to buy airline tickets, new clothing, food, and any incidentals they might need on their trip to the Holy Land. John had advised him against using an ATM since those transactions could be immediately traced. Withdrawing the cash from a teller in a bank was much more secure, despite the long lines and endless paperwork. This tedious process actually worked to their advantage, since it would be days until anyone knew they had been in this bank.

With cash finally in hand, they located a large clothing store in the Aventine section of Rome. They purchased some jeans and loose-fitting Hawaiian-print shirts, along with baseball caps and two pairs of running shoes. Leo also picked out a backpack similar to John's to use as carry-on luggage. They were not about to risk losing the ancient stone brick and had decided to carry everything onboard the aircraft with them.

After changing clothes in the back of the store, they drove around the neighborhood until they found a fenced parking lot. Leo paid the attendant for a month in advance, keeping the spare set of keys John had given him earlier.

He would mail these to the Hotel Amalfi after they arrived in Israel. Leo knew Arnolfo would pick up the car and keep it safe for him.

The pouring rain had almost stopped as they made their way on foot toward a lighted orange sign marking the underground entrance to the *Circo Massimo* metro station, so named for its proximity to the *Circus Maximus*, ancient Rome's largest stadium once used for chariot races. The two men were now in a race of their own.

In Rome, the subway system was known to locals as the *Metropolitana*. The stations were clean but surprisingly drab and utilitarian compared with other European metros. Father Leo loved taking the graffiti-covered trains around town. Compared to driving, the metro was a quicker way of getting in and out of Rome, especially at this hour of the day. Leo had hoped this plan of using the metro would help them reach the airport in time to catch the overnight flight to Israel, but dark clouds had turned the early evening sky into night and the homeward-bound crush of people was filling the trains.

Descending the wet stairs, John and Leo entered the subway. John shook the water from his hair and inhaled the musty scent of the tunnel. "We seem to be spending a lot of time underground lately, Father." John's remark made Leo smile for the first time all day.

Leo looked around the station at the wet commuters milling about. "We can buy our train tickets using cash at that machine over there." He nudged John and pointed to an orange self-service ticket machine next to the entrance. "This metro line connects with the *Ostiense* railway station. From there, we can take a train directly to the airport."

After obtaining their tickets, John paced about the platform, suspicious of everyone, while Leo grabbed a train schedule from a rack on the tiled wall. The crowd along the platform grew until a roar filled the station announcing the arrival of their train. With a loud hiss of air, the doors slid open and the subway cars emptied and filled. Taking their seats, the two rode in silence as they rumbled under the city toward Rome's *Stazione Roma Ostiense*.

After a short fifteen minute ride, the train came to a stop in the station. Leo paused before leaving his seat to peer through the window at the people on the platform. "They might be watching this station, John. This is the main terminal for trains heading south. According to this schedule, the train to the airport leaves in thirty-five minutes, seven thirty exactly."

"Where should we wait?"

"I doubt they're looking very closely at the airport trains," Leo said. He looked around and thought for a moment. "Maybe we should head over to the terminal bar and just wait it out."

"Don't you think they'll be watching the bar?"

"At this point, anything's possible, but with the flooded streets we'll never make it to the airport in time if we try to take a cab, so the train is still our best option."

The two proceeded through the terminal to a wood-paneled Victorian-looking establishment that seemed out of place in a modern railway station. They entered and headed straight for the seats at the end of the bar where they could watch the door.

"Vino?" the burly man behind the bar asked.

"Water, please," Leo said. He knew they had to remain sharp for this last dash out of Rome.

The man grunted and handed them two bottles of water that cost more than wine. Everyone who entered drew their attention, even the women. It was rumored that the fabled Swiss Guard were assigning female security agents to the Vatican after finally starting to admit women into their ranks.

At seven twenty-five, the train to the airport was announced overhead. John began to rise from his stool when Leo grabbed him by the arm and nodded toward two stern-looking men in dark suits who were walking through the entrance. The men looked up and down the length of the bar and began scanning the faces at every table. Two women at the farthest booth from the door shouted out a greeting and began waving. The men smiled and returned the waves before hurrying over to join them

"Let's go," Leo said.

Pulling their caps down low over their eyes, they slung their backpacks over their shoulders and walked out of the bar toward their train. There were twelve railway platforms in the station, and at this hour, all the platforms were full as people hurried back and forth while trains arrived and departed from all directions.

Weaving their way through the rush hour crowd to their train, Leo and John passed two striking young women who turned and giggled at the men's gaudy shirts.

John pulled his hat farther down over his face. "I feel ridiculous."

Leo grinned. "That's the point. Dressed like this, I doubt any security people will recognize us."

It seemed like most of the passengers were well dressed. Dressing well in Italy, especially in Milan and Rome, was a national pastime. There was a sense of pride in the way one dressed in this country. An Italian's clothing was a statement to friends and strangers alike that they were to be respected and that they respected others enough to dress well for them also.

The main offenders in this daily fashion drama were the tourists. You could spot them instantly. This was the look Leo and John had adopted in an effort to throw off anyone who was looking for them. Stepping into the train, the two were ignored by the locals. They were seen only as ingredients of a pervasive vacationer milieu. It was exactly what Leo wanted.

They watched through the windows while the train began to creep away from the station, gathering momentum until it was speeding toward their final stop over the glistening wet tracks that ran parallel to the highway.

John was becoming more nervous by the minute. "I hope the red-eye flight to Israel hasn't sold out yet." He ran his fingers through his hair and looked down at the floor while the streetlights flashed by outside their windows.

"Stay calm, John. It is what it is. If they're sold out, we'll find a place in the terminal to lay low until the next flight."

At last, the train entered the island of light that surrounded the airport before diving beneath the terminal. The platform at the airport station seemed almost deserted as the two men exited the train and walked up the wide marble stairs to the main departure terminal. They scanned the area for security men but saw only a few sleepy-looking passengers pulling wheeled luggage. Leo inhaled a deep breath before he motioned to John and headed directly to the El Al ticket counter.

The Israeli ticket agent looked up as Leo approached. "Good evening, sir."

Leo gave the woman his biggest smile. "We'd like to buy two tickets to Jerusalem please."

"Tonight, sir?" Her tone was formal, and she didn't smile.

Leo's hopes began to fade. "Yes. We need to go tonight."

"We have one flight leaving this evening, but the only seats we have left are in first class, sir. Would you like those?"

Leo breathed a little easier. "Yes, that will be fine. Thank you."

"How will you be paying for those tonight, sir?"

"Cash." He avoided her eyes and tried to look as nonchalant as possible.

Leo was aware that, since they were paying in cash, plus heading for a country high on the terror hit list, they would be scrutinized by Israeli security and Interpol even more closely.

The ticket agent locked eyes with Leo and picked up the phone on the counter. She spoke in hushed tones to an unseen person on the other end. Within seconds, a man in a dark blue suit appeared behind the agent. He studied the two men briefly before speaking in a flat bureaucratic voice. "May I have your passports please?"

Leo and John exchanged glances before surrendering their only means of leaving the country to the obvious airline security man. Taking their passports, he compared them to their pictures, then turned and disappeared into an office area behind the counter. After enduring a long wait watching the joyless agent typing on her keyboard in front of them, the man finally returned with their passports and handed them over to the ticket agent.

With her endless typing finally at an end, the agent stuffed two tickets into paper folders and placed them on the counter with their passports. "Concourse B, to your left. Your plane is on time tonight, gentlemen. Have a nice flight."

Leo and John exhaled slowly. *Almost to the finish line.*

The two men grabbed their tickets and headed across the immense lobby toward the security checkpoint. They were within feet of the metal detector when John suddenly stopped and looked at Leo. "What about the brick with the painting on it in my backpack?"

The look on Leo's face told John that he had completely forgotten about the stone brick from the chapel. "Damn. It's an archaeological artifact, which means it belongs to the Italian government. Actually, it belongs to the Vatican, but we can't say that. They'll never let us leave the country with it. It's a crime to take an archaeological relic out of Italy."

The two men were stopped in their tracks. If they went forward, they would be arrested at the checkpoint. If they turned around and left, they would be stuck in Rome another day, another day running from the unknown and trying to figure out how they would get to Israel.

Leo looked up toward the ceiling as if pleading with God for an answer.

"They won't know it's an archaeological artifact," John said.

"It's almost two thousand years old."

"Yes, but it has a painting of a jet plane hitting a modern skyscraper. I don't think the guards at the checkpoint will think someone two thousand years ago painted it. I'm having a hard time believing it myself."

"You're right. It's too obvious. Good thinking, John. It might raise eyebrows, but it shouldn't get us arrested. Let's go for it."

The two very nervous men made their way toward the tables in front of the x-ray scanner, where they emptied their pockets, took off their shoes, and placed the backpacks on the conveyer belt. The security officer watching the x-ray machine immediately saw the solid rectangular shape and ordered the backpack searched.

"What's this?" The man was holding the ancient stone brick in his hand.

"A heavy souvenir," John replied, trying to keep his voice from shaking. "I wish I hadn't bought it, but it was just so weird I had to have it."

"It's weird alright," the officer said. "It looks old."

"Well, the stone is as old as the earth itself," Leo said. "But the painting can't be any older than 2001."

"That's true," a second security officer said. "I wouldn't want something like that in my house."

"That's what I told him," Leo said, nodding his head in John's direction. "You should see some of the weird art in his apartment."

"OK," the man said, returning the brick to the backpack. "Have a nice trip."

The security men exchanged amused glances and went back to the tedious process of screening the next passenger. Leo and John grabbed their backpacks and walked away from the checkpoint toward their gate, trying to look as if they didn't have a care in the world.

"I really need a drink now," John said, sweat beginning to drip from under his hairline.

Leo's pulse was still pounding. "Me too."

They headed straight for a darkened airport lounge that smelled of cigarette smoke and stale beer. Taking seats at the bar, the two watched their reflections in a mirrored wall and sipped from their glasses of red wine until their flight to Israel was finally announced.

"That's us," Leo said, picking up his backpack.

John followed along through the departure gate and cast one final glance back over his shoulder. No one appeared to be taking any undue notice of them as they walked through the Jetway and stepped into the plane.

The two weary men watched the flight attendants walking up and down the aisle, slamming overhead compartment doors shut and checking seatbelts. Finally, the doors were closed and the lights dimmed as the plane adopted the muted hum of electrical power that preceded the start of the engines. They felt a slight jolt and saw the terminal begin to recede when a small tractor on the ground began to shove the jet backward, away from the gate. John closed his eyes and drummed his fingers on the armrest of his seat while he listened to the four engines come to life one at a time.

The large jet moved away from the terminal on its own power as John opened his eyes and peered out the window at the rows of blue taxiway lights passing below in the darkness. Without fanfare, the plane turned onto the main runway and started its takeoff run. Leaving the ground behind, the jet streaked upward, and the twinkling lights of Rome were quickly extinguished when they entered the base of some low-hanging clouds.

After drinking some bottled water, the two reclined their seats. Within minutes, they were both sound asleep, thirty-five thousand feet above the Mediterranean Sea. They were on their way to the Holy Land.

CHAPTER 13

Jerusalem itself had no international airport. All flights from outside the country arrived at Ben Gurion, located between Tel Aviv on the Mediterranean coast and Jerusalem twenty-eight miles to the east. The sun had risen over the nose of the plane several minutes earlier and Leo and John were now fully awake, watching the scenery grow closer outside their window as the blue and white El Al jet flew in low over the coast of Israel and circled to land.

After touchdown, the aircraft taxied to the ultramodern Terminal 3, where the still-exhausted men shuffled their way out of the big Boeing jet and on through the lines at customs. The two were still paranoid after their ordeal in Rome, and every new situation made them grow progressively more anxious. Israel's international airport reputedly had the tightest security of any airport in the world. Israeli soldiers with automatic weapons were everywhere, along with an invisible security presence no one ever saw, even though it saw them.

Walking through the main concourse, John reached inside his backpack and ran his fingers over the cool, chalky surface of the ancient brick. Satisfied that it was still tucked safely inside, he gave a thumbs up to Leo before they stepped out of the airport into the bright light of the Holy Land.

"God, what a feeling this place has," John said. "I've never been here before. Just think, soon we'll be walking in the footsteps of Jesus, Mary, the Apostles; it's overwhelming."

Leo stretched and watched the wide-eyed tourists flowing out of the terminal. "I experienced the same euphoria on my first visit to Israel many years ago. It doesn't matter whether you're a Christian, a Jew, or a Muslim; the emotions people experience here are powerful. Walking in the steps of our biblical forefathers has a profound effect on those who flock here every year from all over the world. They may not feel it yet, but as soon as they enter the old part of the city and touch the ground where Jesus carried the cross, they will know in their hearts that God is close by."

Father Leo was as excited to be here as he had been on his first visit. It was springtime, and the Mediterranean climate was Eden-like. Breathing in the fresh air, Leo and John stood on the sidewalk in front of the airport. They were wondering what to do next when an old green Land Rover pulled up to the curb next to them. The driver flashed a grin and motioned with his hand. "Leo, John, hop in. We must hurry."

Behind the wheel was a distinguished-looking man with gray hair and a beard. He was dressed in a khaki shirt with the sleeves rolled up, revealing strong tanned forearms and the rough hands of a man who enjoyed working outdoors. In short, he looked like the movie version of an archaeologist.

Leo and John traded looks but remained frozen on the sidewalk while the exasperated driver attempted to wave them into the vehicle. "I'm Lev Wasserman, Anthony's friend. We're not allowed to park here. Get in before we get in trouble with the authorities."

A soldier in the brown uniform of the Israeli Defense Force was already walking in their direction. Leo grabbed the passenger-side door handle and slid into the front seat, while John followed his lead and climbed into the back. Lev waved to the soldier as they pulled away from the terminal and headed off down a palm-lined boulevard toward Tel Aviv and the coast.

"We've been waiting a long time to meet you, Professor," Leo said, extending his hand. "I only wish Anthony could have been with us. I know you two were good friends."

"I considered him one of my best friends," Lev said, shaking Leo's hand and glancing in the rearview mirror at John in the backseat. John's eyes met Lev's in the mirror. "I have to ask the obvious question, Professor. We couldn't use our cell phones or e-mail you about—"

"How did I know what flight you were arriving on? How did I know what you looked like? Those kinds of questions? Well, let's just say I have connections at El Al Airlines. A friend of mine who works at the airport in Rome let me know that you were arriving on this morning's flight."

"Probably that security guy who took our passports," John said.

"Actually, it was the ticket agent," Lev said. "She e-mailed me your photos last night so I could spot you. Nice shirts. I only wish Father Morelli could have made the trip with you. It's hard to believe he's not here with us now."

Leo was watching the palm trees flash by the windows of the Land Rover. "I have a feeling he is here with us now. Why are we headed toward the coast? I thought we were going to Jerusalem."

"Actually, I live on the coast, so I'm taking you to my villa on the beach. Father Morelli loved it there. He was able to relax and work uninterrupted on his many projects. The villa is fairly isolated and large enough to accommodate quite a few people; you'll see. Everyone involved with the Bible code is gathering there today, and a lot of people are looking forward to meeting you. I hope you're hungry, because my cooks are creating a fantastic lunch in your honor."

"You have cooks?" John asked. He felt like he hadn't eaten in days, which was close to the truth. "They must pay professors really well here in Israel."

"Unfortunately, I don't really make that much as a college professor, and my books on archaeology are not what you would call material for the masses, so they're definitely not best sellers. My family was in manufacturing here in Israel and in America. I was an only child, so everything was left to me. I live comfortably, but not extravagantly. I was lucky enough to have a father who appreciated my desire to be a scholar instead of a businessman."

"I thought your field was mathematics, Professor," John said.

"Please, call me Lev. I have two PhDs, one in mathematics and the other in archaeology. When I first met Father Morelli on a dig outside Jerusalem years ago, I went back to school to study archaeology. Anthony's passion for it was infectious. After going on a few excavations with him and digging down through the layers of history, I was hooked. To actually see and touch objects that no one has seen for thousands of years is addicting."

Leo could already feel himself begin to unwind. "Thanks again for picking us up at the airport, Lev. Let's just say the past few days in Rome have been somewhat of a challenge."

"I've heard. There are things we will discuss in time. For now, you are safe. You were friends of Father Morelli, and you are now friends of mine. We all have a lot of work ahead of us, Leo, but first, you must relax. I want you both well rested and well fed. We will work later."

Leo pulled out the small map of Israel he had purchased at the airport gift shop. "Is it far to your house on the coast?"

"We're almost to Tel Aviv. My house is closer to Caesarea, the old Roman port to the north. It's about a forty-five-minute drive from the airport if the traffic isn't too bad."

Leo remembered that distances in Israel were startlingly small to newcomers. A person had only to travel around the country to see just how tiny it really was. Up front in the Land Rover, Leo and Lev heard the faint sound of snoring coming from the backseat. Looking behind them, they saw that John was sound asleep, his arms wrapped around his backpack.

"Anthony was very fond of that young man," Lev said. "He will be a great asset to your church someday."

"He already is. I think John was the closest thing to a son that Anthony ever had."

"Did you bring the stone brick you found in the ancient chapel?"

"It's in that backpack John is holding onto so tightly. Anthony said it would be useful."

"Vital would be a better choice of words, Father. I believe it will assist us in finding something of enormous significance here in Israel."

"Do you have any hint of what we're looking for?"

"We'll be trying to find the answer to that question when the whole team comes together at my house later today. We're hoping that the stone contains additional information, maybe even some subtle engravings, which will help us discover its true purpose. From what Father Morelli said, I have a feeling that a lot of people would like to get their hands on that brick right now."

"John and I were chased all over Rome by security men from the Vatican, and Anthony mentioned in his letter that our lives were in danger. As strange as this might sound, he told me in a letter that I'm supposed to find an object that dates back to the time when Lucifer was cast out of heaven … so basically, I have no idea what I'm looking for."

Lev turned the vehicle to the right as they reached the Mediterranean Sea and headed north along the coastal highway. "You're not alone in this search, my friend. Whatever it is we've been called on to do will be revealed to us soon. I'm sure of it. Do you believe the code in the Bible is the word of God, Leo?"

"Well, I guess I've narrowed it down to the simple fact that the Bible was divinely inspired by God, and the code is in the Bible. Using that reasoning as a premise, and considering everything that's happened over the past few days, I would have to say that I'm becoming convinced that God is using the code to lead us."

"I'm glad to hear you say that, Father, because you will have to open yourself up to the fact that you are being led in the days ahead. You know, I can't help but think back to the days of Moses. Do you think it's possible that God chose something as simple as a burning bush to talk to man thousands of years ago, and is now using a complex code embedded in the Bible to speak to mankind in today's world?"

"That's an interesting concept, Professor." Leo was impressed with the fact that Lev's analogy simplified things and brought the complexities of the code into a biblical perspective. It was the mark of a very intelligent mind. "Doesn't the name Lev mean lion in Hebrew?"

"Yes, as does your name, Leo. You're also a lion."

Leo sat up in his seat. "I seem to be running into a lot of things with subtle meanings lately. John's last name is Lowe, another name that means lion."

"I'm beginning to think that all of God's lions are gathering here now, Father." Lev pulled a cigar from his pocket and glanced over at Leo with the realization that an unrevealed plan was coming together and that he had met someone special, a kindred soul in the search for an unknown truth.

The Land Rover continued along the coast road as the men's discussion revealed that both shared a common bond of scholars who felt a passion for digging down deep and uncovering new realities within their respective fields.

"Have you always lived here, Lev?"

"I grew up on a kibbutz."

"I've always wondered, what exactly *is* a kibbutz?"

"It's a communal farm run collectively and dedicated to the principal that intellectual work, production work, and domestic work are all of equal value. I built my house on the coast and the area surrounding it to resemble the kibbutz I was raised on. My mother and father moved to Palestine back in 1946 shortly before I was born. They were French Jews and were part of the French resistance that fought the Nazis in World War II. One of my uncles was killed by the Germans for hiding some American flyers who were shot down close to his farmhouse. When the war was over, my father wanted to leave Europe as quickly as possible. He and my mother traveled through Cyprus and ended up on a boat bound for the Holy Land."

Leo hadn't realized that Lev's family had been part of the exodus from Europe. "That must have been very difficult for them. Did your father ever talk about those days?"

"He said it seemed peaceful here at first. The British still controlled the area and had been trying to limit Jewish immigration to Palestine. After the Holocaust, tens of thousands of Jews flocked to the region. The Irgun, an underground Jewish organization, fought the British, blowing up their headquarters in the King David Hotel. The Brits finally had enough and pulled the last of their troops out of Palestine in 1948 after the U.N. voted for the partition of the Holy Land into an Arab state and a Jewish state. Jerusalem was supposed to be an international city. After the British pulled out, it was open warfare between the Arabs and Jews. My parents went to live in a kibbutz formed outside of Tel Aviv for safety. I remember the fighting then and have witnessed it ever since."

"You've led quite a life, Lev. I have to admire the Jewish people for preserving their heritage after everything they've been through. Why did you convert to Christianity?"

"That's a strange question coming from a priest."

Leo smiled. "Not really. I just haven't met many Jews who've converted to another religion. They all seem pretty happy with their own beliefs."

Lev lit the cigar hanging from his mouth with a match. "Most are happy with being Jewish. Sometimes, I think they're a little *too* happy."

Leo seemed puzzled. "What do you mean?"

"Well, here in Israel, we're basically a Jewish state, even though the government is supposedly secular, and that causes problems in any society."

As a university professor of theology, this was the kind of discussion Leo relished. "Are you saying that nationalism, along with a predominant national religion, gives rise to radicalism?"

"Yes, in a way, but religion by itself is broader than nationalism and affects people in many countries all over the world. I believe that, no matter where you live, only religious moderation can stop religious extremism."

"So you converted to Christianity because you found it more moderate?"

"No, we Christians can be just as extreme in our beliefs. I'm sure I don't have to tell you that. My late wife was a Christian. She was truly an angel sent from above. We had long talks on the subject of Christ's ministry and how he gave his life to save humanity. She believed we lived in a self-centered world instead of a God-centered world and dedicated her life to looking out for others. She never pushed her Christian beliefs on me, and I never pushed my Jewish ones on her. Out of curiosity and respect for her, I began reading the Christian Bible and the story of Jesus."

"What happened?" Leo asked.

"Slowly, over time, I began to join the ranks of the Sabra, other Jews who believe Christ was the Messiah."

"Was there any one thing that convinced you?"

"Without going into details, let's just say I had a religious experience one day when I was walking with my wife through the Garden of Gethsemane on the Mount of Olives. I converted shortly thereafter."

"Sounds mysterious," Leo said. "However, if you're going to have a religious experience, I can't think of a better place to have one."

Lev smiled. He was starting to like this priest and his easy going manner.

"Did you meet your wife here in Israel?" Leo asked.

"Yes, she moved here to study at the university. She told me she wanted to experience biblical history from a front row seat. We were both young students at the time, and she totally captivated me. We dated for only three months before I begged her to stay here in Israel and marry me. Despite her better judgment, she finally gave in."

"Did she ever miss living back in the States?"

"No, she was very happy here. She had seen the culture in America slowly change over time. The society had become increasingly more consumer-driven and self-centered. The work ethic of the agrarian society that existed before the Great Depression had largely vanished, replaced instead with a dependent society that allowed the government and big corporations to make all their decisions for them. Over the years, we both watched as a whole generation of Americans drifted away from God and civil discourse became less polite and more aggressive. Society was becoming more violent, and just driving down the highway was becoming an exercise in probability, but for some reason, there was no unifying sense of outrage. There was only denial and a detachment from past values."

Lev reached into a cooler on the seat between them and removed two ice-cold bottles of water before handing one to Leo. "I mean, don't the people in your country realize that they have a say in the way their country is evolving? They dutifully pay their taxes and allow the powerful in Congress and Wall Street dictate what they eat, think, and watch on TV. Take for instance the Ten Commandments."

"What do you mean?"

"God's commandments are the very basis for most of the laws in the civilized world, yet a small number of people who deny His existence have sued to have them removed from your courthouses … and they've won."

"I guess sometimes democracy can be plagued with unintended consequences," Leo said. "You know, I grew up in a tough rural section of Pennsylvania. My people worked in the mines. We were surrounded by an Amish community and church-going Christian neighbors who were mostly farmers. Almost everyone in our community worked hard and helped others in need. We even grew most of our food in our own gardens. Most still do. But step out of that little enclave of safety we called our home town and it was like going to another planet."

"Exactly, Father. And if things don't start to change soon, there'll be no turning back. Once the moral fabric of a society begins to tear, it's almost impossible to return to the way things were."

"What do you suggest, Lev? I mean, the problems aren't just in America. The whole world seems to be heading toward moral bankruptcy. I'm just a simple priest, but even I can see that it's going to take something more than just sermons and speeches to bring people to action. Of course, that raises another question. Just what kind of action do we take? I agree that some groups seem to be going to extremes to erase God from our everyday life, but we have to be cautious that we don't move toward a theocracy like those that exist in a few Middle Eastern countries. I'll take a few less public monuments to Christianity any day over a repressive government that dictates my moral agenda."

"It's quite a dilemma, isn't it, Father? Democracy, theocracy, communism, anarchy. Which way do we turn in a world that's so confused? I'm just saying that I hope it's not too late and that the world ends up on the right path, because some of our own young people are beginning to doubt the meaning of faith and the part it plays in their future. That's why I feel the Bible code is so important. If we can prove that God exists and is talking to us again, it will change not only how everyone on earth will begin to look at how they're leading their lives, but how they view their leaders and their neighbors around the world."

The morning sun was rising over a cloudless sky when they turned left onto a long paved driveway lined with olive trees and drove under an arched stone gate topped with a brown wooden cross next to a blue Star of David.

Lev's ancient Land Rover rolled to a stop in front of an enormous Mediterranean-style villa set back from the beach behind a series of sand dunes. A rolling green lawn surrounded the villa's brilliant white stucco exterior, and flowers were everywhere.

Around the back, a sparkling blue swimming pool bordered by tall palm trees separated the house from the sand dunes and the sea. Red-tiled roofs of several dozen smaller houses dotted the landscape, along with vineyards, orchards, and rows of planted fields.

People of various ages could be seen walking about the property, the most noticeable being the young men and women of the villa's security force dressed in olive-colored shirts and matching shorts with automatic weapons slung over their shoulders.

Within minutes of their arrival, the car was surrounded by a group of young people who greeted Lev with laughter and hugs. It was becoming evident to Leo that this man was loved by almost everyone who came into contact with him.

John was just waking up in the backseat. He lifted himself upright and rubbed his eyes, blinking in the sunlight at his surroundings. A smiling group approached the passenger side of the vehicle and opened the doors. They giggled and motioned for Leo and John to follow. "Come with us. We'll show you to your rooms."

Walking toward the villa, Lev stopped and looked back at Leo. "Why don't you two go enjoy a few beers on the beach, Father? We'll find some swimming trunks for you both. I'll call you when lunch is ready."

With that, Lev turned and walked into the villa, leaving a bewildered Leo and John at the mercy of their giggling captors.

CHAPTER 14

The shallow turquoise water of the Mediterranean Sea stretched before Leo and John as they reclined on weathered beach chairs beneath a ragged blue umbrella stuck in the sand. Bathed in the warmth of the moist sea air, Leo squinted in the reflected sunlight and retrieved a cold Israeli beer from the cooler beside him.

"This reminds me of those TV ads for Mexican beer," John said. "You know, the one's where two people are staring at the ocean in silence with two bottles of beer on a table between them."

"Except one of them is a girl in a white bikini, and I don't see anyone who looks like that around."

"No kidding. That brings up a little problem I've been wrestling with lately, Father."

Leo lifted his sunglasses up on his head and looked over at his young friend. "What problem would that be, John?"

"Well, for one, why does the Church continue to insist that priests remain celibate? It's just not natural. I mean, don't you think there would be fewer problems with priests and the way people are starting to view them if they were allowed to marry or have girlfriends?"

"I guess that depends on who you're talking to," Leo said. "If you're talking to those in authority at the Vatican, then the answer would be no. If you're a young man looking at the priesthood, then I think the answer might be different."

John picked up a small sea shell from beside his chair and threw it toward the water. "I guess I'm just hoping that someday, the leaders in the Catholic Church will come to their senses and do away with that bizarre and archaic requirement. Priests should be allowed to have women in their lives. How have you managed to cope with it all these years, Father?"

Leo replaced the sunglasses over his eyes and gazed out at the water. "I haven't always been a saint."

"You, Leo?"

"That's what confession and absolution are all about, my son. I've had two serious relationships in the past."

"With women?" John's eyes were getting wider by the second.

"No, I'm gay. Want some suntan lotion on your back?" Leo was trying hard to keep a straight face.

Like a freshly caught fish that had just landed on the deck of a boat, John's eyes were bulging and his mouth moved without speaking.

Unable to contain himself any longer, Leo burst out laughing so hard he came close to spewing beer through his nose. "Of course with women. I was talking about the years before I became a priest, when I was in college. It was more difficult for me when I was your age. I've always loved women. Still do. But my ability to put my personal desires in perspective with my role in life has become easier with age. Being a priest is a learning process. You don't automatically become a pillar of virtue the day you take your vows. God knows that we are imperfect beings, and he makes allowances for us. I've never believed that the whole celibacy thing should be a central tenet to the priesthood, but I've always kept my vows."

"Wow," John said, looking relieved. "You just described what I'm going through right now. I think about meeting the right woman, getting married, having kids, all of it. I just hope I make the right decision this summer before I enter seminary in the fall."

"You'll find your way, John. Whatever you decide, priest or no priest, you have a good heart. If you want to be a husband and father, I know you'll be one of the best. If you become a priest, you'll be a great one."

"Lunch," a twenty-something girl shouted at the two from the dunes. She had long brown hair and was wearing a white blouse and skintight khaki shorts. She giggled at John before turning her back and running off toward the villa.

John shot Leo a glance and moaned. "See what I mean?"

Leo smiled. He knew the struggle this young man would face in the months ahead would be difficult. It was possible the Church would lose another promising candidate for the priesthood due to its antiquated views of marriage and priests. For now, Leo just wanted an answer to the question of why they were here, and so far, no one seemed to have one.

Beers in hand, they retreated from the beach across a rickety boardwalk that ran through the dunes toward the villa. In the distance, Leo noticed the sun's reflection glinting off something nestled in the dunes farther down the beach. He shielded his eyes with his hands and peered out over the sea swept landscape. Nothing moved. Whatever he had seen was now gone, and the burning heat from the sun-baked boardwalk against his bare feet made him step up his pace. The sound of laughter coming from the villa, along with the aroma of meat cooking on an outdoor grill, put an end to Leo's thoughts about the shining object in the distance as he headed toward the promise of a delicious meal.

Arriving by the pool, Leo and John stopped and stared at a long buffet table piled high with food. There were bowls nestled in ice and filled with Jerusalem salad, a delicious concoction that included olives, feta, pomegranate, and *za'atar*, a seasoning of hyssop and sesame seeds sprinkled with kosher salt. Wide platters ringed with lime wedges held grilled tilapia, known locally as Saint Peter's fish.

There were mounds of pita bread next to bowls of hummus, olive oil, minced garlic, and freshly picked lemons from the groves around the villa. *Shashlik*, spiced ground meat on skewers, along with kebabs of cubed lamb and beef, sizzled on the grill nearby, while dishes of pickled vegetables and baba ghanoush were spaced throughout the buffet next to heaps of freshly picked fruit.

Under big yellow umbrellas, Israeli and French wines populated linen-covered tables, while ice-filled metal tubs holding Cokes and bottles of water were stationed nearby on the stone patio floor. People of all ages were lounging beside the pool, enjoying the feast and the comfortable familiarity of being surrounded by friends who were more like family. The atmosphere had the feel of a holiday to it.

"I think we must have died at the beach and this is heaven," John said.

Leo nodded in agreement as they piled as much food on their plates as room allowed and fell into some poolside lounge chairs. Reaching for a bottle of cold water, Leo noticed Lev standing next to the villa talking to a group of exceptionally fit-looking men. Judging by their appearance, the priest took them for military types.

Lev soon spotted Leo and John by the pool and grinned while raising his glass of wine in a gesture of welcome. Leo and John responded by lifting their bottles of water in a return salute, their mouths too full to grin. Squinting in the late afternoon sun, Leo continued to study the group around Lev. *Could this be the Bible Code Team Morelli had talked about?* His question was about to be answered, because the men, led by Lev, were now walking in their direction.

Several hundred yards away, behind a sand dune to the north, two men with binoculars and cameras packed up their equipment. They walked back to their car parked along the road and sat inside, staring at the villa. The men exchanged glances before looking around to make sure no one was watching as the driver started the engine and pulled out onto the roadway. Slowly, they drove past the villa as the passenger reached for his cell phone and punched in a preprogrammed number.

CHAPTER 15

L eo and John sat happily munching away by the pool while Lev and the three fit-looking men approached them. Two of the men appeared to be in their late twenties or early thirties, while the third appeared to be at least in his fifties. Setting their plates aside, Leo and John stood to meet the group.

"Are you feeling rested, my friends?" Lev asked. "Is the food to your liking?"

"The food is excellent, Lev. I've never seen such a spectacular feast put together in a private home. I feel like a guest at an exclusive resort. We can't thank you enough for your generous hospitality."

"How about you, John? Did you get enough to eat?"

Red as a lobster from too much sun, John stood next to Leo holding a skewer of meat in one hand and a bottle of water in the other. "This is probably one of the best meals I've ever had. My folks back on our ranch in New Mexico used to put on some real parties with lots of Mexican food and barbecue, but nothing like this."

"Well, this is a special occasion," Lev said, winking at the men around him. Let's go inside, and I'll start the introductions." Lev studied John's deepening red color. "You two need to get out of the sun."

The group filed into the villa and entered a cavernous room with a red-tiled floor and a man-sized iron chandelier hanging from the center of a thirty-foot high ceiling. The walls were painted the color of desert sand and lined with artwork, while Persian carpets and white fabric sofas took up the center of the room, giving the space a modern Mid-Eastern flavor. Floor-to-ceiling windows at one end opened up the space to a panoramic view of the sea, while on opposite sides of the room, two wide hallways led away from the great room into separate parts of the villa.

As the men gathered around on sofas, the holiday mood took on a distinctly more business-like tone when Lev stood and faced Leo and John for a moment before speaking. "I want to start off by saying that everyone here is very grateful that you two made it to Israel safely. Those of us involved with the Bible code have been extremely impressed with both of you, especially your involvement in the discovery of the ancient chapel and your ability to shake off your pursuers and make it to Israel without being stopped. I'm sure we'll all get to know one another much better in the days ahead, but before we get to the matter of why we've all been called together at this exact time and place, I want to introduce you to the team Father Morelli was working with for the past year."

The stoic-looking men sitting across from Leo and John smiled in their direction. "Shalom," they all said in unison.

"Don't let their casual looks give you a false impression," Lev said. "Most are experts in their chosen fields, and all of them have devoted the past year of their lives to the study of the code in the Bible."

The man seated next to Lev stood and seized Leo's hand in a vice-like grip. Leo returned the squeeze, causing the man to smile. "I heard you were once a boxer, Father. You still have a good grip."

"This is Moshe Ze'ev," Lev said. "Our chief of security."

"Pleased to meet you, Moshe." Leo watched as John winced in the clutches of the man's iron handshake. At fifty-five years of age, Moshe was the oldest and most colorful member of the three. He was wearing a bright blue fly-fishing shirt, lime-green shorts, and flip-flops. The long, thin muscles of a runner made it obvious that he still kept himself in shape, and his tanned head was completely shaved. His only facial hair was a thick handlebar moustache that he twirled at the ends. Leo knew Moshe's name was, of course, synonymous with the man who delivered the Israelites out of slavery in Egypt—Moses.

"Moshe was a general in the Israeli Defense Force before joining the Mossad, our version of the CIA," Lev continued. "Let's just say he knows more than your average citizen about what goes on in this country and other parts of the world."

A large man dressed in khaki pants with a tight-fitting brown T-shirt stood up. He was six feet five inches tall and looked like a linebacker in the NFL. At the age of thirty-five, he had black hair worn short on top and shaved on the sides and was the only one of the group who did not have any facial hair.

"This is Alon Lavi," Lev said. "Alon was a captain in the Israeli Special Forces and is Moshe's second in command here at the villa."

"I'm happy to meet you, Father. And you too, John."

Leo reached out to shake his hand. "Alon is a Hebrew name, isn't it?"

"It means oak tree," Lev said, cutting in. "Very fitting, don't you think?"

Alon blushed slightly as the Israeli men began to laugh. John stood to shake hands with the big man while making a mental note to be standing close to this guy if a fight ever broke out.

The third man extended his hand toward Leo and John. In his late twenties, with short, dark hair, horn-rimmed glasses, and a beard, he had a decidedly more intellectual look about him than the others. He was dressed in a loose-fitting white shirt that was one size too large and wearing the ever-present khaki shorts that seemed so popular among the staff at the villa.

"Hi. I'm Daniel ... Daniel Meir."

"The Book of Daniel calls you the interpreter of dreams," Leo said,

Lev seemed impressed. "Very good, Father." The Israeli men nodded their approval and obvious respect for Leo.

"It also means one who is pious and wise in the Book of Ezekiel," John added, also earning a few nods of respect from the others.

Quiet by nature, Daniel was embarrassed by the attention. "Well, since you've given me the challenge of having to live up to my name, I hope I don't disappoint you. Of course, one can't help but remember that Daniel was also thrown into the lion's den. I have a feeling history is repeating itself." The room erupted in laughter at the obvious reference to all those present whose names meant lion.

Lev put his hand on Daniel's shoulder and smiled. "Daniel was a cryptographer or 'code breaker' in the ministry of defense and, like me, has a PhD in mathematics."

John was just sitting back down when he noticed the girl he had seen earlier on the beach enter the room from one of the side hallways. She walked right up to Lev and kissed him lightly on the cheek. John suddenly felt self-conscious and began brushing his hair back from his forehead with his fingers.

"Let me introduce you to the final member of the team, running late as usual," Lev said, smiling at the girl. "This is my daughter, Ariella."

Leo took her small but strong hand in his. "It seems we have yet another lion. Ariella is Hebrew for lioness of God. Daniel truly is in the lion's den."

Ariella laughed and swept a strand of long brown hair back over her shoulder. "It's an honor to meet you, Father Leo."

John wiped his hands on his shorts and reached out to shake her hand while uttering a squeaky hello. Ariella smiled sweetly at him before she lowered her enormous brown eyes and turned shyly back toward her father. She was the same height as John, and he couldn't help but notice that her lean tan legs gave her the look of an Olympic swimmer. John thought she was the most beautiful girl he had ever met.

"My daughter has honored me by following in the footsteps of my second career," Lev said. "She just received her degree in archaeology from Hebrew University in Jerusalem."

Leo and John had a newfound appreciation for the individual talents and abilities of this special group of people, a group that had obviously been assembled with a definite mission in mind.

One of Leo's favorite pastimes was looking up the meanings and origins of names that were new to him. Aside from those he had recently met who were named after lions, he was struck by the way all of the Israelis seemed to have names that fit their roles in life. For instance, Alon's last name was Lavi, obviously another lion, and Moshe's surname, Ze'ev, meant literally "son of wolf". *It appeared that Lev had chosen both a lion and a wolf to be in charge of protecting those he loved.*

Then there was Daniel's name—the strangest coincidence of all. As Leo had mentioned earlier, Daniel was called the interpreter of dreams in the Bible, but his last name, Meir, meant brilliant. Putting the two together, Leo saw that the name of the team's chief cryptographer meant *brilliant interpreter*. It was a very appropriate name for a code breaker, and a strange coincidence indeed.

Lev grew serious as he gazed at Leo and John across an immense coffee table hewn from the single trunk of an olive tree. "We would like to extend an invitation. Before I picked you two up at the airport this morning, we all took a little vote. The result was unanimous, and we've all agreed that we would like both of you to join our team here in Israel."

The others nodded silently in agreement.

Leo and John looked around the room and studied the faces staring back at them. *Wasn't this why they had come to Israel in the first place?* Not only had they developed a keen interest in the code, but they were now becoming totally entranced with their new friends in this exotic setting. The Israelis waited for their answer.

"It looks like I'll have to request a leave of absence from my teaching position," Leo said. "It would be an honor, Lev."

Lev fixed his eyes on John. "What about you, John?"

"I believe joining your team is the reason we've come here, Professor. Father Morelli sent us to the Holy Land with a definite purpose in mind, and even if we're not sure what that is right now, I know he wanted us all to be together."

"Good. It's final then. *Baruch haba!*" Lev used the Hebrew phrase for welcome.

Moshe stood from his place on the couch and gave Lev a sly wink. "Why don't we take them downstairs and show them around our little playground?"

Lev smiled when he saw the puzzled looks on Leo and John's faces. "Follow me. I think this is something you will both find interesting." John and Leo traded looks before following Lev and his team down one of the side hallways to an alcove with a staircase descending below ground level. Following a short hallway at the bottom of the stairs, they passed through a double-wide doorway and entered a dimly lit room painted dark gray.

There were two rows of glass-topped tables holding several computer screens and keyboards. Five enormous flat-panel screens lined one wall, and another side of the room had a thick, vault-like steel door in the center. The opposite wall was taken up with an enormous map of Israel and a large erasable board covered in Hebrew writing.

The back of the room held a communications center and was separated from the rest of the space by a floor-to-ceiling glass wall. This area looked like something one would see in a command bunker at NASA and created a futuristic-looking backdrop to the scene. The light from the large screens on the wall infused the area with a bluish hue, while small spotlights scattered in the ceiling created pools of white light around the room.

"I'm not a military man," Leo said, "but this looks to me like some kind of command center."

"You're right," Moshe said. "That's exactly what it is. You're standing in the command center for the Bible Code Team. I copied it from the one I had in the army."

John was amazed. "It looks like you're still in command of an army. This place is really something."

"These are our computer stations, which are connected to a larger mainframe," Ariella explained. "The main computer is programmed with a powerful Bible code search engine. Just enter any word or phrase, and the computer will begin searching in an effort to pinpoint its encoded location in the Bible. Our portable laptops have similar software for field use."

John and Leo walked around the room with Lev, taking in the layout and looking at all of the equipment, while the Israelis continued to study the two new members of their team.

From one of the tables, Alon grabbed a small radio and clipped it to his belt before plugging in the tiny earpiece and boom microphone. He then walked over to the locked vault door and entered a code into a keypad on the wall. The thick steel door opened slowly, allowing Alon to enter the vault and return with a backpack and a large pistol in a shoulder holster. He motioned to John. "Come with me."

John cast a "who, me?" look at Alon. "Where are we going?"

"Outside for a quick patrol of the perimeter."

Sizing up Alon, who truly did seem as solid as an oak tree, John knew it was pointless asking any more questions. Looking back over his shoulder at Leo, he timidly followed Alon up the stairs, looking like a teenager who had just stepped off the bus to boot camp trailing behind his new drill instructor.

Once outside in the bright sunshine, Alon explained to John that the property was surrounded by individual rings of security. Walking past a young man armed with an assault rifle, the two continued along the sand dunes for a quarter of a mile until Alon came to a stop at the perimeter of the property.

"What do you see?" Alon asked.

Looking down the line of shifting sand dunes toward the villa in the distance, John was puzzled by the question. "I'm not sure what you're asking, Alon. I see the ocean, fields of crops, some houses, and the villa over there. Other than that, I just see sand dunes and some palm trees."

"That's all we want people to see."

Opening his olive-colored backpack, Alon pulled out a small shovel and a device that resembled a mini metal detector. Pointing the device at the ground, he began scanning the sandy soil around them. After receiving a strong, audible signal, he began to dig. Barely three shovelfuls of sand later, he exposed the tip of a wire connected to a black plastic box.

"There. That's a motion detector," Alon said. "They're all around the perimeter. When anything crosses this area, an alarm goes off and the exact location of an intruder flashes on a computer screen in the command post by the front gate."

"Pretty impressive, but why are you showing me this? I'm not a security person or a soldier. Do you want me to help you patrol around the villa for terrorists or something?"

"No, I'm sorry, of course not, John. We have our own trained people for that, although in this country, we're all soldiers until a certain age. Something happened a few hours ago that you need to know about."

Alon scooped sand back over the motion detector, and the two began heading back down the line of dunes. They were almost to the villa when John noticed the blue flashing lights of an Israeli police vehicle as it raced through the front gate, followed by two dark-brown military Humvees. Holding his hand to his earpiece, Alon said something in Hebrew into the microphone and began running toward the villa while signaling for John to follow.

* * *

The vehicles skidded to a halt on the circular gravel driveway in front of the house and several uniformed police officers piled out, dragging two handcuffed men dressed in suits with them. A senior officer approached Alon, and after a brief exchange, everyone headed inside.

"What's going on?" John asked. "What are all these police doing here?"

"I believe this has something to do with what I was getting ready to tell you about. Come on. Let's go inside."

The police led the men through the doors of the main entrance, where they came face-to-face with Lev and the rest of his team standing at the bottom of a winding staircase.

"Are these the two men we called you about, Commander?" Lev asked.

"Yes, sir. The license plate on their car matches the number you gave us and they have pictures of the villa on their digital cameras. We stopped them about twenty miles south of here outside of Tel Aviv."

Lev patted the police commander on the shoulder. "Nice work, David. Thanks for helping us out." Lev had known this policeman since he was just a boy, the son of a close friend. "Have they said anything to you?"

"Not a word. Here are their IDs and passports."

"They're not Israeli?"

"Look for yourself, Professor. These guys are Swiss Guards from the Vatican."

The two men in handcuffs shot glances at Leo and John, followed by a quick look back in the direction of the police commander.

"Well, it looks like some of your friends from Rome followed you two here," Lev said. "Undoubtedly, whomever these men take their orders from knows exactly where you two are."

John and Leo were speechless. They believed they were free from the intrigue and dangers they had faced in Rome. Now, in the foyer of Lev's villa in Israel, they had two Vatican security men standing right in front of them.

"What are they going to do with them, Lev?" Leo asked. "Can we speak to them?"

The police commander faced Leo. "I'm sorry, sir, but they're in our custody now. We can't allow you to talk to them, but I assure you, we will find out what they are doing in our country. For now, they will be charged with trespassing. After we find out why they were taking pictures of the villa, they may have additional charges added on."

"Do you know when they arrived from Rome?" Moshe asked.

"According to customs, they checked into the airport three days ago."

"That's before we arrived," John said.

Alon looked at John. "It's also before we knew you were coming."

Lev handed the passports back to David. "There are still a lot of questions to be answered, and we need to let you do your job and see where that leads us. Thank you for bringing them by, David."

Ariella stepped forward and gave the police officer some photos the security force at the villa had taken of the men from a hidden rooftop camera. These included pictures of the vehicle's license plate and one of the men talking on a cell phone.

"One picture is worth a thousand words," Lev said, looking at the photos in the police commander's hands. "I sure would like to know who he was talking to."

The police commander nodded his head. "So would we …we're working on that. I'll give you a call, Professor, if we learn anything else that might be of value to you. Shalom."

"Shalom," the group responded as the police led the two men away.

"That was amazing," John said. "If you don't mind, Alon, I'd like to spend some time learning all I can about the security precautions you guys use."

The Israelis smiled as Alon slapped John on the back. "Then tomorrow we start with target practice. You'll be like a soldier when I get through with you. An Israeli-trained soldier."

"I can't figure out how they knew we would be here," Leo said. "These people are really spooky. Father Morelli said our lives would be in danger— that there are dark forces aligned against us. I only hope those forces don't already have the upper hand."

"At least we had the upper hand today, Father," Lev said.

"True, but those men were human. All the motion detectors and weapons in the world are useless if we come up against a supernatural force."

The others sobered noticeably when Leo mentioned the word *supernatural*.

Leo looked across the foyer and noticed Daniel walking from the hallway with a sheaf of papers in his hands.

"Professor Wasserman, I think you need to see something."

"What have you got there, Daniel?"

"It's a printout of something I just found in that section of the Bible we've been trying to decipher for the past two months."

Lev slipped on his glasses and took the printout from Daniel.

"When were you able to reveal this part of the code?"

"About half an hour ago. I looked around to tell you, but everyone had left."

As one of the world's premier code breakers, Daniel was the typical scholar who tended to get so focused on his work that he was oblivious to all outside distractions.

Lev raised the glasses up on top of his head after reading the first page of the printout. "I think we all need to go back downstairs to the command center and have a little meeting."

Everyone crowded down the narrow stairway into the command center and watched as Lev scrolled through several encoded pages of the Bible at his computer station. He paused to read before looking up at the large screen in the front of the room. "Daniel, can you bring up a map of the area around the Dead Sea on that screen?"

"Sure, Professor." Daniel punched in coordinates on the keyboard, and the large center screen lit up with a multicolored interactive map of the area.

"Zero in south of the Dead Sea. I want to enlarge that area of the desert."

Daniel continued to type, causing the display to zoom in on a sun-baked wilderness known as the Negev Desert.

"There," Lev said, "that's the area Daniel just pinpointed using the code in the Bible."

Leo stared at the screen. "What are we looking at, Lev?"

"Since last summer, we've been trying to pinpoint the location of some-thing we discovered in the code—a physical place that harbors an evolving disturbance in relation to the balance between good and evil in the world. We also found an encoded reference to an object connected to this disturbance. There's something out there. It's probably been there for thousands of years, and we believe it's very important to none other than Satan himself."

"Did I hear you correctly, Professor?" John asked. "Did you say some-thing important to *Satan*?"

"Yes, very important. Daniel just found the exact latitudinal and longitudi-nal coordinates of this area, along with several combinations of words spelled out in close proximity to each other embedded in the Bible. According to the code, these coordinates point directly to an area here on earth reserved for

Satan. It also states that this area is ferociously guarded by him. There is something of great value to Satan at that location, and that is where we must go."

The rest of the team stood in stunned silence. They knew the Bible code was leading them somewhere, but they had not prepared themselves for anything like this. They were being led into the heart of the barren Negev Desert, to a place spelled out as Satan's domain here on earth.

Father Leo took a few steps toward the screen. "Father Morelli indicated to me in a letter that what we are looking for is very old, dating to the time when Lucifer was cast from heaven by God. That much we know. What we don't know is what 'it' is. Morelli also warned that this may have some connection with the *end of days* for humanity. As you might guess, this undertaking could be extremely dangerous, both physically and spiritually. The fact that we must travel to an area said to be reserved for Satan here on earth is especially disturbing to me. I've never read anything in biblical literature that mentions anything about a specific place on earth set aside for Satan."

"How can a place here on earth be held in reserve for Satan?" John asked, incredulous at the thought. "I mean, really, was that an allegorical reference, or do you seriously believe that we'll be entering Satan's actual domain?"

"Let me answer that question," Daniel said. He entered some commands on the keyboard, and a page from the Bible written in Hebrew appeared. Circled in red were the translated words *Negev Desert* crossed by the words *Satan's domain*. Next to these words was the phrase, *the five chosen must enter.*

Daniel looked up from his computer. "As you can see for yourself, this phrase appears to mean a physical spot here on earth. It also gives the exact number of those who will enter this area. The code is usually pretty specific in its wording."

Those who were seeing this for the first time found themselves staring slack-jawed at the screen. But there was more to come.

"Daniel, bring up the next page," Lev said.

Another page of the Torah appeared on the screen. The phrase *that which belongs to Satan*, was spelled out vertically. On top of that, they saw the words *they will give it to God* displayed across the top of the page. To the right was the name *Leo*. To the left of Leo's name were the names *John, Alon, Ariella*, and *Lev*. Crossing both Leo's and Lev's names horizontally was the word *leaders*. Crossing the other names was one word: *chosen*.

Leo had to physically steady himself. Morelli had specifically told Leo that he had been named in the Bible code as a leader, but here for the first time, he saw his name actually encoded in God's book. Lev turned to him and clasped the priest on the shoulder.

"You can't get much more specific than that, Father."

"What does the phrase 'they will give it to God' mean?" Ariella asked.

"I believe it means that five who will enter Satan's domain will be tasked by God to actually take something that belongs to the Devil and give it to God," Lev said.

"How do you go about giving something to God?" Moshe asked. The others nodded in his direction, everyone thinking the same thing.

John felt a chill run up his spine. "And how do you take something from Satan? It seems like every time we find an answer, another question pops up."

Like the humidity from the sea air that flowed through the windows upstairs and crept down the stairway to mix with the cool, air-conditioned environment of the command center, an uneasy silence descended on the group.

Lev put his hand on John's shoulder. "We still have a lot of sorting out to do. I think this would be a good time to settle down and try to find some more answers. One thing I know for sure; soon we will be heading out into the wilderness of the Negev Desert."

CHAPTER 16

Leo awoke with a start. He had been dreaming. In the dream, he had seen a dark storm coming over the desert, and the word *chosen* echoed through his mind. He looked around at the stark white walls of the room in an effort to get his bearings before lifting himself up to see the ocean through the open shutters of the bedroom window. He was on the coast of Israel. He was in Lev's villa. Memories of the events of the past few days were coming back to him as the fog of a long sleep began to clear. *What would today bring?*

Moving slowly, Leo headed straight for the shower and adjusted the water as hot as he could stand it. He placed himself directly under the spray while the green-tinted glass doors fogged up around him. His taut muscles relaxed, and he could feel the pores in his skin begin to pop open.

A knock at the door interrupted the state of pure bliss he was feeling under the pounding stream.

"I'm in the shower."

The door opened. "I know," John said. "I could hear it outside. It's really steamy in here."

"You're starting to test my patience. I take back everything nice I said about you."

"You've been saying nice things about me?"

"Not anymore."

"Everyone's at breakfast, and Lev wants to speak with you. I'll meet you downstairs."

Leo finished lathering up and let the steaming water rinse the soap from his body. When he finally felt half way alive, he stepped out onto the moist tiles of the bathroom floor and grabbed a towel.

Another knock at the door. *This is ridiculous.* "What?"

Lev's voice echoed from the other side of the door. "Just throw your swimming trunks on, Father. We can swim a few laps together before breakfast. We'll eat outside by the pool."

Do they always eat outside here at the villa? "I'll be right down." Swimming a few laps actually appealed to the priest. He usually worked out daily, but exercise had fallen to the bottom of his priority list over the past week.

Walking out into the sunshine, Leo stood at the edge of the pool before diving in and swimming down over the bottom. The cool water felt good against his skin in contrast to the hot water of the shower. He felt invigorated as he surfaced and began to swim the length of the pool. The rhythmic strokes increased his heart rate, causing the tension to melt away as the endorphins kicked in. Lev was still slogging away in the next lane when Leo finished his brief but fast-paced workout and climbed from the water. Drying his hair, he joined John at the outdoor bar and helped himself to some eggs and orange juice.

John spread some cherry preserves on his toast and asked the cook for some more coffee. "This place is like a resort. I could get used to living here."

Leo nodded in agreement. "Lev wasn't kidding when he said he lived comfortably. I wanted to speak with you before we talk to him this morning, John."

"What's up?"

"I think we need to leave for the desert soon, today if possible. I have a feeling there is a time element to all of this. We've got to move quickly if we want to locate whatever it is we were sent here to find."

"I agree. A few more days of this, and we'll never want to leave."

Lev bypassed a towel and let the water drip from his body as he left the pool to join Leo and John. "What a great way to start the day. Maybe after we're finished with our work in the desert, we can all go on holiday together on my yacht."

John rolled his eyes. "You have a yacht?"

"Technically, it belongs to the company my family left to me." He laughed and flicked some water off his tan belly. "But I'm the only one who's allowed to use it."

Leo raised an eyebrow and fixed Lev with a practiced questioning stare. It was a talent he had acquired through years of listening to student's excuses as to why their term papers were late. It was becoming obvious that Lev was very wealthy, but Leo could see that most of his money went to taking care of others and trying to do God's work here on earth. "I thought you said you lived comfortably but not lavishly."

Lev gave Leo a conspiratorial wink as a staff member walked up and shoved a cup of coffee in his hand. He paused to gaze out over the dunes at the sparkling sea while breathing in the aroma of the coffee and taking his first sip. "Have you two thought about your next move?"

"We were just discussing leaving for the desert as soon as possible," Leo said. "We have the coordinates provided by the Bible code now, and I think today would be a good time to head out there."

"You're probably right. I was going to talk to you about how you wanted to proceed. Might as well just jump in and go for it. If you don't mind, I'd like some of my people to go with you. This is still a dangerous country, and running around out in the desert without backup is a recipe for disaster."

"That's not a bad idea," Leo said. The realization that he had no idea about how to proceed was slowly dawning on him. "What do you have in mind?"

"We talked among ourselves last night after you went to bed. What we're actually doing here is attempting to mount a major archaeological project in a matter of days. We're going to need all the help we can get. Whatever is out there in the desert won't reveal itself easily. I'm sending Alon and Ariella with you, along with some staff members from the villa as support personnel. That should get you started while I finish getting the rest of the expedition together here and join up with you in a few days."

Leo finished his juice and set his glass down on the bar. "That's more than generous, Lev. Father Morelli knew what he was doing when he sent us to you. Is there anything John and I can do to get things rolling?"

"You can grab some of those pastries over there. The vehicles are already out front waiting for you."

John threw a look of surprise in Lev's direction. "Wow, you don't waste any time, Professor."

Leo climbed off the bar stool and smiled at Lev. "Why do you always seem to be one step ahead of us?"

"My motives are not entirely selfless, Father. I'm just as interested as you are to see what's out there. It's going to take all of us working together to see this through. Go get ready, and I'll meet you out front."

After dressing and grabbing their backpacks, Leo and John stepped through the large front doors of the villa to the sight of several sand-colored vehicles of various shapes and sizes. A new Land Rover was at the head of the convoy, followed by two large four-wheel-drive military-looking trucks and a large out-of-place-looking vehicle that resembled a motor home. Lev was busy consulting with Alon and Ariella next to the strange looking vehicle, while staff members from the villa loaded boxes of equipment into the trucks.

Leo walked over to the motor home and admired the polished silver exterior before peering up the stairwell inside. The diesel engine was idling, and he could feel the cool air created by the air-conditioning blowing from within. The interior of the front section of the vehicle was sheathed in stainless steel and resembled a commercial kitchen, while the entire rear portion held refrigerated walk-ins for perishable foods and living accommodations for the chefs.

"What in the world is this, Lev?"

"I bought it from a rich Texas oil man. It's a combination mobile kitchen and living quarters. His company was doing some exploration out in the desert, and he sold it to me after they were through. Those oil men like their comforts out in the field. You can prepare enough food for an army with this thing."

"Wow!"

Leo turned to see John standing behind him staring at the motor home. "You really love that word."

John laughed. "Well, it gets my point across."

Lev walked over to one of the trucks and looked inside. After conferring with one of his staff, he returned to join Leo and John. "Everything is loaded in the trucks. You have everything you'll need until the rest of the expedition arrives. Better get going so you can set up camp before dark."

Alon was sitting in the driver's seat of the Land Rover and watched as Leo approached and climbed into the passenger seat beside him. Ariella and John glanced at each other shyly before climbing into the backseat next to each other. Behind them, the engines of the trucks roared to life, and the convoy began to slowly pull away from the villa under a cloudless sky onto the palm-lined highway.

Ariella seemed distracted as she watched the scenery passing by outside her window. "Have you ever been to Jerusalem?"

John felt his heart skip a beat. "Uh, no, I haven't."

She turned and stared at him with her large brown eyes. "It would be a shame to come to Israel and not see Jerusalem. When we get back from the desert, we'll make some time, and I'll show you around the city, especially the old parts."

John couldn't believe his ears. Was he dreaming? She wanted to show him the city. "Yeah, I mean, great. I'd love to spend some time there." *Especially with you.*

Ariella gave him a coy smile and glanced back out the window while they drove on in awkward silence. The highway departed the sandy coastal grass-land, and soon they began to see fields of crops on the fertile Mediterranean plain. Alon's eyes studied every car that passed as the others looked silently out their windows and thought about what they might find in the desert.

The vehicles turned east onto the new six-lane Highway 1 and headed for Jerusalem, drawing curious stares from people in other vehicles. In the subtropical climate, fruit and vegetables grew in abundance, including citrus, avocados, kiwis, guavas, bananas, and mangos. All this bounty came from the region they were passing through. They saw fields of wheat, sorghum, corn, tomatoes, cucumbers, and peppers, along with acres of flowers and vineyards lined with rows of grapevines stretching for miles.

"I never imagined it was so beautiful in Israel," John said, watching the parade of color pass by their windows. "Have there always been farms like this here?"

Ariella waved her hand in the direction of the fields. "They've been doing this since 1909. This country is dotted with two kinds of unique cooperative agricultural settlements. One is called a *kibbutz*. It's a collective community similar to the one surrounding our villa, where the equipment and housing are communally owned and each member's labor benefits the whole group. The other, called a *moshav*, is a farming community or village, where each family maintains its own individual land and any buying and selling are done cooperatively. Both communities are based on social equality and mutual assistance. There is also a security benefit to these communities from the terror groups outside their borders."

John turned his attention from the scenery back to Ariella. "I didn't realize the villa was a kibbutz."

"It's not one in the traditional sense. My father owns the villa and the houses and land surrounding it. He lets people, mostly students, live there free of charge in exchange for providing security, growing the community's food, and taking care of the villa. Because we raise almost everything we eat, the food is free. We also own several vehicles that are available for everyone in the community. They use them mostly for going to school or shopping or just a night out on the town. Some of my father's students are now professors and still choose to live there. We're like a big family that watches out for one another."

"Sounds pretty idyllic to me," John said.

Ariella tossed her long brown hair back over her shoulders. "It is to me. I never want to leave."

"I've lived there for the past five years and feel the same way," Alon said, keeping his eyes on the road. "Lev's promised me a house of my own when I get married."

Ariella giggled. "And when will that be?"

They could see the back of Alon's neck turning red. "As soon as Nava decides she's had enough of flying."

"Who's Nava?" John asked.

Ariella winked. "Alon's fiancée. She flies a helicopter in the Israeli army. You'll meet her soon."

Rounding a corner at the top of a hill, Jerusalem came into view sprawled out before them. The golden Dome of the Rock reflected the sun in the distance while the vehicles crawled through the city in the midmorning traffic. John felt the electricity of discovery. He knew he had come to a special place on earth and wanted to explore all of it. In addition to the beauty he had encountered, the religious significance was overwhelming.

John rolled down his window and stuck his head out to breathe in the aroma of the city. "Can you believe we're actually driving through Jerusalem? Wow!"

Leo smiled to himself. *Wait until he sees the Dead Sea and the cliffs of Masada.*

"What is the name of the desert we're going to?" John asked.

Alon turned in his seat as they came to a stop at a red light. "It's called the Negev Desert. It's a barren wasteland that no one except for nomadic tribes has inhabited since God destroyed Sodom and Gomorrah."

"I remember that from my studies. It is a wasteland. The Romans hated the place, and the British hated it even more. Thank God we have an air-conditioned mobile kitchen."

Everyone laughed and talked as they drove through one of the ever-present checkpoints in Jerusalem until soon the ancient city was behind them. They drove on for a short twenty minutes until they hit Israel's Highway 90 that ran north and south along the west bank of the Dead Sea. Leo still found it hard to believe that the famous biblical landmark was such a short drive from Jerusalem. They turned and headed south, driving for another hour until they reached a deserted roadside park beside the salt-encrusted bank at the southern tip of the Dead Sea.

Taking advantage of the stop, Ariella grabbed her camera and everyone got out to stretch their legs. The waters of the Dead Sea were the most saline on earth. Jagged, twisted shapes of dried salt rose up from crystalline pools, forming towers that seemed more at home on another planet.

Ariella wanted a visual record of the expedition and began snapping pictures. She had stacks of photo albums at home filled with images of all of the archaeological digs she had been on since she was a little girl.

She motioned to the others to come together. "Group picture everyone." All the staff members were used to her incessant photo ops, but they usually complied with only a few moans and groans. As the group gathered together and smiled for the camera, a small half-starved dog with matted light brown hair came limping up on the hot, briny pavement and plopped down right next to John.

Leo watched as John reached down to pet the dog. "Looks like someone has a new friend."

"They always recognize a Franciscan, Leo. Saint Francis was the patron saint of animals."

121

"Everyone knows that," Leo said. "I love animals too. Only humans avoid me."

"That's because Jesuits bite."

Ariella snapped a few more pictures and walked over to join John beside a saltwater pool. He was holding the trembling dog in his arms and trying to give him sips of bottled water. The dog was lapping it up as Ariella reached out to pet him. He turned and began to lick her hand, his brown eyes reaching into her soul.

Fire blazed in Ariella's eyes. "How could someone leave him all alone out here?"

"I can't imagine," John said. "This dog wouldn't have lasted much longer in this environment. Some people seem to lack basic compassion for other creatures. It's like their souls are different from ours, like another species. It really makes you wonder."

"Are you going to keep him?"

"Of course," John answered. "There's no way I'm leaving him out here to die of thirst and starvation."

Ariella looked back at him with a realization that only she was aware of. *John now had two new friends.*

John looked out at the alien landscape. "Isn't this where Sodom and Gomorrah once stood?"

"Supposedly stood," Ariella said. "Some scholars believe Sodom is actually across the border in nearby Jordan, but we're still in the same neighborhood."

"Maybe you can title your pictures 'close to the *supposed* site of Sodom and Gomorrah.'" John grinned at her with the knowledge that a correction was probably forthcoming.

"I believe the actual site is another twenty miles from here, but who knows. We could be standing in the exact spot. This rest stop might be on top of the ancient city of Sodom."

"That's kind of creepy, Ariella."

"I know. Let's get going. I can feel the salt sticking to my hair already."

The group returned to their vehicles, glad to be out of the heat, and soon the small convoy was heading down the highway deeper into the desert.

No one noticed a small car pull in to the rest area behind them and stop. The driver grabbed a camera from the center console and began taking pictures of the salt ponds before turning his camera on the departing vehicles. The passenger pushed his sunglasses back on his head and took out his cell phone. He punched in an international number and waited for an answer.

CHAPTER 17

The parade of vehicles motored steadily along the paved roadway, every-one mindful of the fact that they would probably not see a gas station in the near future. Extra fuel was pulled behind one of the trucks in a large tank, while another pulled a tank full of water.

In the Land Rover, the abandoned dog now sat happily between John and Ariella in air-conditioned comfort, munching away on some roast beef John had confiscated from the mobile kitchen.

The small convoy traveled south for another fifty miles before it rolled to a stop along the side of the highway. Looking out through the windows of their vehicles, the occupants scanned the vast emptiness of the Negev Desert that stretched as far as the eye could see.

Magnificent desolation. Leo had heard astronaut Buzz Aldrin use the same words to describe the moon when he stepped out onto its surface for the first time.

The Negev Desert was one of the most isolated and desolate places on earth. Ringed with gray mountains in the distance, they could see nothing green. Except for a few hardy species of insects and snakes, the only signs of life in this arid sea of rock and sand were the Bedouin tribes who still passed through the area, clinging to their traditional nomadic ways.

Two thousand years ago, the Nabataeans controlled the ancient spice and incense route here where the caravans crossed from India and Southern Arabia to the Mediterranean. Scattered ruins of their culture could still be found among the shifting sands. The area had changed little since that time, and for the most part, the Negev remained wild and free from modern civilization.

The motorized caravan lurched forward once more before turning off the paved highway and heading deeper into the desert where there were no roads. They traveled another two hours at an agonizingly slow pace, skirting sheer cliffs that dropped into deep, shadowed canyons before the convoy drove up onto a flat crater-filled plateau. Alon glanced at his GPS and brought the Land Rover to a stop.

"I guess this is it," Ariella announced from the backseat.

Leo looked out across the forbidding landscape and watched the shimmering waves of heat rising in the distance. "I sure hope so. I don't think my backside could take much more bumping along over these rocks and holes."

The other vehicles pulled to a stop around them, a modern-day version of a wagon train in the desert. They dismounted their trucks and stood under the sun, gazing at the strange beauty of the immense wilderness before them.

The desert here was surrounded by cone-like mountains and vertical cliffs ringing their position. Nearby, the plateau ended at the edge of a precipice that dropped several hundred feet into a canyon below. There were stories of people becoming disoriented by the optical illusions created by the canyons running through the flat plateaus and driving right off a cliff before they realized it was there. This was definitely not a place to be exploring after dark.

The color of the loose sand was golden, with red and white patches of soil pushing through in places. The air was still, and the absence of sound was slightly unnerving to those accustomed to lives around people and the attendant noise of TVs, music, and traffic. It seemed peaceful, yet for some reason, the place gave the new arrivals a vague feeling of apprehension. The atmosphere especially affected Father Leo. He looked at the angle of the sun and asked the others to immediately begin setting up camp in a race against the approaching darkness.

The small band of men and women began working together in the laborious task of unloading the trucks, pitching tents, and organizing supplies, while the cooks cranked up the mobile kitchen and were slicing and dicing their way to dinner. In the dusty orange haze of the desert sunset, the camp was just beginning to take shape when they all heard the sound.

A rhythmic thump, thump, thump could be heard in the distance. The noise grew louder, then fainter as it crisscrossed the floor of the canyon below.

Everyone in camp stopped what they were doing and listened. Whatever it was, it was getting closer to their campsite.

The sun had just dipped below the horizon, allowing the group to see rapid bright-red flashes of light shooting up into the sky from the edge of the desert where the plateau met the rim of the canyon. With everyone's attention riveted on the lights, a dark fast-moving shape materialized from the rim and flew up and over the camp, followed by another. Blowing sand swirled over the vehicles and tents, entering the nostrils and mouths of the startled and confused group as they shielded their eyes.

Slowly, they began to grasp their situation. Two large Blackhawk helicopters were circling their campsite and preparing to land, their flashing red strobe lights reflecting against the vehicles and desert floor around them.

The group instinctively turned their backs to the landing aircraft, pulling their shirts up over their faces in an effort to keep from breathing in the swirling sand. The helicopters began touching down next to the camp and quickly shut down their engines, one after another, until the whine of the turbines and the chop of the rotor blades came to a halt.

Leo and the others brushed away the fine grit that covered their clothing and filled their hair as the helicopters' doors began to slide open, revealing familiar faces peering out from inside.

Ariella was the first to spot Lev. "Father! What are you doing here? How did you ...?"

"I'm sorry, little one. We tried to reach you on your cell phones and radios, but nothing seems to work right out here. Our signals were probably blocked by the canyon walls. But the radios seem to be working fine now. Moshe finally convinced one of his high-ranking cabinet friends to authorize the use of these helicopters. We didn't plan on having them so soon."

Everyone was overjoyed at the arrival of Lev and the other staff members from the villa, including a dusty but grinning Leo. "I didn't think we'd see you for another few days."

Lev winked before reaching into the helicopter and pulling out a case of wine. "Tonight, my friend, we eat, drink, and dance. Tomorrow, we work."

John looked confused. "Did Lev just say we were going to dance?"

Ariella threw her head back in laughter. "It's an Israeli thing."

CHAPTER 18

THE NEGEV DESERT—DAY 1

The two groups came together and continued to set up the camp, designating separate areas for different purposes. Lev instructed one of the helicopter pilots to radio the villa, and soon, another convoy of trucks full of equipment was en route.

The cooks threw more meat on the grill in anticipation of the new arrivals while Leo helped some young people carry long folding tables into an enormous screened mess tent Lev and his staff had erected next to the mobile kitchen.

John and Ariella took charge of setting up generator-powered lights to illuminate the area around the perimeter where another group was busy setting up a row of large ten-person tents with a series of portable latrines nearby.

Around nine o'clock at night, a line of headlights could be seen in the distance. The second convoy, bringing more supplies and additional staff from Lev's villa, soon rolled into camp, spurring another round of unloading and organizing. There were twenty-four people in the new group, half of them women. They had been summoned to perform various roles, including security, medical, communications, archaeological excavation, photography, transportation, and supply. The helicopters were being secured for the night by their crews and would remain with the expedition, as it was now being called, for as long as they were needed.

Alon and Daniel began work on setting up a special communications facility in the center of camp. It was an improved version of the inflatable tents designed before the Gulf War for the harsh desert environment. It came complete with its own power source and the air-conditioning necessary for the sensitive electronic equipment.

Antennas began to sprout up around the perimeter of the new facility like a giant spider web. One of the vehicles in the second convoy was a huge four-wheel-drive tanker truck full of water, which was conveniently placed between the kitchen and a second inflatable tent used for showering.

Exhausted from the day's work, everyone in camp finally gathered around the steaming platters of food that were coming in a steady stream from the kitchen to the tables in the mess tent. Candles provided a soft, flickering light while a CD of classical music played in the background. Bottles of Israeli wine were passed around, and soon, the evening began to take on the aura of an impromptu party in the middle of the Negev Desert.

Lev and Leo sat at one of the long tables and enjoyed the stillness of the moment. Leo was still amazed at how the Bible had led them to this spot in the middle of nowhere, and he was anxious to learn more about his new friends and their work on the code.

Lev reached over and poured some white wine in Leo's glass. "We share a common bond, Leo, a bond formed by our faith in Christ and the knowledge that our numbers are slowly dwindling. I believe this group here tonight represents one of many seeds that will soon spread throughout the world. In fact, I would call them all *chosen* ones."

That got Leo's attention.

"What do you know about those who are mentioned in the code as chosen, Professor? Have you found any more names in the Bible listed as chosen for this task?"

"So far, we only have the five names Daniel found. No one else here is mentioned in the code, but they all support our mission. Even though all these people have gathered here at this time and this place to do God's bidding, only those whose names are encoded in the Bible will be tasked with retrieving the object we were sent to find."

The two men looked around at the others from their place at the end of the table. They were enjoying the camaraderie of this special group of men and women who had volunteered to help solve an ancient mystery, despite a clear warning about the danger they all faced.

John entered the tent, wearing fresh jeans and a clean white T-shirt borrowed from a staff member.

"I see the new shower tent has been christened," Leo said.

"What a great idea, a tent with running water. I feel like a new man. There's nothing like a cool shower before dinner, even if it is almost midnight."

Lev winked at Leo. "I'm glad you enjoyed it. Living this close to the desert all our lives has helped us learn a few tricks to keep comfortable."

Ariella entered the tent with the stray dog wrapped in a towel.

"What on earth are you doing with that dog?" Lev asked.

"He needed a bath too. He smelled terrible. Since he's staying with us, he's going to be well-groomed."

The mess tent had taken on the din of a popular bistro at happy hour. Everyone was chatting all at once and enjoying the sumptuous meal created by the cooks. Alon seemed happier than usual and had his arm draped over the shoulder of one of the female helicopter pilots. Ariella introduced her to Leo and John as Alon's fiancée, Nava. The couple apparently had not seen each other in months and couldn't take their eyes off each other.

John and Ariella retreated to a far corner of the tent to engage in some quiet conversation while the former stray dog slept soundly at their feet after having made the rounds of every table and receiving his fill of handouts.

"Those two are starting to look like a couple," Lev said, watching his daughter and John alone at a table. He sighed before turning his attention back to Leo. "Do you have any knowledge of group dreams and prophecy, Father?"

"Well, my specific area of study is ancient Christian sects and how they came to form the Catholic Church, but I recall several documented cases of group dreams occurring throughout history among the faithful. Some are what I would call inspirational dreams that have a positive effect and can spur people on to achieve great things in the name of God. Others seem to be more prophetic in nature, predicting either catastrophic or miraculous events. These dreams can also be a warning, offering instead a vision of things to come for those who refuse to heed God's word."

"Can these dreams come from somewhere other than God?" Lev asked. "I mean, could Satan inspire group dreams in people?"

"Well, I guess when you're talking about dreams with religious overtones, there's really no way to tell. A lot depends on the content of the dream and what you may or may not be asked to do in them. Mental institutions and prisons are full of people who did some really bad things they believed God had told them to do in a dream."

Lev shifted uneasily in his seat. "I haven't mentioned this before, Leo, but many of us here have been having dreams about coming to this desert together, including myself. I guess there's been some concern about where these dreams are truly coming from."

This was getting interesting. "What exactly do you see in your dreams, Lev? I mean, are there any explicit verbal instructions, and do you all dream the same thing?"

"For the most part, we all see a terrible storm over the desert."

Leo felt a sudden chill as the hair raised up on his arms.

"I don't know if Morelli told you, Father," Lev said, "but I've had the gift of prophecy since I was a child."

Leo put his glass down and looked Lev right in the eyes. This man was serious. Leo had a knack for being able to tell if someone was telling the truth or pulling his leg. In his entire career as a Jesuit priest, he had met only one other person who had the gift of prophecy, and that person was the previous pope.

"Do you mean you actually see things that happen in the future?"

Lev looked embarrassed. "Well, yes. It's only happened a few times and I never know when it will occur again. When I was a student, I told one of my teachers in school that I had dreamed about the American president being shot and killed. The next day, President Kennedy was assassinated. I also dreamed about the World Trade Center being hit by airplanes the night before the attack."

Leo was dumbstruck. A real-life prophet here and now in this day and age. Morelli must have been totally beside himself when he met this man. One of his main goals in life had been to meet a real prophet living in today's world. Morelli had believed that by meeting a modern prophet whose prophesies could be verified, he could validate stories from the Old Testament about the prophets of old.

"But you said others in your group have been having dreams about coming to the desert."

"Only lately. Those of us mentioned as chosen have had the same dream for the past two weeks. We're all praying that these dreams are coming from God and not somewhere else."

Leo thought for a moment. "Have any of the others had prophetic dreams in the past?"

"No, and we're not sure that these dreams are even prophetic, because nothing we saw in the dreams has happened yet."

"Is there a common thread to these dreams other than the storm and the desert?"

Lev ran his hands through his hair and breathed in deeply. "Yes. Besides seeing a storm, we all heard a voice telling us that we were chosen."

Leo took a long sip of Israeli wine and reclined in his seat as he thought about what Lev had just told him. "Until it's proven otherwise, I would have to say your dreams come from God. If it makes you feel any better, I've had the same dream, and Father Morelli instructed me not to trust anyone with this task who wasn't specifically listed in the code as being chosen."

"I have to admit, I was starting to wonder if you had dreamed the same dream as the rest of us," Lev said. "I felt relieved when I saw the word chosen encoded with our names in the Bible. That does seem to verify that these dreams come from God, even if none of us has any idea why we've been chosen, or for what. What we do know is that all of us have been brought together in what, in my opinion, is way more than just a coincidence. I guess we're just going to have to be patient until the code reveals the real reason we've all been summoned here."

"I'll drink to that," Leo said, hoisting his half-full glass of wine.

Lev touched his glass to Leo's. "A toast to dreams and codes and all true messages from God."

The two men continued to hold their glasses in a salute, looking straight into the eyes of one another, knowing, at that moment, that God had truly ordained this conclave in the desert. They placed their glasses on the table, and Leo leaned close to Lev in an effort to keep their conversation private. "I'm probably being redundant telling you this, Lev, but there are fifteen prophets who have books named after them in the Bible. Elijah was the first to perform miracles in a battle between God and the deities of the pagans. I sincerely pray you will be our Elijah in the days to come. God has given you the gift of prophecy for a reason, and you must use it wisely, both for the sake of everyone here tonight and maybe even the world itself in the days to come."

Lev frowned at the comparison between himself and the prophets of old. "You don't pull any punches, do you, Father?"

"Only in boxing when I was in the ring with a weaker opponent."

Lev had enjoyed his discussion with Leo. The priest had a gift for listening and condensing other's concerns down to their very essence. Yawning, he realized he needed a few hours of uninterrupted sleep before their work began in the morning. He stood and stretched before turning back toward Leo. "The gift of prophecy is a difficult thing to describe, Father. I've been struggling with it all my life. I used to get periodic flashes of things before they happened, but now they're becoming stronger and more frequent. I can only tell you that something bigger than anything I have ever seen before is coming. We need to have a meeting tomorrow after breakfast with everyone in the camp. I'll go over what we know up to now, and hopefully, that will help us in our plan of action in the days to come."

"Get some rest," Leo said. "I have a feeling we won't be getting much over the next few days."

The tables in the mess tent began to empty as Leo followed Lev out into the rapidly cooling desert air. Both men stared up into the star-filled heavens in silence. This initial gathering of those called to this spot in the middle of an empty wilderness was coming to an end, and one by one, they felt their way into darkened tents, where they collapsed onto their cots. Soon, sleep overcame all who were not on sentry duty on their first night in the Negev Desert.

CHAPTER 19

THE NEGEV DESERT—DAY 2

A dusty yellow ring that seemed painted around the sun provided a hazy backdrop over the awakening camp. As the day wore on, the pastel horizon of the dawn gave way to a brilliant clear-blue sky, and the unrelenting heat began to make itself felt across the desert. Breakfast in the camp had ended an hour earlier, and people scurried about, finishing projects they had started the night before.

Out in the desert, the sound of gunfire echoed against the surrounding mountains as Alon introduced John to military weapons. The big Israeli commando had taken John under his wing, becoming a surrogate big brother to him. Much to John's relief, Alon had pointed out that the Hawaiian print shirts John and Leo were wearing were glaringly inadequate for the harsh desert environment, so he had furnished them both with some long-sleeved white cotton shirts, khaki shorts, and olive-colored hats that had soft wide brims that hung loosely down around the sides.

"What kind of backpack is that, John?" Alon asked, peering at a small hole beginning to form around the bottom.

"A cheap one. I bought it a few months ago, before I came to Europe. Didn't have much money."

"I think what you're carrying deserves better." Alon walked over to a truck and pulled out a general issue military backpack like those used by the Israeli army. "Here, John. Put the brick in this. It's made of Kevlar. This material will even stop a bullet."

John had given Alon and the others a chance to examine the brick the day before at the villa. They were all full of curiosity at the strange painting of a jet hitting one of two tall towers and the obvious reference to the disastrous 9/11 terrorist attacks on New York City. The same question was on everyone's mind: how did that image get painted two thousand years ago on a stone brick found under the Vatican? Most puzzling of course was the question of why. Lev and his team had still been unable to find any clue to the brick's significance or its relation to what they were looking for in the desert.

The stray dog was already gaining weight as John continued to make sure he had plenty of food. He had decided to name him Camp, since he was now recognized by everyone as the official mascot of the entire camp.

Returning from a scouting mission of the region, the turbine engines of one of the helicopters drowned out any conversation as Leo and Lev emerged from the dust created by the spinning rotors and called for everyone to gather in the mess tent.

Lev stood up first. "Shalom, everyone. This morning we scouted the area around our campsite, taking pictures and looking for signs of life or anything out of the ordinary. There's probably no one around us for at least fifty miles. Because of the sensitive nature of our work here, that's probably a good thing. I want to turn this meeting over to my daughter, Ariella, so she can explain the archaeological aspects of the mission and also go over any hazards we might encounter out at the excavation site just to the south of our camp."

Ariella brushed the hair back from her face and stood up next to her father. "This morning we used ground-penetrating radar and took some infrared pictures of an area revealed to us by the code in the Bible. The images from these two sources reveal some unusual anomalies in the substructure of the earth beneath the sand. There also appear to be remains of several man-made objects close-by. This is the area where we will begin our excavation, so be very careful in your digging. We have learned from the Bible code that something very old lies in this area of the desert, and many of you have heard that this object is connected to none other than Satan himself. Be that as it may, this is where we will begin our search. If anyone here decides they want to leave, please raise your hand, and we'll make sure you have a seat on a truck leaving for Jerusalem within the hour."

Predictably, everyone in the tent looked to their right and their left, but no one raised their hand.

"Good. Any questions before we get going?"

One of the young female staff members from the villa spoke up. "I've never been on an archaeological dig or anything like this before. What do we do?"

"There are several archaeologists here who will guide you out at the excavation site. Just follow their instructions and work at your own pace. Drink plenty of water, and see the medic if you start to feel weak or dizzy from the heat."

Lev pulled an unlit cigar from his mouth and stepped forward. "Also, a lot of you have asked me who the leader of this expedition is. We discussed this subject among ourselves this morning and decided the leadership will be shared equally between Father Leo Amodeo and myself. If you have any needs or concerns, feel free to ask either one of us. If we disagree on anything, we'll put it to a vote in front of the whole camp."

"We really should get moving, Father," Ariella said. "Are there any more questions?"

No one spoke. They were all deep in thought as they lifted themselves away from the tables and began to file out of the tent to the waiting vehicles. Climbing up next to Lev in the back of one of the trucks, Leo glanced at Ariella sitting in another vehicle and wondered what it would have been like to have a child like her. "That's some daughter you have, Lev. She's smart and takes charge when things need to be done."

"Believe me, I know. Since she was a little girl, she's been very independent and headstrong. My wife died when Ariella was only ten, so I've had to raise her pretty much by myself."

"Maybe we should have made her one of the leaders," Leo said, causing both men to chuckle. He looked at Lev and studied the furrowed lines around his eyes, remembering their conversation of the night before. Was it possible that he was sitting next to a prophet; one that people would be talking and reading about a thousand years from now?

The truck lurched forward, and the small line of vehicles drove the short distance to a spot in the desert pinpointed by Daniel from the coordinates he had discovered in the code.

As soon as the trucks stopped, Ariella jumped out and began taking GPS readings of the site. Lev followed her with a bundle of wooden stakes with small white flags attached and directed the staff to pound them into the ground around the perimeter. Daniel then used a surveyor's instrument to take laser sightings over the surface, marking an area where the group began placing more stakes, this time with yellow flags, inside the perimeter. In the very center, all the flags were red and formed a large circle.

By nine in the morning, the sun beat down on the site with a fiery stillness as Ariella instructed the others to start digging along the perimeter by the white flags. They were assisted in their digging by a small backhoe that had just arrived from Jerusalem. In an effort to provide some shade, reinforcements from camp, including the cooks, had been called in to help erect an enormous canopy with open sides over the area where they would be digging. A much smaller open-sided tent was erected close by for use as an onsite archeological headquarters for the excavation.

Under the cover of the smaller tent, laptop computers and photographic equipment filled half the space. In the other half, several members of the team were busy sketching detailed drawings of the site on two portable drafting tables that had been mounted atop a wooden floor hastily assembled to keep the sand at bay.

Several staff members were assigned to pass out water to everyone on a regular basis in the oppressive heat as the team continued to dig, reaching the five-foot level along one section of the perimeter by midmorning.

John removed his cap and shook the sweat from his hair before stepping into the shade of the site headquarters tent. Looking up from his computer, Daniel noticed John's crimson face. He reached into a nearby ice chest and handed him a bottle of ice-cold water. "John, do you have that brick with you?"

"It never leaves my side." He hefted his new backpack up onto the table next to Daniel's computer and removed it for him to examine. "What are you looking for?"

"I've been searching through the Bible looking for anything in the code that mentioned that brick. I'm pretty sure I've just found what we've been looking for."

"Have you told Leo yet?"

"I just called him on the radio. He's on his way over."

John watched the pages scrolling on the computer screen while Daniel picked up the brick and held it in his hands, turning it over as he inspected it. He saw right away that there were no inscriptions that could be seen with the naked eye.

The anticipation John felt was nerve-wracking. "Can you show me what you've found?"

Daniel put the brick down and motioned for John to join him in front of the computer just as Leo's jeep came roaring up to the tent and slid to a stop.

"Thanks for getting here so quickly, Leo," Daniel said. "I was about to show John the section that mentions the stone brick you found in the chapel."

Leo could barely contain his excitement. "We've been dying to know more about that brick ever since we laid eyes on it."

Daniel pointed to a page on the screen containing a section from the Bible. Several words and phrases written in Hebrew were interconnected and circled in red. "This is the grid where I found the reference to the stone brick. The words *terrorist attacks* were the first ones that jumped out at me. Next to that are the words *New York*, followed by the date *September 11, 2001*. Now, if you look down at the bottom of the page, you will see the words *stone brick* and *wall of the chapel* located between two phrases. The first phrase reads *it is the key*. The second one says, *the attack is painted on the key*."

Leo felt his heart race. "So what this is saying is that the brick is a key of some sort?"

"Exactly, and it goes even further. Cross over to the edge of the page, and you will see the words *the key will unlock that which belongs to Satan*."

Leo picked up the brick and studied the painting. "I believe this image was painted on the brick with the intention of getting our attention. Morelli told me that the code is like a time lock revealed only to the right people at the right time. This brick was not meant to be found or even understood until this exact time in history. Before 9/11, the painting would have been interesting, but meaningless."

"At least now we know it's a key of some sort," John said.

Leo handed the brick to John. "John, you need to watch this brick like a snake in the room until we need it, whenever that may be. I think Lev will be overjoyed with this new information. Have you told him yet, Daniel?"

"No, he drove back into camp to get some more supplies. I thought you might like to surprise him with the news."

The three men sat in the shade of the tent, drinking cold water and taking turns examining the ancient brick, while, at the excavation site, Ariella was in her element, digging in the dirt. A female staff member by the name of Maya was working next to her in the trench and paused to take a drink from her canteen. "You know, Ariella, Satan's not going to let us dig something out of the ground that belongs to him, load it on a truck, and just drive out of the desert with it. What do you think we're really looking for?"

"In archaeology, you just keep digging until something is slowly revealed. You can't rush it. We're going to have to take our time and be patient. That's what makes the experience so exciting. It's like unwrapping a present and you can't wait to see what's inside."

Maya removed her pale blue baseball cap and poured water over head, letting it drip off the ends of her short black hair. "There are all kinds of rumors going around camp. Some of the staff are really spooked. One of them even decided he'd had enough and quit. He rode back into town with the truck that brought the backhoe out here this morning."

"You know as well as I do, Maya, that some people are just not cut out to … hello?" Ariella's spade had just struck something hard in the sand. "What's this?"

"It looks like metal," Maya said. "Should I call Lev on the radio?"

"Good idea. Ask him to bring my camera."

Ariella produced a brush from her pocket and began brushing away the sand from the object while Maya grabbed her radio and called Lev who was still back in camp. The excited chatter on everyone's radios alerted Leo and the others to rush out to the site to see what Ariella had found.

Arriving at the freshly dug trench, they saw that Ariella and Maya had just finished removing most of the sand from around the top of a buried object. "It's metal alright," Ariella said. "It looks like the paint's been burned off by something really hot."

News of the discovery was spreading. Everyone stopped what they were doing and began to crowd around as Ariella and Maya continued to reveal more metal, making it obvious that they had uncovered only part of a much larger object buried below.

Lev had finally arrived with Ariella's camera and began shouting orders. "Everyone grab a shovel. We need to enlarge this trench, but be very careful. We'll take a reading with the metal detector to get an idea of its size and dig around it, then work our way in."

The enthusiastic group began to dig without thought to the heat, and within an hour, the burned remains of a vintage World War II era military truck began to materialize.

Ariella jumped up on the edge of the widening excavation and began taking pictures. "This is probably one of the man-made objects we spotted with the infrared pictures we took earlier."

Farther away from the truck, one of the workers pushed a shovel into the ground, and a definite crunch could be heard.

"Stop!" Ariella shouted. She ran over to the area where the worker was standing and jumped down into a newly excavated area where a second object had been discovered. Once again, she began to methodically brush away the dirt, gradually revealing something that caused those around her to gasp. She had just uncovered the unmistakable face of a blackened skull. As some of the workers unconsciously began to back away, Leo made the sign of the cross and uttered a silent prayer.

As the significance of their discovery began to sink in, Lev knelt down to assist his daughter, slowly revealing a complete skeleton next to the remains of the truck. Burned bits of clothing, along with leather boots and metal buttons with insignia, were all that remained of what obviously had once been a military uniform.

Ariella wiped some dirt off her forehead and looked up at Lev. "What do you think this is, Father?"

Lev peered down at the skeleton. "I'm not sure. I think the better question would be *who* is this? These remains could be from the fighting during the 1940's. It looks like this vehicle took a direct hit from a bomb of some sort. Let's take some pictures of the buttons and the insignia and e-mail them to the university in Jerusalem. We should have some sort of identification of the uniform within a few hours."

Daniel, working on a hunch, grabbed a metal detector and began walking in a straight line away from the perimeter. The needle on the meter spiked, and he heard a loud tone in his earphones. The sound faded before increasing in intensity again as he approached an area where the detector registered another large metal object. He made some notes and walked back to the excavation to confer with Lev and Ariella.

"I think what we have here is an entire convoy of trucks," Daniel said. "The readings go on in a straight line, and the objects are roughly the same size as the one we just uncovered. There is one object smaller than the rest at the end of the line. It's about the size of a car."

Lev looked out over the site. "Let's dig that one up first. It's probably the commander's vehicle."

One of the men jumped into the backhoe and they struck out for the end of the line along with several workers. Within twenty minutes, they began to uncover the burned remains of a jeep. Some of the drab olive paint was still evident, but nothing else remained to give any hint at the country of origin.

Digging more carefully now, Ariella began to use a small spade. She worked the soil around the jeep until she began to see bones. They were the blackened bones of a hand. Replacing the spade with a brush, she gently spread the soil away from around the bones until she spotted the edge of a small white piece of paper lying close-by in the sand. Reaching down with her fingers, she gently lifted up what appeared to be a partially burned photograph and held it in her hand. Tears began to form in her eyes. The scorched but well-preserved picture was that of a young woman and a baby, and somehow, Ariella knew that she had just uncovered someone's husband and father.

* * *

It was past noon, and the sun was directly above the site, turning the desert floor into a furnace and prompting the medic to call for a halt to any further work until the temperature fell to safe levels. Lev lifted his daughter from the site as everyone gathered around and Father Leo blessed the body of the soldier. With a sense of overwhelming sadness, they all climbed into the back of a truck and rode back to camp in silence.

While lunch was being prepared, the group recovered in the refrigerated air of the communications tent. Pictures of the items Ariella had found were e-mailed to the university and within the hour, the team had received confirmation that the military convoy they had just uncovered was British. In a strange twist, they were informed that, coincidentally, a thirty-man patrol had vanished in this desert in 1948 when the British had been in the process of pulling out of Palestine after the U.N. partition of the Holy Land. All efforts by the British government to locate the patrol had failed due to strange weather phenomenon that hampered the search until they were forced to quit. The final report read, "Loss of unit in presumed military action with unknown aggressors."

"They never knew for sure what happened to those men," Lev said. "At least their families can have some closure now."

"Do you think it has anything to do with what we're looking for?" Leo asked, hoping Lev had some sort of picture in his mind of what had happened out there in the desert.

"Probably just a coincidence." Lev seemed lost in thought, as though something else was troubling him.

Moshe was at the communications console, finishing a conversation on his satellite phone, when he looked up at the two leaders. "We have a political issue to worry about now. We've uncovered a military grave site, and it's already getting attention in Jerusalem and in England. We need to step up our operations."

Leo glanced over at Lev. "What do you think about going to a twenty-four-hour schedule? It will be cooler at night, and we still have a lot of ground to cover."

The sweat was beginning to dry on Lev's head in the coolness of the tent as he ran his hands through his hair. "I'll have another generator and some more floodlights flown out tonight. One of my staff got heat exhaustion today and had to be flown to the hospital in Jerusalem. Some more of my top people are flying out here in a few hours to help."

"We also have another problem," Moshe said. "The young man who quit this morning and hitched a ride into Jerusalem on one of our trucks has vanished."

"What do you mean vanished?" Leo asked.

"He jumped out of the truck when it came to a stop at a red light and ran away down a side street."

Alon entered the tent, catching the last part of the discussion. "He must have been pretty freaked out about something."

"No, there's more. We checked his name against our database and couldn't find him. He's not one of ours."

"How the hell did that happen?" Alon practically shouted.

Moshe twirled one end of his moustache. "He must have found his way onto one of our trucks on the way out here last night. He never would have made it through security onto the grounds at the villa, so it probably happened when the trucks stopped for gas in Jerusalem. We have a lot of new students living at the villa now, and many are still new to each other. He probably just kind of blended in after everyone was getting back into the trucks from the restrooms. He was smart enough to know that we would be on to him today, so he pretended he'd had enough and hitched a ride out of camp."

"Great security." Alon was beside himself. Although Moshe was the security chief for the entire organization, Alon had been given direct command over camp security, and it had been breached.

Alon spoke through clenched teeth. "Have we found out who he is or what he was looking for?"

Moshe watched Alon continue to seethe. "We don't have a clue at this time. He could have been one of those Vatican security people who have been following Leo and John."

"That thought had crossed my mind," Leo said.

Moshe wanted to help calm Alon. "Well, it's too late to do anything about it now. We've run a security sweep of the camp to check for bugs and explosives. Nothing's turned up. Why don't we all go over to the mess tent and have lunch? We can't resume work on the dig anyway until it gets cooler."

"That sounds good to me," John said, feeling hungry as usual. "I think I'll go check on Ariella and see if she's hungry too."

Lev winked at Leo. "Good idea, John."

The men walked toward the mess tent, discussing the day's events and planning for the work ahead that night. Alon was so angry about the security breach he was unable to talk. His face was red, and he brushed off any attempt to make him feel better. The others decided it was better to leave him alone for a while.

For the next few hours, the camp came to a virtual standstill courtesy of the blazing afternoon heat. Alon's fiancée, Nava, entered the mess tent and sat next to Ariella. She leaned in close and spoke in a soft voice. "I need to get Alon out of here for a while before he drives me and everyone else crazy with his security precautions. We've been engaged to be married for a little over a year now, and I can count the times we've been together on one hand. My schedule as a military helicopter pilot is so demanding that I'm afraid we're going to drift apart. Do you have any ideas?"

Ariella thought for a moment before answering. "Why don't I get John, and we'll all go on a little picnic to a place I know close-by?"

"That's a nice idea, Ariella, but don't you think it's a little too hot for a picnic? Where is this place?"

"There's an oasis I've been to that's like a little paradise in the middle of the desert. It's surrounded by palm trees and has a clear freshwater pool. There's even a spring-fed waterfall. The problem is, it's about seventy miles to the west of here, and it would take hours to get there by land." Ariella gave Nava an exaggerated wink, hoping she would catch the hint.

"Not if you have a helicopter." Nava smiled. "I'll have Gabriella fire up the chopper while I go find Alon. You and John grab the food and wine and jump onboard."

"Who's Gabriella?"

"My new copilot. You should see the looks on the other soldier's faces when we land and they realize two girls are providing their air cover."

* * *

After obtaining a basket full of fruit, cheese, and wine from the mobile kitchen, the group of happy campers climbed onboard the helicopter and lifted off across the desert toward the oasis. Alon had initially balked at the idea of leaving the camp in the wake of a security breech, but one look from Nava alerted him to the fact that this outing with her had a higher priority.

John decided against taking the backpack containing the ancient brick and asked Leo to keep an eye on it until he returned. Sitting by the open door of the Blackhawk next to Ariella, he looked down and watched the desert rush by below. "How do you know about this place, Ariella?"

"I did some research for a college project there one summer. We were looking for a species of fish that lives in the spring. They live only in this one spot on earth and are highly endangered. That's why we try to keep the location a secret from everyone except the Bedouins who've used the oasis for hundreds of years. Its thirty degrees cooler next to the waterfall, and I always wanted to go back there with someone special to share it with." Ariella stared into John's eyes when she said this, giving him a clue to her hidden meaning.

Soon, the helicopter was circling low over a lush green dot in the middle of the stark landscape. They landed at the edge of the oasis and trekked under the palm trees to a large pool of crystal-clear water. A tall rock formation towered above, where a pristine spring at the summit created a waterfall that fell twenty feet into the turquoise pool beside them. Without hesitation, the group stripped off their shoes and ran for the water, diving fully clothed into the cool depths.

Rising to the surface and floating on their backs, they frolicked in the water while the tension of the day slowly faded away. John backstroked toward Ariella, squirting a mouth-full of water up into the air before turning over to face her. "I've been wondering, Ariella, how did you become so interested in history?"

"I used to go with my father on all his archaeological digs around the world. I grew up digging down into exotic ancient cities and discovering beautiful objects of art that had been hidden for thousands of years. I never thought of doing anything else with my life after that. How did you end up becoming a priest?"

"I'm only a candidate for the priesthood. I haven't taken any vows yet. I'm still not sure if that's what God's calling me to do or if He has something else in mind for me. I truly believe God leads us to where we need to go if we listen. Sometimes, I think about having a wife and children someday."

Ariella studied his face before diving down to the bottom of the pool and surfacing next to him.

"Maybe someday you will." She grinned through the water streaming down her face. "What was your major?" Ariella winced. "I can't believe I just asked you that."

John laughed and pushed the wet hair out of his eyes. "History and anthropology."

"Really? Most guys I know hate history. Once they find out my passion is all about the past, they lose interest and want to talk about other things. But you … you're different. You love history, you love animals, and you love God." Ariella became serious. She gazed into his eyes and grabbed him around the neck, bringing his face against hers and kissing him slowly. She trembled at his touch while he took her in his arms. They kissed again. She had never trembled at anyone's touch before. They paused with their noses touching, staring into each other's eyes before she smiled and pulled away. She continued to watch his reaction before plunging her head underwater and swimming back down to the bottom of the pool.

John was in a state of shock as he treaded water, but he knew at that moment that things had changed. Here in the middle of the Negev Desert, halfway around the world from where he was born, John had just made a life-changing connection. He knew beyond any shadow of a doubt that he had found the one girl he wanted to spend the rest of his life with. Life really was strange and wonderful.

Ariella returned to the surface and took him by the hand. Together, they swam to the bottom of the pool, where she showed him the small fish that lived under the waterfall. They popped up under the pounding water from above and swam to the bank at the edge of the pool before climbing out and lying on the warm sand while the sun dried their bodies. They lay there, drinking wine and eating fruit and cheese, talking together as though time would run out before they had the chance to say everything they wanted to say.

Alon and Nava had quietly slipped away from the others for some time alone. They had climbed to a shallow pool on top of the falls and were sipping wine in the cool water while peering down on the others below. Nava's name meant beautiful in Hebrew, and Alon was having a hard time keeping his eyes off of her.

Since the Israeli military required its pilots to maintain a high level of physical fitness, Gabriella had decided to swim laps by herself in an effort to stay in shape and avoid looking at the love-struck couples around her. Her boyfriend was a fighter pilot stationed in Tel Aviv, and she felt a twinge of jealousy that he wasn't with her now in this beautiful spot. She spotted Nava above the waterfall with a glass of wine in her hand and made a mental note. *No more flying for her today.* Finished with her laps, she left the coolness of the pool and grabbed a bottle of water before joining Ariella and John on the shore.

John pulled a bottle of wine from the basket. "Would you like a glass, Gabriella?"

"Only if you want two impaired pilots flying you back to base." She cast a glance up at Nava laughing loudly and playing in the water with Alon.

"Good call," John said. "Have you two seen much action fighting the terrorists lately?"

Gabriella shook the water from her short blonde hair and fixed him with cool blue eyes. "We're always on alert here in Israel. Sometimes we have to take out their leaders when we get intelligence that they're traveling somewhere down a road in a car. They never see us. The first hint they have that we are in the area is when the car they're riding in blows up after we've fired a missile at it from several miles away. I think we're a pretty good deterrent to the ones who want to live to see their grandchildren."

"What scares you the most about fighting the radicals?"

"It's usually no contest in a firefight, at least, not with us anyway. But you can't defend against a brainwashed nut job strapping on explosives and walking into a restaurant or mall. With better intel and advanced technology, we're getting more adept at picking those people out. What really scares me is the possibility of one of those morons getting their hands on a nuclear bomb. I only hope they realize that, if they ever attack us with a nuke, we'll turn their country of origin into a sheet of melted glass."

"The problem today is trying to figure out who the bad guys are," Ariella said, wringing the water from her hair. "We have the usual suspects all around us, but they don't always represent a country in the traditional sense. The days of huge enemy armies marching across our borders are over. I'm afraid that one day a small group in a cave somewhere will get their hands on a bomb and we'll have no one to retaliate against, giving them free reign to do it again."

"Ariella's probably right," Gabriella said. "Attacking their country of origin could be counterproductive, especially if you're dealing with someone like Bin Ladin who even hates his own country. I think the real problem is the hatred and evil that exists in the world today, and it would take an act of God to change that."

Gabriella looked down at her watch and sighed as she noticed the time. "I guess we need to think about heading back to camp."

Amid the groans and child-like pleas for "just a few more minutes," the group slowly made their way back to the aircraft. The magical time spent at the oasis had ended, and soon, they were flying back to their hot, dusty camp in the middle of the Negev Desert. The break had allowed Alon and Nava to reconnect and pushed Ariella and John into the realization that they were now more than just friends.

The sun was setting as the chopper set down outside the camp perimeter. Lev cast a slightly disapproving glance at the group as they emerged in their damp clothes, but nothing was ever mentioned about the outing. He was glad to see that his daughter had finally found someone she was interested in. It was time for her to begin to find her own way in the world and not feel obligated to watch after him all the time. He turned back toward the camp and uttered a silent prayer for the safety of everyone who had willingly come to this place in the desert to unearth a mysterious object in God's name.

The night was much like the night before, except that the young people had built a tall bonfire and were singing and dancing out in the cool dry air of the desert. Two more generators and extra floodlights had arrived, and the new crew members would be working throughout the night at the excavation site. Alon was going from person to person, checking IDs, running laser fingerprint scans, and reporting back to Moshe. He wasn't going to be burned twice.

After dinner, Ariella took a brief nap and was up again at midnight. She drove alone in a jeep to the dig and found her father checking on the staff's progress. Lev was standing next to Leo and Daniel at the edge of one of the trenches, looking at a diagram of the site, and work around the excavation was now at a fever pitch. The floodlights created an oasis of light in the middle of a sea of sand as the sound of generators and the backhoe working nearby made it impossible to speak in a normal tone and the staff had to shout to be heard.

"Where's John?"

Lev cupped a hand over one ear. "What?"

Ariella raised her voice a few degrees. "I said, where's John?"

"Oh. He's asleep back at the camp. We didn't want to wake him. Some of us need to be fresh for the next shift.

* * *

In the darkness of his tent, John awoke and fumbled for his shirt and pants. He stretched, laced up his boots, and grabbed his backpack. Standing outside, he paused to breathe in the cool desert air while gazing up into the black sky overhead. He marveled at the sheer numbers of brilliant stars above. The night seemed especially full of stars in this part of the world. He looked around the camp at the remaining embers from the bonfire and thought of coffee. The mess tent was dark, so he decided to head out on foot in the direction of the lights at the excavation site in the distance.

Walking out into the desert, John stumbled along in the darkness, mindful of the numerous holes and crevices he had seen during the day and wishing he had remembered to bring a flashlight. He was halfway to his destination when he first heard the sound. *Was that an animal?*

A low, guttural growl flashed from out of the darkness. Raised on a ranch, John knew the sound was not the usual snarl of any carnivore he had ever heard before. He quickened his pace. The growling seemed to follow him. It was almost directly behind him as he looked over his shoulder and began to run toward the floodlights. He could see nothing in the darkness around him as he ran as fast as he could over the uneven terrain, but the growling was louder and getting closer. He could almost feel the warm breath of exhalation on his neck as his boot caught on a rock and he stumbled forward.

He landed in a shallow rock-strewn hole and lay motionless in the sand as the snarling seemed to come from all directions. John lifted up to his knees and spun around in a circle in a frantic attempt to locate the predator. His heart was pounding, and his breathing was coming in short shallow gasps. *Calm down!*

He picked up a rock and clenched it in his hand. Peering in the direction of the lights in the distance, he realized no one knew he was out here in the dark all alone.

The snarling and growling grew even louder as he raised his head a few inches above the edge of the crevice. The distant lights of the camp were suddenly blotted out by something in the darkness. A shape. Something was definitely there.

He ducked back down into the shallow depression and lay on his back, staring at the stars. The brick in the backpack dug into his skin as he fought

150

to control his fear. Any moment now, the thing out there would be on him. A bright light suddenly flashed in his face.

"What are you doing down there in that hole with that rock?" It was Alon, his flashlight shining in John's face. "And where's your security escort?"

"I didn't know I needed one."

"You do now. New rule. We had a security breech yesterday, and if you leave camp, you have to have an escort for your own safety."

John stood up and brushed the sand from his shirt. "Did you hear an animal growling out here?"

"No. I still want to know what you were doing in that hole."

"I tripped. How did you know I was out here?"

"The security post back in camp saw you leave and radioed me you were on your way to the excavation site."

John was starting to wonder if he had imagined it all. "I'm sure I heard an animal growling."

"I don't know of any big animals out here in the desert. Nothing for them to eat. Come on. I'll take you to the dig. We'll have some coffee. Our guys brought some Starbucks. I love that stuff, especially the Italian roast."

They were walking toward the lights when a geyser of dust shot up into the air from the center of the excavation. Alon and John could hear shouting and see people running toward the cloud of dust hanging over the site while their radios came to life with a constant stream of excited chatter. The lights of the camp behind them began coming on one by one, providing even more evidence that something big had happened. Alon and John began to run.

John was trying to keep up with the former Special Forces soldier who was shouting into his radio and rapidly leaving him behind. "What is it Alon? What's happened?"

"The backhoe just disappeared into the ground. Come on. We need to hurry. Someone might be hurt."

Arriving at the dig, they saw a large group of people standing back from a huge hole in the ground that had just opened up and completely swallowed the backhoe and its operator. The piercing lights of the backhoe could be seen shooting skyward, resembling searchlights at a grand opening, while the sound of the diesel motor could still be heard revving wildly below.

Lev was shouting commands to the staff as he moved to the edge of the hole and stared down in horror at the wreckage of the backhoe. "We need to get down there. Now!"

Daniel grabbed his arm. "Careful, Professor. The sides of that crater are still unstable and might cave in."

Lev stepped back from the rim and motioned to Alon. "Call the chopper. Tell them to hover overhead and lower someone down there. We've got to see if that man is still alive and get him out."

"Yes, sir, I'm calling them now."

The group stood by helplessly as they heard the sound of the helicopter's turbines in the distance run from a whine to a full-throttled chop before lifting into the air. Within seconds, the chopper was overhead, and a staff paramedic was rappelling down a rope into the void. Leo could feel nothing but overwhelming admiration at the efficiency of the Israeli-trained men and women as they pulled together when danger presented itself.

Although they could see the lights from the backhoe, they could not get close enough to the edge to see if the driver was moving.

A yellow rescue stretcher was lowered into the large pit, and after several tense minutes, they saw the backhoe operator being winched into the chopper along with the paramedic. When they were safely onboard, the helicopter tilted sideways in an arc and flew the short distance back to camp where the man would be taken to the medical tent.

Alon walked over and stood next to Lev. "I just heard over the radio that the operator of the backhoe had some deep cuts and a few broken bones, but they think he'll live. They're going to stabilize him and then fly him to Jerusalem."

"Thanks, Alon. Praise God the man is alive."

John stood back from the rim and peered down at the twisted shape of the now-silent backhoe, its lights still pointing eerily skyward. "That's one big hole in the ground."

Ariella stood beside him. "This is probably the subsurface anomaly we saw with the ground-penetrating radar yesterday. There's probably some sort of cavern under us."

"Let's get everyone back away from this area right now," Lev said. "This whole region is obviously unstable. We're going to have to approach our excavation in a whole new way. We'll have to wait for daylight to resume operations."

Two hours later, a small pool of light framed a patch of desert sand outside the entrance to the communications tent, where the group had gathered back in camp. Everything had been moved away from the gaping hole in the ground, and the exhausted group was sitting quietly inside, contemplating sleep, when one of the sentries ran into the room. "Look outside!"

Leo jumped to his feet. "What is it?"

"You've got to see this for yourselves."

The group hurried outside, where they beheld a sight in the distance that would remain with them for the rest of their lives. Coming from the center of the excavation was a brilliant red glow emanating from the newly formed hole in the ground. It lit up the sky above them. A sound resembling the cries of a wounded prehistoric beast filled the air as everyone edged toward the camp's perimeter to witness the surreal sight before them.

"I think we've awakened something," Lev said.

No one would sleep tonight.

CHAPTER 20

THE NEGEV DESERT—DAY 3

Over the camp, dawn was approaching. Small groups huddled together around campfires as they watched the red glow fade away with the arrival of the sun. The site was eerily quiet now and they could see nothing moving in the distance.

The camp's leaders were sitting in the mess tent, drinking coffee, and trying to decide if they should even consider going back to the excavation site. The bizarre reddish light and eerie sounds that emanated from the vicinity were enough to call a halt to the operation right then and there before anyone else was hurt, or worse.

John poured his second cup of coffee while Camp lay curled up at his side. "I think we need to notify the government, or army."

"And tell them what?" Alon said. "That we've been led out into the desert by a code in the Bible? That a giant hole appeared in the desert and we saw strange lights and heard weird noises coming out of it? Some of our friends in the army already know we're out here, and they're available if we need them."

Lev asked one of the cooks to make him some eggs and returned to his place at the table with the others. "Last night, I decided that we needed a geological survey of the area before we go back there. A professor friend of mine teaches geology at the university. He used to work with the oil man I bought the mobile kitchen from. Nava flew him in this morning. He's out at the site now, doing a survey."

"I just talked to him on the radio," Moshe said. "He told me he had to gather some more data about the substructure around the hole before we go anywhere near it. He wants to use one of the choppers to take a second set of ground-radar images from the air and then set off some small explosions around the perimeter for a seismic profile of the area."

"No. Absolutely no explosives," Lev said from across the table. He was holding his head in his hands, not even bothering to look up. "We have to go down into that hole as soon as possible. I just want his best guess."

"That's lunacy," Alon barked. "It's too dangerous. I've set up a security perimeter around it, and no one goes anywhere near that hole until it's been declared safe."

Lev raised his head and looked around the room. His eyes were bloodshot from lack of sleep. He seemed exhausted to the point of disorientation.

"It will be much more dangerous the longer we wait. I sense we've awakened a dormant force, one that is now gaining strength as we speak. This is the evil force the code warned us about. This force is protecting something down below us and the longer we wait, the stronger it becomes. Our chances of finding whatever it's protecting diminishes by the hour."

Moshe frowned. He was alarmed at Lev's state of exhaustion. "How do you know what's down there without a survey?"

Leo became uncharacteristically defensive. "If Lev says something is down there, then we have to believe that it's down there. We don't need a survey."

Moshe wasn't convinced. "Are you sure, Lev? I mean, you look terrible. When's the last time you slept?"

"I sleep as much as I need to. Time is running out. Trust me on this, Moshe."

At the opposite end of the tent, John, Ariella, and Daniel sat together with a diagram of the excavation site, furiously scribbling notes and engaged in an animated discussion. When they were finished, Daniel grabbed the diagram and placed it on the table in front of the leaders. "We believe that the cave-in was simply the result of the backhoe breaking through a thin part of the earth's crust that covered a large underground cavern."

Ariella pointed to the diagram. "According to the ground-radar studies already done, this anomaly in the substructure beneath the desert floor was really the top of a dome covering a cavern below. The weight of the backhoe was just enough to break through into a large chamber. The walls of the cavern are solid rock, so there's no longer any danger of another cave-in. All we have to do is anchor ourselves from above and rappel down into the chamber below."

"How extensive is this subterranean cavern?" Leo asked.

"The radar images we've taken show that it's gigantic. We're on top of it right here where we stand. John says it's comparable to Carlsbad Caverns in New Mexico."

"She's right," John said. "I've reviewed the data. This thing is composed of multiple passageways and chambers, both above and below each other. It's a gigantic three-dimensional maze."

Alon pulled the map closer to study it. "What about that strange red glow and all those weird sounds we heard?"

"That's the part that bothers me," Ariella said. "I'm not so much worried about a cave-in as I am about that odd reddish light. I spoke to the geologist about it before he went out to the site this morning, and he said that, theoretically, we could have released some trapped gas that looked red in our halogen floodlights. I definitely smelled the odor of sulfur when I was out there. As far as the noise is concerned, who knows? We could have disturbed a pack of wolves or something in the area."

"I think we disturbed a lot more than just wolves," John said. "I've never heard wolves that sounded like that before. It was otherworldly."

Lev looked up from the diagram. "There are no wolves in the Negev Desert. What we're facing is much worse. I think it's time to put it to a vote. All those in favor of returning to the site and seeing what's down there, raise your hands. If there aren't enough votes to go, we pack up our stuff and leave today."

Everyone in the room was focused on Lev. No one flinched or raised an opposing view. Leo was the first to raise his hand, followed by Lev, Ariella, Daniel, and John. Soon hands began to rise all around the tent, until everyone present had their hand in the air.

"Good," Lev said. "Grab your stuff and let's get to work. I'm sending a team down into the cavern."

CHAPTER 21

The gaping crevice stood silent before them. Alon, John, Ariella, and Leo had been tagged as team one, the team chosen to descend into the first chamber of the cavern. Team two was composed of Lev, Daniel, and Moshe, along with the two helicopter pilots and a paramedic from the staff. This team was the designated rescue team if something happened to team one. Long metal spikes were being driven into the ground to secure the ropes that team one would use in their descent to the floor of the cave. Their preparations had taken longer than anticipated, and the sun was now high overhead. It beat down on the camp with waves of choking heat that mixed with the dust of the desert.

Nava and Gabriella maneuvered their helicopter next to the site as team one tested the headlamps of their helmets and strapped into special climbers' harnesses. They threaded long color-coded nylon ropes through carabiners, slipped on heavy leather gloves, and connected the earpieces in their helmets to radios attached to their belts. Alon went first, slowly backing his way over the edge. He fed the rope through the metal carabiners and descended along the rock face, passing the twisted wreckage of the backhoe, until he had reached a solid rock floor forty feet below the rim.

Once the team settled on the floor of the cavern, they saw that they were encircled by a sheer wall of rock that made the surface seem even farther away. The backhoe was wedged precariously above them between two large outcroppings of rock. It was obvious to them that the slightest movement could shift its balance, causing the whole machine to come crashing down on top of them.

Seeking a safer area to begin their exploration, they inched their way around the cavern until they came upon a massive slab of rock leaning inward against the wall surrounded by some rotten timbers and an old rusted lantern.

"Someone's been down here before," Ariella said.

"Yeah," Leo agreed. He ran his hand over one of the rough wood timbers sticking up through the sand. "It looks like someone tunneled down here sometime in the past and then covered it back up."

John approached the giant rock and peered around it. "Hey, check this out. There's a tunnel here."

Ariella looked over his shoulder while Leo squeezed in between them. "Yeah. It's almost perfectly round, like it was bored out with a machine."

"Or fire," John said, running his fingers over the tunnel wall. "The rock here is solid black, like it was melted."

Leo stopped and considered their next move. The decision was made for him when Ariella switched on her helmet light and brushed past, heading into the tunnel without flinching. The men exchanged glances and took off in pursuit. In her excitement to see what lay ahead, Ariella was quickly leaving the men behind.

"Slow down, Ariella," John shouted. "We don't know what's down here."

She turned and looked back over her shoulder. "Only one way to find out."

With their macho image shattered, the men continued to follow her through the tunnel as they snaked their way deeper into the earth.

Before the team had entered the cave, they had forgotten to switch on their radios, so Alon asked everyone to stop and turn them on before they proceeded any farther into the underground labyrinth. Instantly, they were greeted by Lev's near-hysterical shouting from the surface.

"Ariella! Leo! Can you hear us?"

"Yes, we read you, Lev. Is everything alright?"

"Some kind of large black cloud just formed above us. It came out of nowhere. It's as dark as night up here. The wind is really starting to pick up, and the sand is blowing so hard we can't see more than five feet in front of us. Something's happening, and you all need to get out of there. Now!"

Before they had time to react, Ariella screamed from somewhere ahead of them in the tunnel. The men ran forward, rounding a corner where they came to an abrupt stop. Ariella was standing perfectly still with her back to them.

She was facing what appeared to be an old woman dressed in black flowing cloth from head to toe with only a slit at the level of her eyes. The figure was standing in the middle of the tunnel, blocking the way, a gargoyle-like senti-nel placed there to keep intruders from passing farther into the cave. Without warning, blood-red light shot from unseen eyes hidden beneath the robes. In an instant, the group realized that this was no old woman. A loud, piercing howl began to emanate from the thing as Leo thought for an instant that he saw it begin to change shape.

"Run!" Alon shouted, grabbing Ariella by the hand and pulling her away from the black-robed figure. They ran, stumbling over the few rocks on the smooth floor, their hearts pounding and their breathing coming in rapid gasps. Reaching the end of the tunnel, the group fell against each other into the open cavern. Looking up, they saw, to their horror, that the sky had turned black, when only minutes before, bright sunlight had flooded the area.

The wind was blowing violently above them, causing dirt and debris to swirl about the circular walls of the cavern. The otherworldly howling was becoming louder and shriller, while the unmistakable smell of sulfur filled the air. John had been the first to exit the tunnel under the mammoth slab of rock, followed by Ariella and Alon, leaving Leo standing between them and the thing in the tunnel.

In the open cavern, the three outside began to make their way to the ropes, feeling their way along the rock wall. The wind was beginning to blow even harder. Loose rocks from above started to tumble down on the backhoe, caus-ing it to roll sideways. It began to slip from its perch, sliding an inch at a time from the ledge. With the screech of metal against rock, it tilted farther and finally dropped straight down into the cavern below. John was the first to see it falling. He turned and shoved Ariella back into Alon under the protection of the thick slab of rock over their heads, but it was too late for him to follow. He hugged the wall and prayed as the backhoe crashed in front of him and a jagged piece of twisted metal slammed into the rock directly beside his head. Slowly, he took in a breath and opened his eyes. He was alive. The backhoe had missed him by inches.

John could feel Ariella's small hand tugging at his shirt and pulling him back under the rock slab. The three huddled together, bathed in the smoky red light coming from the tunnel. Leo stood his ground in front of the entrance, peering inside at moving shadows beyond the opening. Would the thing, whatever it was, come after them?

He remained standing at the entrance, a human barricade between the tunnel entrance and the others, afraid to blink while staring into the reddish gloom. He rubbed his eyes and looked again. In the haze beyond, he could make out something moving just within his field of vision. His eyes burned as he continued to stare into the void. He saw something move. He focused and then recoiled when he saw what appeared to be the shape of an ancient winged beast silhouetted against the misty red light.

Leo reached into his shirt and pulled out the large golden pectoral cross given to him by Father Morelli. Placing the cross in front of his body at arm's length, he began to pray loudly. He kept his eyes focused directly ahead at the thing in the tunnel. John could hear Leo praying in Latin and recognized bits and pieces of the prayers; they were directly from the rite of exorcism.

The others backed as far as they could into a space under the rock slab while Father Leo continued to pray. They tried to shout for Leo to move away from the tunnel, but their words were lost in the churning wind and deafening shrieks of the entity. The wreckage of the backhoe blocked their way out, and the thing in the tunnel blocked their way forward.

Leo braced himself before the entity, watching it flicker and change shape like something from another dimension trying to enter the earth plane. A wall of heat struck Leo and the others, causing them to shield their faces with their hands. The howling intensified as the group grew more terrified by the second.

Leo had been frozen by fear with the knowledge that the thing was most likely a demon, but he continued to pray. He was gripped with the Jesuit warrior's desire to fight in God's name. The thing was advancing. It was almost in front of him when he pulled a small bottle of holy water from his shirt pocket and began to sprinkle it against the walls of the cave. He then began tossing handfuls of the liquid directly at the thing. The water hissed as it struck the entity, and the howling abruptly stopped. The red light began to fade, and the temperature started to return to normal.

Leo saw that the thing in the tunnel was gone. Whatever it was had disappeared into the gloom beyond. The wind outside began to calm, and the black clouds above evaporated into the dusty blue sky. In the sunlight filtering down from above, only silence surrounded the team at the bottom of the cavern.

"Leo! John! Can anyone hear me?" It was Lev shouting again on the radio. "The clouds just vanished. The wind stopped. Is everyone OK down there?"

Alon spoke into his radio. "We're all in one piece, Lev. Can you have Nava fire up the helicopter and have them lower a line to us. We're going to have to dig ourselves out around the backhoe."

"We're sending the second team down to help you. Hang on," Lev shouted.

The four leaned against the wall and tried to steady their breathing. They had all clearly been terrified. Brushing the sand from their hair and clothing, the group paused to examine each other for injuries. There was no doubt in any of their minds that they had just encountered a supernatural being. It was a malevolent force that none of them ever imagined existed in reality. It not only existed, but they had seen it with their own eyes. It had appeared right in front of them and tried to harm them.

Father Leo continued to hold his cross in his outstretched hands, watching the entrance of the tunnel for any sign of a return by the entity. Within minutes, the team from above had reached the cavern floor and had cleared a way around the backhoe to reach the shaken group.

Soon, Nava had the big, gray Blackhawk positioned over the gaping hole. She watched the paramedic begin winching both teams onboard and glanced at the temperature gauges in the cockpit. "Let's get everyone out of there as soon as possible. I think that sandstorm did something to the engines; they're starting to overheat."

The helicopter hovered overhead until both teams had been hoisted out of the cavern. Nava then angled it away and streaked for the camp while keeping a close eye on the gauges.

John grabbed a blanket and wrapped it around Ariella. "You're shaking."

"So are you ... I think we all are," Ariella replied through chattering teeth. "It's over a hundred degrees out there ... why are we so cold?"

Moshe and the medic grabbed more blankets and wrapped them around the others. "You're in shock," the medic said. "I want you all to go directly into the medical tent when we land. You need rest and fluids."

As Nava and Gabriella guided the big chopper toward its landing pad in camp, the medic took Leo's pulse and frowned before hooking him up to a cardiac monitor. "What did you guys see down there?"

Leo pressed his fingers to his temples and stared at the floor. "A demon."

The medic turned pale. The eyes of the other members of the rescue team grew wide as they involuntarily recoiled. *A demon?* Lev studied the priest. "Did you say … a *demon*, Father?"

"Yes. At first it looked like an old woman covered in black robes, but the eyes … they weren't human … I saw glimpses … glimpses of a winged beast when it changed shape."

Moshe looked shaken. "It changed shape? You've got to be kidding."

Everyone grew silent, but the image of the thing in the tunnel continued to dominate the thoughts of those who had seen it. *Had they really just uncovered an ancient nest inhabited by one of humanity's oldest enemies?* The shaken medic reached into his bag and pulled out a plastic bottle filled with capsules. "The doctor just looked at Father Leo's heart rate on telemetry and wants him to take a sedative." Leo shook his head and pushed the medication away.

Lev reached out and put his hand on Leo's shoulder. "No arguments right now, Father. Doctor's orders. You've just been through a terrible ordeal, and I feel partially responsible. I should have seen something like this happening."

"You can't blame yourself, Lev. There's no way you could have known what was down there. That thing we saw in the tunnel was very powerful … I'm sure we only witnessed a fraction of its power … and it plays tricks with people's minds." The priest watched the surface of the desert slide beneath the open door as the helicopter skimmed the earth. "We all knew we were in the vicinity of an area claimed by Satan. He's still protecting something of great value to him … and he knows we have come for it. Based on what we saw today, I don't think there's any question that we're dealing with a demon, a very powerful demon left by Satan to guard whatever's down in that cave. The tunnel is the way in, and I suspect that the object we are looking for is located somewhere past the spot where we encountered the entity."

"What about the Bible code?" John asked. "Has anyone come up with any new information about this area since we arrived?"

"Daniel and Moshe have both been working nonstop," Lev said. "It's like the code has become a black hole when it comes to encoded messages about the forces we are up against out here."

With shaking hands, Leo lifted a bottle of water to his lips and took some large gulps. "We've got to keep looking … there's bound to be something. If we want to have any advantage at all over that thing guarding the tunnel, we'll need to know more before we go back down there. I mean … we still don't even know what we're looking for."

Camp the dog was barking furiously beside the landing pad when the helicopter swooped in and touched down. He ran beneath the whirling blades and scratched at the sides until the door slid open and he saw Ariella inside shaking uncontrollably. He began to whimper and followed along behind the team, refusing to leave their sides as they entered the medical tent. Still cold, Ariella picked up the worried dog and held him in her lap. The dog seemed to have a calming effect on her and the shaking slowly ceased as her body temperature returned to normal.

The only member of the team who required medical attention was Father Leo. He was showing pronounced symptoms of dehydration, prompting the doctor to start an IV and give him fluids intravenously. He remained resting on a cot with his eyes closed while Ariella quietly led Camp outside and motioned for John and Alon to follow.

Away from the confines of the tent, they breathed in the fresh air and felt the warmth of the sun against their bodies. Life was a gift … and no one had to tell them how fortunate they were to still be able to enjoy it.

John brushed the hair back off his forehead as they headed for the mess tent. "After what we just saw, I think this might be a good time to bring up the fact that I've been having strong dreams about a dark storm over the desert since I arrived in the Holy Land."

Ariella stole a glance at Alon. "We were wondering if you were having those dreams."

"Come again … how do you … what do you know about my dreams?"

"All of us who were listed as *chosen* in the Bible are having them … something special is happening to all of us. Those who were meant to go down into that cavern out there are all having the same dream."

"When were you going to tell me about this?"

"It had to come to you without any suggestion from us. It's a gift from God, John. If you were meant to receive it, it had to be without any prior knowledge."

"Has Leo said anything about having these dreams?"

"Yes, he told my father about it the night we arrived in camp."

"This is too much, Ariella. Group dreams? Do you guys know what any of this means?"

Ariella took him by the hand. "We believe those mentioned in the Bible code as chosen are the only ones experiencing them. My father dreamed about this spot in the desert before the rest of us, which leads me to something else I have to tell you ... my father is a prophet, John.

"A prophet?" John stopped walking. "You're kidding."

Ariella gave him a patient smile. "No, I'm not kidding. There's something going on here that none of us fully understand yet, but it's important. It could even be the most important thing to happen in the past two thousand years. We are being allowed glimpses into God's realm through our dreams. My father believes it's similar to living in the era when the Old Testament was written, only these events are happening now, in our own time."

John looked off into the distance and thought of the words in the Bible when the Hebrew prophet Joel quoted the apostle Peter. *"In the last days, God says, I will pour out my spirit upon all people. Your sons and daughters will prophesy. Your young men will see visions, and your old men will dream dreams ... Before that great and glorious day of the Lord arrives."*

Alon and Ariella waited quietly until John turned his attention back to them and they began making their way slowly across the camp. Once they were in the calm shade of the mess tent, they found a table and poured tall glasses of cold lemonade.

Ariella brushed her long hair back into a ponytail and secured it with a hair band. "My father is the only one who seems to know anything about what is happening down in that cavern. He's made some connection with that thing down there."

A connection? John felt like someone had just poured ice water down his back.

"He still has no idea what the demon is protecting ... or why it's protecting it," Ariella continued, "but he said he's pretty certain that we'll all recognize whatever it is once we find it."

Just like the seal in the catacombs, John thought. Once again, they were searching for an object that would reveal itself only when they laid eyes upon it ... only this time the object was guarded by a demon, and apparently, Lev had made some kind of connection with it. John was well aware that demons were capable of great deceit. They could influence anyone they came into contact with ... or anyone open to suggestion. He was finding it difficult to adjust to everything he had just been told as chills ran up his spine.

Glancing at Ariella, John decided to keep quiet until he learned more. The news that Lev had made some connection with the entity was weighing heavily on him. He would have to talk to Leo as soon as possible ... but keep an eye on Lev.

As if on cue, Lev entered the tent and took a seat next to Alon. "I hate to repeat myself, but what I said earlier still holds true."

"Refresh my memory," Ariella said. "What are we talking about?"

"The longer we wait, the stronger that thing out there becomes. Ever since that demon appeared today, I've started to get some powerful flashes of what I believe are its thoughts. I feel it's drawing its strength from Satan himself and that others like him may be on the way. Despite the danger, we have to go back into that cave tonight. If we wait any longer, we may never find what we were sent here to retrieve."

"There is also the possibility that we might end up like that British convoy out there," Alon said.

John wondered if he had heard Alon correctly. "Am I missing something again?"

"The British have no record of any military action in this area. The remains of those British soldiers we found out there show they didn't die from combat injuries. Whatever happened to them occurred so quickly that they didn't even have time to radio for help. The charred bones we found indicated they died from extremely high heat, only there was no shrapnel or residue from explosives found anywhere at the site. We're starting to think they encountered the same malevolent force we saw today in the cavern. If that's true, anyone who enters the area is at risk of meeting the same fate."

"Alon's right, my friends," Lev said. "I think we should send everyone away from this area except for the team that goes back down into the cavern tonight."

"You can't be serious, Professor," Alon said. "The team that goes back down there, *if* anyone goes back down there, will need some serious backup."

Lev finished off his lemonade and poured another glass from the metal pitcher. "Any weapons will be useless against it. Having more people here only means more people will die if the demon unleashes its full fury against us. That thing down there could take out the whole team and the entire camp just like it probably did with the British convoy. You can double that probability if another one like it shows up."

John felt himself getting lightheaded. He knew it was either the heat or the encounter with the entity in the tunnel. "We all owe our lives to Leo. Without his intervention, none of us would be standing here talking about it now. Going back into the cavern without Leo would be a huge mistake, and it's up to him alone to decide if he wants to risk facing that thing down there again."

Lev sat back and closed his eyes. "You're right, John. Maybe I am rushing things a bit. Leo needs to rest before we discuss it with him."

"Discuss what with me?"

The group turned to see Leo standing behind them, holding his IV bag over his head and munching a sandwich.

John jumped up from his seat at the table. "Father … you shouldn't be up walking around. The doctor said you needed to rest."

"I know, but I feel great. Pull this needle out of my arm, and give me a cup of coffee."

Lev turned to the medic who had followed Leo into the tent. "There's just no arguing with an ex-boxer exorcist priest."

The medic smiled at his noncompliant patient. "Fine, but you can forget the coffee for now. Coffee's full of caffeine, and it's a diuretic. You need to keep the fluid we just gave you."

The majority of the camp's staff filtered into the mess tent behind Leo, but no one seemed interested in eating. The usual gaiety that had dominated their gatherings over the past few days had taken on a somber air, and the staff seemed interested only in the close comfort of each other's presence. By now, everyone had heard about the events that had occurred in the cavern, and the reality of their situation was becoming more apparent as talk centered on the evil that lay beneath their feet.

John swirled the lemonade in his glass and looked across the table at Alon. "I can barely remember what my family looks like anymore. So much has happened over the past week."

"What we're doing is very similar to combat, John. In the army … whenever I was far from home and locked in a life-and-death struggle with a formidable enemy, nothing else mattered but the job of survival. It's like I became another person, and thoughts of home and everyday life seemed like a distant memory." Alon reached out and clasped John on the shoulder. "I've been watching you, John. You're a brave and smart man. You'll do fine."

John looked at Alon and wondered what it took to mold a man like him. A lethal force to those who stood in his way ... and fiercely protective of his family and friends, he was also kind and almost overly sentimental at times. Even though John had never been a soldier, he realized that Alon was right. Their present life and death struggle with a terrifying enemy was just like war, and the camaraderie they shared and the bonds that were being formed were just as strong.

At the end of the tent, Leo and Lev were engaged in quiet discussion and it was clear that the two leaders were already formulating a strategy for reentering the cavern. When both stood, everyone knew that a decision had been made and a plan was about to be revealed.

Lev looked around at the Bible Code Team before facing the rest of the staff and quietly calling for everyone's attention. "In a few hours from now, a team led by Father Leo will reenter the cavern. He will be joined by John, Alon, Ariella, and myself. The five of us will be supported by a second team in the helicopter led by Moshe. This team will include Daniel, a paramedic, and our two helicopter pilots, Nava and Gabriella. The two teams of five will be the only one's allowed in the vicinity. We've decided that it's just too dangerous for the rest of you to remain in the area. Because time is a factor, we will leave the camp in place and evacuate the entire staff back to the villa in the next few hours. Moshe will be in charge of the evacuation and making sure that everyone is out of the area except for the two teams that will remain."

A murmur went up under the tent. A young man stood and shouted from the back of the tent. "We're not leaving you, Professor!"

A few tables away, a young woman stood up. "Yes, we're not afraid. God has called us all here together in the desert. We're not leaving you alone."

"Thank you, everyone," Lev said. He pushed his glasses up into his mass of curly gray hair. "By now we all know that we've been called to this place by God, but only five of us were chosen to enter the cavern tonight. The five names of those who will go were specifically found encoded in the Bible, and I firmly believe that this is God's way of telling us what he wants us to do."

Leo leaned forward and placed his hands on the table. "Some of you have heard rumors about what occurred in the cavern this morning. I will tell you now that we face an evil entity that grows stronger by the minute and that there may be more than one of them down there now. They are endowed with terrible powers and can play tricks on the mind."

"We believe an entire British convoy encountered the entity out there over sixty years ago," Lev added. "Thirty heavily armed soldiers were no match for it. Every one of those men died a horrific death. Those who will be on the first team tonight were chosen by God for a reason, and we believe He has given us His blessing and divine protection in this mission. The second team will only be supporting the first team from a distance. If they don't hear from the team down in the cavern after midnight, they have strict orders to leave the area at once. The first team will have no backup from the second team after that time period. We will be left in God's hands at that point."

Both men looked around at the silent faces staring back at them. The mess tent had taken on the aura of a church, and it seemed an appropriate time for Father Leo to ask everyone gathered together, Christian and Jew alike, to join him in a prayer. After everyone bowed their heads, the priest clasped his hands together and closed his eyes.

"Father, we beseech you. Grant us your protection in the hours ahead. We face your avowed enemy, Lucifer, and his dark angels here on earth. We call upon you to give us strength as we do battle against him in your name. We call also on Michael the Archangel to come to our aid with his most holy army of bright angels in this fight against an unspeakable evil, and we humbly ask you to bless us as we strive to be worthy of your everlasting grace. Grant us your peace in the days ahead, and protect those of us who enter that dark world below tonight. Give us your holy armor against the demons we face in your name, and throw down your mighty sword against them. If any of us shall perish, please forgive us our sins and welcome us into heaven this very day. Amen."

Father Leo raised his head and scanned the room. Everyone remained with their heads bowed, lost in his words.

Then one of the Jewish staff members asked to say a prayer for the safety of the Christians. *"Baruch ata Adonai, Eloheinu melech ha-olam. Blessed are you, Adonai, our God, ruler of the world. Protect our Christian friends in their fight against the evil that lies beyond in the desert and give them the strength of Almighty God, for they are our brothers and we are theirs. Amen."*

Leo broke the silence that followed. "I want to thank all of you who will be leaving camp for your service to this expedition and your willingness to stay in the face of great danger. Those who are evacuating back to the villa, please grab only your personal belongings and find a place in one of the trucks or other vehicles. We want everyone out of the area within the hour."

The camp sprang into accelerated activity as the two teams of five prepared for this last ditch effort to find the unknown object hidden by Satan in the desert. Alon assisted Nava while she flushed the sand from the air intakes and went through a complete preflight check of the helicopter. She didn't want any mechanical problems tonight. Gabriella, meaning *God is my strength* in Hebrew, was performing preventive maintenance on the rescue hoist they would use to lower the first team down into the cavern.

Out at the excavation site, everything around the cavern had been loaded onto trucks and transported back to camp. The crushed backhoe had been winched up out of the cavern with the help of two large truck-mounted steel cables and a large bulldozer that had just arrived from Jerusalem. Now, only a large, bare hole remained in the desert floor.

Since the camp was being abandoned in place, there was no equipment to be packed away, and soon, those leaving were ready to go. Within minutes, a small convoy began to roll out of the desert toward Jerusalem. From the rear window of the mobile kitchen, the little brown dog began to bark at the ten team members who were remaining behind. They all stood alongside the path of the departing vehicles and waved until the convoy faded into the distance.

Lev turned away and motioned for Leo to accompany him to his tent. When they were inside, Lev invited the priest to sit while he poured each of them a small glass of wine. He sat and gazed out of the open tent, watching the orange globe of the sun sink past the horizon.

"I've been thinking since this morning, Leo, that, if we were able to identify the entity down in the cave, we might have the upper hand when we go down there tonight."

"I've thought a great deal about that," Leo said, "and I think I already know what it is we're dealing with. Right before I took out my cross, the demon was changing shape. He appeared briefly to look like some sort of winged beast.

It probably already knew I was a priest, but when it realized what I was about to do, it focused its full attention on me just long enough for me to recognize it. I believe we're dealing with none other than Agaliarept himself, the grand general of hell. He was known among the Assyrians and Babylonians as one of the most malevolent forces in the Middle East and has long been considered by the Church as one of the most terrible of all demonic entities. In the Old Testament, he was described as one who conceals himself in black robes and dwells in the vast desert wastelands. He is represented as a strange jackal-like creature with wings and is known to be a messenger of the Beast. He is the most ruthlessly destructive demon of them all. He possesses the power to discover all secrets and represents the destruction of human life itself."

Lev took a last sip of wine before setting his glass aside. He had heard of this demon in a mythological context as the dark angel of the fatal winds, or a carrier of plague. People of the Middle East recognized him as a pestilential being representing chaos. He was especially good at stirring up enmity and distrust among men. Now, led by a Catholic priest and an Israeli Christian prophet, five human beings were deliberately entering the demon's domain in God's name to search for an unknown object, an object that the grand general himself was bound by Satan to protect. It was almost too much for any of them to comprehend.

"It sounds like you know exactly what we are up against, Leo. I should have realized you had some idea of what it was you came face-to-face with this morning. Is there anything else we can do to prepare?"

"I think we've done all we can. God has chosen his lions; the rest is in his hands. The confrontation with the entity this morning was just a prelude to the real battle yet to come. What really haunts me is how easily it gave up. I would have thought it would have come at us with everything it had. It's almost like it's leading us into a trap."

Lev raised his glass to Leo in a final salute. "Well, if it's a trap, then we'll all be in the trap together."

CHAPTER 22

God's chosen ones were running late as they made their preparations for the coming battle. It was after ten o'clock when they finally congregated in the communications tent to run the Bible code software on their laptops one last time. It was their final chance to gather as much insight as possible into what awaited them below the surface of the desert.

John strapped on his backpack before approaching Leo and pulling him aside. "I need to talk to you, Father. I'm worried about Lev."

"Lev? What's wrong with him?"

"Ariella said he's made some connection with the demon. He even told us himself that he's been receiving flashes of the thing's thoughts. What if it's influencing him in ways we don't understand yet?"

"I don't think you have to worry too much about Lev, John. He's been in tune with the entity's emotions ever since it appeared to us. The demon is communicating with Satan now, and despite its desire to keep its thoughts and activities a secret, its unconsciously revealing itself to the professor. I'm convinced Lev was born with a gift … he's a lot more sensitive than the rest of us to the presence of evil forces."

"But what if it works the other way? What if the demon can pick up on Lev's thoughts? If it knows our plans, it could endanger the whole mission."

"When you're dealing with the supernatural force of a demon, anything's possible. From everything I've read on the subject, anyone who comes into close contact with one is vulnerable to its power to read minds. There are scores of famous stories in the church about exorcists who've had to fight the mind control capabilities of demons."

"But you're the one who confronted the demon down in the cavern today, Father. It was you who saved all of our lives. Why isn't it trying to communicate with you?"

"I don't think it's trying to communicate with anyone. It's trying to protect something. We're not dealing with the demonic possession of a person here. We're dealing with the possession of an area here on earth, and the demon will protect its territory with all of its fury."

The thought of facing an enraged demon that could read their minds seemed totally unreal to John. He didn't feel like a brave man, but he knew he had to face his fears and go with his friends down into a dark and terrifying place … a place from which they might not return. Like a young soldier before battle, he needed reassurance from someone like Father Leo that they all weren't just going blindly to their deaths. "Do you think you'll be able to expel it from the cavern like you did this morning, Father? I mean, as an exorcist with God on your side, wouldn't the demon be afraid of you now?"

"All Jesuit priests are required to study the rite of exorcism, John, but that doesn't make us exorcists. I've never even been present at an exorcism except for today, and I'm not sure that would be considered a true exorcism. That title is reserved for those priests who specialize in such things, and from what I've heard, they don't live long, happy lives. I carried the cross and holy water into the cave because we were entering an area said to be inhabited by Satan or one of his servants, and like any soldier of the cross, I wanted to be prepared. The entity hasn't been banished from the area by my presence. All I did this morning was ask for God's help in allowing us to escape. The demon is still down there, and I'm afraid he'll be even better prepared for our return. It probably knows what we're planning now, and it's expecting us."

"Well, I hope you have a few more gallons of holy water with you, Father, because I have a feeling we're going to need it tonight."

"Here, John, take this." Leo handed John a bag containing nine plastic bottles filled with holy water. "Hand these out to the rest of the team."

"They might be Christians, Father, but they're not Catholic. Won't they be offended if we ask them to carry around holy water?"

"It's their choice, of course, but I'd like everyone to have one just in case."

"Where did you get these?"

"I filled them up from the camp water supply this morning and blessed them."

"Of course. I keep forgetting. Any water blessed by a priest makes it holy. It could even be Evian or Perrier. Just think, sparkling holy water."

Leo couldn't help but laugh out loud at John's innate ability to keep things light in the face of overwhelming odds.

Across the tent in front of his computer, Daniel was running the code program when it suddenly froze on one page. "Professor, have you got a minute?"

"What have you got there?" Lev said, peering over his shoulder.

"I've discovered an exact position of the excavation site in a different section of the Old Testament."

Lev pointed to the screen as the rest of the team gathered around. "It looks like these numbers here denote the same latitude and longitude we first saw in that section of the code that led us here initially. Next to our present geographical location are the same five names of everyone who's going into the cavern tonight. Underneath that, in the same grid, we see something else."

Leo moved in between Daniel and Lev. "You're right. That is interesting." His eyes fell upon the encircled phrases—*dark guardians*, *Satan's most fearless*, and *fire*, along with the phrase, *they will bring forth a great bounty*. These words lay sandwiched between the position coordinates and the names of those chosen to descend into the cavern. Above that was another phrase that puzzled everyone. There were only two words ... *The Book*.

"What do you make of that, Professor?" Daniel asked.

Lev stared at the screen. "I wish I knew, but I'm afraid time for any more analysis is running out."

The two teams continued looking over Daniel's shoulder at the glowing screen, everyone applying their own personal interpretation to the meaning of the last two words.

Lev felt the anxiety level rising within the tent as he ran the last phrase over and over in his mind. *The book.* Was there something they had missed?

"Do you think we're supposed to take a Bible with us?" John said, breaking the silence.

Lev grabbed his equipment and started for the door. "Right now, all I know is that every minute we wait, that thing out there grows stronger. Grab your gear and let's head for the chopper."

The sun had long since dipped below the horizon and the teams could feel the stored heat rising from the desert sand. In the darkness, they passed through pools of light created by the overhead flood lamps as they made their way to the waiting helicopter.

Nava and Gabriella climbed into the cockpit and donned helmets equipped with the latest night-vision technology for operations in total darkness. They would need that technology tonight.

The team members climbed onboard and settled into the back. Nava could hear the click of seatbelts behind her as she flicked a switch over her head, sending a signal to the engine. Soon, the whine of the turbines drowned out any other noise as the blades above began to spin faster and faster, causing the cabin to vibrate with power. Nava pulled back on the controls and the chopper leapt into the air at an angle, eventually leveling out en route to the excavation site.

Before anyone had time to dwell on what the next few hours would bring, they were hovering directly over the cavern. The descent team strapped into their climbing harnesses and put on their helmets while Alon remembered to instruct them to turn on their radios. One by one, the five members of the descent team were guided to the door by the paramedic and lowered into the darkness. They dropped along the vertical walls of the cavern while the helicopter's strobe lights painted the scene intermittently with red and white flashes that filtered through the blowing sand.

The last to touch down, Leo felt for the cavern floor with his boots before unhooking himself from the line attached to the chopper, severing the last physical tie they had to the outside world. The team looked up at Gabriella and saw her waving to them from behind her cockpit window as the chopper lifted higher into the sky and passed out of sight. The sound of the blades beating the air quickly faded until the only thing that remained was the silence of the stone walls around them.

The five team members glanced around nervously, no one wanting to speak, lest they wake the thing that dwelt below in the tunnel. With Leo in the lead, they picked up their gear and made their way across the floor of the cavern. Reaching the overhanging slab of rock at the entrance to the tunnel, they heard a loud, static-like hiss burst from their earphones. Everyone winced as they grabbed their headsets before Nava's soothing voice filled their ears.

"Team Two calling Team One. Radio check. Can you read me, Alon?"

Alon hit the button on his microphone and answered. "We read you loud and clear, Nava. Thanks for scaring the pants off us. Where are you now?"

"We're flying east over the camp toward the Dead Sea. We'll land about twenty miles from your location. We left a satellite phone at the surface by the edge of the cavern so you can contact us when you get out. We can be at your location in seven minutes if you need us."

"Thanks. What time do you have?"

"It's exactly 11:00 PM. You don't have much time."

The others watched Alon's face in the glow of their lights as he spoke into the radio. "Remember, if you don't hear from us by midnight, leave the area at once. If we don't make it out, there's no sense in losing any more people in an attempt to rescue us."

Nava's voice echoed in their headsets. "Godspeed to you all. We'll see you soon."

CHAPTER 23

The radios were now quiet as the five adjusted their equipment under the leaning slab of rock in preparation for entering the silent tunnel before them. Leo glanced around at the others and paused. He looked directly at John and spoke in Latin. "*Ad maiorem Dei gloriam.*" For the greater glory of God. It was the Jesuit motto. The team passed through the dark opening, cautiously descending the sloping floor of the tunnel into the labyrinth below. Microscopic electrical impulses crossed the synapses of their nerve endings, causing their hearts to beat faster as they approached the spot where the demon had first appeared to them. Their breathing increased to short, rapid gasps with the anticipation of its return.

Ariella's eyes were wide and moving quickly from side to side. "Maybe you did scare it off, Father Leo."

Leo squinted ahead in an effort to see beyond the reach of his light into the total darkness ahead. "I seriously doubt it. Even though we don't see it, the demon knows we're here."

"This rock looks volcanic," Lev said, reaching out and running his hand over the smooth black rock of the tunnel wall. It's almost like we're in the hollow part of an ancient lava tube."

"What does that mean?" Alon asked.

"Nothing of significance really, except maybe to a geologist. It probably means that this cave was formed eons ago by volcanic activity. Usually caves that have large caverns were formed in limestone hollowed out by flowing water. Our ground-radar images show that there are large caverns below us.

It's possible that we are in two distinctly different cave systems. The one below is probably limestone, and the one we're in right now was created by heat. I didn't see any indications of extinct volcanoes on the geologist's map. The surveys the oil companies made of this area years ago either missed them or failed to chart them for some reason."

"I think I know why they weren't charted," John said. "If I remember my college geology classes correctly, lava tubes were rough and twisting, not smooth and straight with ninety degree turns. I'm starting to believe this tunnel was created artificially by tremendous heat from a source hot enough and focused enough to melt rock in straight lines."

Lev studied the wall again. "Good point, John. The black color threw me off. Volcanic activity usually doesn't create tunnels this straight and symmetrical. I'm glad you paid attention in geology class."

The team shrugged off the conflicting geologic evidence and continued their descent farther into the cave. Every noise seemed amplified and set their nerves on edge, while every bend of the tunnel caused them to pause for a moment before descending deeper into the demon's territory.

Alon peered down at the tiny glowing numbers on a new laser pedometer he was using to measure their progress. "I think we're about a quarter mile inside the cave now."

Leo stopped for a moment and looked back at the others. "This could go on for miles. There's no end in sight. Do you sense anything at all, Lev?"

"Nothing, but we have to keep going, Father. We have no choice."

Everyone nodded in agreement, and the nervous group set off again down the sloping floor of the seemingly endless black tube. After walking on for another fifteen minutes, Ariella noticed the color of the rock had begun to change. She walked up close to her father and pointed to the tunnel wall. "The rock looks lighter now."

"I think the darkness is starting to lose its grip," Lev whispered. "Everyone stop. Turn off your lights."

The others looked around in confusion but did as Lev instructed. They were enveloped in darkness as soon as they turned off their lights. Soon, their eyes began to adjust, allowing them to see what Lev had suspected. Ahead, where the tunnel made a slight curve, a diffuse bluish light was barely visible, making the dark walls around them appear lighter.

Despite his fear, the prospect of discovery ignited John's curiosity. It was a curiosity mixed with dread, like the feeling one gets when they see a car accident up ahead on the highway. He didn't want to go any farther, but he couldn't stop himself. "What do you think the source of that light is, Professor?"

Lev switched his light back on. "Your guess is as good as mine. Let's keep moving."

As the others fell into step behind him, the creeping sensation of impending doom took hold, but Leo shook it off as they continued deeper into the cave. Walking down the sloping floor, the light continued to grow in intensity until finally they rounded a ninety degree bend and suddenly stopped. To their utter amazement, a bright, light-filled space lay beyond.

Leo pushed down a sudden urge to run and breathed in deeply before taking a few hesitant steps to the end of the tunnel. Casting a glance back at the others, he turned to face the light and stepped into an enormous glowing cavern.

Lev followed and stood transfixed at the entranceway. "This place is massive, Leo."

Ariella pushed around them. "Oh, my God. It's huge."

The rest of the group inched their way out of the tunnel and stared in silence while their senses adjusted to the unexpected radiance of the mammoth space. Right away it was obvious that the color of the rock had changed dramatically. Instead of the black coal-like surface of the tunnel, the walls of the chamber they were now standing in were light blue and had a luminescent, opal-like quality to them.

Leo touched Lev on the shoulder and pointed to the wall next to the opening of the tunnel they had just come through. The initials, *GB*, were carved into the rock. *Someone had been this far before.*

"What do you think GB means?" Lev asked.

"I have no idea," Leo said, "but evidently someone has come through here before us."

John leaned closer and saw the faint outline of an inscription below the initials. He reached out and brushed his hand across the lettering.

"Can you read it?" Ariella asked.

"No, but Leo probably can. It's Latin. I think learning that language is kind of a job requirement for Jesuit priests."

Leo moved around John and studied the inscription. "It says … *Leave it in place.*"

The mystery of the cavern had just deepened. Was this some sort of reference to the object they sought? It seemed likely to Leo, but who or what had left the inscription totally baffled him. Latin was definitely not around when this cavern was formed, and, up until now, they had assumed that they were the first humans to ever set foot in this area. This inscription was a warning. *A warning to them.*

"Let it alone for now, Father," Lev said. "I have a feeling time is growing short."

Leo reluctantly pulled himself away from the wall and joined the others as they explored the cavern. Walking over the level floor toward the center of the chamber, they looked up along the smooth curving walls and saw that they were in a perfect dome that towered at least six stories above their heads. A total of four dark tunnels intersected the cavern, matching the four points of the compass, while directly under the uppermost point of the dome was a raised platform-like structure created from angled white stone. There was no doubt in anyone's mind that they had just stumbled into something not found in nature. The cavern was different from anything that existed in wild caves, and each new discovery was making it more and more apparent that this space had been created by someone or something with a plan.

A low-intensity bluish glow seemed to pulse from the walls with the regularity of a heartbeat as the team looked at one another with a sense of wonder. Leo's mind reeled. This hollowed out area looked more like a cathedral than a cavern. The raised formation in the center even resembled an altar.

Watchful of their surroundings, the group continued to listen for the sound of anything approaching as they cautiously made their way under the top of the dome. They were astonished when they looked up and saw luminescent patterns that appeared to represent constellations of brilliant white stars all around them. The star-like pinpoints of light covered the entire surface of the cavern's walls and ceiling, like those projected onto the curved interior dome of a planetarium.

"This place is magnificent," Lev said.

"It's beautiful," Ariella added, turning in a circle as she gazed at the glowing ceiling full of diamond-like stars.

Leo placed his hands on his hips and looked toward the top of the dome. "There's something not right about the location of the constellations."

"They're reversed," Lev said. He pulled at his beard and squinted at the placement of the stars above his head. "We're looking at the stars as they would appear to someone at the edge of the universe looking toward the earth. This is a view of our heavens from very far away."

"Yes ... that's it," Leo said. "This view of the stars is the opposite of what we would see from our vantage point looking up into the sky from the earth."

"My God, it seems like every new discovery we make is another puzzle." Alon said. He was becoming more confused by the minute with all this talk of reversed views of stars. "How could anyone on earth know what the stars look like from the edge of the universe?"

"Any modern astronomer could figure it out," Lev said, "but judging by the look of that tunnel we just came through, I have a feeling this place is probably millions of years old. Ancient man had no knowledge of astronomy or distant galaxies, so looking at it from a biblical point of view, I would have to say that this is a representation of a view of the earth from heaven above, a view only God would have had of the world when this cavern was created."

"But the code specifically pinpointed this area as one reserved for Satan here on earth," John said. "Why would God's view be represented here?"

John's last observation jolted Leo. "Of course! God's view. I think we're looking at the stars as Lucifer did when he was still one of God's angels ... before he wanted to rule heaven and was cast out by God."

"You think this was created to give Satan the view he once had before the war between heaven and hell?" Ariella asked.

"Yes ... I mean ... this is just a theory, but I believe that Satan is recreating a scene here on earth that he can never see again from heaven. As strange as it may seem, for some reason, he's using God's view to house something of great value to him."

They all stood in awed silence and continued to gaze upward, absorbed in the spectacular star-filled ceiling, while Ariella walked ahead and ascended some glistening stone steps to the raised area in the center of the cavern. She continued to study the ceiling and the surrounding cavern before she looked down at the floor and let out a gasp. "Everyone, come look at this."

The others raced up beside her and were shocked when they looked down at the floor beneath them. It was transparent, the color of black polished onyx with hints of cobalt blue infused throughout. They were standing over a crystal abyss, and the effect was dizzying, like being in a glass-bottomed boat and looking down into the deep blue of the ocean with no bottom in sight. The solid void seemed endless, making it impossible to tell how far the magnificent gem-like stone continued into the depths of the earth.

John bent down and ran his hand over the smooth surface of the floor. There was no dust; the area was as clean as an operating room. Dropping to his knees, he pressed his face close to the floor and peered down into the translucent depths below. "Wow. What's that?"

The others crowded in around him and stretched their necks, straining to see.

"Yeah, what is that?" Alon said.

Below them, encased in the lucid stone, a rectangular object was clearly visible. It was red in color and looked to be approximately twelve inches wide and fifteen inches long.

Without warning a muted, thunder-like rumbling filled the large chamber. The earth beneath their feet seemed to shift, and then all was quiet again. The team huddled closer together—the rumbling and movement had totally unnerved them. Father Leo removed the large golden cross from under his shirt and held it tightly in his hands as he began to pray silently.

Tiny beads of sweat formed across Ariella's forehead as she whirled around and peered into all four tunnels for any sign of the thing she knew had to be near.

"I'm afraid our time alone here is coming to an end," Lev said. "The demon is close by."

"Yes," Leo said, "I think we all just felt his calling card. Demons can manifest themselves in a hundred different ways, none of which we would expect. It could enter the room as a beautiful woman, and then suddenly change into some horrific manifestation of pure evil. It might appear a hundred yards away … or right in front of us."

The sudden rumbling had awakened the fear everyone had so far refused to acknowledge. Ariella's fingernails were digging into John's arm. "Why doesn't it appear?"

John winced as he gently patted her hand. "I don't know, Ariella. I'm surprised we've made it this far."

"So am I. That thing we saw yesterday has to be around somewhere. It's not going to let us come in here and do whatever we want without a fight." The hair began to stand up on the back of her neck. "I'm afraid we've made a terrible mistake."

"The book!" Lev shouted. He was pointing down at the dark red shape they had all been looking at before the rumbling started. The others strained in an effort to make out the details of what Lev was seeing.

Leo was focusing all of his attention on the object lying below in the clear blackness. "I'm not sure I'm seeing anything I could describe as a book."

Lev seemed almost agitated. He pointed back down into the translucent abyss. "The Bible code mentioned a book. Look! What else could it be?"

The red shape began to materialize in Leo's field of vision. The object's outline became clearer to him. "Oh, my God, you're right. I see it now."

Slowly, one by one, they all began to see the outline of what indeed looked like a large red book.

"It is a book," Ariella whispered, as if revealing a secret.

"That's got to be what we're looking for," John chimed in. They all studied the transparent floor in an effort to make out the details of something that had probably occupied this cavern since the beginning of time.

Lev knelt beside John and placed his hand on the floor directly over the book. The others watched as he closed his eyes and concentrated with every ounce of his God-given ability. Time passed as another distant rumble came from below. The ground shook again, this time stronger and lasting longer.

"Oh, my God," Lev said in a weak voice. His eyes were closed, and he was sweating profusely. He seemed to be in some sort of trance.

Leo knelt beside him and placed his hand on his shoulder. "What's happening?" He glanced over at Lev's face. "Lev ... are you alright?"

"I know what it is, Leo. Oh, my God. We're all in more danger than I thought."

Everyone froze. *More danger?* They looked around the cavern for any physical sign of a threat. Lev stopped speaking and remained transfixed on the red object beneath him. Despite Leo's pleas for him to speak, he remained statue-like on the cold transparent surface.

With Alon's help, Leo lifted Lev to his feet.

"Lev, what is it? Open your eyes and talk to me."

With visible effort, Lev slowly began to open his eyes. His gaze had a faraway look, as though he was seeing something in another dimension. At last, he began to mumble. His breathing was labored and his words were unintelligible as the others strained to hear. His body shuddered before he finally broke loose from his trance-like state and shouted out loud. "It's a Bible!"

Comprehension evaded the group as they tried in vain to understand.

"Did he say ... a Bible?" John asked.

Leo tried to think. *Why would Satan be protecting a Bible?*

Lev continued to tremble while Ariella poured some cool water on his forehead.

"He's not making any sense," Alon said.

Lev's faraway look evaporated. He was transported back to the present from a distant vision. He looked around at the others before turning to Leo and grabbing him by the shoulders.

"It's the ... it's the Devil's Bible, Leo."

Leo physically stepped back away from him. He was sure he had misunderstood what the man had just said. "The what? Did you say—the Devil's Bible?"

The team was shocked into the first stages of disbelief. What in God's name was Lev talking about? Everyone knew that there was only one Bible— the one and only true book that was born from the hand of God. The idea of Satan having his own Bible was beyond their grasp. It sounded like a bad script from a horror movie.

Could it be? Leo wondered. *Could Satan actually have his own written version of the events that had occurred since his banishment from heaven by God? Was this the Devil's church here on earth?*

Questions and doubt began to flood his mind. The inevitable theological dialogue resulting from a book inspired by Satan could shake the very foundation of the world's three monotheistic religions. It could wreak havoc with mankind's belief systems and play right into Satan's hand.

A thousand possibilities ran through Leo's mind, but one fact stood out above all others. Nothing good could come from the hand of a dark angel cast from heaven by God himself. This was evil in its purest form.

Ariella looked down into the darkness at the red object encased beneath her. "I know this is what we're supposed to take from Satan and somehow deliver to God." She was beginning to shake uncontrollably as she glanced about the cavern. The others followed her gaze to the object below and were overcome by the aura of pure malevolence flowing from the area around it.

Certainty and resolve was beginning to replace doubt and fear in Leo's mind, but he was still holding on to a secret belief that maybe they were doing the wrong thing by being there at all. Maybe they should just leave it alone and run away from this place as fast as they could. This could very well be the biggest crapshoot in history.

"We have to take it," Lev said, seeming to read Leo's mind. "I sense there is great evil coming from this spot, and the darkness will only spread if we fail to carry out the mission God has set before us. We must remove that book."

"That thing is covered by solid stone," Alon said. "How are we supposed to get to it without drilling equipment or explosives?"

The others looked around at each other with the realization that they had missed the obvious. There was no way to access the book encased under several feet of solid stone.

Leo found it increasingly hard to think. He had to clear his mind. What did the chapel they had discovered under the Vatican have to do with this monument to Satan here under the desert? Had he given this enough thought? He had to assume the two were surely interconnected somehow. The letter! In Morelli's letter to Leo, he had written that the object they would be searching for in the Holy Land was very old, dating back to the time when Lucifer was cast out of heaven. This must be it.

For a moment, Leo felt certain the right answer was floating somewhere within his grasp before he began to second guess himself again. Was the demon playing tricks with him? His mind played through a half-dozen scenarios before the priest realized that he needed strength and feedback from the others. He put the obvious question to the group out loud. "I trust what Lev has said, but if this is really the Devil's book, I have to ask, does God really want us to touch such an evil thing? We have to be absolutely certain that we are doing the right thing."

"Maybe taking it away from here neutralizes it somehow," John said. "We've been talking a lot over the past few weeks about how the world is backing farther and farther away from God, and we've seen in the code that this is an area that harbors an evolving disturbance in the balance between good and evil in the world. Something's causing the great shift away from the world's belief in God. Maybe this is the answer."

Leo's thinking began to clear, and he realized that whatever they had to do, they had to do it quickly. "John, give me the stone brick."

John and Leo's eyes met. The ancient stone brick from the chapel!

"How did we forget about that?" Ariella said. She was dumbfounded at how they could have forgotten such a critical piece of the puzzle.

"The demon's trying to cloud our thinking," Leo rubbed his temples. "I can feel it."

John's palms were sweaty as he slid the backpack off his shoulder and reached inside to remove the mysterious brick. He lifted it out just as a searing heat flashed from inside the stone. "What the ...?"

The heat pressed into John's flesh. His hand was on fire. He opened his hand and watched the brick fall to the gem-like floor below. It shattered into pieces the moment it hit.

The group froze in place. Had they already failed before they had started? Ariella took in a deep breath and bent down to examine the remains. She removed a small spade from her backpack and flicked the largest broken piece over. A pulsating light lit up their faces and the team began to back away— *Now what?*

Encased within the broken piece of brick was a glowing, rectangular crystal. It began to pulsate with the same bluish glow that emanated from the walls of the cavern. Ariella's eyes widened. Instinctively, she bent down and reached her hand toward it.

"Careful," John said. "That thing is really hot."

She prodded it with the tip of her finger. "It's cool."

Wrapping her fingers around it, she pulled the crystal-like object loose from the stone and held it up. Her face was bathed in its brilliant light. "Look." Her eyes widened farther. "It has the image of a golden sword inside."

Everyone stared at the beautiful image with wonder.

"It's the key," John said, his mind racing ahead of the others.

Could it be? Leo thought. He glanced back at Lev. "Your call, Professor."

Lev wiped the sweat from his forehead and looked around. "Let's start looking for something we can match it with. There has to be a connection here somewhere."

The five found it difficult to take their eyes away from the image of the golden sword as they slowly moved away and spread out, looking for anything that might possibly be a link between the pulsating crystal and the book encased below.

Alon was focused on the cavern's walls when he crossed in front of one of the black tunnels and stopped. *Were those eyes staring out of the darkness at him?* He began to slowly back away, his voice failing. John was looking up at the ceiling for clues when Alon backed into him. John twisted around and felt his heart begin to race. Two vacant, yellow eyes were glaring at the group from inside the tunnel. "Father Leo."

The others turned and saw Alon and John backing away from the terrifying sight.

"Stay where you are," Leo said to the group. "No one run." Instinctively, they began to move to the center of the cavern, away from all of the entrances.

They were watching the menacing eyes framed in blackness when they heard a muffled growl from behind and turned to see a black-robed figure standing motionless inside the cavern.

Leo swiveled his head. "Oh, my God, there are two of them."

"Look again, Father," John said, looking into one of the other tunnels. "There are three of them."

Leo wheeled around and saw another pair of unearthly yellow eyes following their every move from the tunnel John was staring at. He held up his large golden cross and quietly told the others to take out their bottles of holy water. They formed a tight circle and huddled together, no one saying a word.

A low rumble broke the silence as a misty, dark cloud began to form inside the cavern, blotting out the luminescent stars above. Leo began to pray, as did the others.

Bright red light shot from the eyes of the black-robed figure standing inside the cavern, while the smell of sulfur filled the room and the temperature began to rise.

Leo was praying with all of his power, beseeching God to intervene. He knew that facing even one demon was a losing proposition in most cases, and now they were facing at least three that they could see. *Satan had called in the reserves.*

The black-robed figure began to change shape back and forth, allowing the group to see glimpses of the demon's gargoyle-like silhouette. Satan's second in command, Agaliarept, his winged, jackal-like general over hell began to howl, filling the space with an unearthly sound. His blood-red eyes were watching their every move. He rose up as if to fly away before suddenly disappearing from their view. From the blackness of the tunnels, the growling intensified, while inside the cavern around them, a hideous, echoing voice chanted in an ancient, long-dead language. The group spun around to the sight of two more sets of yellow eyes watching them from the other two tunnels.

Leo studied their situation, his analytical Jesuit training forcing him to weigh all their options. Apparently, only the most powerful demon, Agaliarept, had eyes the color of blood, while the other four demons possessed yellow eyes, making it easier to differentiate between Satan's grand general and the lesser demons who guarded the tunnels. Five against five—but odds mattered little in a battle with the supernatural.

"They're in all the tunnels!" Alon shouted above the din of howling and chanting.

"We've got to get out of here!"

"It's too late," Lev told him, "they're blocking the exits."

John grabbed Alon by the shoulders. "The book! We've got to get the book."

"The book ... are you crazy? Those things will probably kill us all before we even touch it." Alon was beginning to tremble. Even a man built like an oak tree had his limits.

Leo had to do something. Anything. "Sprinkle the holy water in front of yourselves!" he shouted. Praying in Latin, he held the cross in his outstretched hands and commanded the entities to depart while the others began to pour their holy water around in a circle.

Suddenly, Satan's general appeared directly in front of them. He had been there all along, and only the last-minute command to use the holy water had prevented him from entering the circle, or worse, entering one of the team members. The hideous demon glared right into Leo's eyes before becoming vapor-like and fading from sight.

The terrifying sight of the malevolent yellow eyes staring out from the black robes of the demons in the tunnels was beginning to unnerve the group. *What were they waiting for?* In the blink of an eye, the demons disappeared from their hiding places and materialized inside the cavern. The feeling of evil was electric as they flickered and blurred before disappearing once again. The events were becoming more and more chaotic, disorienting the team.

"Where did they go?" John shouted.

Leo held his cross high. "They're still here. Join hands and pray."

A strong wind blew over the group as the vibrating hum of thousands of tiny beating wings echoed off the surrounding walls. In an instant, a massive swarm of bright red flying insects filled the cavern and surrounded the team. The insects discovered that they were blocked by the ring of holy water and began circling the group in a maddened frenzy.

The temperature in the cavern began to rise, causing the holy water to slowly evaporate into steam above the transparent floor. The petrified group could feel the rising heat on their exposed skin as the vapor rose around them, and then, without warning, the insects were on them.

God's chosen five screamed and shouted in agony while trying in vain to protect themselves from the savage insects. Leo crossed himself and prayed for salvation. *Had God abandoned his chosen ones?* Above the sound of the insects and their own screams, they could hear the demons laughing all around them. It was now only a matter of time as the blood flowed from their wounds and their vision began to cloud into blackness.

Feeling that she was about to lose consciousness, Ariella dropped the rectangular crystal from her hand. It struck the transparent black floor, causing a brilliant light to shoot from within, filling the cavern with the shining image of a gigantic golden sword directly over their heads.

The insects stopped in midair. They seemed to melt before turning into a foul-smelling dust that drifted onto the floor and over all the surfaces of the cavern. The demons stopped their dreadful laughing and fled to the tunnels.

Leo shielded his eyes as he looked up at the golden image hovering above them. "Saint Michael's sword!"

But Satan's general and his demons were far from through. The swirling wind enveloped the team again, and the heat became unbearable. The yellow eyes of the four lesser demons could be seen keeping a death watch from a distance inside the tunnels.

Without warning, a loud crack reverberated throughout the cavern. The floor trembled slightly. Their vision blurred as the minor shake transformed itself into a violent, full-blown earthquake. The five fell to the floor, unable to stand. Chunks of the once-beautiful ceiling began to fall; piece's of it barely missing the group.

The ground continued to tremble, causing a large crevice to open up beneath them. The rumbling stopped. All was quiet. They waited. The earth began to rumble again. It grew louder and louder until a geyser of water blasted from a widening fissure in the floor and tons of water gushed into the cavern from somewhere below.

The sudden earthquake had shattered the onyx-like floor, and Leo could see that the Devil's Bible was now exposed. The demons in the tunnels shot from their hiding places in an attempt to retrieve their master's prized possession. With the realization of what was about to happen, Leo staggered to his feet. The demons were about to retrieve the unholy book and take it to another hiding place. He had to act.

The rest of the team members were in a life-and-death struggle against the elements. The water was rising in the cavern, and they were still weak from the attacks by the insects and the scorching heat. With their strength failing, they saw Father Leo standing in the calm embrace of prayer, his large golden cross clasped tightly to his chest as a cloudy vision appeared before him.

The demons began to wail and screech. Agaliarept reappeared next to one of the tunnels … cowering from the misty apparition beside Leo. Suddenly, a strange, transparent fire erupted around all of the entities and they began to disappear, one by one. The fierce wind slowly dwindled to a soft breeze, while the circling black cloud above evaporated into nothingness.

Ariella looked dazed. "What happened?"

"The earthquake must have fractured an underground aquifer," Lev answered, bobbing about in the rising water.

"No, I mean the demons. Why did they leave? Did they take the Devil's Bible?"

"I don't see it," Lev said.

Alon shouted to the others and held up his arms. "Look! Our wounds are healing!" They all looked to see the deep bites from the insects miraculously fading away.

"Father Leo. He blessed the water!" John shouted. "We're all swimming in holy water." He looked over at the smiling priest who was still clutching his cross and trying to keep his head above the rushing torrent. The apparition that had appeared next to him was now gone.

Their relief was shattered when, without warning, thousands of bubbles began to rise around them. The team started to panic as the cool water looked like it was beginning to boil. They held their breath, waiting for the next attack from the demons.

Leo shoved his head underwater and peered into the depths below. He saw a dark shape rising toward them. Leo strained to focus and braced himself as the blurred object loomed closer. Suddenly, the red book shot from the surface and splashed down into the water beside them.

"The Devil's Bible!" they all yelled in unison.

Without hesitating, Alon reached out and grabbed the book. He swam over to John and threw it into his backpack. They had miraculously succeeded in obtaining Satan's Bible, but their priority now was escaping from the quickly flooding cavern.

The water was gushing forth with tremendous force and had already covered the tunnel entrances. *Maybe they hadn't succeeded after all.* The walls had lost their glow, requiring the team to switch on their lights. Trying desperately to think of a way out, they continued rising toward the solid top of the dome.

"Can't we swim down and out through the tunnel?" Ariella shouted. "It slants upward, away from the cavern, and part of it might be above water."

"No way," Alon answered. "That tunnel is too long … it's probably totally underwater by now."

"I can't believe God would let us get this far only to let us drown," John sputtered.

Leo held the cross out of the water. "Pray everyone."

Instantly, the golden image of the sword appeared once again on the ceiling above, followed by a thunderous crack like the one they had heard before. The rising water stopped and quickly began to recede, causing a mist to form with the sudden pressure change within the cavern. The dog-paddling group felt the fractured floor beneath their feet as the last of the water disappeared into the fissures caused by the earthquake.

They lay on the floor, huddled together in the mist-filled cavern, barely able to make out the openings of the tunnels around them. Everything looked different. *Which tunnel should they use?*

Leo shined his light around the walls in an effort to find what he was looking for, but the murky atmosphere within the cavern was making it difficult to see. There! His light flashed across the initials carved into the wall. "That's the way we came in." Leo lifted his hand and pointed in the direction of the tunnel.

The others breathed in before slowly lifting themselves to their feet. Their respite was short-lived when they were seized by horror at what they saw and heard next. The fissures beneath them began to widen with a sound like paper tearing, while the transparent floor of the raised area in the center seemed to liquefy before their eyes into a thick, black substance that flowed out over the cavern floor.

"Run!" was all Leo could manage to shout. No one hesitated. They ran as fast as they could into the black tunnel they had entered from, slipping in the thin torrent of water that was still draining back into the cavern. More rumbling from below prompted them not to look back as they felt a searing heat behind them. *Run!* Their lungs were bursting for fresh air, and they knew they couldn't stop to catch their breath.

They continued to run through the tunnel as fast as they could and had almost reached the exit when a loud explosion rocked the ground and walls around them, hurling them to the floor.

A second explosion erupted underground. They looked back to see a yellow wall of flame flowing through the tunnel and heading their way. Lifting themselves up, they made their way forward again before staggering out of the tunnel into the cool air of the open pit. They threw themselves to the ground behind the leaning slab of rock just as the flames shot from the tunnel mouth and curled around the huge stone.

Crawling, they retreated to the farthest corner of the open cavern while flames and smoke belched from the fiery opening. A loud roar that mimicked the death throes of an exploding volcano could be heard from deep inside the earth. The noise was deafening, and the acrid smell of the fire was making them all choke. It was becoming impossible to take in a full breath of air.

Alon withdrew a grappling hook with a rope attached from his backpack and threw it over the edge of the pit onto the loose sand of the desert floor above. He gave the rope a mighty tug and the hook came flying back down on top of them, almost hitting Leo in the head.

Without waiting, Alon picked it up and threw it back up over the edge. The others now backed away as he once again pulled on the rope.

"It's holding!" Alon tightened the straps on his gloves and began climbing hand over hand until he reached the top and heaved himself over the edge. Looking down at the others, he wrapped the rope behind his back and yelled for Ariella to grab on. The flames were now shooting wildly from the entrance of the tunnel. The heat was becoming unbearable as the confines of the pit transformed it into an oven.

Alon pulled with all of his strength while Ariella inched upward using both hands and feet until she reached the top. Grabbing her by the hand, Alon flung her over the edge onto the sand. On the cavern floor below, the others began shouting out in pain. They were roasting alive.

A new noise filled their ears as a bright light flooded the area from above. They all looked up, shielding their eyes from the dust, smoke, heat, and light. Over the rumble of the ground beneath them, they could make out the sound of something familiar. It was a helicopter.

Alon watched with exhausted relief as a webbed canvas rescue net came flinging out of the door of the Blackhawk and landed in the cavern below. The wash from the rotor blades beat the smoke back and stirred up the sand as the three men shielded themselves from the flames and felt for the webbed net. Ariella and Alon could hear the shouts from below and feel the heat radiating from the cavern as they groped for their goggles in the swirling sand and peered over the edge into the inferno.

In the fiery glow, they could plainly see the rescue net with the three men clinging to its webbing. It floated upward behind the helicopter that was now powering away from the flames engulfing the entire cavern. Ariella fell to her knees and began to weep, deep sobs coursing through her body. Alon picked her up and carried her away from the edge of the glowing pit into the cool desert air.

The Blackhawk flew low, swinging in an arc over the moonlit desert to where Alon and Ariella had taken refuge on a small hilltop several hundred yards away from the flaming cavern. The helicopter's searchlight illuminated the area as Nava lowered the rescue net holding the three men to the ground before tilting away and circling back for a bouncy landing at the base of the hill.

Leo, Lev, and John lay in the sand as the hazy white light from the full moon, combined with the yellow light of the fire in the distance, created a surreal pattern of flickering color around them. They were a little red from the heat, but no burns were visible as Alon and Ariella rushed to their sides and began pouring what little water they had over their bodies in an effort to cool them as much as possible.

They raised themselves up on their elbows and gulped in the cool air of the desert night with the knowledge that the sudden arrival of the helicopter had saved them from being burned alive in the radiant heat inside the cavern.

Ariella laid her water bag down and held her father close, feeling his pounding heart through his shirt. He patted her on the head and stroked her hair. "I'm alright, little one. That water felt good. Thank you, dear."

"That was quite a ride," John said. He rose to his feet and shook the water from his hair. "Thank God for the chopper. Another thirty seconds down there and we wouldn't be standing here now."

Alon looked down at his wrist and saw that his watch had been ripped off by the insects. "What time is it?"

"It's after midnight," John answered. They turned to see Moshe, Daniel, and the paramedic walking up the incline to the top of the hill. The medic began checking everyone for injuries they might not have noticed in their adrenalin-fueled escape from the cavern. He had once been a combat medic in the same army medical unit with Ariella, and they had both seen fellow soldiers fail to detect severe wounds in the heat of battle.

Leo led the group in a short prayer before they scanned their surroundings. The moon was so bright they had no trouble discerning their deserted camp in the distance. The immediate threat had passed, but they all sensed the presence of the entities somewhere out there around them.

Moshe reached down and grabbed Lev by the arm, lifting him to his feet. The two old friends looked at one another as they had many times in the past after a battle. They had been together during the six-day war in 1967, rushing headlong into the old part of Jerusalem when the Israeli army captured that part of the city and took control away from the Arabs. It had remained under their control ever since.

Lev looked down at his watch and eyed his old friend. "If my watch is right, it's almost one o'clock in the morning. You should have been out of the area at midnight."

"We got lost," Moshe winked. "We thought we were headed for Jerusalem."

John reached in his backpack and held the book up for all to see. "I think we need to get this thing out of here as soon as possible."

"Is that what we came for?" Moshe asked.

"Yes," Leo said, taking the book from John. He paused for a moment, knowing the effect his next words would have on those who had yet to learn the nature of the object. "It's the Devil's Bible."

Moshe and Daniel stood motionless, unable to speak. The words were incomprehensible to them. Daniel thought he had misunderstood. "The *Devil's* Bible?"

Leo looked down at the book. "Yes. We're taking it back to the villa … John's right …we need to get out of here as soon as possible."

Moshe and Daniel remained frozen in shock while Leo shoved the book into the backpack and handed it back to John.

"Let's go," Lev said. "Grab your gear, and let's head down to the helicopter."

Nava and Gabriella had stayed with the chopper. They were coordinating with other forces in the area by radio when they saw the group descending the hill toward the aircraft. Gabriella began sniffling from her copilot's seat.

"What's wrong with you?" Nava asked.

"I didn't think we would ever see them again."

Nava looked back out her window and saw the pale, drawn looks of the faces of those who had just escaped from the cavern. "Oh, my God. They're in shock."

Without waiting, she began firing up the engines.

Ariella climbed onboard and began strapping herself into her seat. "I'm freezing."

"Me too," John said. "Just like the first time when we encountered the demon."

The members from the support team began to cover the five shaken survivors with warm blankets and shoved cups of hot coffee into their hands. With everyone inside, the engines throttled up to a crescendo and soon the aircraft was flying over the bright desert floor under the moonlit sky.

The helicopter was barely in the air when a dazzling light signaled a massive explosion that rippled across the ground below them. The desert above Satan's underground cathedral erupted in tall, shooting flame.

The flames they saw were not the same flickering yellow ones they had seen pouring from the tunnel. Instead, a straight tower of blue and white fire was seen rising out of the ground. It resembled a twenty-story blow torch reaching toward the sky.

Nava flipped off her night-vision goggles and circled the dancing cylinder of fire. "Look at that. How is that possible?"

"What's fueling it?" Gabriella shot back.

Leo pushed his way into the cockpit between the two pilots and stared through the front windows at the ground around the fire. A thick black liquid was now spreading out over the floor of the desert from the base of the tower of flame.

He turned around and shouted to the others. "Oil. That black liquid we saw down in the cavern was oil."

Lev held his head out of the chopper's door into the rushing slipstream and gazed down at the sight below. He pulled his head back inside and looked around at the group. "Leo's right. It looks just like an oil-well fire down there."

Leo grabbed Lev by the shoulder. "Your country is about to become very rich, Lev. It seems God has taken Satan's domain here on earth and transformed it into a much prophesized gift from God to the people of Israel."

The others stared in disbelief as the helicopter continued to circle the area from a safe distance above. The open cavern was overflowing with viscous oil covering the nearby desert in a widening pool of fire. The scene had a biblical aura about it.

Nava glanced out her side window at a second helicopter that had joined them off to their right, while at the same time, she heard Moshe in her headset talking on the radio to officials in Jerusalem. Israel's leaders were being apprised of events in real time and were mobilizing experts to send out to the desert to contain the fires and plug the huge natural oil well.

Low on fuel, the two choppers reluctantly angled away from the miraculous sight and headed north toward Lev's villa. Everyone onboard was staring back in awe at the tower of fire when Nava gave a shout from the cockpit. "Hey, you guys, look at this."

Down below, next to their now-deserted camp, a geyser of water was shooting into the air and flooding the desert around it. "You've got to be kidding," John said. "Fire and water? That must be coming from the same underground aquifer that flooded the cavern."

Two Israeli jets screamed by overhead as Leo glanced at Lev. He saw the other man give a tired smile in his direction. They both knew what this meant. God had not only delivered the wealth of oil to the Negev Desert, but given the nation the water it would need to turn the barren wasteland into a bountiful garden full of food-producing farms. They were witnessing a miracle not seen by man since biblical times.

Both realized they had been part of God's plan as viewed through the third lens of scripture. They were two modern men blessed and called on by God to be his tools. Lion soldiers in the service of the Almighty.

From this moment forward, Leo realized that people around the globe would now have tangible proof that the Bible was a living text that continued to reveal God's word in new and exciting ways. Its message to the world had not stopped with events that happened only in ancient times. Instead, it was guiding their lives in the present, as it was always meant to do, proving itself to be a timely book now and for the future. The passage in the code that read *they will bring forth a great bounty* echoed in Leo's mind.

John was watching Ariella towel her hair dry in the back of the helicopter when she started smiling sweetly at him.

"What?"

"God saved our lives tonight, John. He saved us for each other."

John was at a loss for words. He reached out and held her close, knowing that it was becoming increasingly evident that he could no longer imagine life without her.

Behind them in the desert, water continued to gush from the newly formed crevice in the ground. Farther in the distance, the pillar of fire lit up the sky, while in the canyon beyond, a strange reddish glow highlighted the towering cliffs. If anyone had been near enough to hear it, a chorus of shrieking and growling noises could be heard coming from the darkness.

CHAPTER 24

A constant stream of vehicles came and went from Lev Wasserman's villa. Both teams had arrived by helicopter before dawn and most went straight to bed. Those who needed some minor medical attention were first treated by an Israeli doctor before trudging upstairs to their rooms.

Almost everyone slept until after noon when they awoke and slowly made their way downstairs. They gathered in the kitchen and out by the pool under a brilliant blue sky, where they enjoyed some simple food cooked to order by one of the chefs. After enjoying orange juice, coffee, and pastries, Lev gave Leo a tour of the grounds around the villa, while out on the beach, Ariella and John were breathing in the fresh sea air and walking in the surf, followed by Camp the dog.

Moshe was in the underground command center, scanning the satellite pictures of the Negev Desert and focusing in on the images of what remained of their camp. Israel and the rest of the world had awakened to the news that a vast oil reserve had been discovered in the desert, while simultaneously, water from an unknown aquifer was flooding an area nearby, creating a wetland of lakes and waterfalls.

News crews were tramping about in the water and circling overhead in helicopters with their cameras. People in Israel were celebrating in the streets, while the rest of the world watched as images of the tower of flame in the desert flashed onto their TV screens.

Rumors of oil in Israel had been circulating for years, and now, by what could only be called a miracle, the country was about to share in the wealth of the Middle East. Additionally, Israel's leaders had always considered using irrigation to create farmland in the Negev Desert in an effort to produce more food for its growing population, and now water was pouring from the earth, a biblical gift from God.

Watching the flat screen TV over the bar, Gabriella and Nava were sitting with Alon and Daniel under the roof of the open-air kitchen by the pool, devouring turkey club sandwiches and downing ice-cold bottles of Coke.

"Just look at those pictures of the desert," Nava said, looking up at the screen. "The whole area is totally flooded. The newscasters are calling it a miracle."

Daniel kept his eyes glued to the TV. "If people only knew the whole story, they would know just how much of a miracle it really is."

"Look," Gabriella said, "there's the camp. You can see some of the equipment and the antennas from the communications tent sticking up above the water. And look there, in the distance. You can still see the fire jetting out of the hole in the cavern." She paused to watch the scene. "How long do you think this will go on Daniel?"

"No way to tell. A lot depends on the size of the aquifer and oil deposit below, not to mention the pressures that have built up on them over time. It always amazes me that some of the most barren places on earth seem to hold the greatest treasures."

"Well, it certainly looks like the Negev Desert is going to be a Garden of Eden now," Gabriella added, unable to take her eyes off the screen. "I just keep thinking of that awful place that's been down there all this time, with those grotesque demons guarding it. It really makes you wonder if there are any other places like that in the world."

Alon took a sip of his Coke and turned away from the TV. "I think that almost everyone knows that the human race has always been surrounded by evil, but to actually come face-to-face with it, to look it right in the eye as a tangible entity, is something that's so unreal that I think a lot of people are going to have a hard time believing us. I'd like to think of myself as a man who could stand up to almost anything, but what we saw down in that cavern last night was something I hope I never see again as long as I live. I'll tell you one thing though; it's made my faith in God even stronger than it was before, and that was pretty strong."

Walking through the vineyards with Lev, Leo was deep in thought. He gazed out beyond the sand dunes at the blue water of the Mediterranean and marveled at the rhythms of life. The tide came in and out every day without fail, just as life ebbed and flowed. Daylight and darkness, life and death, everything had a rhythm.

The very presence of a book inspired by Satan didn't surprise him. It was the classical yin and yang, the good versus evil that had existed since men came into the world. But why exactly did it exist? The philosophical questions raised by its existence would be endless. Was it some kind of Nihilistic thesis? When was it written, and what did it say? And most chilling of all, was Satan really the inspiration for its existence?

Leo stopped next to a row of merlot grapes and turned toward Lev. "Did you recognize the writing in the book?"

"Daniel seems to think it's a form of cuneiform writing. It resembles some Mesopotamian script found on ancient tablets near Babylon."

"Has he been able to decipher any of it?"

"Not yet. There's nothing to compare it with. There's no telling how old it is or when it was written."

"What's your gut feeling then?"

"I've been thinking about that all morning. I mean, there's no telling what's inside that damned thing. Maybe it's an antithesis of our own Bible, with its own version of the history of creation and an entirely different set of commandments. I can tell you one thing, though ... that book was written with a definite purpose in mind, and I doubt it's a love letter for humanity."

Leo held a rosary in his hand as the two men turned down a path leading between two rows of grapevines. "You know, Lev, many people throughout history have also used God's book as an excuse to do some pretty evil things, but you're right; those are the kinds of questions we need to explore if we want to find out why we were sent to find a book inspired by Satan at this point in history. I keep thinking of Morelli's analogy of the Bible being infused with a series of time locks, so I'm guessing the answers will come when God wants us to have them."

Leo continued to wonder if the Devil's Bible identified its followers with stories of their own ancestors. In other words, did Satan have his own version of an iniquitous opposite to Abraham? Did he send a figure into the world to spawn a legacy of evil among man? Could this explain the age-old question of why there were both good and evil people in the world? The Cain and Able dichotomy.

Leo watched the young sentries who voluntarily patrolled the fields without complaint. They were the continuation of a long legacy of good versus evil as they struggled to defend their families and friends against terrorist attacks.

As the two men walked along manicured paths, Lev pointed out the individual family houses scattered over the park-like setting of the compound's two hundred acres. After Lev converted to Christianity, he and his wife had started this community together in an effort to provide a kibbutz-like atmosphere for Christians in Israel. His late wife had been passionate about the land and was instrumental in the farm's design. Her handprints were on everything, from the decision on where the vineyards and vegetable gardens would be planted, to planning and supervising the construction of the villa and all the houses on the farm.

As Leo took in the beauty of the grounds, he thought of the courage it took for Lev and his wife to create such a place. "What do your Jewish friends and neighbors think of a Christian kibbutz in their midst?"

"They don't have a problem with it. We're all still Israeli citizens and are bound together in our fight to protect Israel and our homes at any cost. I respect and support my Jewish brothers and sisters, and they do the same for me. My family was a little concerned when I converted, but since they weren't strict Orthodox Jews, it wasn't such a big deal. Again, we believe the issue of religious moderation is central to tolerance of other religions and everyone getting along."

Lev pulled a cigar from his shirt pocket and lit it with a match. "Every year, as a group, we attend several celebrations around the country at various Jewish communities, and we've always been welcomed. There are several Jewish families living right here on the compound; they have their own synagogue next to our chapel. That's why you see both a Christian cross and the Star of David over the gate in front of the villa. I would like to think that someday we will see a mosque here, but from a security standpoint, that's impossible right now. I have a lot of Muslim friends, and they agree that the radical elements within Islam are tearing down their own houses with mindless violence. It seems we all still have a lot of work to do."

As the two men turned to walk back to the villa, enjoying the sunshine and taking in the fresh sea air, Leo found that the mysterious book they had discovered in the desert continued to dominate his thoughts. He wondered if the book had been in the world all this time, waiting to herald the arrival of the evil one so that his followers could dispense his message of hate and destruction throughout the world. If that were true, it could very well be the key to Armageddon and the Antichrist's rise to power someday. Until the book was translated, Leo knew the answer to these questions could only be imagined, like distant objects seen through the fog.

Lev stopped along the path and snapped a small bunch of grapes off a gnarled vine. "You know, Leo, it wasn't until I converted to Christianity that I learned that Jews and Christians think of the devil in different ways."

Leo smiled the knowing smile of a Jesuit theologian who had pondered this subject for hours on end. "I know, it's strange, when I was still in seminary, we learned that the Jewish view of Satan differed quite a bit from the Christian version. In Judaism, the word Satan means challenger or accuser. He is believed to have the evil purpose of searching out men's iniquity, an accuser who appears to wander the earth functioning like some kind of celestial prosecutor. In the Book of Wisdom, the devil is represented as the being who brought death into the world."

"That's a very good way of putting it, Father. In my Christian education, I was taught that the devil was the malevolent force behind the engine that drove the evil covering the globe. Once among the highest of God's angels and known as the *brightest in the sky*, he rebelled against God and was cast down from heaven, where he waged war against those who obeyed God's commandments and who believed in the testimony of Jesus. Lucifer is now the ruler of the demons, entrenched among us with frightening anger where he sows hate and sorrow in men's hearts. I think these differing views between the two religions have caused Christians to be much more fearful of the evil one's presence."

Both men looked at each other with the realization that what they had seen in the desert the night before had proven beyond any doubt that their fear was justified.

CHAPTER 25

The warm night water of the Gulf of Mexico flowed past the beaches of Texas. The nutrient-rich brew of plankton in the water supported the famous gulf shrimp that swam in its current and grew to enormous size. From time to time, the Mexican shrimp fleet plied these same seas along with the local boats from Texas and Louisiana. The radios in the wheelhouses crackled with a mixture of English, Cajun, and Spanish, giving rise to competition among the multicultural fleet that passed back and forth over the continental shelf, dragging their nets along the smooth white bottom in the search for seafood gold.

In the early morning hours, one of the aged and brightly painted Mexican boats passed close to the coast, drawing little attention as it blended in with the lights of the fleet. There was, however, a noticeable difference between this crew and the others. For some reason, they seemed more interested in the comings and goings at the entrance to the Houston ship channel inside Galveston Bay than they did in catching shrimp.

Time and fuel meant less profit in this struggling industry, but instead of passing over the shallow Gulf bottom, scooping up shrimp, the boat's long black nets remained dry and coiled up on the deck. Maybe the crew was wary of past run-ins with Texas shrimpers, or maybe they were just looking for a place where they could dock and buy supplies. Whatever the reason, it was apparent they had made a decision as they turned north and headed straight up the ship channel.

Although it was almost one o'clock in the morning, the nautical traffic in this port was still busy as the small boat continued unchallenged past the entrance. It glided by grain silos full of wheat and rice and gigantic oil refineries that hissed and growled with towers of flame and escaping misty vapors that were revealed by thousands of lights that turned night into day.

Highlighted by a single halogen lamp on the deck of the shrimp boat, the tall, bearded captain appeared Hispanic, as did the crew. They were foreigners in a strange land, and as they glided along in the dark humid air over the murky water, they gathered together and looked out upon the huge glowing city. Then they did something strange. They placed small woven mats on the rear deck before dropping to their knees and bowing down to the east, toward the holy city of Mecca.

The boat motored beneath the stern of a gigantic oil tanker docked next to a vast refinery, drawing the attention of an alert crewmember leaning over the ship's railing. Because he was a Muslim, the crewmember aboard the large ship immediately noticed the scene on the deck of the shrimp boat below. *This was not right.* The Mexican flag fluttering over the small boat reminded him of a visit he had once made to the largely Roman Catholic country, but these men were obviously Muslims, like he was, and this was the wrong time of day to be saying their prayers.

His mind began to race and a sickening fear rose in his throat. Radical Islamic terrorists had caused great harm to his religion over the past few years, and he was afraid they were about to make it much worse. He watched as the colorful shrimp boat pushed through the oily water beneath the tanker. The frightened crewman thought for a moment and weighed his options. He had to tell the captain. They must notify the American Coast Guard!

He started to run franticly along the deck toward the bridge, tripping as he strained to keep the Mexican boat in sight. Racing up a flight of metal stairs, he paused and grabbed the railing to glance over the side. He watched as the tall, bearded man on the boat below looked up at him, his face highlighted by the surrounding industrial lights reflecting off the water. The man smiled and raised his hand as if he was waving goodbye before disappearing through the door of the wheelhouse.

The crewmember could now clearly hear the words of the men praying on the deck of the innocent-looking boat. They were speaking in Arabic, and the prayers were the prayers of martyrs asking for Allah's blessing. He looked on in horror as they passed the bow of his ship and continued up the channel toward Houston. It was the last sight his eyes would ever see.

Inside the shrimp boat, the bearded man attached some wires to a square box-like device the size of a home dishwasher. He looked at a picture of his family and closed his eyes, uttering a final prayer before flicking a switch.

A blinding flash of white light that was seen from hundreds of miles away erupted from the small boat as it vaporized. The giant ship beside it, the refinery, and a large portion of the city close-by were also instantly gone, while at the same time, the signature mushroom-shaped cloud of a one megaton nuclear detonation rose in the confused sky above the bayous and houses and freeways of America's fourth largest city. The explosion was eighty times more powerful than the bomb that exploded over Hiroshima in 1945. Everything within two miles was leveled except for some of the strongest buildings made from reinforced concrete. Ninety-eight percent of the population within this area was instantly killed.

The blast left a crater two hundred feet deep and one thousand feet in diameter that quickly filled with water from Galveston Bay after the initial shockwave. Nothing recognizable remained within a mile of ground zero. Three miles away from the center of the explosion, virtually everything was destroyed. Single-family residences within that area had been completely blown away; only their foundations remained. Within this area, fifty percent of the population lay dead, with another forty percent actively dying or injured and moaning in agony.

Farther out, about five miles from where the shrimp boat carrying the bomb had been converted into molecules, most buildings were heavily damaged. The windows of tall buildings had been blown out, and first responders would find the contents of the upper floors of these buildings scattered on the streets below, along with the people who had been inside.

Those out in the open within this five mile radius had experienced third-degree burns from the initial fireball, while those inside close to windows had been shredded by the flying glass and bullet-like pieces of debris. It was a scene of unimaginable horror, but this was only the beginning. Within thirty miles of the blast, a lethal dose of radiation had been delivered through the air. Death would occur within hours to most of those within this area.

The wind on this night was blowing north at seventeen miles per hour. The massive amount of dirt and debris that had lifted up into the grayish purple-tinged mushroom cloud now began to follow the wind for hundreds of miles before gradually falling back to earth. This material was also lethally radioactive, and death would soon visit entire families up to ninety miles away within two to fourteen days.

Farther away, about one hundred sixty miles from where the bomb had exploded, people would experience extensive internal damage to their digestive tracts and white blood cells, with the resulting loss of hair and unexplained cancers that would ravage them and their children in the years to come.

It would be ten years before the levels of radioactivity in these areas would again be considered safe, but for now, a large part of the country had been rendered an unlivable graveyard. America's worst nightmare had just occurred.

CHAPTER 26

Snorkeling over the reef in the clear water of the Mediterranean coastline, John and Ariella were spearing fish for lunch. They had been in the water for almost an hour when Ariella swam up next to John and pointed to her divers watch. Reluctantly, they headed for the shore until their feet touched sand and they struggled through the surf up onto the beach. Ariella smiled as she held up a string of good-sized snapper. Camp ran up to John and sniffed at his single, small mackerel, before running off to chase an errant crab scurrying across a sugar-white sand dune.

Their morning fishing expedition over, the two headed across the weathered boardwalk toward the villa and joined the others at the poolside bar.

"Nice fish, John," Daniel said.

"I probably should have thrown it back." He cast a glance at Ariella. "Now she's going to force me to eat it."

"That's right," Ariella said. "That's the rule around here. If you keep it, you eat it."

"Maybe Camp would like it," Nava said, winking at Alon.

On cue, Camp's new crab friend pinched him on the nose. The little dog yelped and raced through the dunes to the safety of his human friends. "I think he's had enough seafood for today," John said.

Everyone was talking and teasing John about his miniature fish while an American news channel provided background noise. The newscasters were going on about the discovery of a large oil field in Israel when the red banner of a news bulletin flashed across the screen. With the events of the night before still fresh in their minds, everyone wondered if something else had occurred in the desert and turned their attention to the flat screen TV over the bar.

One of the television journalists held his hand to his earpiece and turned to his stunned-looking female co-anchor. His face took on a pale, vacant look. He paused for a moment; he seemed to be having trouble collecting himself before he looked directly into the camera and took a deep breath before speaking. "Ladies and gentlemen, we have just received news of an unbelievable nature. If this bulletin can be confirmed, our worst national nightmare has been realized. We're hearing just now that a nuclear explosion has occurred in an American city, totally vaporizing an area within a mile of the blast and devastating an area for five miles around that. The city is Houston, Texas."

Everyone by the pool stopped what they were doing and stared at the TV screen in total disbelief. It was one of those moments when, years later, people would recall exactly where they were when they heard the news. The television journalists were silent for a moment, not knowing what to say next or if professional decorum had rules for their emotions at a moment like this.

The female newswoman tried to compose herself before continuing. "We've just learned that apparently, sometime around 1:00 AM Central Standard Time, a small fishing boat entered the Houston ship channel from the Gulf of Mexico. Shortly thereafter, those onboard detonated what is believed to be a nuclear bomb in the center of one of the largest petrochemical industrial areas in the world. The scene was captured on tape by security cameras just before the blast. Authorities say it is an obvious attempt to knock out some of the country's largest refineries and cripple the economy, with the added benefit of taking the lives of as many Americans as possible in the process."

Daniel slammed his orange juice down on the bar. "It's 9/11 all over again."

"No, it's much worse," Nava said. "Now the bastards have nuclear weapons."

Ariella leaned close to John as tears began to flow, mixing with the drying saltwater of the sea on her tanned face. Her mother had been an American, and she had distant relatives who lived in Texas. Returning from their walk through the fields, Leo and Lev joined the others in front of the TV just in time to see the first pictures from Houston spring to life on the screen. Before their eyes was a scene of unbelievable horror.

News of the attack spread throughout the villa prompting Moshe to put the compound on the highest alert. The Israelis had played out this scenario in their hearts and minds many times over the years since the attacks of September 11. They had hypothesized that, if one city was attacked anywhere in the Christian or Jewish world, it could be the beginning of a coordinated series of detonations in other cities around the globe.

Some of the brightest minds in think tanks on both sides of the Atlantic had run the numbers, and the laws of probability and supply and demand won every time. Since the old USSR had collapsed, several nuclear weapons had gone missing, and people with a lot of money could buy anything. The laws of probability, plus the laws of supply and demand, equaled nuclear weapons in the hands of terrorists.

Tel Aviv was less than twenty miles from the villa and was a highly prized target of terrorists. Jerusalem was officially considered off the list for now, since the Dome of the Rock and the El-Aqsa Mosque, two of the most holy sites in Islam, were located on the Haram esh-Sharif in the old section of the city. But times were strange and getting stranger, and even though many believed the holy city was probably safe from attack, the radicals were seized by a fervor resembling mental illness, and therefore, theoretically, everything was on the table.

The staff switched the channel to CNN, where they were already interviewing government officials. Security consultants were blaming the explosion on radical Islamic terrorists, or RITs, the acronym used by many in the intelligence community to identify this newest enemy to world peace.

"No surprise there," Alon said when he heard the latest bit of news.

The TV networks were pulling out all the stops and using every resource available. Unnamed sources within the CIA and NSA were quoted as saying that they had already gathered enough evidence to begin building a case against those who had attacked America.

Everyone at the villa watched the reaction from around the world as the global community joined in the rising tide of sorrow and fear beginning to circle the world. Leo was struck by the timing. When God brought forth his bounty, such as the oil and water now washing over the desert, Satan seemed to strike back with yet another depraved assault against humanity. *Was the painting of a nuclear explosion on the seal they had found outside the ancient chapel a warning after all?*

While everyone sat frozen in front of TV screens throughout the villa, Daniel was about to make a discovery that would remove any doubt from their minds.

CHAPTER 27

Daniel liked to work alone. Possessed with a brilliant mind, he was totally absorbed in his work on the Bible code. He was one of those people who could solve a Rubik's Cube in less than a minute. When not busy working on codes, he loved cooking French food and collecting fine bottles of wine from vineyards around the world. Despite his service in the higher echelons of the Israeli military, those who knew him well considered him a Renaissance man. No one would have been surprised that he had retreated to his computer in the command center to work on the code in the face of the tragedy in Houston. He needed the time alone to reflect on man's inhumanity to man, and working on the code allowed him to think.

The glow from the computer screen highlighted his intellectual features. His tussled brown hair and beard, along with his round horn-rimmed glasses, gave him the look of a perpetual student. He scrolled through endless permutations in the code for the hundredth time in an effort to find some clue to the meaning of the chapel under the Vatican. Ever since he had found the first mention of the chapel in the code months earlier, its significance had eluded him.

In 1993, American astronomers Shoemaker and Levy had discovered a comet streaking toward Jupiter, and after measuring its speed and trajectory, they estimated that it would hit the gigantic planet on July 16, 1994. Several years later, after the collision had occurred as predicted on that date, when Daniel had been a mathematics student at the Hebrew University, Professor Lev Wasserman was trying out a new skip sequence in the code when he discovered something that shocked him to his core. Encoded in the book of Isaiah was the mention of a collision of a comet with Jupiter on the exact same date ... July 16, 1994.

The precise date of the comet's impact with the planet had been encoded in the Bible three thousand years before the actual event had occurred. The day Lev shared this discovery with Daniel was the day Daniel Meir became convinced that the code was proof of a higher power at work.

He was just about to turn off the screen when he noticed some words highlighted in red. Right in front of him was the phrase ... *under the Vatican*. He stopped and scanned the page up and down, looking for something, anything. There! To the left of the phrase, the words *holy chapel* jumped out at him.

Perspiration formed across Daniel's brow and trickled down his temples while he continued to scan the page for other hidden words. He didn't have to scan for long. Across the bottom of the page was the longest phrase in the code he had seen to date ... *God will send his chosen guardians to take the book to the holy chapel.* That was it! That was the chapel's secret. It had been constructed to receive the book. Daniel thought back to the passage that said *they will give it to God.* The answer to how they would give the book to God was right in front of him.

Then, something else caught his attention ... two more phrases. *Satan will bring fire to the world* and *his forces will come for the book.* Running up horizontally from the bottom, he saw another phrase pop up on the screen ... *the evil one will strike back.* The encoded messages were coming at an exponentially faster rate. He sat transfixed as the computer continued to reveal more hidden phrases ... *The book holds Satan's plan* and *Tribulation until God takes the book.*

Daniel ran his fingers through his beard and stared at the screen. For some reason, God wanted Satan's book taken to the chapel ... and He was using His chosen ones to do it. *But for what reason?* He read two of the phrases over again; *the evil one will strike back* and *his forces will come for the book.* Was the attack on Houston Satan striking back? What next? Chills ran up Daniel's spine as he realized the danger they were all in.

He had to tell the others. He hit the print button and ran off a copy before running upstairs and outside to the poolside bar where everyone was transfixed in front of the TV. No one moved or spoke as they watched the images of the devastation in Houston scroll across the screen. Daniel grabbed Leo by the arm and shoved the printout into his hand.

Father Leo's face drained of color before he turned to John. "John, where's the Devil's Bible?"

"Alon and I decided to lock it up in the weapons room until we leave for Rome."

"From now on, John, we can't let it out of our sight. I don't know why I didn't think of it sooner. The book must always be in the possession of one of us ... one of the chosen."

"That room is made of solid concrete, Leo. It's got a thick steel door like those used in bank vaults. Besides, no one could possibly get into that room with all the security they have around here."

"We can't underestimate the power of the book or those who may want to take it. We're dealing with supernatural forces that dwell in an entirely different realm from us, and no amount of concrete or steel will keep them out. The book needs to be kept in the possession of one of the five who took it ... one of the chosen. I just pray that we're not too late."

The tragic news of Houston was pushed into the background as everyone jumped from their chairs and raced through the villa and down the stairs to the command center. No one spoke. They all stood looking at the locked steel door as Alon began punching the combination. A series of clicks, and then, slowly, the heavy door began to swing open. The group stood by and held their collective breath while Alon and Leo stood at the entrance and waited.

As soon as the door was halfway open, Alon reached in and switched on the lights. John's backpack was still lying on the floor where he had left it. Everyone rushed forward, trying all at once to crowd through the doorway. Leo knelt down by the backpack and peered inside. He exhaled a sigh of relief and reluctantly pulled the nightmarish object out into the open.

The Devil's Bible was obviously a very ancient book. It was thick with a red covering made from some unknown type of material. The front of the book was covered in raised black symbols ... unknown symbols from a dark world. Excluding the mysterious symbols, no other markings were present.

Leo hesitated before opening the cover and leafing through the thick parchment-like pages. There was no doubt in the priest's mind that this book was a real instrument belonging to Satan, and he felt a panicky need to drop the book to the floor. The mere touch of it sent shivers up his spine. He sensed a malevolent force beginning to permeate the very air they were breathing, and he knew the power within was strong.

Without warning, something flashed in the periphery of Leo's vision just as a warm breeze touched their faces. He stepped back with the realization that there was something in the room with them. He grabbed a flask of holy water from his shirt pocket and quickly doused the book with the liquid. A loud thump shook the building. It was followed by a low snarl that was heard by everyone as the smell of something dead and rotting began to fill the air.

Everyone began to cough and gag in an attempt to rid themselves of the noxious odor, while several broke and ran from the room in an effort to get as far away from the odor and intense feeling of fear they felt in the book's presence.

"I think that smell is coming from the Devil's Bible," Ariella shouted.

Lev leaned closer before stepping back and holding his hand over his nose. "It is!"

Leo quickly doused it once again and prayed. Slowly, the odor started to subside, along with the evil presence they had all felt was so close just moments before. It was as if the book was a living entity, dying in the absence of its master.

Could it be decaying? Had the book been somehow protected from disintegrating under the sands of the desert, encased inside Satan's cathedral? Leo examined the unknown writing on the cover before realizing that he needed Daniel's talent with computers. "Daniel, could you come here for a moment?"

A look of horror crossed Daniel's face as he approached the book as if it were alive. "What do you want, Father?" He felt like his heart was going to stop. The thing repulsed him, and he wanted nothing to do with it.

Lev held his hand up in front of Daniel before walking over and running his fingers across the raised symbols on the cover. "What's on your mind, Leo?"

"We've got to scan this book page by page into the computer so we can analyze it later. I'm concerned the book itself might be changing somehow, and we can't risk losing what's written inside. This book could very well hold a code like the one in God's Bible … a code that we can use in the future."

People who broke codes for a living possessed a special curiosity when it came to solving puzzles. That was why most of them entered the field in the first place. This same driving curiosity was now pushing Daniel to overcome his revulsion at being so close to pure evil as he looked around at the others before slowly reaching out and taking the Devil's Bible from Leo's hands. "Any idea what this thing is made from?"

"Looks kind of like leather," John said.

Holding it at arm's length, Daniel walked over to his computer station and laid the book on the scanner. "I'll clip a piece off the back cover and send it to the lab for testing." He snipped a small piece from the corner, and then, with a scholar's methodical touch, he began to scan it, page by page, until the entire text was uploaded into the computer. The exact nature of the material the book was made from was still unclear, but Daniel noticed that water had obviously not harmed the book when the cavern flooded.

A unique curiosity was also the hallmark of a good archaeologist, and Ariella was no exception. The ancient book seemed to mesmerize her as she reached out to touch it. Lev's hand shot out and grabbed her by the arm as if he had seen a poisonous snake on the table.

"I think enough of us have touched it. We still don't know what kind of power it has."

Ariella nodded and stepped away, knowing that her father had undoubtedly felt something dark and evil within when he had touched the book.

When Daniel was finished, Leo took the book and placed it in a waterproof plastic bag. He then placed it inside a clear container filled with holy water and slid the whole package inside John's backpack and handed it to him.

"Never *ever* let that book out of your sight again until we get back to Rome," Leo said.

John looked directly into Leo's eyes. "You can depend on me, Father. Where I go, this book goes."

Everyone's nerves were shot. Events were rushing at them from all directions, and Leo was growing fearful that things would spin so out of control that the team would reach a point where they would be unable to emotionally and psychologically process it all.

The nuclear attack in America, together with another close encounter with an unseen force within the command center itself, was creating an environment of constant fear. The fear of the unknown, coupled with the fear of what lay ahead in a worsening global situation, would soon drive everyone into overload.

What they all needed now more than anything else was reassurance and a break from the constant pressure. Many of them had still not come to grips with what had occurred in the desert the night before and were in a mental state of detachment resembling battle fatigue.

After Leo discussed the situation with Lev, he motioned for everyone to follow him upstairs. He led them outside and over the wooden walkway across the dunes until they came to a stop at the water's edge. Father Leo stared straight out at the sea. He didn't look back, and he didn't speak as his puzzled followers gathered behind him. With no hint of why they were there, God's chosen warriors sat on the warm sand and felt the spray from the sea bathe them in the briny perfume of the ocean.

Leo kept his back to them and waited. The steady rise in animated chatter over the roar of the surf, punctuated by the occasional laugh, was evidence to the priest that the tension was beginning to drift away, like the sea foam that blew from the rippling edge of the encroaching tide.

Like most solitary people who sought natural settings to think, Leo knew that environments like waterfalls and beaches produced tens of thousands of negative ions in the air. These invisible molecules were believed to produce biochemical reactions in the blood that increased the levels of the mood chemical serotonin, helping to alleviate depression and relieve stress. Some said it was the action of the pounding surf that produced the euphoria, while others said it was simply the relaxing atmosphere of the beach itself. Whatever the reason, Leo knew the environment was a perfect setting for the group to decompress together for awhile.

Inhaling some deep breaths, Leo turned to his curious audience. "Before I begin, I want you all to know that you're a very special group of people. It has truly been a blessing to get to know each and every one of you, and to be a part of your extended family."

Ariella smiled at the others. "Oh boy, we must really be in trouble."

A few nervous laughs erupted from the group, but they kept their eyes focused on Leo.

"A short time ago, Daniel discovered some new information in the code. This new information is suggestive of the fact that we might have interfered with Satan's plan for the world by taking his Bible. Also ... and the reason isn't quite clear yet ... God's chosen ones have been given the task of taking the book to the ancient chapel we discovered under the Vatican. With that being said, we can be sure that Satan will now come at us with everything he has."

Everyone let out a gasp.

"Satan is very angry now, and it's conceivable his influence was behind the attack on Houston. His increasing influence on mankind could be the driving force behind God sending us out into the desert to retrieve the book. As impossible as it may sound, I think we may be witnessing the beginnings of a second war between heaven and hell, and God is calling his chosen together as soldiers. A growing number of people have fallen away from God's teachings over the past few years, and because of it, the world is now standing at the edge of a precipice."

The group sat blinking at Leo, not really knowing what to expect next. Lev pulled a cigar from his shirt pocket and put the unlit stogie in his mouth. "I don't think I want to see another Sodom and Gomorrah. Why don't we get you and John back to Rome with that book today?"

John raised his hand. "Won't that be a little difficult, since all commercial flights have just been canceled in response to the attack on Houston?"

Lev gave him a wink. "We'll figure something out."

CHAPTER 28

The spotless Gulfstream jet sat baking in the sun on the tarmac at Ben Gurion Airport. Anyone in the aviation community knew that this aeronautical work of art was one of the finest private jets on the market and came with the added benefit of transatlantic capability.

The plane was being fueled as Nava guided the big Blackhawk helicopter in for a landing in front of the hanger. Camp barked as he stuck his head into the slipstream, becoming the envy of every dog who had ever stuck his head from the window of a moving vehicle. He was reveling in the ultimate dog game of feeling the wind in his face and flying across the land faster than any dog on earth. Sitting beside him in the back of the helicopter was Ariella, accompanied by John, Leo, Lev, and Alon.

The chopper hovered briefly before finally touching down on the hot cement. As the rotor blades revolved to a stop overhead, Leo looked out at the sleek outline of the gleaming white jet and noticed the blue logo of the Carlton Oil Company painted on the fuselage. "That jet doesn't happen to belong to the same oil man you bought the mobile kitchen from, does it, Lev?"

"Yup. It belongs to Jeb Carlton. He loaned it to us with no questions asked after I called him this morning and hinted that we were partially responsible for finding the oil in the desert."

"What's it doing in Israel? Is he here now?"

"No. He has several aircraft based around the world. His home office is on a ranch outside Midland, Texas. We've been friends for years. I spent some time on his ranch once … almost got bitten by a rattlesnake. That part of Texas is almost as barren as the Negev Desert."

"When do we leave?" John asked.

"As soon as that fuel truck moves away." Lev watched the driver unhook the fuel nozzle from the wing.

Leo and Alon jumped from the chopper, followed by John and Ariella. These four would be flying to Rome, while Lev remained behind at the villa.

"Are you sure you can't come with us, Lev?"

"I'd love to, Leo, but someone has to stay here and coordinate things. Besides, we're on high alert here in Israel, and I need to be close-by in case anything else happens."

Ariella stood on tiptoes and kissed her father goodbye through the door of the helicopter. She reached down and gave Camp a kiss on the nose while her father held him tightly on a leash to keep him from jumping out and following behind. "Goodbye, Father. I'll call you as soon as we get to Rome."

"I put the satellite phone in your bag. You can call me from wherever you are. I'll see you soon. Take care of yourself, little one. I love you."

Nava gave Ariella a thumbs-up and waved to Alon while the engines of the Blackhawk came to life and the aircraft rose slowly into the clear blue sky. Lev continued waving to Ariella as she grew smaller below, while Camp whimpered and squirmed in the seat beside him.

The four turned from watching the helicopter depart and climbed a short set of stairs into the plush cabin of the jet. A female flight attendant pulled the door shut behind them and shoved a red lever down, sealing the cabin in preparation for flight, while up front in the cockpit, the two pilots adjusted their seats and began going through the mandatory preflight checklist.

Outside, near the tail of the aircraft, one of the Rolls-Royce engines started with a strong thump, followed by the run-up of the second engine on the opposite side. Puffs of gray smoke shot from the rear of both engines as the cabin vibrated with the steady hum of power.

After receiving clearance to taxi from the tower, the captain released the brakes and the thirty-million-dollar executive jet began to roll away from the hanger toward the runway.

John removed his backpack and set it on the floor next to his seat before stretching out next to Ariella on a beige leather sofa that lined one side of the cabin. Across the aisle, Leo and Alon faced each other in oversized leather seats separated by a polished walnut table. Alon shoved a vase of fresh flowers aside and placed a pack of cards in front of Leo and winked. "Do you play cards, Father?" Leo smiled back as he gathered up the cards and began to shuffle the deck.

A flat screen TV in the front of the cabin was showing nonstop pictures from Houston on the Fox network. It was a vision like nothing any of them had ever seen before, and anyone with an opinion agreed that the vicious 9/11 attack on New York paled in comparison. Reporters in the field were telling shocked viewers that at least one hundred thousand people were dead and thousands more were overwhelming emergency rooms in the parts of the city that had not been touched by the initial blast or ball of fire that spread across the landscape.

Portable military hospitals had been rushed to the area, and the countryside outside the city resembled one enormous M*A*S*H triage area. Things were so bad that patients were actually laid out in the open across the lawns of local hospitals. It was like the famous scene from the movie, *Gone with the Wind*, when rows of Civil War wounded filled the streets of Atlanta. Radioactivity readings were through the roof, and many secondary casualties would soon fall victim to the invisible poison that drifted through the air.

Turning into position for takeoff, the pilots shoved the throttles forward. The jet picked up speed and raced over the rubber-scarred concrete until it lifted off midway down the runway and climbed into the air at a forty-five degree angle. The emotions of the four passengers were mixed as the plane streaked upward on the way to its assigned cruising altitude of forty thousand feet. They were on their way across the Mediterranean to the Eternal City, and the ancient chapel was waiting.

The flight attendant remained seated in the back of the cabin across from Ariella as the plane continued to climb and everyone's ears popped in the changing pressure. She was the same height as Ariella, but slightly frail looking, with long blonde hair and blue eyes. Her name was Sarah, and Ariella quickly learned that she was from Abilene, Texas. They talked about Texas, chicken-fried steak, and tubing down the Guadalupe River north of San Antonio in the summer.

"What got you interested in flying?" Ariella asked.

"Daddy's a pilot. For the past few years he's been working as Jeb Carlton's chief pilot. That's how I got this job. I used to work for an airline, but the people nowadays have become so rude and demanding that I quit after a few years."

"It must be a lot of fun flying all over the world."

"I usually fly the local runs around the country, but a few nights ago, I had a really powerful dream about Jerusalem and decided to ask for this trip."

Ariella's eyes widened and she let out an unconscious gasp.

Sarah immediately picked up on her reaction. "I'm sorry, did I say something wrong?"

Ariella forced herself to smile while casting a sideways glance at John. "No, my ears just popped. What was in your dream?"

"Well, like I said, I was dreaming about Jerusalem, but then I was standing out in the desert, and I definitely had a feeling that something was about to happen. I saw a storm coming and then the wind started to blow and I heard a voice telling me I was chosen. Why do you ask?"

"Oh, just curious. I know a lot of people who've been having strange dreams lately."

Sarah's eyes became vacant as she thought back to the dream. "Yes, it was strange. I kept thinking about it all the next day and when I heard that one of the company jets was flying to Israel, I jumped at the chance to come."

Ariella noticed that the girl's movements were almost trance-like as she twirled her hair in her fingers and turned to stare out the window at the sun glinting off the blue sea below.

Ariella leaned close to John. "Did you hear what she said?"

"Yeah, this is really weird. I think we need to have a little talk with Leo about her."

"I agree. This is just too much of a coincidence. There's a connection here somewhere."

The jet leveled out and the noise from the engines fell from full power to cruise as Sarah unbuckled her seatbelt and walked forward to begin preparing lunch for her guests.

John reached across the aisle and tapped Leo on the shoulder. "Can we have a word with you, Father?"

"In a minute, John. I'm a little busy at the moment."

226

"But this is really important, Leo."

"So is this." Leo watched Alon from the corner of his eye and tried to keep a straight face as he showed John the four kings he was holding in his hand.

"Ok," John said, "but we really need to talk when you're through."

Up in the front of the cabin, Sarah was quietly humming to herself as she pulled some food trays from the freezer compartment. She reached up to grab some napkins when she caught the first whiff of something burning. She stepped back and looked at the oven, but then remembered she hadn't started cooking yet. She froze. An in-flight fire was a flight crew's worst nightmare.

Within seconds, a misty, red-tinged smoke began to drift through the cabin. Sarah let the trays fall from her hands and jerked open the cockpit door to alert the pilots. She was horrified to see that the cockpit was also filling with smoke, a reddish smoke that was punctuated by the acrid smell of sulfur. A piercing alarm began to sound as a series of red lights flashed on the instrument panel in front of the pilots.

While the mystified crew was trying to process the flood of conflicting information from their instruments, the starboard engine suddenly flamed out and stopped. Confused by this sudden series of events, the copilot called air-traffic control and declared an emergency, while the captain performed a one hundred eighty degree turn back toward the airport.

The plane was still over the Mediterranean with nowhere to land, but the crew had no choice except to descend in a controlled emergency dive. The pilots donned full facemasks, while small yellow oxygen masks fell from the ceiling in the passenger compartment and dangled in front of the five souls who were now beginning to gasp for air.

John and Ariella grabbed two masks and placed them over their faces, breathing in the fresh air while staring into each other's eyes, wondering if their future together would be only a brief dream before the jet slammed into the sea below. Leo's winning poker hand was scattered on the floor as he and Alon slipped their masks over their heads and tightened their seatbelts. Without warning, the second engine flamed-out, leaving the jet totally without power. The multimillion-dollar jet had just turned into a heavy glider and plummeted toward the water below.

The captain fought for control of the aircraft and shouted for Sarah to pre-pare the passengers for a water landing. Inching her way back into the cabin,

Sarah strapped herself into a seat and held an oxygen mask to her face. She looked around the cabin and lifted her mask just long enough to instruct her passengers on how to brace themselves for a crash landing.

Alon noticed the absence of sound from the engines. "Both engines are out!"

"Airplanes can still land without power from the engines," Sarah said.

"They just can't choose their landing site," Alon replied, flashing Sarah a soldier's smile that he and his comrades had adopted in the past when faced with overwhelming odds.

Time was now running out for the jet as it neared the surface of the water twenty miles off the coast.

"Put on your life jackets," Sarah shouted to her passengers. "They're stowed under your seats. Remember not to inflate them until you've exited the aircraft. If you inflate them too soon, you'll bob to the ceiling as the plane begins to sink, and you won't be able to get out. When we get close to the water, I'll call for you to assume crash positions."

The smoke in the cabin had become intense and was interfering with the pilot's ability to see out of the cockpit. They were attempting to level out when the blue of the Mediterranean Sea loomed in front of their windows and the jet slammed into a wave. The right wing submerged first, ripping it away as the plane began to cartwheel over the sea, tearing the main cabin open and scattering pieces of the aircraft along the path of destruction. The jet flipped two more times before finally coming to a stop and taking another wave over the top of the fuselage. Sea water rushed in and what was left of the main cabin quickly began to sink.

CHAPTER 29

Moshe ran into the villa, shouting and gesturing like a crazy man as he ran up the stairs and heaved himself into Lev's room.

Standing in front of his bathroom mirror wearing only khaki shorts, Lev was busy trimming his beard with a pair of scissors. In the mirror, he saw the reflection of Moshe standing in the doorway, tears streaming down his face.

"We just got a call from Nava," Moshe blurted. "She heard over her radio that the jet just crashed into the Mediterranean."

Lev dropped the scissors in the sink and stared into the mirror before turning to face Moshe. In his mind, he could still see Ariella's face as she waved goodbye to him from the ground as the helicopter lifted into the air. His daughter, his beautiful Ariella. Anyone but her!

One of the female staff members came running into the room behind Moshe. "Oh, no, God. It can't be!" She pulled her short black hair back with her hands, stretching the skin on her face and making her eyes look cat-like as she stared at Lev and Moshe, the tears flowing down her face.

As news of the crash sent a wave of sadness over the villa, some gathered downstairs, not knowing where to go or what to do, while others walked out to the beach to stare at the sea, hoping for a sign. Somewhere out there, God had just decided the fate of their friends.

Many wept and prayed for a miracle, but most knew that a high-speed jet crash was usually not survivable, even in water. Only a few hours before, they had all been together, safe at the villa, watching a tragedy unfold on the other side of the world. Now tragedy had visited their world.

Lev sat on the edge of the bed with his head in his hands while Moshe stood by silently, his hand resting on his old friend's shoulder. Lev choked. He raised his head and looked up at Moshe through tear-filled eyes. "Call the chopper. We're going out there to look for them. There might be survivors."

CHAPTER 30

The main cabin had sunk to the bottom of the Mediterranean, where it had come to rest in the inky blackness for the past hour. Pieces of wreckage still floated about on the surface of the water, and the smell of jet fuel lingered in the air. Miraculously, there had been survivors.

Sadly, the pilots had not survived the initial impact; their cockpit was crushed when it nosedived into a wave as the plane cartwheeled over the water. When the sea rushed into the cabin, Sarah's emergency training kicked in. She unbuckled herself from her seat and pulled an emergency ring by the door, releasing a life raft that automatically inflated when it hit the water.

John had struggled to free Ariella who had been knocked unconscious and was still strapped in her seat. Leo and Alon had been flung from the aircraft through a ruptured hole in its side but suffered only cuts and bruises. They had paddled their way back into the sinking plane and helped John free Ariella before the cabin began its downward plunge to the sea floor.

The four bobbed to the surface, where John held Ariella's limp form in his arms. She began to moan and slowly regained consciousness as they floated amid the pieces of wreckage. "What happened?"

"The plane crashed, Ariella," John said.

"It what?"

"Try not to move too much. You might have a head injury."

They found Sarah floating on her back, holding onto the inflated raft. She was wracked with fits of coughing from inhaling sea water. Unable to climb into the raft, Leo and Alon swam up beside her. The men then gently lifted both women over the sides and climbed in next to them. Aside from some cuts and bruises and one possible concussion, the group had survived the crash relatively unscathed.

John looked over at Leo while he stroked the water off Ariella's forehead. "How did we survive that?"

"I don't have a clue, John," Leo said. "We were probably going in excess of two hundred miles an hour when I saw the right wing slice into a wave. Hitting the water at that speed is like hitting concrete."

The group sat in the sloshing water inside the raft, too much in shock to feel any emotion. Ariella was now completely awake but still had no memory of the crash. They scanned the surface of the water for any sign of the pilots, but they all knew in their hearts that the men had now joined centuries of ancient sailors on the bottom of the Mediterranean.

Squeezing the mixture of jet fuel and sea water from her hair, Sarah reached into a bag stowed in the raft and activated the jet's emergency locator beacon. She then produced a first aid kit and began tending to the minor wounds when Leo suddenly sat up and began frantically searching the sea around them. "The book, John! Where did you put the backpack?"

John's eyes widened. "I put it next to my seat on the floor of the cabin ... and that's the last time I saw it." John leaned back and covered his face with his hands. "It's probably on the bottom of the ocean by now."

Leo slumped in the raft, unable to think anymore. Survival was now their only priority. They would have to deal with the loss of the book later. He remembered the reddish smoke in the cabin and the smell of sulfur. *Satan finally got his Bible back after all.*

* * *

Nava's large Blackhawk helicopter landed in front of the villa within minutes of being notified of the crash. She kept it on the ground just long enough to allow Lev and Moshe to climb onboard before she practically jumped the chopper back into the air and sped out over the beach, skimming the waves en route to the scene.

They flew in the direction of the crash with grim determination. Only the whitecaps of some breaking waves were visible to the searchers as they scanned a vacant blue sea around them. Continuing on, they were finally able to see ships and helicopters in the distance, and within minutes they were passing over an Israeli Navy vessel that was rushing to the scene.

Circling overhead, Nava watched several inflatable speedboats drop from the large ship and race toward a small yellow life raft bobbing in the middle of a floating debris field. A navy chopper swung in front of them and flew in low over the drifting wreckage before coming to an abrupt hover as two pararescue divers jumped into the water.

"There are survivors," Gabriella shouted into her headset microphone. Lev and Moshe strained to see between the tops of the swells. Everyone back at the villa listening to the radio transmissions from the helicopter began to jump and shout for joy. People had survived. But how many?

Lev and Moshe finally saw the life raft and began to count. There were five. Unless they had been picked up by another aircraft or boat, two were missing. They scanned the horizon in an effort to see any bright-colored life jackets floating nearby.

Nava flew her helicopter in beside the navy chopper and radioed the Israeli Navy for permission to pick up survivors. As the big Blackhawk came in low, Lev looked down and suddenly burst out in tears when he saw the face of Ariella looking up at him from the small raft rising over the crests of the waves in the water below. His body was wracked by sobs of joy as everyone was quickly winched aboard and he was finally able to hold his dazed and shivering daughter in his arms once again.

Nava was hovering less than twenty feet above the surface preparing to depart when John suddenly shouted something to Leo before jumping from the open door and splashing into the water below.

"What's he doing?" Nava shouted. "Has he lost his mind?"

John was swimming like a madman toward something bobbing in the water. A small speedboat from one of the ships arrived and pulled up alongside of him just as he reached the object and pulled it to his chest. Two burly Israeli sailors reached out and yanked him from the water while he held the backpack above his head for everyone in the helicopter to see.

"What kind of idiotic stunt was that?" one of the sailors said to him. "You could have been killed. No piece of luggage is worth that."

"This one is," John said.

As soon as he was winched back aboard the helicopter, John opened the backpack. The Devil's Bible was still resting securely inside, untouched by the crash. Leo could only smile with relief. They had the book, but they were still in Israel. Leo started to speak, but Moshe held up his hand. "I'll say it for you, Father. Now, one more time, John: never *ever* let that book out of your sight again."

Nava tilted her Blackhawk toward the shore, and after a short but speedy flight, they were landing on the roof of the hospital in Tel Aviv, where they would spend the next few hours being X-rayed and prodded until the doctors were satisfied that it was safe to send them home.

Sitting next to each other in the hospital waiting room, Ariella and John began describing Sarah's dream to Father Leo.

"You're kidding," Leo said. "She actually said she heard the word chosen?"

They both nodded their heads. "Those were her exact words, Father."

Leo had to think this one through. "Give her some time to rest after we get back to the villa, Ariella. If she is truly one of the chosen, God will reveal His plan to us soon enough. I have a feeling she is here for a reason, so if she starts asking questions, tell her the truth."

As the helicopter lifted off from the hospital roof, everyone who had been in the crash sat frozen in silence. Their nerves were frayed, and their expressions had taken on the thousand-yard stare, a look frequently seen on fatigued combat soldiers who had witnessed horror that exceeded their imaginations.

Within minutes, they were landing on the lawn in front of the villa, where they were surrounded by all of their friends who tearfully welcomed them home and escorted them to their rooms. Ariella was trying hard to let Sarah decompress in a strange environment, but after hearing all the whispers surrounding her arrival at the villa, Sarah insisted on learning the truth behind their flight to Rome. Ariella led her upstairs to a dorm-like room, and while some of the girls from the villa gave her dry clothes and some food, Ariella began telling Sarah about the dreams and the Bible code and the special group of people who were called *chosen*.

In the wake of the colossal news story from the United States dominating the airwaves, the crash of a private jet in the Mediterranean was never mentioned by the media. The search for the missing pilots would continue into the night and on through the next day, even though the searchers were convinced that the two brave men were now resting in God's arms at the bottom of the sea.

CHAPTER 31

Light from inside the villa cast yellow boxes of color across the brick walkways outside the windows as the sun dipped below the horizon. Upstairs in his room, Leo awoke from a brief nap, unable to sleep any longer. He wandered down to the poolside bar where he found John sitting quietly by himself with the backpack at his side. Leo poured two glasses of wine as they looked at one another with unspoken relief at being alive. They sipped their wine in silence before deciding to walk out and sit on the beach. In the gathering darkness, the sound of the surf pounding against the shore provided a rhythmic backdrop to their discussion.

Leo was deep in thought as he gazed out into the total blackness covering the sea and held the wineglass to his nose, inhaling the multilayered aroma. "I think we should have paid more attention to what the code was trying to tell us before we rushed off with the book today."

"I know, Father. That crash was no accident. Something was with us on that plane. It's like some form of enveloping energy follows the book wherever it goes. If I hadn't spotted this backpack when I did, it would have washed back up on shore and then someone or something would have recovered it. No doubt it would have found its way back into that desert or another hiding place somewhere in the world."

"We've got to get that book to Rome somehow," Leo said, "but I don't want to risk trying to fly with it again."

"How about traveling over land?"

"Too risky. We would have to cross Lebanon and Syria before we reached Turkey."

"Yeah, those are fun countries."

"Exactly. That's why I think our best bet is to go by boat."

"Couldn't the same force that destroyed the jet do the same to a boat? I mean, don't you think one rescue at sea is enough for a while, Father?"

"True, but I'm not sure if the force we're facing is coming directly from the book itself or from farther away. Something is trying to keep the book from leaving the Holy Land, John, and it's capable of reaching out and bringing down an airplane."

Leo twisted the base of his glass in the sand. "When we rushed to get on the plane, we failed to take any precautions, and we were almost killed. This time, we've got to be more vigilant. I've really got to think this one through, because time is running out."

"Well then, Father, I guess we need to find an unsinkable boat that can take us to Italy."

Leo laughed out loud as he finished his wine. "I think we both know who we need to talk to. Let's go find him and see what he's probably already worked out for us."

They rose and wandered through the dunes to the silent villa before finding Lev sitting quietly in his upstairs library under a single lamp, absorbed in a book. Lev noticed the two enter the room and pushed his reading glasses up on his forehead, his wrinkled brow furrowing over his bushy eyebrows as Leo and John took seats across from him in matching green wingchairs.

"Ah, what a day, my friends," Lev said. "I don't know whether to feel sorrow or happiness. The attack in Houston has brought great sadness to the world. But on the other hand, God has given me back my Ariella. It's like a giant hand reached down and snatched all of you from a certain death. I had to come up here to read for a while. It helps to clear my head."

"What are you reading?" Leo asked.

"Revelation. I thought it was appropriate at a time like this."

"You'll have to pardon me, sir," John said, "but I don't think reading Revelation would clear anyone's head."

"No, you're probably right, my young friend, but I was trying to find some insight into the events of the past few days. I only wish we could have found a warning about the attack on Houston, but sadly, predictions about the future only happen by chance. It's all part of God's plan after all. We can never be in complete control or have knowledge of everything. After the attack this morning, we entered the words "Houston" and "nuclear bomb" into the code program, and immediately, the computer found an encoded reference to the event, including the exact hour the bomb would explode. Unless you know specifically what you're looking for, the only way to find predictions is to accidentally stumble across them like they did with the encoded message of Yitzhak Rabin's assassination. After he was killed, the researchers went back and found the name of the assassin, but his name wouldn't have meant anything to them beforehand. The Bible code keeps giving us snippets of information, like God whispering in our ears."

"What's on your mind, Lev?" Leo asked, sensing that something else was troubling him.

"I've just finished talking with Daniel. He's begun to translate the Devil's Bible."

John literally jumped up from his chair. "You're kidding. That's great!"

"I don't know if *great* is the word I would use, John. I may have an inquisitive mind, but reading the words of Lucifer is not a task any Christian should take lightly."

"Has he been able to learn anything so far?"

Lev put his copy of the New Testament aside and leaned forward. "You were very wise to have the book copied for future study in case anything happens to it, Leo. The information we've found so far is invaluable. When Daniel's computer program started translating from the back of the book forward, it became clear why the dark angel is so anxious to have his book back. It appears that Lucifer has his own version of Revelation, and it's already started."

"I must have missed something," Leo said, his emotions sliding from excitement to dread. "Did you say that a different version of Revelation has already started?"

"Yes. The book itself is like an unholy relic. Some of our own holy Christian relics are able to perform miracles in God's name. The Devil's relic, if that's what we can call it, has the power to cause great evil in the world.

That's the most likely reason it was hidden here on earth. Apparently, Satan's timetable and God's timetable for the end of days don't agree."

Leo stood and began pacing the room. "Then if that's true, why were we sent to bring something like that out into the world?"

Lev stirred in his seat. "According to what Daniel has been able to decipher so far, the Devil's Bible has made an appearance in the world once before and was sealed back up to await the end of days. It has the power to jumpstart the reign of the Antichrist before the rapture, causing millions of Christians to remain here on earth to suffer before God can gather them up."

"That's impossible," Leo practically shouted. "God would never allow it."

"That's why we were sent to retrieve the book and take it to the chapel under the Vatican. God wants it destroyed, Leo. We are to be His instruments in preventing Satan from rushing the biblical timetable. God is sending us to protect those who have given their lives over to Christ … we're soldiers in a celestial war now … and there are going to be casualties, Father."

Leo's mind was reeling. "You say the book has made an appearance once before?"

"Father Morelli told me of an old archaeologist priest who worked alone out in the Negev Desert back in the late 1930s. He was one hundred years old when he died last year. He was Morelli's mentor and taught him about the area under the Vatican. His name escapes me, but there were stories from some Bedouins in the area that he found something out there and then suddenly left the country."

"Gilberto Bianchi," John said. "That was his name. Father Morelli was his successor."

"GB," Leo shouted, startling both Lev and John. They looked at him, waiting for some kind of explanation. "GB … the initials carved into the wall of the cavern where we found the Devil's Bible!"

"Wow … you're right." John said. "That's who must have tunneled down there before us and then covered up that section of the cavern where the backhoe fell in. Remember those old timbers and that lantern we found next to the tunnel entrance?"

Leo looked puzzled. "There's only one problem. How would he have known where to look? Even if he knew about the code, he lacked a computer to unravel it."

"He could have been counting sequenced letters in the Bible by hand and accidentally stumbled across the coordinates of the cavern," Lev said. "A few people who believed in the code before computers tried to find it using that method, but it was painstakingly difficult, and it took years to find even one or two words spelled out, so most researchers gave up. It's my guess that he didn't even know what he was looking for. He might have simply found a set of coordinates in the Bible and followed the lead like any good archaeologist would do."

"Still, there's no way he could have gone down there all alone," Leo said. "And even if he did, the book was encased under six feet of solid rock and guarded by demons."

Lev ran his hand through his gray beard and looked up at Leo. "I think he was allowed to take it, Father. It probably wasn't encased under the stone when he found it."

Leo's mind was racing. "But why take it and then return it?"

Lev faced a wall of shelves that were filled with books … books that had become like friends to him over the years. "I've been sitting here thinking about that. It was the same time the earth was being ravaged by World War II. That was when the Holocaust occurred. At least fifty million people around the world died. We'll never know the true number. It was the single darkest hour in mankind's history. The first nuclear bombs were used then, and for the first time in history, we had been given the means to destroy ourselves."

Leo stood in front of the room's only window and looked out into the darkness. "So you're saying that Satan had a hand in allowing the book to leave the cavern?"

"Exactly, Father. Like I said before, it's my theory that Bianchi was allowed to bring the book out into the world once he discovered it. Then later, sometime during the war, he realized what it was and connected it to the events that were happening. He must have been horrified by the book's power to unleash so much misery around the world."

"That's a good hypothesis, Lev, but how could he have returned it to the cavern and carve out a warning to 'leave it in place' without the demons stopping him?"

"I think God probably had a hand in protecting Bianchi when he returned the book to the desert. The priest was an unwitting participant in Satan's attempt to show God his power. Lucifer continues to deny that God is more powerful than he is. He probably couldn't resist showing off a little and used a priest to do it."

"This is unreal," John said. "The Devil's Bible has been lying out there ever since, waiting for someone of Satan's choosing to remove it so it could make an appearance in the world again sometime before the end of days ... only we beat him to it."

Leo looked uncomfortable. Too many things just weren't adding up. Father Morelli had been very close to Bianchi, but Morelli obviously knew nothing about the book. Leo could only guess at whom Bianchi might have confided in. Surely, he must have told someone at the Vatican about something so monstrous and evil after he discovered what the book was capable of. Maybe that's why there was so much interest in them from the Vatican security people, if that's who they really were.

"We also received the lab results from the sample of the book we took," Lev added. "The DNA shows that the cover is made from the skin of a jackal. We're still not clear on the symbolism involved, but we do know that the Antichrist will be born of a jackal, so that's not too surprising. What bothers me the most is the evil that seems to flow from it. I'm convinced now more than ever that it must be destroyed, and that God alone will have to do it. It's up to those chosen by God to keep the Devil's book from falling into the wrong hands and deliver it to the chapel. Without Satan's Bible, those who would change the biblical timetable laid out in the Book of Revelation will be rendered powerless."

Leo's face turned pale. The darkness outside seemed even darker. "They're going to pull out all the stops to prevent us from reaching the chapel now. This is an extremely dangerous time, not only for us, but for the whole world if we fail."

"How come God doesn't just zap the book into oblivion?" John asked, peering at the backpack lying on the floor beside him. "Why does He need our help to destroy it?"

Leo turned away from the window and smiled. "God works in mysterious ways. Surely you remember that old saying, John. God has always involved man in the war between good and evil. We have to be participants in our own salvation. That's the way it's always been and that's the way it will always be."

Lev clapped his hands together and stood. "We have to leave right away. I'll make some calls and have my crew prepare the yacht while you two gather anything you may need for the trip.

"You were right, Father," John said, grinning. "We didn't even have to ask about the boat. The man already had a plan."

Lev picked up the phone and called Moshe and Alon before heading for the door. He stopped and looked back at his two American friends. "This time we all go together." He reached for the door and paused again. "And, John, don't forget the book." He winked before turning to race down to the command center.

* * *

Lev burst through the command center doors and saw Daniel sitting alone in front of his computer.

"Hi, Professor." Daniel looked up at him with bloodshot eyes.

"Grab your laptop, son," Lev said. "We're leaving."

Alon and Moshe entered the center and headed straight for the weapons room. They grabbed several radios and a multitude of weapons from the racks on the walls, including automatic rifles, pistols, grenades, and explosives.

Upstairs, lights were coming on all over the villa as John and Leo ran to their rooms and threw some clothes into their backpacks. With a backpack full of clothes on one shoulder and the backpack containing the Devil's Bible on the other, John sprinted down a long hallway to Ariella's room and knocked on the door. She opened it and stood there for a moment before she grabbed him around the neck, pulling him into the room and kissing him deeply. John responded, forgetting for a moment why he was there.

"We've got to go, Ariella."

Ariella closed the door and arched her eyebrows coyly. "Where?"

"We're taking your father's yacht to Italy."

"Just you and me?"

"No, all of us. We're taking the Devil's Bible to the Vatican, and we really need to hurry."

"Oh." Disappointment etched her face. "That's why you came to my room."

John's eyes widened. "What did that bump on the head do to you?"

Ariella laughed as she turned to retrieve a bag from her closet. "What bump? I feel fine."

John shook his head and hefted the ever-present backpack containing the book over his shoulder. "I promise you that, when I get rid of this thing, we'll never be apart again."

Ariella flashed him a sensuous smile while grabbing some clothes from a pile on her bed and stuffing them into her bag. John opened the door and they both ran straight into Sarah in the hall. "I want to be on the team," she said. "I know this is why I'm here now."

Ariella looked at John and hesitated before answering. "Are you sure, Sarah? I mean, your dream pretty much confirms that you were meant to be here, but this is a big commitment. We're getting ready to head back out into the Mediterranean, and there could be a repeat of what happened earlier today."

"I'm sure, Ariella. I've never been so sure of anything in my life."

"Ok then. Come with us. Welcome to the Bible Code Team."

Down in the communications center, plans were being made for a hasty departure across the Mediterranean. Lev sat at a console, wearing a white dress shirt and khaki shorts. His tanned and calloused feet slipped in and out of his flip-flops as he talked to the ship's captain on his cell phone. Alon had doubled the sentries around the perimeter and placed the villa on high alert for any suspicious activity. For security reasons, only those with a need to know were informed of the new mission now unfolding around them.

CHAPTER 32

The yacht was located about twelve miles north of the villa in the ancient port of Caesarea. Moshe and Alon departed the grounds at 2:00 am in a small car, followed by Daniel and Sarah who caught a ride with several of the cooks in a large truck full of provisions. Nava and Gabriella had been notified and were now airborne in the Blackhawk en route to the villa.

Leo and Lev made some last-minute arrangements before jumping into Lev's old Land Rover, while John and Ariella grabbed Camp and piled into the rear seat. John never let the backpack out of his sight, taking one more peek inside at the clear container holding the red book before giving Leo a thumbs up. Thirty minutes behind the other departing vehicles, the Land Rover rolled out onto the highway and began speeding up the coast toward Caesarea.

Lev was the first to see the headlights of a large white SUV turn onto the road behind them. It sped up and kept pace.

"That's not one of ours, is it, Father?" Ariella said.

Lev looked into the rearview mirror. "No, it's not. I'll speed up a little and see what they do."

The SUV matched the Land Rover's speed as the two cars raced down the highway. The large vehicle inched closer, pulling to within a few feet of the Land Rover's rear bumper.

"Whoever they are," Lev said, "they don't care about keeping a low profile."

Lev lifted a military walkie-talkie from the front seat next to him and called Nava in the helicopter. "We have company."

"How many?"

"Looks like only one vehicle for now. A big white SUV … and they don't seem to be worried about keeping a low profile."

"Be there in three minutes."

The occupants of the SUV hadn't counted on the Bible Code Team having air support as the Blackhawk swooped out of the sky and fell in behind the tailing car.

Speeding down the highway, a man in the front passenger seat of the SUV pulled out a pistol and aimed it from his side window at the Land Rover ahead. He began firing, shattering the Rover's rear window and causing everyone inside except for Lev to dive down in their seats.

From the rear seat of the SUV, a third man produced a light machine gun and leaned out of his window. He looked up and aimed the gun at the Blackhawk before making the fatal mistake of pulling the trigger, firing off a series of bursts at the helicopter overhead and sealing the fate of everyone inside his own vehicle.

Nava and Gabriella exchanged glances as they pulled up and circled around, coming back into position behind the SUV. Gabriella studied a computer-generated display through her helmet eyepiece and chose her weapon. "Got him in my sights."

Nava held the chopper steady while simultaneously keeping an eye on the occupants inside. The man with the machine gun crawled into the back of the SUV and lowered the rear window before aiming straight up at the helicopter.

"Now would be a good time, Gabriella," Nava said with a hint of sarcasm.

With the push of a button, a rocket erupted from a side pod on the helicopter and streaked toward its target. Within seconds, the SUV was a flaming, unrecognizable heap of wreckage on the side of the highway. The large gray helicopter sped by overhead as Nava and Gabriella high-fived each other in the cockpit.

John stared through the shattered glass of the Land Rover's rear window at the flames receding in the distance. "Whoever they were, they definitely miscalculated you, Lev."

Leo was growing weary of the intrigue. "My God, who are these people? Did the police ever get any information from the two you caught spying on us at the villa?"

"Nothing," Lev said. "They refused to talk. The police could only charge them with trespassing and had them deported from the country."

"Well, it looks like they still have friends around; only this time, they did a little more than trespass."

The Land Rover pulled into the harbor in the early morning darkness. The lights from the yacht were ablaze, highlighting members of the crew who could be seen scurrying about the decks, making the boat ready for sea. The "small" yacht Lev had told them about earlier was actually a luxurious two-hundred-thirty-foot-long super yacht. The boat had a dark blue hull and white superstructure, and the main deck sat at least twenty feet above the water line. As soon as the Land Rover came to a stop, it was surrounded by crew members who helped Lev and the others carry all of their equipment up the gangplank to the yacht's main deck.

The Blackhawk had arrived with the Land Rover and was circling the harbor, sweeping the docks with strong searchlights looking for anyone who didn't belong. Satisfied the scene below was clear of intruders, the two women landed the helicopter at the end of the wharf, but kept the engines running.

While the turbines continued to whine, Nava climbed out of her armored seat in the cockpit and stepped out onto the dock. Her long black ponytail hung from the back of her helmet and swished back and forth as she walked over to speak with Alon. After a quick embrace and a few words, she waved in the direction of the helicopter and turned to board the yacht with Alon, leaving Gabriella to take control of the Blackhawk. Alone now, Gabriella lifted the chopper into the air, where she would remain overhead until the boat was safely out of the harbor.

Leo and Lev made their way up an interior stairway of the yacht to the darkened bridge. Only the red battle lighting and the greenish glow from the radar display highlighted the men's faces as they conferred with the captain and scanned the periphery of the harbor. Besides the helicopter overhead, several of Moshe's most experienced men, armed with sniper rifles and night-vision goggles, had been secretly placed in concealed positions around the harbor to avoid any surprises.

Leo poured himself a cup of coffee from a pot nearby and settled into a raised seat next to the captain's chair. He took a sip from the steaming cup while brushing the long gray-streaked hair from his face and peering out on the reflections from the yacht's lights on the water.

The priest's hands were still shaking slightly from the encounter with the SUV on the highway. "I don't like this newest development. Those were real people with real guns out there on the highway behind us, not supernatural beings. There is more to this than meets the eye. Not only are we threatened with invisible satanic forces, but we're also forced to deal with what appears to be a very organized effort by some very mortal individuals who want to obtain the Devil's Bible for their own reasons."

Lev pulled on a dark blue windbreaker with the yacht's logo embroidered on the front. "I don't like it either. At least we can fight humans with conventional weapons, but the fact that someone knows what we have and wants to possess it at any cost is another factor we have to consider. I'm beginning to wonder if Jeb Carlton's jet was brought down by supernatural forces or if it was sabotaged by the same people who came after us tonight."

"I don't think the plane was taken out by sabotage," Leo said. "They would have risked losing the book in the crash. Why don't we put Moshe to work on this and see what he can come up with? He has the kind of connections most security agencies can only dream about. If anyone can find out who the people chasing us are working for, he can."

"He's already on it," Lev said. "He just talked to the Israeli police who are on the scene back on the highway going through the wreckage of that SUV. They're looking to see who it belonged to and trying to ID the bodies inside. He's also made some calls to Rome. Some friends of ours are already starting to scout around. I'm sorry to say this, Father, but Moshe doesn't much trust the Vatican, especially since we found those two Swiss Guards spying on the villa."

"I can't blame him. I'm having some doubts myself."

Lev winced when he told Leo that one of his men distrusted the Vatican. He admired this priest and considered him a part of his family, but he had also seen the passage in the Bible code that spoke of dark forces within the Church working against them.

The yacht's captain was outside on the deck in front of the bridge, smoking and watching the activities of the crew on the deck below. His name was Alex Pappas, a Greek who carried himself with the pride of thousands of years of Greek sailors who had plied these waters before him. In his mid-thirties, he was considered young for a ship's captain. His short black hair provided a stark contrast to his spotless white uniform, while his hazel eyes reflected the color of the sea he had lived on for almost his entire life. His father had been the captain of the yacht, Christina, the yacht that once belonged to Aristotle Onassis.

He flicked the remainder of his lit cigarette overboard and gave the order to release the lines connecting the yacht to the dock. The crew began drawing in the thick nylon rope and coiled it on the deck as Camp ran back and forth, barking at the dockhands on the concrete wharf below.

The captain entered the bridge and took his place at the controls. With the flick of a toggle switch on a hand controller, he increased the RPM of the engines and the bow and stern thrusters came to life, slowly pushing the large boat away from the dock. With the boat now moving toward the center of the harbor, the huge brass propellers under the stern began to spin, driving the massive blue and white yacht out of the marina.

Moving past the breakwater protecting the harbor, the captain kept the boat centered in the channel until they passed the end of the jetty and entered the Mediterranean Sea, where he ordered the helmsman to increase the speed, pushing the bow higher as it slipped through the waves into deeper water.

Only the lights from distant ships far out at sea punctuated the darkness before them as the boat headed west across the open ocean toward Europe and the Italian coast. No one onboard knew what awaited them in the current climate of world events, nor could they imagine what forces might already be at work to keep them from making their destination. Despite the fact that they were now moving away from land, everyone onboard remained on high alert for any hint of an attack against them or their boat.

Wearing only a thin black polo shirt and white shorts, Leo shivered in the chill from the wind as he descended the stairs from the bridge. He was making good on his promise to take every precaution and walked the entire length of the boat, blessing the decks with holy water and praying for their safe passage across the sea. Although he was surrounded by the best Israeli-trained security men and women in the world, he recognized that the fate of those onboard this ship remained in God's hands, for only He knew what truly lay ahead for them all.

John and Ariella were standing side by side on the yacht's rear deck, watching the lights from the shore recede. They marveled at the phosphorescent glow given off by the plankton stirred up in the ship's wake. The moon was rising in the distance as the two lovers held each other tightly. They kissed unashamedly in full view of both Leo and Lev, who sat with Moshe at a table on the rear deck. John and Ariella felt they had nothing to hide now.

Leo had come to know John as a fine man who had honestly looked at the priesthood for his life's vocation, but it had become obvious that God had called on him to marry and start a family with Ariella instead. The priest drank his coffee in silence. He enjoyed seeing how happy these two were in each other's presence. There was no need to ask if John would be withdrawing his application from Jesuit seminary, when and if they returned to America.

The hiss of water passing along the hull provided a backdrop for what was so far turning out to be an uneventful cruise. Leo had volunteered to give John a break from watching over the backpack containing the book and kept it next to him on the teak wood deck below his chair. He eyed it with revulsion and wondered why the entities hadn't shown themselves since they had left port. Leo felt a chill as he remembered the reddish smoke in the plane's cabin just before the jet had crashed into the sea. Like any confrontation, the wait could sometimes be worse than the event itself.

The priest leaned back in his chair and stared up into the star-filled sky. The quiet isolation of the sea, along with the rhythmic hum of the motors as the yacht pushed through the open water, began to lull him into a mood of complacent introspection.

His thoughts were interrupted when he heard the voice of one of the ship's crewmembers speaking to Lev.

"Sir, we have a radio call for you from shore. Would you like to take it on the bridge or in the salon on the main deck?"

Lev let his cigar smolder in the ashtray. "I'll take it in the salon."

Casting a glance at Leo and Moshe, he leaned his body against the roll of the deck and followed the sailor through the glass doors into the plush aft salon. He crossed the blue marble floor, taking the receiver and remembering to push the green talk button on the ship to shore radiophone before he spoke.

"Hello?"

"Hello, Professor Wasserman?" It was David, the Israeli policeman. He had just come from the scene of the burned out hulk of the SUV. "We've discovered the identities of the men inside the vehicle that attacked you on the highway. They appear to be Swiss citizens."

"Vatican security men?"

"At first, we thought so, but their Vatican security IDs were fakes. They've been living in Rome for the past two years, but we haven't been able to learn who they really worked for."

"Thank you for keeping me informed, David. Is there anything else?"

"No, except for the fact that we found a detailed blueprint of your yacht on the highway next to the wreckage. You might want to take some extra precautions and make a sweep of your boat for anything suspicious."

"Thanks, David. We'll take it from here. Let me know if you learn anything else."

"You got it, Professor. Have a safe cruise."

CHAPTER 33

The sunrise crept over the stern of the yacht as it made its way west across the Mediterranean. The wind was light, and the water was smooth, allowing the bow to cut through the sea with little effort. Gray dolphins played in its foamy white wake while taking turns lagging behind and turning sideways to gaze up at the crew through one eye peeking above the surface.

Lev descended the stairs from the bridge and approached the lounging group warming themselves in the sun on the back deck. He was barefoot and wearing a blue-and-white-striped T-shirt with dark blue shorts. His tanned arms were covered in white hair that reflected the sun as he ran his hands back through the thick mop of gray hair hanging in his face.

"Anyone care for a tour of my little boat?"

"I'd love to see the rest of it," Leo said. They all stood and followed Lev up to the bridge.

The yacht was a beauty. Built in Holland in 2002, the boat was immaculate. Two decks rose above the main deck, with the bridge on the uppermost deck almost forty feet above the waterline. The entire superstructure was brilliantly white, while the hull was painted a glossy dark blue trimmed with two gold stripes that ran the entire two-hundred-thirty-foot length just below the main deck.

"What do you call her?" Leo asked.

Lev's face suddenly became somber.

"Carmela. She was named after my dear wife."

"That's a beautiful name, Lev," Leo said, wondering why he had not taken the time to ask Lev more about his late wife. People at the villa talked in hushed tones when her name was mentioned.

After a quick tour inside the bridge with all of its high tech equipment, Lev led the group outside to the top deck behind the bridge, where he showed them a small sunken pool next to an extensive outdoor bar, complete with widescreen TV and barbecue grill.

"This looks like a mini version of the pool area back at the villa," Leo observed.

"I copied it as near as I could with the limited space available on a boat. An outdoor entertainment area needs to have a pool, a bar, and a grill, in that order."

Ariella giggled at her father as he pointed above to an assortment of antennas and two radars that spun constantly, scanning the horizon. Lev loved his electronic gadgets, and this was a source of much amusement to Ariella, as it had been to her mother.

While Lev explained the navigation capability of the boat, Leo and John's attention was drawn to the helipad located behind them with a small dark-blue helicopter secured to the deck.

"Oh, I see you like my little bird." Lev smiled. "We use it quite a bit actually. That's why Nava came on board. It's used mostly for going back and forth to places on shore and spotting schools of tuna for our supper." Written in gold script on the fuselage of the helicopter was the name, *Little Carmela.*

The group left the sun-drenched top deck and crowded through a tight interior stairway that descended below to the lavishly furnished mid-deck salon. The front section of the salon was furnished with two cozy booth-like tables that faced a rich cherry-wood bar topped with black granite. Two flat screen TVs above the bar were usually reserved for watching sports, but unfortunately today, the thrill of soccer, basketball, and football were replaced with images from the aftermath of the attack on Houston.

Several crewmembers were standing in front of the TVs watching the news of the attack, their youthful exuberance flattened by the overwhelming evil displayed across the screens before them. They were all dressed in the yacht's standard uniform of dark blue shorts and blue and white horizontally striped polo shirts with the name of the yacht, Carmela, embroidered in gold on the upper left chest.

The aft portion of the salon held a spacious seating area surrounded by large horizontal windows that ran the entire length of the space, giving it a bright and airy feel. Oversized glass doors opened outside onto a covered deck furnished with several tables and built-in bench seats that followed the curve of the outside railing.

Descending some exterior stairs to the main deck, they entered the grand salon. Inside, the group beheld a more formal area that resembled a five-star hotel lobby and included a grand piano and expensive artwork from around the world. This area of the yacht contained a large dining room and a fully equipped gourmet kitchen large enough for a team of chefs to prepare a dinner party for at least fifty guests. Blue marble flooring ran the entire length of the salon, where several multicolored fabric couches faced the heavy glass doors that led out onto the main deck.

Beyond the doors lay the main deck, the focal area for most of the entertainment that occurred on the boat. The first half of the deck closest to the salon included a seating area and bar that was covered by a blue-and-white-striped fabric awning, while the last twenty feet of the stern section was left open to the sky, so that guests could sit under the sun or the stars and watch the yacht's wake recede into the distance.

The group paused to watch a pod of dolphins play nearby before descending down another narrow stairway to an area below the main deck. They trailed along behind Lev as he passed through a dark, wood-paneled hallway lined with brass side railings. Antique brass lamps gave off a soft yellow glow and provided a fitting ambiance for Lev's collection of classic oil paintings of sailing ships at sea. This region of the yacht was reserved for guests and contained twelve staterooms, all beautifully decorated, with their own private baths.

To the rear of the guest's quarters, a large, garage-like space held some of Lev's favorite toys. Next to a room full of scuba diving equipment, two speedboats and several jet skis crowded the area in front of a large hydraulic door that could be lowered at the stern, providing direct access to the water.

Below this deck lay the engine room. It gleamed from top to bottom and was the pride of the yacht's engineer. Anyone who spilled oil on the immaculate floor did so at their peril. Twin turbine engines propelled the craft through the water at a speed greater than most small speedboats, and oversized fuel tanks carried a sufficient amount of diesel for a voyage across any ocean in the world.

Lev looked at Leo and John, beaming like a proud father. "Well, what do you think of her? Isn't she magnificent?"

"Magnificent would be a good word," Leo said. "Palatial would be another that comes to mind."

"I'm glad you approve of her, Leo, because I hope you'll be spending a lot of time at the villa and on this boat in the future, my friend."

Leo had never traveled in such wealthy social circles in his simple life as a priest, and a man like Lev was an enigma to him. Rich and smart, he also possessed a heart filled with love. He was generous to a fault and protected those in his care like a lion.

With the tour finished, Lev excused himself from the others and made his way forward to his cabin. The stress of the past few days was showing on his face when he slid beneath the covers of his bed for a much-needed nap. He had just fallen asleep when a knock on the door awakened him. "What is it? Is the boat sinking?"

A nervous-sounding voice echoed from the other side of the door. "No, sir. I'm sorry to disturb you. Father Leo wants to talk to you, sir. He says it's very important."

CHAPTER 34

L eo was pacing the bridge when Lev found him. Obviously worried, his green eyes looked out over the rolling sea in the direction of the Italian coast. Over the course of the past few days, the priest had barely slept, and his scarred left eyelid drooped more than usual. His hand trembled as he took a sip of yet another cup of coffee.

"Why don't you go below and try to get some sleep, Father?"

"How far are we from Italy?"

"At this speed, we're already two-thirds of the way across the Med. Alex told me we should be approaching the southern Italian coast sometime later this evening."

"Have you given any thought as to where we will dock?"

"We usually go into Fiumicino when we bring the yacht to Rome. It's a large harbor close to the city and a good place to buy provisions, but …"

"We'll stand out like a sore thumb there," Leo said.

"You read my mind, Father. Moshe and I have been looking for somewhere less conspicuous and farther down the coast. A place where we can sneak into a small harbor in the middle of the night, somewhere they won't be expecting us."

"What about docking at a harbor on the opposite coast?" Leo asked. "Maybe somewhere along the Adriatic Sea."

"Let's take a look." Lev called Alex over as he opened a polished wooden cabinet and pulled out several sea charts of the Italian coast. Even though he enjoyed his electronic gadgets and could have easily looked the same information up on the navigational computer, he was still a traditionalist at heart and loved his large paper charts.

Alex spread one of the charts out flat with his hands while Lev drew a mental line from the east coast of Italy to Rome. "I think any of these ports on the east coast are too close to the city. If anyone is watching the harbors there, we would be spotted in an instant. How about farther south … on the western coast?"

"Mmm." Leo rubbed his chin and ran his finger over the map. "Have you thought about a port on one of these islands here?" The port he had pointed to was located on Lipari, one of the Sicilian islands close to the west coast of Italy. It was small and populated with a scattering of bars, restaurants, and hotels.

Alex studied it for a moment and nodded his head. "I've docked there before. It's out of the way, and no one on the mainland would know we were in the area. I personally wouldn't want to take the Carmela into that port."

Lev continued to stare at the chart. "Why not?"

"If the volcano on that island is active, it makes the whole place smell like sulfur. The smell gets into everything and the whole boat stinks for days."

Leo and Lev exchanged glances simultaneously.

"Let's cross that one off our list," Leo said with a straight face. "We probably need to be somewhere along the coast on the mainland."

"How about this harbor?" Lev said. He was pointing to the port of Maratea along the southwestern coast about 180 miles south of Rome.

The captain's face immediately lit up. "No problem. I've been in that harbor dozens of times. Small, discrete, and it can accommodate a yacht of this size. It's perfect."

"Good," Lev said. "That actually works out better for us from a logistics standpoint."

Leo placed a ruler over the map and measured the distance to Rome. "I think it might be a good idea to have a place near Rome to go to if we need to escape the city in a hurry. We could use Father Morelli's country house. It's about forty-five miles south of Rome … near the village of Sermoneta. He left everything to me, so technically, I own it now. I'll call the caretakers and let them know some special guests of mine might be stopping by."

"You're getting good at this, Father. I'm beginning to think you have some Israeli commando training behind that Roman collar."

"I have a feeling you and Moshe were already in the process of making plans. I just wanted to check on things."

Lev gently took the cup of coffee from Leo's hand and looked him in the eyes. "Why don't you call the caretakers from your cabin, Father? There's a phone by your bed. I'll have some lunch sent down."

"You haven't slept either, Lev."

"I'm heading for my cabin too. We're in capable hands with Alex at the helm … and Moshe and Alon are onboard to watch over things."

Lev set the coffee down and put his hand on Alex's shoulder. "Captain, this priest is barred from the bridge until I say so."

Alex winked. "Aye aye, sir."

Leo knew he had lost this battle. He rose slowly from his seat and ran his hand across the stubble on his face before giving Lev a weak smile and sauntering off down the hallway that led to the stairs and his cabin below. Once inside, the exhausted priest closed the door and sat on the edge of the bed to remove his shoes. He lay back on the soft comforter and rubbed his eyes in an effort to clear his thoughts. Dreams flooded his mind as sleep overcame him while he lay there still fully clothed with his legs dangling over the side of the bed.

Lev had lied. He had no intention of going to his cabin, at least not for another thirty minutes. He descended the stairs into a secure area below the bridge and opened a stainless steel door. Inside was a room bathed in red light that resembled the combat information center on a warship.

Lev paused and let his eyes adjust to the darkness before walking over to a console next to Daniel and Moshe. He looked up at a multicolored electronic image of Italy on the big screen above their heads. "Have you found anything yet?"

"Not yet, Boss," Moshe replied.

"Keep at it. Leo and John are going to need all the help we can give them once we're in Italy."

CHAPTER 35

While Leo slept, the yacht sailed on throughout the day. The calm sea and warm air formed a blanket of humidity that clung to the surface of the water as the big boat sliced through the tranquil ocean. News from America continued to dominate talk onboard, giving the Bible Code Team even more motivation to gear up mentally for the task ahead.

It was early evening, and the sun was setting on their port side, creating a melancholy visual effect over the yacht as it headed north and passed through the strait separating Sicily from the mainland of Italy. The decks were softly lit with dozens of tiny white lights strung overhead, while next to the grand salon, the chefs were preparing dinner in the galley.

Leo had awakened with a start, encircled by his comforter after seven hours of fitful sleep. He showered for a full thirty minutes in the black-and-gold-streaked marble shower and let the hot water flush the beach sand from his pores. He picked out a bottle of shampoo emblazoned with a French label and lathered up his thick hair twice before grabbing a washcloth and scrubbing the rest of his body until he finally felt clean.

Feeling refreshed, Leo turned off the water and emerged into the steam-filled room. He donned a white terry cloth bathrobe with the Carmella's blue and gold logo embroidered over the left side of the chest and looked into the mirror. Running his hand over the stubble on his face, he reached for a shaving kit by the sink before turning on a tiny flat-screen TV mounted at eye level on a cinnamon-colored wall. From the corner of his eye, he glimpsed the images on the screen while he shaved. Pictures of Houston still dominated the news and Israeli officials were telling journalists that Israel was on full alert now as new threats were being aimed in her direction in the aftermath of the nuclear attack in America.

Smoothing on some aftershave, Leo exited the bathroom to discover that someone had removed all of his clothing, and that a blue dress shirt and tan slacks had mysteriously appeared on his bed. Knowing who was probably responsible for the theft of his clothes, he smiled to himself as he tried on the pants. A knock on the door ended his luxurious seclusion.

Leo opened the door to find John standing in the hallway dressed for dinner. "I found these new clothes hanging in my closet when I woke up. This shirt's an Armani. What gives?"

Leo pointed out his own new clothes. "I'm sure Lev has something to do with it. Where's Ariella?"

"She's still dressing. Evidently, there's a big dinner party planned for this evening, and she won't let me see her until she comes out of her room."

"Sounds like someone has a surprise for you. Come in while I look for some shoes."

"I wanted to talk to you about Ariella, Father. I ... "

"Listen, John, it's been pretty obvious to everyone around that you two were meant for each other. The priesthood isn't for everyone, and you don't owe anybody an explanation. God has chosen our callings for us, and they're all equally important. You're a devoted Catholic, and you'll be a devoted husband and father someday. Besides, if all Catholic men became priests, we wouldn't have any more Catholics."

John stood awkwardly in the doorway and smiled at Leo's last remark. He had agonized over his decision and felt that he was letting the Church and his mentors down, but it was evident that he was destined to take a different path ... a path that he and Ariella would walk together. Whatever lay ahead for them, John knew the Church would always remain a central focus in his life, and that, no matter what, he had made a life-long friend that he could call upon in the years ahead.

"It's funny how life takes us in different directions when we least expect it," John said. "A few weeks ago I thought my path was set ...then I met Ariella."

John's expression reminded Leo of his own struggles when he was considering seminary years ago. "Every time I come to a fork in the road, John, I feel I'm being led. Let's go topside and see what that girl has in store for you."

They walked out into the wood-paneled hallway and up the narrow stairs to the main deck. The members of the Bible Code Team were all dressed for the occasion, sipping their wine and chatting nonstop in anticipation of a relaxing evening aboard Lev's yacht.

Alon and Nava were nursing sunburns from sitting in the upper deck pool too long, while others had escaped the sun by napping. Almost everyone had skipped lunch and all were ravenous as the smell of garlic and lemon-seasoned Mediterranean cooking mixed with the sea air and wafted from the kitchen out onto the deck. Camp had captured the hearts of the Carmela's crew and had his own bowls of food and water inside the main salon. The little dog had claimed one of the couches and was sleeping soundly.

As everyone mingled on the back deck, the sliding glass doors to the grand salon opened and Lev stepped out with Ariella on his arm.

John gasped silently as she stood before him, a vision of pure femininity. He had never seen her in a dress before, and she looked even more gorgeous than he thought possible. She wore a knee-length white silk dress emblazoned with a red and yellow Calder-like pattern. Her long brown hair was pulled up on top of her head, and long gold earrings and light makeup highlighted her already perfect features. Her brown eyes positively beamed as she gazed at John, somehow knowing the effect she was having on him and giggling at his weak-kneed and slack-jawed response.

Dressed in a dark blue sport coat with an open white shirt, Lev led his daughter out on deck and handed her off to John. He clasped John on the back as they stood face to face for a brief, silent moment. Without saying a word, he had said it all. *Welcome to the family.* John's affection for both Lev and Ariella was growing daily, and Lev's unspoken blessing had a humbling effect on him, especially since he had only known the two of them for such a short period of time.

Night had fallen as everyone flowed into the yacht's main dining room and gathered around the long, highly polished Koa wood table. The flickering light from the candles reflected on the faces of the guests, giving the scene a subdued aura of elegance. Ariella and John sat next to each other while Lev took his place at the head of the table with Leo to his right. A beautiful gilded chair at the far end of the long table was always left empty in memory of Lev's late wife.

"Something smells delicious," Leo said.

Moshe beamed from across the table. "It's my wife's cooking."

"Moshe's wife, Hadar, is actually one of the most famous chefs in Israel," Lev said. "She always accompanies us when we sail on the yacht."

The hungry diners could hear the sounds of a busy kitchen in the background as Daniel noticed the newest member of the group, Sarah Newton, standing shyly in the doorway. He caught her attention and motioned to the empty seat next to him.

Ariella glanced at John before looking over the table at Father Leo and giving him a conspiratorial wink. Despite the fact that Sarah's dream was similar to their own, they had both been secretly worried that Sarah was not one of the chosen … that bringing her with them was a mistake. Their fears were finally put to rest by Daniel earlier in the day when he had discovered Sarah's name encoded next to the word *chosen* in one of the books of the Old Testament.

Leo watched Sarah as she smiled at the others around the table. He was instantly struck with the realization that she truly was one of the chosen, and that could only mean that there had to be others like her out there somewhere. He filed away a mental note to discuss his theory with Lev. They needed to begin searching the Bible right away for names of those chosen by God.

In honor of their Italian destination, Hadar and the other chefs had prepared an elegant meal that began with a typical Mediterranean salad, including lettuce, tomatoes, olives, artichoke hearts, and feta cheese, drizzled with garlic-infused, lemon-scented Italian dressing. This was followed by *saltimbocca alla romana*, veal slices rolled with prosciutto and sage. The main course was *abbacchio alla cacciatore*, lamb cooked in anchovies, garlic, wine, chilies, and olive oil. The dinner was topped off by a *timballo di ricotta*, ricotta cheese baked in a tart with sugar, lemon, brandy, eggs, and cinnamon—Ariella's favorite dessert.

Sitting next to Ariella, John could barely take his eyes away from her. The idea of exposing her to any more danger was weighing heavily on him. The need to protect her was strong, but he knew that she would scoff at the idea of needing to be protected. She was a strong-willed, independent woman who had once been an Israeli soldier and had faced danger as well as, or better than, most men. Falling in love with a woman like her came with a whole new set of challenges, but John was more than up to the task with a quiet strength that matched Ariella's. Glancing at her profile, he knew that somehow they would work it all out. For now, he had to stay focused on making sure the object in the backpack beside his chair made it to Rome.

With most of the cooking done, Hadar joined Moshe at the table across from Nava and Alon. "Where did you find such a beautiful dress, Sarah?" Hadar asked.

"Yes, it is beautiful. I found it hanging in my closet this afternoon." Sarah smiled and glanced over at Lev and Ariella. "I think there are fashion elves roaming this boat."

John saw Ariella biting her lip to keep from laughing. "Yeah, Leo and I were wondering the same thing. How come we all have these great new clothes that just happen to fit us?"

"Oh, the clothes." Lev threw his head back in laughter. "Ariella and the staff obtained your sizes and ordered the clothes delivered to the boat when you first arrived at the villa. I thought you would enjoy a little overnight cruise along the coast after we came out of the desert. I don't think anyone here could have predicted the events that have happened since Leo and John arrived. It turns out that we got to take our little cruise under totally different circumstances from what I had originally planned. We didn't know about Sarah then, but luckily, she and Ariella are about the same size. Please … accept these clothes as a gift from us to you."

Sarah blushed as Ariella held up a glass of wine in her direction and gave her a warm smile. The rest of the table followed by raising their glasses in a toast to Lev and Ariella … who had proven, as always, to be generous and beloved hosts.

"What are our plans once we reach shore?" John asked to no one in particular.

The lively talk at the table tapered off as everyone's eyes rotated in Leo's direction. John had pretty much nailed what everyone else was thinking. Leo set his glass aside and folded his hands on the table.

"I don't really have a solid plan at this point except to get the book back to the Vatican as quickly and safely as possible. It will obviously be too cumbersome and hazardous for everyone to accompany us all the way, so I think this is something we'll be deciding on later tonight."

Lev looked down the table at Moshe and gave him a barely perceptible nod.

Moshe twirled one end of his moustache and looked down the length of the table. "According to one of our scenarios, it may be advantageous to use as many of you as possible."

Leo smiled with the knowledge that Moshe and Lev had probably been making plans all along based on various perceived threats. It was a generational habit all Israelis shared from living their entire lives surrounded by an enemy bent on their destruction.

Leaning back in his chair, Lev surveyed the table and took a final sip of wine. "We're planning on holding a briefing scheduled at 5:00 am for the entire staff. We still have some details to work out in support of the final dash to the Vatican, but all of our efforts will be to support that mission. It will be vital that everyone is prepared to do their part, no matter how small it may seem. Until then, let's enjoy our last evening aboard and try to relax before we dock, because tomorrow will be very busy indeed."

As the dinner slowly ebbed to a finish, everyone pushed their chairs back and filtered outside. Strolling along the main deck, they could feel the fresh sea breeze and see the twinkling lights from the Italian shore as the boat moved along the coast toward its destination.

At one of the outside tables, Leo joined Lev and Moshe who were smoking Cuban cigars obtained by the yacht's captain in Panama the last time the boat had passed through the canal. John and Ariella were coiled up on a couch next to Camp in the salon, and Alon and Nava had retreated back to the pool on the top deck to nurse their sunburns with a bottle of champagne.

"My God," Lev said, looking at some of the young couples cuddled up around the boat. "This yacht is starting to look like the Love Boat. I think now would be a good time to go up to the operations center."

"Operations center?" Leo quizzed. "I must have missed that on the tour."

"We wanted you to sleep this morning and felt that if we took you into the ops center, you'd be awake the rest of the day. Come on. We have something to show you." The three men slid out of their deck chairs and climbed the exterior stairs to the bridge.

Daniel and Sarah had left the table together after dinner. They made their way up to the railing in front of the bridge and stopped to look skyward at the stars. Along with all his other talents, Daniel was also an amateur astronomer and had taken to giving Sarah a verbal tour of the cosmos. She gently touched his arm as she pointed to a distant star and asked him its name. They stared into each other's eyes for just a moment before a dawning awareness of the three men standing behind them interrupted the spell.

"There must be something in the water," Moshe said as he threw his head in their direction. Leo and Lev stifled their laughter before they entered an area behind the bridge and descended the small stairway leading to the ops center. Once inside, Leo had to let his eyes adjust to the darkness in the red light of the room. Realizing that Moshe and the others would need his expertise, Daniel reluctantly excused himself from Sarah and headed inside. She turned away to face the sea with the picture of Daniel's face still in her mind before descending to the deck below to join the others.

Inside the communications center, the yacht's executive officer was at his console, scanning cell phone and satellite transmissions on shore with the help of a large mainframe computer capable of breaking encrypted codes. In front of a bank of computer screens, Daniel resumed a project he had been working on before supper. He had been absorbed with searching for encoded messages in the Bible all day, and his brief respite with Sarah was the only free time he had allowed himself.

Moshe stood next to the female communications officer and studied the lighted image of the Italian coast. He looked at Leo and noticed the puzzled look on his face as he listened to all the radio chatter. "We're trying to pick up any cell phone or radio traffic about the yacht's arrival in the area," Moshe explained. "If it looks like we're going to have a reception committee, then we'll have to alter our plans."

Lev had been uncharacteristically quiet since they entered the operations center. "Daniel found something encrypted in the Bible this morning that you might find interesting, Father."

Was this going to be *good interesting* or *bad interesting*, Leo wondered. "Let's have a look."

Lev ran his hands through his hair and looked over the row of computer screens. "Can you bring it up on the main screen again, Daniel?"

The multicolored screen came alive with green letters forming a matrix. Circled in red were the words, *Leopold Amodeo* and *John Lowe*. The names were crossed by encoded script that read *they will journey with the book to Rome*. Then, at the bottom of the page, the most chilling words of all … *the Antichrist will read from it.*

The Antichrist? Leo felt the bile rise in his throat. "What do you think that means?"

Daniel turned in his seat and faced him. "The first part apparently confirms what we already knew. You and John must be the ones who will take the book to the chapel. However, the reference to the Antichrist took us by surprise. This is the first time we've ever seen his name encoded anywhere in the Bible. Of course he's mentioned openly in Revelation … in the New Testament, but we've never seen it encoded before … except …"

"Except what, Daniel?" Leo asked.

"Except in the section of the Devil's Bible we deciphered."

Leo stared at the words on the screen. "That would make sense in Satan's book, but this was found in God's Bible. This is an enigma if I ever saw one." *The Antichrist will read from it.* "What is the code trying to tell us?"

"It's a mystery to us too," Lev said. "This is the message I knew would keep you awake all day if you saw it. For now, all we can do is keep searching through the Bible and pray we can find something else that will help clarify that statement."

A primeval fear was rising within the Jesuit warrior. Was it possible that the Antichrist was alive and now living in the world of men? The forces at work against them seemed to be multiplying by the hour. As disturbing as this last revelation was, Leo had to force himself to put this latest puzzle aside and concentrate on the mission at hand. "Can you all show me how you develop one of your scenarios?"

"Sure, Father," Lev said. "Moshe, punch up the one we discussed before dinner."

The large screen before them changed to display all of the towns and roads between the harbor at Maratea and Rome.

"As you can see, there are several main roads leading from this harbor toward Rome. This will work nicely in our plan because it allows us to pick and choose the best routes and vehicles for the trip to the city. Then we look at all the possible ways someone could spot you or ambush you on the road. We try to put ourselves in the other guy's head. A plan of action is developed for every conceivable threat, and an offensive and defensive scenario develops from all the pieces. Moshe has just finished running an especially intriguing scenario that I think holds the best chance of success against a force that, for all practical purposes, we know nothing about. If you don't mind, we'd like to work on it some more and eliminate some of the bugs before we present the final version to you at the 5:00 AM briefing."

"That's fine by me, Lev. I'm just a simple priest, and the closest I've been to an operation like this is watching a program about military planning on the History Channel."

"You're much more than a simple priest, Leo. This is a spiritual mission run like a military campaign, and you're the ultimate general. You have to realize that you could be the hope of the world, and there are dark forces out there that are well aware of your presence and what you're doing. We can only assist you in the earthly fights, but you're the one who must defeat the invisible ones that will come at you and John."

The yacht rolled slightly, giving Leo an excuse to grab the edge of the console to steady himself. After a few awkward seconds of not knowing what to say next, he excused himself and walked out into the hallway and down to the main deck. He made his way forward to the bow and stopped to gaze out across the dark water at the lights along the coast.

Being at sea must be a lot like being in outer space, he thought. Everyone onboard is separated from terra firma on a self-contained vessel cast upon a great void, traveling from one point of land to another, unable to survive outside the warm enclosure of their ship in the middle of an unyielding sea. The crew onboard could safely venture out of their craft in port, but at sea, the boat was their whole world.

Leo imagined that, if only they could just keep on sailing right by the coast and never touch land, maybe the book would remain out of the hands of those who would use it to work their evil against the world, a world that was already so saturated with hate that all it needed was the strike of a cosmic match against the fuel of intolerance that had formed like a puddle of gasoline across the globe.

Father Leo stood at the railing. He felt the salt spray in his face and the cooling breeze blow through his hair. The wind ballooned his half-buttoned shirt away from his chest as he closed his eyes and wondered how a small, insignificant priest could possibly accomplish anything against such odds.

CHAPTER 36

The Carmela was still miles from the harbor as dawn approached. It was 4:00 AM, and the night crew had awakened everyone onboard. This was, after all, not a luxury cruise, although it had seemed like one at times. Lev and his staff had done everything in their power to make life a little easier for those who would soon be going ashore in the final dash to Rome. They would all be facing a terrifying enemy as they made their way to the city—and some might not return.

The chefs had set up a breakfast buffet in the main salon for the large group who filtered in and gathered on sofas and chairs with plates of food on their laps and steaming cups of coffee in their hands. A large screen in the front of the room came alive with images from Daniel's computer as he readied the presentation. Alon stood against the back wall and dimmed the lights so that Moshe could go over the scenario he had been working on almost all night long. The old former general had fallen into bed and slept for only two hours before his 4:00 AM wakeup call.

Moshe stood and walked over next to the screen. He was barefoot, wearing baggy white shorts and an orange fly-fishing shirt. His eyes were bloodshot from lack of sleep as he twirled the ends of his immense handlebar moustache and scanned the room for any sign of a reluctant participant. Everyone had to perform their part seamlessly or the plan would collapse.

"This will be what we in the military call a multipronged assault," Moshe began, pointing at the screen. "What this means to a civilian is that many of you will be going in different directions at different times in different vehicles.

Our goal here is to create as much confusion as possible for anyone who might be watching us or trying to intercept the Devil's Bible before Leo and John can deliver it to the Vatican. In order to do this, we will be sending several of you out in groups of two, all heading for Rome. One couple will be racing up the coast in one of the Carmela's speedboats to the harbor at Fiumicino on the outskirts of Rome, while the others will be in different cars on separate highways heading toward the city. All of you will be carrying a backpack identical to John's when you leave this boat so that anyone who might be watching won't know which one of us has the book. It's a version of the old shell game."

The group began to experience a hybrid mixture of emotions, a subtle crossover between fear and excitement. Those gathered together in the salon looked at one another in anticipation as Moshe finished his part of the briefing and handed off to Lev.

Wearing his usual khaki shorts and white shirt with the top two buttons undone, Lev rose from his seat and stood barefoot in front of the group. He took a sip from his coffee and paused to clear his throat. "The real Devil's Bible will, of course, be with John and Leo. They will be departing in the helicopter with Nava before dawn while we are still at sea. The rest of you will leave the boat after we dock and head out from the harbor in rental cars as a diversion. The helicopter will drop Leo and John off in the countryside on the outskirts of Portenza, this village here." Lev pointed to a map on the screen with a red laser pointer.

"The helicopter will then return to the yacht while Leo and John walk into town and catch the morning train to Rome. Moshe and Alon will drive one of the rental cars to the same village and stand by outside the train station as a backup until Leo and John catch their train. If there are no problems, they will return to the Carmela, where they will board the helicopter and fly to the airport outside Rome with Nava. Moshe and Alon will then take a rented van and drive from the airport to the train station where they will meet Leo and John."

"Why not just fly Leo and John right to the Vatican?" Ariella asked. The others all shook their heads in agreement and waited for an explanation.

Moshe moved in next to Lev and continued. "This plan requires diversion and confusion in order for it to work. These people are smart, and they probably know we're in the area. We will be launching the helicopter right before we enter the harbor when the sun is just starting to rise. All of the lights will be turned off to make it look like we are being secretive about it. If they're watching, they will naturally assume that the helicopter is en route to the Vatican and tell their people watching the highways and train stations to head for Rome. This will provide a window of opportunity for Leo and John to board their train unobserved. Then, after all the cars race away and the helicopter returns to the yacht, they'll be totally confused."

"Wow," John said. "You guys think of everything."

"Military scenarios are like a big chess game," Moshe continued. "Every move requires a counter move, and you must be constantly at least five steps ahead of your opponent. Lev and Ariella will remain aboard the Carmela in the operations center to coordinate communications and send help if needed. After we know that Leo and John are safely on the train en route to the city, the yacht will leave the harbor at Maratea and head north to Rome. That will create yet another distraction to anyone watching."

A young voice spoke up from the back of the room. "Will we be using our cell phones?"

"No cell phones," Lev said. "Your backpacks will contain secure radios and satellite phones to contact the yacht and stay in touch with each other. It's important that all of you stay in communication with the yacht as you drive to Rome using different highways. Even though we have ways to track you, we need to have voice communication with you at all times until you meet up with the yacht when she docks at Fiumicino Harbor, about thirty miles west of the city."

Lev took another sip of coffee and scanned the room. "Are there any more questions?"

No one spoke.

"Ok, then, let's get going."

Everyone filed outside to finish their coffee and watch the horizon for the coming of the sun. In the early morning darkness, they could hear the sound of the helicopter's engines come to life up on the top deck.

John approached Ariella and stood in front of her with his backpack slung over his shoulder. She bit her lip, trying to avoid the tears she knew were close. John saw through the ruse and held her tightly. "Don't worry. I always feel safe when Leo's around for some reason. I think it's safe to say we have God on our side."

She nodded her head and put on a brave smile as she had done in the past when she bid farewell to others who were leaving on missions to defend those they loved. Kissing her gently on the cheek, John turned away and climbed the exterior stairs to the helipad.

John saw that Leo was already strapped in and climbed onboard with his evil burden. All lights had been extinguished throughout the boat, and Nava had intentionally left the flashing red strobes of the helicopter turned off.

The yacht was now nothing more than a black hole in the sea as the rotor blades spun faster and Nava pulled back on the controls, slowly lifting up and away from the Carmela as the yacht passed beneath them in the darkness below. As soon as the chopper had departed, the captain ordered all the lights switched back on. The Carmela's outline was now illuminated as she made her turn toward the small harbor situated under tall cliffs that hugged the shore.

On a narrow road that skirted the cliffs above, a small car was parked at a scenic overlook. Two men had been watching the progress of the yacht through binoculars as it moved north along the coast. Earlier, they had seen the lights of the boat suddenly go out, causing them to lose sight of her. Panicking, they scanned the darkness, unable to see anything until their eyes adjusted enough to see the shape of the boat in the dim moonlight. They had watched with curious interest for several minutes until the lights came back on. *Why did they do that? The helicopter was gone!*

They cursed as one of the men dialed a number on his cell phone while the other continued to watch the yacht turn into the channel leading to the harbor. Suddenly, the man observing the yacht shouted and grabbed the shoulder of the man speaking on the cell phone. Looking skyward, he pointed excitedly to the dark, dragonfly-like shape of a helicopter highlighted by the moon as it passed over the coast before disappearing behind the hills.

* * *

A row of rental cars reserved by Moshe through a third party in Italy was lined up along the dock next to the Carmela. By now, the glow of the impending sunrise could be seen over the distant hills as the yacht rocked gently against the lines that secured her to the dock. Activity erupted on the boat as two backpack-toting staff members ran out onto the main deck and clamored over the side down some nylon webbing into one of the yacht's speedboats. The small boat's powerful motor roared to life before it raced away past the breakwater at the harbor entrance and headed north along the coast toward Rome.

At the same time, four other staff members carrying identical backpacks bolted from the main deck and ran down the gangplank onto the dock. They jumped into two small white rental cars and sped away from the harbor in opposite directions. They were followed by four more backpack-toting members of Lev's staff who also raced away in white rental cars. They would be taking roads leading away to the east before turning north toward Rome. Then, Daniel and Sarah and Moshe and Alon, all raced away from the harbor in two different cars, heading in two different directions.

A group of curious locals stood along the dock watching with amused stares as the scene unfolded around them. One of them turned to another and wondered aloud why all those people wanted off that boat in such a hurry. They all laughed before turning their attention back to their work of mending torn fishing nets.

As soon as all the vehicles were away, the helicopter returned and circled to land on the helipad. Nava jumped out and purposely left the chopper's doors open so that anyone watching could see that the helicopter was empty. Now, everyone left onboard the yacht could only wait for Moshe and Alon to call and let them know that Leo and John had made it safely onto the train.

Standing on the cliffs above, the two men watching stood motionless. They were completely dumbfounded by the scene. At least a dozen people had sped away with identical backpacks in identical cars heading in different directions. Then, the helicopter had returned to the yacht with no one onboard except for the pilot. *Had it just been scouting the area?* They had already called Rome and informed their associates that the book was probably on the helicopter. Sweat caused by the adrenalin-fueled response to fear ran down their collars as one of the men opened his cell phone and hit re-dial.

CHAPTER 37

L eo and John were literally hiding in the bushes. Twenty minutes earlier, the helicopter had dropped them off in a darkened field. They watched the traffic on a narrow road leading into the village of Portenza before slinging their backpacks over their shoulders and walking quickly out of the brush onto the edge of the road. Dressed casually in polo shirts and jeans, the two looked like tourists backpacking through the countryside.

"It seems like only yesterday that we were trying to get *out* of Italy," John said, squinting at the sunrise peeking over the surrounding hills. "What time does our train leave?"

"Six forty-five exactly," Leo said. "Italian trains are always on time, so we can't be late. From what I could see when we flew in, the village should be just ahead."

The two picked up their pace, peering inside every vehicle that passed for signs of out-of-place men in suits. John nudged Leo when Moshe and Alon drove by in their rental car without acknowledgement. Keeping a low profile, the two Israelis continued into town and parked a block away from the train station so as not to draw any attention to Leo and John.

Entering the outskirts of the small town, Leo and John made their way through sleepy streets to an Italian train station built in the typical style of the 1930s. The interior was spacious, with high ceilings towering above, supported by square green marble columns. The Italians seemed to love the colors of green and yellow, and this building was no exception. The entire station was done in a green and yellow color scheme, with green and yellow tiles on the floor surrounded by yellow-tiled walls. Even the signs displaying arrival and departure times were yellow.

The only deviation from this theme was the brown wooden ticket window where Leo and John purchased their tickets using cash. Daniel had painstakingly made some false IDs for them, but the agent didn't seem interested and never asked for identification.

Taking a final look around the inside of the station, they passed through a pair of immense two-story wooden doors onto a concrete platform located outside above the rails. Stealing glances at the other passengers lining the platform, they took seats on a bench resting against the station's red brick wall. Both felt the same edginess that had gripped them when they had escaped from Italy the week before. It was 6:35 am, and they could see the bouncing headlight of a train approaching in the distance. If nothing happened in the next ten minutes, they would soon be on their way to Rome.

The dark blue train screeched to a stop, and a few passengers stepped off while an equal number clambered onboard. Leo and John climbed the metal steps into a dingy railway coach that was beginning to show its age. They turned down a narrow, window-lined passageway and walked through the smoke-stained car while peering into separate wood-paneled compartments built to hold six passengers each on facing brown-upholstered bench-type seats.

"Here's one," Leo said. He stepped into a vacant compartment and looked through the oversized window at the now-empty train platform for anyone that seemed suspicious. John eyed the seats and stuffed the backpack onto an overhead shelf before sitting by the door.

A sudden jerking motion signaled movement as the engine began pulling the train away from the station. The aged train slowly increased speed until the scenery was flashing by their windows in a blur of green. Leo was restless and stood, pacing the compartment and poking his head out into the narrow passageway. "I think I'll get some coffee and a paper in the dining car."

"Do you want me to come with you?" John asked.

"No, you'd better wait here with the backpack. You want some coffee?"

"That'd be great," John said. He closed his eyes and leaned back in his seat as Leo exited the compartment.

Leo peered into every compartment as he walked through the connecting passages toward the front of the train. The only other passengers he saw appeared to be the local Italian gentry who seemed surprised when they looked up and saw someone who appeared to be a tourist within their midst. *Not good*, he thought. Anything that made them stand out from the crowd was not to their advantage, and he and John seemed to be the only tourists on this train.

Stepping into a wood-paneled coach from another era, Leo approached a marble-topped counter and ordered a small cup of dark espresso. He grabbed a paper and tried to look casual, sipping his coffee and glancing at the pictures of the devastation in Houston spread across the front page under bold headlines in Italian. A sense of urgency gnawed at his already unsettled stomach.

The priest folded the paper and offered it to an attractive middle-aged woman standing next to him. They made small talk for several minutes before Leo decided that it was probably unwise for him and John to remain separated for too long. He ordered coffee to go for John and tapped his fingers nervously on the counter as he and the woman next to him continued to smile at one another. She turned and leaned forward while laying her hand on his. "It's a long ride into Rome," she said. "Why don't we have another cup of coffee and sit at one of the tables?"

It was obvious to Leo that he had been a little too charming. Forgetting John's coffee in his haste to retreat, he excused himself from the disappointed woman and began making his way toward the back of the train.

Entering one of the tight connecting passageways, Leo stepped right into the path of two well-groomed men wearing suits. Leo froze and tried to think as the train swayed from side to side over the worn tracks. He had looked into every compartment on the way to the dining car, and these men hadn't been in any of them. He held his breath as the two men squeezed past with only barely perceptible nods.

Walking quickly through the next car, Leo looked back over his shoulder at the men who appeared to be continuing on toward the front of the train. The train lurched around a bend just as he reached his compartment, forcing him to grab the edge of the doorway before stumbling inside. It was empty. *No John ... no backpack.* He stepped back and looked up at the compartment number posted on a bronze plaque over the door. It was the same compartment they had been sitting in.

Looking up and down the empty passageway, Leo felt his heart beating in his chest as panic began to settle in. Abandoning the need to maintain a low profile, he raced toward the end of the train, systematically looking into every compartment until he came to the end. *No John.* He turned and retraced his steps, wondering what to do next. He knew that he hadn't passed John when he was returning from the dining car. In his panic, had he missed him somehow when he searched the rear section of the coach? He swirled around just as a thin wooden door opened, almost hitting him in the face. It was John holding the backpack.

"What are you doing?" Leo asked breathlessly. "This is not a good time to disappear on me."

"I had to use the bathroom, Father."

Leo worked to slow his breathing. "Sorry, John ... guess I'm a little jumpy ... but from now on, we stay together. If one of us goes to the bathroom, the other waits outside the door."

"I know, Father. That was a dumb move. I should have waited until you got back. Did you get my coffee?"

"I forgot, but we can't go back to the dining car. I just passed two guys in suits heading in that direction. I could swear that I looked in every compartment on the way there, but I missed those two somehow. Anyway, it's probably nothing, but I think it's safer to stay in our compartment until we reach Rome."

The two returned to their compartment as the long blue train left the fields behind and began hugging steep mountain cliffs. Speeding through a series of tunnels, it turned inland again and passed through the remote and wild regions of Basilicata and neighboring Calabria, two of the poorest regions in Italy. Greek, Roman, and Norman ruins dotted the landscape outside their windows. Calabria still retained its frightening reputation for crime and banditry thanks to the *'ndrangheta*, the violent first cousin to the mafia. Due in part to the Aspromonte and Sila mountain ranges, the rugged landscape they were traveling through had blocked change and left the region much as it had been for the past one hundred years.

The train snaked its way northward back to the coast, where it moved through Naples into the Lazio region of Italy surrounding Rome. Every stop was a cause for concern due to the constant parade of passengers that got on and off the train at every station.

Leo pondered the fact that they had escaped any undue attention on their passage through southern Italy and that so far, no attempt had been made to take the book from them. Leaving the rural countryside behind, they continued on seemingly unobserved, watching the suburbs of Rome come into view outside their windows. Both grew quiet with anticipation, knowing that soon, they would be arriving at the large Termini railway station in the center of the city. Their journey to the ancient chapel was almost at an end.

CHAPTER 38

After making sure Leo and John had caught their train to Rome without incident, Moshe and Alon had returned to the yacht via a dusty rural road through the hilly farmland. They wanted to make sure they weren't being followed before circling back to the harbor.

Once onboard the yacht, they climbed the stairs to the helipad and jumped into the waiting chopper with Nava. In less than a minute, the chopper lifted off and skimmed the waves until they passed over the rugged coastline, staying low and speeding north through twisting valleys on their way to the airport outside of Rome.

All of the teams were now on their separate diversionary paths to the city. They were under orders to enter the city and drive around to see if they were being followed, then speed to the harbor when the Carmela arrived in Fiumicino harbor.

Daniel and Sarah had been the team chosen to drive to Morelli's seventeenth-century house. It was located forty-five miles south of Rome along a narrow, tree-lined road in a valley below the ancient hilltop town of Sermoneta. The immense reddish-colored structure was the size of a small palazzo and was fronted by a circular gravel driveway with a four-hundred-year-old fountain in the center topped by the weathered statue of an angel. The house had been built among the remains of the abandoned medieval village of Ninfa, and the entire area had been converted into lush gardens, where clear streams and waterfalls punctuated the strikingly beautiful grounds surrounded by crumbling ruins.

Sarah's eyes grew wide as the house came into view and they stopped next to the fountain by the entrance. "Oh, my God, Daniel. Look at this place!" "It's really spectacular. Father Morelli had excellent taste." A middle-aged couple came rushing down the front steps.

"*Buon giorno*. Welcome," the man said. "Father Leo called yesterday and told us you were coming. You must be Daniel." He bowed slightly from the waist. "And you must be Sarah."

"*Si. Piacere di conoscerla*," Sarah said.

The man and woman beamed, while Daniel stared at her with his mouth hanging open. "I didn't know you spoke Italian."

"I'm a woman of mystery," Sarah said, laughing. "I just told him that we were pleased to meet them."

The couple grabbed their bags from the trunk and led them up the stone steps through weathered front doors, all the while speaking to Sarah in rapid Italian.

"They act as though we were long lost relatives just returning home from a long trip," Sarah said. "Wouldn't it be fun to live in Italy for awhile someday?"

Daniel just smiled and took Sarah by the hand as they passed through the doorway into a large entrance hall with inlaid terrazzo floors. To their right was an enormous ballroom-sized space with gilded wall coverings and crystal chandeliers. A magnificent curved marble stairway led to the rooms above, while a wide hallway passed through the center of the building to an open country-style kitchen and dining area with red brick floors and sienna-colored walls.

The caretakers insisted on feeding their new guests, and after showing Daniel and Sarah their rooms upstairs, they escorted them back down to the rustic kitchen. Throwing a loaf of freshly baked bread onto a cutting board, the man winked as he told the two how romantic the surrounding gardens were and encouraged them to explore the grounds after lunch.

Covering approximately thirty acres, the estate had a gentrified rural ambiance that included a swimming pool surrounded by marble statues and extensive terraced flower beds. The most striking feature of the house was a twelfth-century medieval stone tower that was constructed five hundred years before the house was added. The tower dominated one end of the structure and could be reached by a long hallway that led from the kitchen.

After they were finished with lunch, the two briefly explored the grounds before Daniel went to work, setting up his laptop computer and communications gear in one of the upstairs bedrooms. With nothing for her to do at the moment, Sarah informed Daniel that she was going off to explore the tower.

An hour passed before Daniel was satisfied that all his equipment was functioning properly. He wandered through the house carrying a large duffle bag and climbed the winding stairs of the tower before opening a wooden trap door into the room at the top. Looking around at the thick stone walls, he spotted Sarah gazing at the grounds below through one of the medieval arrow slits. "Hi. I thought you might be getting lonely up here."

"This place is gorgeous," Sarah said. "Just look at all the flowers."

"It's really beautiful. Makes me wish we were here under different circumstances."

Sarah turned away from the opening and gave him a sympathetic look. They both stared across the room at each other before Daniel opened the bag, exposing an Israeli-made Uzi submachine gun and a shotgun. "Sarah, do you know how to shoot a gun?"

"I used to shoot skeet with my father at his gun club."

"Perfect ... you take the shotgun. I have no idea what dangers Leo thinks we might face out here in this beautiful spot, but we have to be prepared. If any of the others have to make a run for it out of Rome, this is where they will come."

"Do you think anyone else knows about this place?"

"It's possible. Morelli entertained a lot of people from the Vatican here, so this house is probably common knowledge to the security men there. The question is whether or not anyone who might be after the book will correlate this location with any of us."

"You used to be some kind of Israeli commando or something, didn't you?"

"I was in crypto." He saw the puzzled look on her face. "I was a code breaker. I saw some combat on the Lebanese border when we were fighting Hamas, but I was never a commando. You're probably thinking of Alon."

"Oh, the big guy, Nava's boyfriend."

"Yeah, that's him. He can really tell you some stories."

"I'd rather hear yours." She crossed the room and stood close, looking up into his eyes. They reached out and held each other tightly, listening to each other's heartbeats in the stillness of a twelfth-century medieval tower built for defense. It reminded them both that they were locked in a battle with humanity's oldest enemy in a setting eerily appropriate.

Daniel gazed down at Sarah's head nestled on his shoulder. "We need to keep a watch over the grounds and the highway leading here. This tower is as good a spot as any. I can stay up here while you get some rest."

"That's OK. I couldn't sleep now if I wanted to. I'll take the first watch."

They held each other for a while longer before Daniel kissed her lightly on the cheek. "There's also a walkie-talkie in that bag. Use it if you need me in a hurry." With that, Daniel disappeared through the trap door and descended the tower stairs. Sarah picked up the shotgun and made sure the safety was on before returning to her lookout spot at the slit in the ancient tower wall. The contrasting beauty of the gardens below made danger seem very far away.

CHAPTER 39

The air traffic control tower at Leonardo da Vinci Airport was keeping Nava's helicopter in a holding pattern while a United 747 passed by on final descent for a landing. Next in line, she navigated the small chopper carrying Moshe and Alon to an area designated for private aircraft. Now they would wait.

In the harbor at Maratea, the yacht shuddered as the engines came to life. The Carmela slowly eased away from the dock and passed through the entrance of the harbor, picking up speed as she made her way north along the coast in a part of the Mediterranean known as the Tyrrhenian Sea. They were now destined for Fiumicino, homeport to some of the finest luxury yachts in the world. Fiumicino was a large fishing town on the central Italian coast known for its great seafood restaurants, but more importantly, it was also home to Rome's main harbor and the busy Leonardo da Vinci Airport. This strategic location would make the port an excellent choice for their new temporary base of operations.

Shortly after noon, the yacht entered one of the most exclusive marinas in the world and was being secured alongside the dock next to the speedboat that had arrived hours earlier. Listening to the radio chatter from the teams in rental cars now heading for the harbor, Lev and Alex drank coffee and gazed out at all the other boats through the windows of the bridge. They knew that, even if the yacht had not been spotted yet, there was no longer any need for secrecy as far as the boat's location was concerned since the Devil's Bible was no longer onboard. All the pieces were in place, and it was now up to Leo and John to deliver the book to the chapel under the Vatican. Only the specter of the unseen forces that surrounded them stood in their way.

At the airport, it was time to go. Nava fired up the chopper, while Alon and Moshe piled into a rented minivan and headed for the train station in the center of the city. If traffic wasn't too heavy, they would arrive at precisely the same time as Leo and John's train from the south.

Back on the Carmella, Ariella leaned against the railing on the main deck and watched a tiny blue speck in the sky grow larger until the shape of the yacht's helicopter loomed overhead before touching down on the top deck. Nava jumped out and waved to her before Ariella turned her attention back to the dock.

Inside the bridge, Lev sat idly watching a crewmember wash the salt spray from the windows when he noticed a bright red Ferrari speeding along the dock. It slowed and pulled to a stop next to the yacht. One of the Carmela's crewmembers, who had supposedly gone ashore to buy supplies, jumped out of the driver's seat and ran up the gangplank to the yacht's main deck. Without a word, the crewman tossed the Ferrari's keys to Ariella and stood aside while she bounded down the ramp with her backpack and jumped into the car.

Lev jumped to his feet and ran out onto the upper deck, followed by Alex. "Ariella! Where are you going?"

She paused long enough to toss her head out the window and throw him a kiss before roaring off alone toward the city.

"Damn that girl. She's more headstrong than her mother, God rest her soul. What can she possibly be thinking? Where is she going?"

"You know where she's going," Alex said.

Lev hung his head and walked slowly back into the bridge. Yes, he knew where she was going.

CHAPTER 40

Focused beams of particle-filled sunlight passed through windows set high above, casting shadows onto the polished marble floor from the statues that lined the hallway in this section of the Vatican. Cardinal Marcus Lundahl was walking quickly, his black and scarlet cassock flowing behind him over the cool, smooth surface of the wide corridor. His assistant followed behind, almost running to keep pace with Lundahl's long strides.

Arriving in front of a single elevator, the two stepped inside and faced the closing mirror-like doors. Twenty feet away, two Vatican security men dressed in black suits were running toward the elevator and waving for them to wait. Instinctively, Emilio reached his hand out to prevent the sliding doors from closing. Lundahl swatted the priest's hand aside, never taking his gaze away from the approaching men as the doors came together before the suits arrived. Inside, Emilio cast a sideways glare at the cardinal as the two descended into the bowels of the Vatican in silence.

The elevator stopped at the very bottom level, where the cardinal exited into yet another long hallway that led off to his right. Emilio followed along behind until they reached the thick glass entrance of the security complex, the Vatican's equivalent of a police command center.

Opening the door, an older man with a short-cropped military-style haircut stood aside for the cardinal. He was the same man Leo had seen with the cardinal the day Morelli died. The man's name was Francois Leander. Swiss by birth, he was also the chief of security for the Vatican. "Good morning, Cardinal."

Francois glanced down the long hallway behind the cardinal and saw the two men in suits bolt from a stairway and begin running toward them.

"We've had a serious security breach, Francois," Lundahl said. He turned and watched the men running in their direction. "I want you to seal this facility immediately. Let no one in or out."

"Yes, sir. Right away."

Lundahl then shifted his gaze to his assistant. "Emilio, you can go now. I don't think I'll be needing you anymore today."

"But ... Your Excellency, I ..."

Francois opened the center's bulletproof glass door and gestured toward the hallway. Emilio looked pleadingly into the eyes of the cardinal. "We have a full schedule today, Eminence, and—"

"Thank you, Emilio, but we don't have time to argue." The security chief now had his hand on Emilio's chest and literally pushed the priest back through the doorway. He slammed the heavy glass door shut just as the two security men reached the enclosure. The look on Emilio's face changed from quizzical to pure fury. The men in suits banged on the door and shouted, demanding to be admitted. Their features were contorted in rage, knowing their shouts could not be heard behind the thick glass.

Francois smiled at the cardinal before they turned their backs on the scene outside and headed for the communications section of the complex. "I don't know why you kept that disgusting little spy of a man around you for as long as you did, Cardinal."

The cardinal stopped and put his hand on the chief's shoulder. "I've always believed in the old saying; *keep your friends close and your enemies closer.*"

The entire staff stood when the cardinal entered and looked around the room. He made the sign of the cross and walked through the complex, stopping to shake each man's hand in turn. Lundahl then took a seat in front of a console before flipping a switch that illuminated a large screen in the front of the room. The picture from a solitary hidden security camera immediately came into focus. Before them on the screen was the image of the pink-stoned wall of the hidden chapel in the catacombs below.

Drumming his fingers on the console in anticipation, he turned and looked at the man sitting beside him. Father Anthony Morelli smiled back at him. "Soon, Your Excellency, very soon."

CHAPTER 41

L eo was sweating. The Roman spring was turning into the hot Roman summer as the temperature soared past ninety degrees. Locals kept saying they
had never seen it so hot this early in the year. The foyer of Rome's main train
station was packed. Volumes of humanity flowed in and out of the *Stazione
Termini* as Leo and John made their way out into the *Piazza del Cinquecento*.
Looking like tourists, they were immediately surrounded by unofficial tour
guides, taxi drivers, flea-bag hotel representatives, and various other unsavory
characters trying to separate them from their money as quickly as possible.

Leo's imposing figure, along with his knowledge of fluent Italian street
slang, soon dissipated this crowd when they realized they were not dealing
with a tourist.

Looking around, there was no sign of Moshe and Alon. Leo had hoped
they would be waiting for them when they arrived. Knowing Rome like he
did, he realized that it was unwise to linger in the area next to this station any
longer than necessary.

"Give me the backpack, John."

"Don't worry, Father. I've managed to bring it this far, and it's not getting
away from me now."

"Do you see that man over there looking our way?" Leo pointed to a huge
Italian man in the center of a group of tough-looking men across the street.
"This station is home to some of the best pickpockets and thieves in the world.
Alon would have a hard time keeping that backpack if that guy over there
wanted it."

John followed Leo's gaze to the man who was now looking right at him. He thought for a moment before slowly handing Leo the backpack containing the book while Leo handed him the decoy backpack. The large man had obviously come to some conclusion and was now walking in their direction. He was within twenty feet of Leo when a white minivan skidded to a stop between them. Alon slid the side door open and jumped from the van, allowing the large man approaching to see the nine-millimeter pistol stuck in his waistband. Game over. The large man's eyes widened as he backed away into the safety of his group and began to once again scan the environment, like a predator on the African savannah looking for new, less dangerous prey.

Moshe gunned the minivan's engine and lurched away from the curb into the rush of late-afternoon Roman traffic at the height of tourist season. "Where to now, Father?"

"The Hotel Amalfi. It's where I always stay and it's right across the street from the Vatican. The owner is a friend of mine and he's expecting us."

Moshe used the van's horn as he wound his way through traffic. "Do you think that's wise, Father? I mean, if this is a place where you are known to stay, the phone might be tapped. They could even be watching it."

"I e-mailed the owner. Besides, they probably don't think I would be bold enough to come back to my regular hotel. It's probably the safest place in Rome for us to be right now."

The van weaved its way down the *Via Crescenzio* past the *Castel Sant'Angelo*, the same enormous castle where they had climbed out of the catacombs with Morelli into a basement storeroom. Leo glanced up at the summit of the massive round building and fixed his gaze on the colossal bronze statue of Michael the Archangel with unfolded wings, sheathing his sword with his right hand. Created by the eighteenth-century Flemish sculptor, Peter Anton von Verschaffelt, the statue seemed to speak to Leo, telling him everything would be alright. The priest said a silent prayer as they passed below, praying to the powerful angel to protect them one more time.

They rounded a corner and came to a stop several doors down from the hotel. The men checked the area in an effort to spot anyone looking at them with more than a casual interest. The street was especially quiet for this time of day, but anyone could be the one who might be watching to see if they showed up:

the single man in a suit casually strolling by, the old lady with a shopping bag, the young girl with a dog. Security people knew all the tricks.

Moshe opened the driver's door and stepped out into the street. Alon placed his hand on the gun in his waistband as they sat in the van and waited for something to happen. The young girl with the dog crossed the street while the old lady with the shopping bag disappeared around the corner. The man in the suit slowed his walk as he passed by the van and said hello, smiling to no one in particular before continuing on his way.

It was time to go. The men grabbed their backpacks and exited the van. They stood together on the deserted sidewalk, and after another quick look around, they headed straight toward the hotel and bounded up the steps and through the welcoming Victorian doors.

Arnolfo practically leapt from behind the desk and grabbed Father Leo in a warm bear hug. "Thank God you made it safely, Father. I've been sick with worry since I got your e-mail. I've been keeping a close watch around the hotel for suspicious persons like you asked me. Did you see the girl with the dog?"

"I knew it," John said. "She's the one I figured they would use. It was so obvious."

"She's my daughter," Arnolfo said, trying to keep from laughing and embarrassing John any further. He looked at Leo. "Didn't you recognize her, Father?"

"It's been years since I saw her last, Arnolfo. She's much older now."

"I know, *Santa Maria*, tell me about it. She's been watching the street for you. Please, come with me into the kitchen in back so we can have some private talk."

"Good idea, sir," Alon said, glancing back at the front doors.

They were just crossing the lobby heading for the back of the hotel, when the sound of screeching brakes on the street outside literally made the men jump. Alon drew his weapon and stood before the group while Arnolfo grabbed a baseball bat from behind the reception desk and stood beside Leo.

One of the front doors swung open and Ariella stuck her head in. "Hi, guys."

Alon lowered his gun as the others let loose a collective hiss of the air they had been holding in their lungs for too long.

"Breathe, everyone. It's just me."

John rushed around Alon and grabbed her in his arms. "What are you doing here? How did you …?"

"The communications people on the yacht have a GPS fix on you at all times. I just asked them where you were, and bingo, here I am."

"A GPS fix? I don't have a—"

"The sensors are embedded in your clothing."

"Nice. Remind me to never lie to you about where I'm going."

"Just remember never to lie to me." Ariella laughed and looked around the room. "Are you guys really getting ready to play baseball?"

Arnolfo adopted a sheepish grin and put the baseball bat back behind the counter.

Leo and Moshe exchanged glances. They felt uncomfortable with the sudden turn of events, but both knew Ariella had a right to be there. She was, after all, one of the chosen and had braved the terrors in the desert, proving herself to be a strong and willing equal to any of the men.

"We need to get going," Moshe said.

Arnolfo led the way down the narrow back hallway to a small family-sized kitchen. The hotel lacked a restaurant and provided only drinks or late-night sandwiches for the guests. Arnolfo poured some wine while the group gathered around the heavy wooden kitchen table and began discussing their plans for entering the catacombs below the Vatican.

Leo looked around the table. "Does anyone have any idea where we can enter the area where the chapel's located? We can't just walk through the Vatican, and I don't want to go all the way back to the entrance under Mamertine Prison in the Forum."

John had one arm draped around Ariella's chair. "How about that tunnel we used the last time? The one under the *Castel Sant'Angelo*. We could go back down through that manhole the same way we came out."

Leo thought for a moment. They had almost been discovered by security men when they climbed up into the castle's basement storeroom with Morelli. He weighed their options, wondering if there was a way in without being seen or stopped by security.

"How about *my* basement?" Arnolfo asked. His face was a mask of innocence and simplicity.

Leo shot him a glance. "*Your* basement? Do you mean that wine cellar down below?"

"Yes, Father, that's it."

"Thank you, Arnolfo, but the area we need to get into is much deeper than that."

"There is a tunnel below, Father. My grandfather covered it up because he was afraid the children would find it and get lost down in the catacombs. Also, the smell is not so good."

The others sat up and pulled away from the kitchen table as if it had suddenly become electrified. Leo stood and began pacing, staring at the floor and running his fingers over his chin. "Let's go look at it."

Arnolfo led the way through a plain wooden door in the kitchen down a tight, winding stairway. He pointed to the narrow steps beneath their feet. "Careful, Father. These steps were carved two thousand years ago by the Romans. I think they had smaller feet than us."

They continued down until they were standing in a chamber hollowed out of solid rock and filled to the curved ceiling with hundreds of bottles of wine.

"I remember you telling me about this wine cellar, Arnolfo," Leo said. "I had no idea."

"Some of this wine has been here since before we were born, Father."

"Where's the entrance to the tunnel you told us about?" John asked.

Arnolfo looked down at the floor. "You're standing on it."

The group studied the two-inch thick stone blocks that covered the floor as Arnolfo grabbed a shovel from a dusty corner. Placing the edge of the shovel blade between two large rectangular stones, he pried the edge a few inches high while Alon and Moshe lifted it up and shoved it aside. After lifting several more stones, they revealed the hard-packed dirt beneath. Arnolfo began digging, and within minutes, he had struck the wooden cover his grandfather had placed there over fifty years earlier. He gingerly pried the rotting wood up, and immediately, the room filled with the dank smell of the ancient tunnels beneath.

John turned his nose up at the smell. "I love the smell of catacombs in the morning."

"It's late afternoon," Arnolfo said, not getting the joke.

Leo looked around at the others before glancing at Arnolfo and pulling Moshe aside. "I think it would be better if you stayed here with Arnolfo and guarded this entrance."

"What?" Moshe looked offended. "Lev gave me strict orders to stay with you."

"We have Alon, and besides, I'm not entirely helpless. I don't want to leave Arnolfo and his family here without someone like you to watch over them. If the Vatican security men come to the hotel, you're the only one who can keep this entrance safe if we need to make a hasty retreat."

"I see what you mean, Father. No one will follow you down that hole."

Everyone gathered around and peered down into the dank opening. Air began to rush in and out from the tunnel below, as if they had uncovered the hidden lair of a sleeping prehistoric animal that was breathing deeply in its nest.

Arnolfo pulled a wooden ladder away from the wall and lowered it through the narrow entrance while Alon pulled a headlamp from his backpack and was the first to descend to the tunnel floor below. One by one, the others disappeared through the hole until only Arnolfo and Moshe remained in the wine cellar above. Arnolfo called out to Leo as he descended the ladder. "Do you want me to come with you, Father?"

Leo poked his head back up through the opening. "No, my friend. We need you to stay here with Moshe and help keep a watch over this entrance and the street outside the hotel."

Moshe held up his walkie-talkie. "I'll lock the door at the top of the stairs and call you if there's any trouble."

Leo reached the floor of the tunnel and switched on his light. The illuminated group was looking around and trying to decide which way to go when, without warning from above, the figure of a man descended the ladder behind them. It was Lev.

Ariella ran to him and stretched her arms around his neck. "Father! What are you doing here? I thought you were going to stay with the boat."

"I could say the same thing about you. I had an overpowering need to be here with the rest of you. We all started out together in the desert, and we should all be together for this."

A feeling that something wasn't quite right had been nagging at Leo all day, and now, with Lev's arrival, he realized what had been bothering him. "I don't know what we were thinking. All of us who descended into the cavern under the desert and retrieved the book should be here now. We're all a critical part of the plan."

Lev switched on his headlamp. "I know. We almost made a terrible mistake. I started thinking about the section of the code that said *we* would give it to God. That could only mean that the same chosen ones who discovered the Devil's Bible in the desert are supposed to deliver it to the chapel under the Vatican. Once more, God is whispering to us and saying that we must follow his plan. It fills me with terror to think of what else we might have missed."

Lev's last sentence got everyone's attention. They all made a mental checklist of anything they might have forgotten. Alon was the first to break the spell of self-doubt that had the team frozen in place. "Well, we're all here now, so let's go."

Everyone grabbed their backpacks and let the beams from their lights guide them through the tunnel into the maze of the catacombs.

Alon looked back over his shoulder from his place in the lead. "Are we headed in the right direction, Father?"

"We'll soon find out." Leo could surmise from dead reckoning that the tunnel they were in now ran in the general direction of Vatican City, but they were in uncharted territory, and since only he and John had been to the chapel before, he wanted John's opinion.

"What do you think, John?"

"This tunnel is probably very close to the one we used before, Father. We passed a lot of intersecting tunnels before we ended up in the area beneath the Basilica where we discovered the ancient chapel. This has to be one of them."

The shaft of light from Arnolfo's wine cellar receded in the distance as they pressed on to what would most probably be another confrontation with a force they still knew very little about. No one had to say it, but they all knew in their hearts and minds that their final battle with evil lay ahead in the darkness beyond.

CHAPTER 42

A lon continued leading from the front. His head was on a swivel, peering ahead and then behind as they made their way toward the jumble of
chambers and tunnels. The memory of the last time they had been in a tunnel
was still fresh in his mind. "Did you bring your holy water, Father?"

"I've got plenty. How's everyone doing?"

"We're fine. This can't be any worse than the last time," Ariella said,
instantly regretting her words. Already, the dank smell of the catacombs, along
with the lack of fresh air, was beginning to make them all a little lightheaded.
Everyone dreaded another encounter with the demons, and for some reason,
the fear they felt here was even stronger than that they had experienced in the
desert.

Arriving at the end of the tunnel where it dead-ended into a larger tunnel,
John pointed excitedly to the wall straight ahead. "Look, Father."

Morelli's yellow chalk mark was on the wall of the intersecting tunnel in
front of them, pointing to the right. They turned in the direction of the arrow,
picking up the pace with the anticipation of getting to their destination as
quickly as possible.

The group shined their lights down every tunnel they crossed in an effort
to mark their progress. They were in a gigantic ancient maze, and even though
a tunnel might look familiar, they could easily get turned around and start
heading in the opposite direction.

Leo was behind Alon when they rounded a corner and entered a large
space where the ceiling rose almost twenty feet. Leo stopped for a moment to

get his bearings and called out to the others. "I think we're under the Basilica. The tunnel to the chapel is a little farther ahead."

Alon was preparing to call Moshe on his radio when a bright light suddenly filled the space.

"Vatican security! Halt!"

The five shielded their eyes from the light as several uniformed and plain clothes Vatican security officers flooded out of side tunnels and surrounded them.

A short middle-aged priest with heavy eyebrows stepped forward accompanied by a young dark-haired officer with cold gray eyes. "May I ask what you are all doing down here? This area is off-limits—and you are all trespassing."

Leo immediately recognized Emilio. He thought hard, dozens of explanations running through his mind. Why hadn't he prepared for something like this? He uttered the first words that came to mind. "We were touring the catacombs and got turned around. These are some of my friends, Emilio."

The diminutive priest stared at Leo with contempt. "What a coincidence that you got lost right under the Basilica, Father. I think we both know why you're down here. Unfortunately this is now a matter for the police. You are under arrest. Please come with us."

Leo shot Alon a glance and faced Emilio. "Since when do priests arrest people?"

"I'm not arresting you, Father; they are." He pointed to the group of stone-faced security men surrounding them.

Alon had been given strict orders from Lev to protect Leo and the book at all costs. He moved next to Leo and felt for the nine-millimeter pistol under his shirt. Lev looked him straight in the eye and the unsaid message was immediately understood. Alon slowly moved his hand away from the hidden gun.

Several of the security men began removing handcuffs from their belts while advancing toward Leo and the others. Alon counted six of them, two holding automatic weapons pointed right at them. John and Ariella stepped back as Alon shielded Leo and gave Emilio a look that would wither most men. Sensing danger, Emilio put his hand up in front of the advancing security men. "I don't think those handcuffs will be necessary. I hope you will all have the good sense to behave yourselves. Please follow us."

Alon was seething at his inability to do anything. Even though he was now a Christian, his Jewish heritage was screaming out to him. Jews had gone with uniformed men without a fight in the past, and he was not about to let history repeat itself. He glared at Emilio. "Where are you taking us? We haven't done anything wrong."

Emilio returned the stare before catching himself and forcing a tight smile in an attempt to project a more fatherly figure. "May I remind you, sir, that you are trespassing on Vatican territory and that we have the right and duty to take you all to our police station. Hopefully, we can straighten this entire situation out in more pleasant surroundings."

The Bible Code Team looked at one another with resignation for the moment. Their thoughts were melded together with the knowledge that they would have to sidestep this situation quickly. The book had to reach the chapel, and without knowing exactly why, they knew it had to be delivered soon.

Leo tried to think. What if they searched the backpack? The security men would be sure to search them when they reached the police station.

Alon was livid. Lev's words ran over and over again in his mind. *Guard the book with your life!* No matter what happened, he would never let these men get their hands on the book. Leo could tell by looking at Alon what was going through his mind. He knew he was powerless to stop him if one of the security men tried to grab the backpack holding the book.

Emilio led the way, heading in the opposite direction away from the Vatican and the hidden chapel. The tunnel widened as they made a sharp right into a small chamber and stopped. Two of the security men in black suits looked at each other nervously and motioned to two other security officers with automatic weapons standing behind Leo and the others.

Ariella moved between Leo and Alon and whispered in their ears. "They're going to kill us."

Without warning, Emilio stepped forward and snatched the backpack from John. At the same time, the two security men behind them raised their weapons. It was the last act of their lives. Two bullet holes appeared in their foreheads as Leo turned to see Alon crouched in a classic handgun combat position with his nine millimeter extended in front of him, smoke rising from the barrel. Alon swirled around just as two other security men pulled their weapons, but it was Lev who fired this time, dropping both killers to the ground.

Emilio never looked back. Followed by the remaining panicked security men, he ran for his life down a side tunnel, clutching the backpack and disappearing into the maze under the Vatican.

Alon shouted at them to drop the backpack and took off in pursuit. Leo reached out and grabbed him solidly by the arm. "Stop, Alon. I have the book."

Alon turned to face him, his eyes bulging. "What? I thought John …"

Leo grabbed Alon by the shoulders. It was like stopping a bull that had seen a red flag waved before its eyes. "We switched."

Alon began to focus on the words, his pupils growing smaller as his body slowly began to release itself from combat mode. "You what?"

"We switched. Back at the train station." Leo drew a breath. "I have the book now. They only got a decoy backpack."

Alon turned and looked at John, who was nodding to him with his mouth hanging open. He scanned the chamber around them before returning the warm gun inside his waistband. Their Israeli protector began to take some slow, deep breaths as he had been trained to do following a lethal engagement. It was a method designed to steady his nerves and purge his system of excess adrenalin, allowing him to face the next threat with a clear head.

Lev dropped the clip from his gun and reloaded as easily as if he were reaching for a beer in the refrigerator. Older bulls reacted differently than younger ones after a battle. Lev had been a battle-tested soldier before Alon was even born.

John dropped to one knee, sick to his stomach. The bile rose in his throat as he looked at the dead security men around him. He had never seen death close-up like this before. Ariella knelt beside him and brushed the hair out of his face before gently pulling him back to his feet.

Leo continued to watch the tunnel where Emilio had retreated. "We've got to reverse course and get to the chapel before our friends find out they have the wrong backpack and return with reinforcements."

Alon called Moshe on the radio to alert him to their situation, but the signal was pure static. Either they were too deep for the radio to work, or it was purposely being jammed by someone.

Alon looked at the others. "We're on our own. Let's get moving."

CHAPTER 43

PAKISTAN – THE NORTH-WEST FRONTIER PROVINCE

The giant Russian-made rocket transporter rumbled out of its underground hiding place at the base of the mountains. Behind it was a solitary military truck full of men wearing checkered turbans and carrying automatic rifles and rocket propelled grenades. They followed a rocky path, skirting populated areas while looking skyward and chanting prayers in their native tongue.

A spring thunderstorm had just passed and the skies were beginning to clear, but the men in the small convoy were not worried about satellite surveillance above their position. They had practiced daily and knew that their mission would take only a few minutes. After that, their fate was no longer important.

After plowing over the rough terrain and traveling another mile, the massive, dull-brown vehicle slowed to a predetermined stop. The crew of the transporter waited. They radioed their leader in a nondescript safe-house in the nearby town of Chitral and scanned the horizon as the rag tag group of men in the truck behind them jumped out onto the wet soil. Awaiting final instructions, the men spread out and formed an armed ring around the perimeter of the rocket launcher.

When confirmation finally came, the Taliban commander ordered the crew to activate the hydraulic pads that dropped from beneath the transporter onto the uneven rock-strewn plateau, creating a stable platform for launching.

Simultaneously, the Cold War-era Russian Su-18 intercontinental ballistic missile, code named the Satan, was raised to its full upward position at the rear of the vehicle.

Inside a cramped space behind the driver's compartment, two technicians were activating the targeting computer that would send the rocket on its way. The commander stood outside and scanned the skies. He was looking for signs of a predator drone in the vicinity, but intellectually, he knew that if an unmanned enemy aircraft had already spotted them, they would be dead before they ever saw the missile that attacked them.

Vapor rose into the cloudless blue sky from the side of the rocket as the freezing volatile fuel began to warm and vent to the outside. Predetermined target coordinates were confirmed by the crew, and the computer now took over the countdown. The men had done all they could; the rest remained in the hands of Allah and the gods of technology.

They jumped from the cab of the transporter and ran toward the waiting truck in the distance just as a fiery blast erupted from the nozzles at the base of the rocket. Fire enveloped the truck as the thrust from the engines sent the giant, deadly arrow skyward, leaving a white plume of smoke in its wake.

In a matter of minutes, the spent rocket would reach its apogee and the nuclear warhead would separate, beginning a six-thousand-mile-per-hour descent to its target below. Thousands of years of history, along with some of the most holy sites known to man, were about to be vaporized. The target was Jerusalem.

CHAPTER 44

The Carmela bobbed calmly at her dock in the yacht-encrusted Porto Romano Marina inside Fiumicino Harbor. The citizens of Rome flocked to the beautiful harbor and beaches nearby in the summer for weekend getaways and were unaware of the events occurring over two thousand miles away in the rugged mountains of northern Pakistan. Inside the yacht, the scenario was reversed. Alarms were going off and the crew was in a state of panic. Many seemed unable to move as they stood in front of TV screens scattered around the boat and watched the world situation spiral out of control. Air raid sirens were now blaring in Tel Aviv and Jerusalem as the Israeli military tracked the inbound warhead heading their way.

The United States had been on a virtual lockdown since the nuclear attack on Houston. Widespread hysteria had set in around the country and revenge was in the air. As people around the country feared another attack, rumors swirled inside and outside the government as to who had finally committed the unthinkable act of nuclear terrorism on America. Inside the Oval Office in the West Wing of the White House, the president and his advisors were huddled in a feverish debate about their next course of action.

One more incident like the one in Houston would be the tipping point toward a holocaust of unimaginable proportions aimed at anyone America and Israel believed was responsible. The entire world was now on high alert, and nerves were frayed at the highest levels of every government on earth. Unlike the major powers, terrorists didn't have hotlines with their enemy to allow cooler heads to prevail. They just struck without warning.

On the bridge of the yacht, Alex was frantically trying to raise Lev and the others on their radios in the tunnels under the Vatican. Lev's words before he departed the ship echoed in the ship captain's mind. *We've got to get that demonic book into the chapel soon. The world has been on the verge of a total meltdown since we took it from the desert. We've become soldiers in a war between heaven and hell, and this is one war I don't want to lose, for all of our sakes.* Alex tried once again to raise them on the radio, but only static hissed from the speakers on the bridge. He felt helpless as he pounded his fists on the radio and listened for a response.

Unable to reach Lev, the Carmela's captain walked out on deck and lit a cigarette. He gazed out across the dazzling harbor at all the gorgeous people lying in the sun on the decks of their boats. Eating from picnic baskets and playing with their children, they were totally unaware of the horror that was about to befall the world's holiest city as they enjoyed life to the fullest. *What if Lev and the others don't make it to the chapel?*

* * *

South of the harbor, at Morelli's country estate, Daniel had called the yacht for instructions. He wanted to know what he and Sarah should do in view of the impending attack on Israel. Unable to reach Lev, the communications officer on the yacht had told him to stay where he was. Daniel held the satellite phone in his hand and paced back and forth outside by the fountain in front of the house, wondering why he and Sarah were staked out in a village so far from Rome. Wouldn't he be of more value back on the yacht?

Sarah came down from the tower and called him into the house. The caretaker's wife had already laid out a simple meal for them in the kitchen and placed a bottle of red wine on the table. Daniel uncorked the bottle and filled Sarah's glass halfway to the top before pouring his own. They ate their meal in relative silence, neither one knowing what or who they should be guarding against.

Sarah stood up and walked around the kitchen. "Why don't we just get in the car and drive to the yacht?"

"Because Lev and Father Leo decided that we should remain here for some reason. Believe me, if I knew, I'd tell you."

"But it doesn't make any sense. I'm not complaining, Daniel, it's just that I kinda want to know what we're doing here."

"So do I, but Lev always has a plan, and he's never let me down. He's honest and smart and possesses a psychic ability to know what people need to do and where they need to be. I'd trust him with my life ... so for now, we wait and keep a close eye on that road."

CHAPTER 45

L eo and the others raced toward the chapel under the Basilica through the maze of tunnels. Leo couldn't be certain exactly where he was, but he had retraced their steps as closely as he could remember. Stumbling forward, they came to a Y-junction ahead of them. Right or left? John pointed to the left, and they all took off in that direction. Within minutes, they had arrived at an area both Leo and John recognized. Above them, the wall Emilio had constructed to keep Morelli from entering the catacombs was now open, the broken bricks strewn about. Only darkness lay beyond the gaping hole. If anyone was on the other side, they were hiding in the darkness.

Gradually, as if in a dream, a figure stepped through the opening and stood before them. Leo focused his eyes on the familiar red-headed man wearing a Roman collar.

"Anthony …?" *Father Morelli?* Leo rubbed his eyes and backed away. *Was this some kind of demonic trick?* Everyone present had known Morelli and had been deeply touched by the news of his death, yet all were hesitant to approach him. Morelli descended the pile of rubble and stood in front of a shocked Father Leo.

Leo just stared at Morelli with disbelieving eyes. "This can't be." Leo grabbed his old friend by the shoulders, halfway expecting his hands to pass through a ghost-like vision.

Morelli hung his head in shame. He knew he had purposely lied to his closest friends and feigned death for reasons he had not been able to share with them. "I pray that you can all forgive me … but we had to make everyone believe I was dead so that I could intervene on your behalf while you went to Israel to find the Devil's Bible."

Leo's mind was reeling. "You … you knew about the book!" Leo was caught between the emotions of surprise and anger. "Why the charade? You've been my friend for over thirty years … and suddenly you can't trust me?"

"We were trying to convince others that I was dead and that the search for the book was over while you and John went to Israel. Real grief is hard to fake, and you were being closely watched. Vatican security had just learned that I was the target of an assassination plot by Emilio's men and it was necessary that they believed I had died a natural death. Unfortunately, the attention shifted to you and John when they discovered both of your names in the code and found out you were on your way to Israel."

"They know about the code?"

"A lot of people know about it; it's not a secret. They may even know things we don't."

A look of comprehension was beginning to cross Leo's face. "How long have you known about the Devil's Bible, Anthony?"

"Since Father Bianchi told me about it on his death bed. He told only one other person, and that was the last pope, whose cross you're now wearing under your shirt. That cross was meant to be used by the leader of those chosen to enter the cavern. Bianchi was used by Satan to take the book out of the cavern before he realized what he had unleashed on the world and returned it to its hiding place under the desert. It wasn't until after Lev showed me the Bible code that I knew only the chosen ones would recognize the object in the cavern for what it was and be allowed to take it against Satan's will when the time was right. Only God could lead you to the book through the code. That's why I couldn't tell you about it. No one on the Bible Code Team was allowed to know about the book in advance. Its existence was a closely guarded secret. Even Lev was unaware of what he was looking for. If I had told any of you about the book, and you weren't one of the chosen, all of you would have been killed by the demons while you were trying to remove it."

Leo just stood there. The situation had an unreal quality to it, and he was having a hard time trying to process everything. The tension was finally relieved when John stepped forward and embraced Morelli. "Glad to have you back, Father."

The others still held back, not sure of what would follow next. Slowly, with the realization that his old friend was still very much alive, Leo's suspicion began to fade.

"Do you have it with you?" Morelli asked.

Leo swung the backpack off of his shoulder and opened it up. Morelli peered inside at the object he had known existed—but was forbidden to see. The red book looked innocent enough to him, but he could sense the evil inside.

"Close it up. I don't want to look at it anymore," Morelli said. "We have to reach the chapel before it's too late. Things are happening in the world, and we have to stop them. Follow me."

The group fell in behind him, their senses on high alert for any unfamiliar sound or quick movement. Within minutes, Morelli found the tunnel he was looking for and veered off to the right. After leading them up a slight incline, he stopped next to the pinkish-colored stone that marked the outside wall of the ancient holy chapel.

Leo and John stood next to Morelli in silence. The joy they felt at finally arriving back at this special place pushed aside their fear and exhaustion. The others gathered quietly behind them, no one wanting to say a word. They had finally arrived at their destination. Now what?

John ran his fingers over the rock. "I know where I've seen this stone before. This is the same pinkish stone we saw in buildings all over Israel."

Alon moved to the wall and studied it for a moment. "It's limestone from the Holy Land. Ancient buildings all over Israel are constructed from it. How did it get here under the Vatican?"

"I have no idea," Morelli said. "My best guess at this point is that ancient Christians transported the stone here somehow and used it to construct this chapel with a definite purpose in mind."

Morelli quickly spotted the section of the wall they had sealed back up when they first discovered the chapel. "The stones are just piled on top of each other with mud in between, so the wall should be easy to push in."

Alon put both hands against the wall and shoved. It gave way quickly, the stones falling into the chapel with the muted sound of stone hitting stone. In their excitement and haste to gain entrance to the chapel, the men began knocking more bricks loose with little thought to the structural integrity of the surrounding wall. Suddenly, a loose stone fell from a spot above, striking Morelli on the head and knocking him unconscious.

Everyone stared in disbelief at the limp figure of Father Morelli lying on the tunnel floor, blood running from a small gash on the top of his head. Leo rushed to his side. "Oh, my God. I can't believe it. We've got to get him to a doctor."

Lev grabbed Leo by the arm and lifted him to his feet. "There's no time for that now. Ariella was a field medic in the army. Let her tend to him."

"I'm not letting him die in this tunnel with help only a few stories above us."

"I'm afraid the help above is from God now, Leo. If we don't get that book into the chapel right now the whole world will suffer. Father Morelli is a Jesuit, one of God's soldiers. Soldiers get injured in battle, but the others must keep going. I promise you, Ariella will take good care of him."

Leo was torn but realized that Lev was right. Time was running out, and they had to go forward without Morelli. Leo made the sign of the cross over his friend and said a prayer for his recovery before turning away to face the gaping hole in the wall. Ariella cradled Morelli's head in her lap and held pressure on his wound while the others found themselves shining their lights into the dark, empty space of the ancient chapel. They paused to collect themselves before stepping across the rubble into the large room beyond.

Leo, Alon, and Lev stood silently inside the chapel, while John began frantically looking around.

"Where should we put the book?" John said.

Leo took in the surroundings. He had no idea. He set the backpack down and slowly pulled the Devil's Bible from within. It was still sealed in plastic covered by the outer case filled with holy water. The group formed a circle in the middle of the chapel and stared down at the book. No one had a clue as to what they were supposed to do next.

Alon rested his hand on the radio strapped to his belt, inadvertently pushing the antenna wire farther down until it clicked into place. The radio suddenly came to life as they all heard the strained voice of the yacht's captain calling them. "Lev, Alon, anyone … can you hear me?

Alon keyed his mike. "Yes, Alex, we read you. What's wrong?"

"Oh ... thank God I finally reached you. A missile was just launched a short time ago from Pakistan. It's heading straight for Israel ... probably Jerusalem!"

"Oh, my God," Lev said.

Alex shouted into his radio again. "They think it might have a nuclear warhead."

The team stared at one another in disbelief. *Not again.*

John grabbed Leo by the arm. "I thought bringing the book here would stop these kinds of events from happening in the world."

Leo was lost, all emotion draining from his body. Nothing in the Bible code had told them what to do next. *Would it even matter?* "Lev, do you have any ideas?"

"Give it to God."

"What are you talking about?"

"We have to give it to God ... place it on the altar."

Leo was staggered by the response. *Why hadn't he thought of that himself?* Lev had stated the obvious. Without waiting a second longer, Leo picked up the case holding the book and began walking toward the altar. A rush of hot wind suddenly blew against their faces while, at the same time, the acrid smell of sulfur filled the air. The same reddish glow they had seen in the desert began to radiate around them. They could hear low, guttural growling coming from every side of the room as they jerked their heads around, realizing to their horror that they were surrounded by six black-robed entities advancing on them, their yellow eyes staring out from behind the slits of their black robes.

Leo and the others froze. There wasn't enough holy water in the world to defeat six demons bent on retrieving their master's unholy book. Father Leo began to pray. Their time had run out and they were obviously defeated before they had even begun. Six against four. The odds mattered little to Leo in what he believed were his last moments on earth. He cast a final helpless look at the demons surrounding them. *God, please let death come quickly!*

CHAPTER 46

Above ground in Vatican City, people were gathered shoulder to shoulder in Saint Peter's Square. Many had gathered to pray in the aftermath of the attack on America, sensing the worst was yet to come. Many of the older Italian people seeking comfort in front of the huge church had lived through the horrors of World War II, and they knew how fragile peace was in a world so engulfed by fear, evil, and suspicion. One small flame could ignite a whole forest, and they had lived in the forest before.

The clear blue skies were beginning to be replaced by an army of rapidly moving black clouds flowing over the city like a dark curtain. A hot wind began to blow, while an eerie haze formed in front of the Basilica, causing people to shrink with fear. Dust and paper flew from every crevice and swirled about Vatican City, forcing people to shield their eyes and seek cover.

Without warning, a young girl fell to the pavement and her eyes rolled up in her head. She began to speak with a strange, otherworldly voice in a language those close to her knew was not Italian. Two priests nearby grabbed the girl and began carrying her toward the church.

The people began to shout. "What's happening?" They began to pray ... *Father, deliver us from evil!*

The skies became darker as the wind grew in its ferocity. Solid objects like trash cans and chairs bounced across the pavement as people instinctively began running across the square in the direction of the church. Mothers grabbed small children as whole families ran from their homes toward the Basilica.

They were blinded by the swirling dirt and debris, groping their way forward in the darkness until they reached the steps of the world's largest church.

Together, the multitude stumbled and fell through the gigantic doors while turning to look back over their shoulders at the scene outside. It was now as dark as night, and the wind had a reddish cast to it.

CHAPTER 47

In the chapel below, Leo and the others drew together in a tight circle. *This is impossible*, Leo thought to himself. *This chapel is holy.* God would not allow Satan or his demons to enter this sanctified place. He grabbed a bottle of holy water from his shirt and began dousing the floor around them. "In the name of Jesus Christ our savior, we command you to leave!"

A garbled voice echoed around the room. "We are too many for you, priest. Give us our Bible!"

The others huddled behind Leo as he clutched the book and continued to throw the last of the holy water around them in a circle. They knew their weapons were useless as the temperature in the room began to soar and the choking smell of rotting flesh filled the air. The men began to retch, falling to their knees, facing the altar.

A hollow, cruel-sounding voice suddenly came from behind them. They turned their heads and saw the chilling sight of the demon, Agaliarept, his hideous winged form rising in the reddish smoke that drifted upward in the chapel. Satan's greatest and most malevolent demon was towering above them in the darkness. Hell's general was standing in a holy chapel, unfazed by his surroundings.

The demon flickered, like the image of something moving in the rapid pulse of a strobe light. "Your holy water is no use to you here, priest." The demon lowered his head, his glowing red eyes boring holes through Leo. *Why is this happening?* Leo thought. *Was it possible the chapel had never been sanctified?*

Alon had had enough. He brought the pistol from beneath his shirt and fired at the demon. There was no effect as Alon emptied the gun. "Curse you, you evil thing from hell!"

The demon became furious, rising even higher. Alon was suddenly flung through the air by an invisible force, his body slamming against the wall of the chapel, where he sank to the floor, unconscious. The case filled with holy water enclosing the book shattered in Leo's hands, forcing him to drop the Devil's Bible to the floor. The sound of laughter echoed through the chapel. "Run, priest, run. You're no match for those of us who now inhabit this church. Where is your God now?" The voice changed and mimicked a deep-voiced human chanting a guttural litany in an ancient language that had existed before time.

John inched his way over to Alon's limp form. He tried to lift him up and attempted to shield him with his own body from any further harm. He felt the probing eyes of the demon piercing his very soul and wanted to flee from the chapel but stood his ground between it and Alon.

Darkness was enveloping the men as they began to lose their vision. They were overcome by weakness, the life force slowly ebbing from their bodies.

Lev grabbed Leo by the shoulder. "We've got to get out of here."

Leo looked up, the demon mysteriously appearing and disappearing in their field of vision. "What are you talking about? We have to put the book on the altar."

"We'll never make it. We're all going to die if we stay in here."

Leo staggered to his feet and headed for the book. Lev grabbed him from behind. "You've got to leave, Leo. You're not the one."

"What? But if I'm not—"

The demon suddenly appeared next to Leo. The smell was overpowering. Leo and Lev were forced to back away, unable to stand up against this embodiment of pure evil any longer. They moved back and huddled against the chapel wall by the entrance, averting their eyes from the sight of the demon.

Lev grabbed Leo by the arm and began leading him out of the chapel. John saw what was happening and lifted himself to his feet, staggering toward the book. "I'll do it, Father."

The demon turned on him in a fury. "You're not even a priest. Your soul is mine."

Leo pulled loose from Lev and instinctively lashed out at the demon, trying to physically punch him as hard as he could.

The demon laughed as Leo's body flew through the air, his head hitting the floor. Lev grabbed him under the arms and began dragging him toward the opening in the wall. John wisely began to back away. Because of Leo's intervention, he had temporarily been spared from the demon's wrath. He moved to Alon's side and began to inch him out into the tunnel by himself when he realized that two more pairs of hands were helping him. Morelli had regained consciousness, and he and Ariella were helping John pull Alon to safety.

The heat and wind escalated in the chapel while, outside in the tunnel, Lev laid Leo on the floor beside Alon. Away from the presence of the demons, Alon began to wake up and slowly regain his senses. They knew they were powerless in the battle with the demons, and it was useless to try to return to the chapel in the face of such overwhelming odds.

The terrified group sat huddled together, lost in the haze of battle and thinking of retreat, when they saw the lights of men approaching from out of the darkness of the catacombs. Leo lay on the tunnel floor, drifting between consciousness and the black void enveloping him. He lay there, breathing in and out, his vision cloudy, when he saw the light in the distance ... a golden light in the sign of the cross. With his last ounce of strength, he lifted his head and looked upward at a sight he never expected to see. Striding toward him was the unmistakable image of a tall cardinal, his black and scarlet robes flowing behind him. The large golden pectoral cross hanging from his neck reflected the light from the group's flashlights. It was Cardinal Lundahl.

Several priests and cardinals were following behind him. They stopped and stared in open-mouthed horror through the hole in the chapel wall. The sight within caused them to take several unconscious steps backward.

The black-robed entities flew about inside the chapel, screeching and wailing as the huge demon moved to the front of the altar, growling and forcing everyone except Lundahl to move even farther away from the opening with a strong, evil-smelling wind.

Slowly regaining his strength, Leo was trying to stand. He looked at the cardinal with disbelieving eyes.

Cardinal Lundahl stepped forward and put his left hand on Leo's shoulder while making a sign of the cross with the other. "We're glad you made it back to us, Father."

A strong movement within the chapel shook the ground beneath their feet, and bricks and rocks began to fall from the ceiling above.

Morelli looked up at the cardinal. "We don't have much time, Marcus."

Leo was completely baffled. He looked from Lundahl back to Morelli, not knowing what to believe anymore. "Time for what?"

Morelli looked Leo in the eyes. "Cardinal Lundahl is the one."

"The one for what?" Leo shouted.

"He is the only one mentioned in the code who must face the demon in the chapel. You and the others were only meant to retrieve the book and bring it here. Marcus is the one who must face the evil within that room on the other side of this wall. That bump I got on the head prevented me from telling you that before you all entered the chapel."

"But Lev knew. I remember him telling me in the chapel that I wasn't the one."

"Somehow, he sensed in the midst of the encounter with the demon that you weren't the one chosen to deliver the book," Morelli said.

"He's right, Leo," Lev said. "That's the first time I've ever retreated in battle, but I knew we weren't supposed to be there this time. We needed rein-forcements, and I believe they have arrived."

The ground shook violently again as more bricks fell around them and a series of hideous growls could be heard inside the chapel. The cardinal looked at Morelli and the others with a mixture of sadness and resignation. "I must go now."

"May God be at your side, Marcus," Morelli said.

The solemn chant of men praying in Latin echoed in the tunnel as the priests and cardinals doused Lundahl's clothing from their vials of holy water before he walked to the entrance of the chapel. Without looking back, the cardinal ducked and squeezed his tall frame through the opening in the wall before disappearing into the red mist beyond.

CHAPTER 48

After the cardinal had disappeared into the chapel, the demon could be heard laughing with a hideous cosmic voice that seemed to come from everywhere at once, like an echo connected in a never-ending stream. With the fearlessness of youth, Alon and John wanted to follow, but Lev and the others held them back. Morelli stood beside them and looked through the opening. "He has to do this alone. Whatever you do, don't enter the chapel."

"But why?" Alon asked, his voice trembling and his body shaking. "We're the ones who found that damned book and brought it here. Why does he have to go in there alone? You heard what that thing said; one priest is not enough."

Morelli winced and pulled at his Roman collar. "He's a cardinal, a Prince of the Church and the one God has chosen by name to enter and face the demon. We must not interfere."

They all stood looking through the opening as another series of violent quakes shook the ground and the crumbling ruins of the catacombs around them. A few glanced up at the ceiling above, not knowing how much more shaking the ancient tunnels could withstand before the entire area caved in.

Leo stuck his head into the chapel, momentarily catching a glimpse of the cardinal standing before the demon and speaking to him. The creature's hideous face was now inches from Lundahl's, breathing in and out and filling the air around them with a warm and nauseating stench. *The Devil's breath.* Time seemed to stand still as more rumbling and growling noises could be heard from within. Suddenly, the cardinal cried out.

In the blink of an eye, the room filled with a brilliant light, and the foul smell of the demon was replaced with the aroma of roses. Leo stared unbelievingly at the sight that began to unfold around Lundahl. Seven enormous angels encircled him, bathing the cardinal in their golden light. They were beautiful. Their shining brilliance made it difficult to look at them. Their features were blurred, but Leo could still see their faces and the kindness that flowed from within.

Leo's mind was barely able to absorb what he was seeing. Somehow, he knew that these were no ordinary angels, but archangels, God's most powerful and faithful soldiers. The others gathered around the opening and stared at the astonishing sight before them. The priests and cardinals who had accompanied Lundahl immediately dropped to their knees and began to pray. Leo, Morelli, Lev, John, Ariella, and Alon stood transfixed in front of the opening, unable to speak or move.

The cardinal was now standing with his arms outstretched. The dazzling light emanating from the angels reflected off the cardinal's golden cross as they spoke to him in inaudible tones. Only Morelli seemed to know what they were saying and began to tell the others. "They're identifying themselves one by one to the cardinal and the demon."

Morelli paused for a moment, a smile spreading across his face. "The first and tallest one is the archangel, *Michael*, meaning *he who is like God*. He is God's most faithful angel, and his main function is to rid the earth and its inhabitants of fear." The angel spread his long wings and held his sword high before turning to face the demon, his mere presence forcing Satan's most powerful soldier to recoil in fear, for these two had met in battle before.

Morelli paused again. The otherworldly voices of the archangels that only he seemed to hear had caused his entire facial expression to change. "The next one is *Ariel, the lion or lioness of God*. This archangel is a fierce protector."

Ariel spread her luminescent wings forward around the cardinal and looked sweetly back at Leo and the others. Her presence gave comfort to those watching from outside, especially Ariella, who saw the angel's eyes meet hers for a brief second.

"The third is *Chamuel*," Morelli said, "meaning *he who sees God*, and he is endowed with the power to protect the world from fearful and lower energies like demons." Chamuel advanced on the lesser demons, causing them to shriek in fear and take on a vapor-like appearance. The angels were also communicating with each other and looking over their heads at a vision only they could see.

Morelli looked upward in an effort to see what they were looking at but could see only the stone ceiling. Despite the fact that he had the look of total peace on his face, his whole body was shaking.

"What about the others, Father Anthony?" Ariella asked.

Morelli shook himself loose from the grip the experience was having upon his physical body and peered back into the chapel. After a full minute of silence, he staggered away from the opening, unable to go on.

Leo watched Morelli with concern, waiting for his friend to regain his strength, when, without warning, Father Leo suddenly found himself seized with the ability to hear the archangels speaking within the chapel. Tears of joy began to stream down his face. The angel's voices were the most beautiful sound he had ever heard. Leo knew no choir in the world could stir such emotion. He inched closer to the opening and listened before speaking to the others.

"The fourth archangel is *Gabriel*," Leo said. "His name means *God is my strength*. He is known as the angel of resurrection and is the patron archangel of the clergy." The others gasped at the mention of his name, and the priests in the tunnel crossed themselves. He was considered by many to be the rock star of all angels. Gabriel had placed himself between the demons and those outside the chapel.

Leo felt himself losing control. His body was not responding, and he feared that he was on the verge of collapse. Gabriel turned and looked directly at him with an expression of understanding and kindness no human would ever be able to imitate. He fixed the priest with his unearthly eyes, giving him the strength to go on. Leo could no longer feel his body. He had been transported into another dimension, a dimension filled with joy. He was looking into the eyes of Gabriel, the very angel who had been present with Jesus at the Resurrection.

Leo wiped the sweat from his brow with the back of his hand. "The fifth archangel is *Raziel*, meaning *secret of God*. He knows all the secrets of the universe and how it operates. The sixth is *Uriel*, meaning *fire of God*. This angel illuminates situations and gives prophetic information and warnings to mortal men who are receptive to his messages."

Leo strained to hear the last of the archangels give his name. "The seventh archangel is *Raguel*," he said to the others, "which means *friend of God*. His chief role in heaven is to oversee all the other archangels and ensure they work together in harmony."

Leo stepped back from the opening on the verge of total collapse. In all their lives, these men of God could never have imagined in their wildest dreams that they would ever be blessed enough to be in the presence of an archangel, much less seven of them. Tears of joy streamed from everyone's eyes as they watched the scene before them.

The cardinal stood steadfast, surrounded by the seven archangels. He then shouted at the demon, forcing it to grow physically smaller. It had become quiet and was cowering in a corner of the chapel.

The cardinal advanced on the demon, the angels surrounding him. "In God's name, we command you to leave this holy place." He walked in a circle, spreading holy water and sanctifying the chapel. The winged demon, Agali-arept, recoiled even farther into the corner while the lesser demons shrank from the sight of the angels. The Devil's general began to shriek, his features contorting in obvious agony in the presence of so many powerful beings from heaven.

Lundahl now prayed to the angels surrounding him for their intervention, calling out their names in the order he had received them and asking for the demons to be cast out from the chapel. The lesser demons in the chapel were becoming transparent, as if they were slowly evaporating before the eyes of the cardinal. The black-robed figures literally floated through the walls, leaving only Satan's second in command to face the cardinal and the archangels.

The demon paced, flickering in and out of the earthly plane he had entered, swinging his monstrous head from side to side like a primitive beast, weighing his options. The hideous ancient tormentor of humanity summoned all his strength and called forth a burning wind that blew throughout the chapel.

The archangels grew brighter, causing the demon to shriek in apparent agony before he suddenly seemed to gain strength from an unseen source and grow in size again. The monstrous demon advanced once more from his corner, heading toward the cardinal and the archangels. He then lifted up into the air on outstretched red and black leathery wings, taking flight around the chapel, hissing and growling, his eyes changing from red to yellow and then to black before he landed in front of the wall by the altar. Behind the demon, a reddish pattern began to form on the stone of the chapel wall, spreading outward like bloody streams from a wounded river.

The cardinal felt the presence of Satan himself. He began to tremble but stood steadfast, refusing to let the demon see his fear. In an instant, the archangels formed a line between the cardinal and Satan's hissing and spitting general standing defiantly in front of the bloody apparition spreading across the wall behind him.

The angels seemed to be speaking to someone. They stood in front of the shrieking demon, their golden light emanating around them. Without warning, a brilliant white light filled the chapel, and a feeling of total peace flowed through those witnessing the event. It was as if God himself was present among them.

In an instant, the apparition forming on the wall withered from sight, and Agaliarept once again fled to a corner of the chapel. His eyes were hollow pools of darkness that gave no indication of emotion. He seemed trapped and abandoned as he gave up a final, pathetic howl—becoming nothing more than a misty shadow before finally fading from sight.

The terrible burning wind in the chapel abruptly stopped, and the red mist hanging in the air slowly disappeared. Only the defeated echo of the demon's final moments could be heard traveling underground through the tunnels. The archangels formed a circle and looked inward at one another, uttering words from an ancient language, while the brilliant white light illuminating the chapel began to fade, leaving the golden auras from the archangels to fill the space around them with an otherworldly glow.

The angelic visitation came to an end as suddenly as it began. All of the angels except for Gabriel slowly began to drift upward through the ceiling of the chapel, where they disappeared in a star-like burst of blue light too bright to look at. Leo shielded his eyes before looking at the ceiling in sad fascination, wishing they were still there, when he noticed Gabriel above him. "I have a message for you, Leo." Gabriel was speaking to him.

Leo was unable to respond. He could only listen and squint upward into the eyes of the dazzling winged figure of the angel above him. Gabriel spoke again. *"He who will heal the world will soon come, but for those who do not believe in Him, existence will be darker before that day arrives."*

Leo had just received a prophetic angelic message, one he knew was meant not just for him, but for the whole world. This was a sacred communication from God, and Leo was humbled that the archangel had entrusted it to him.

His message delivered, Gabriel drifted back toward the front of the chapel, where he touched the stone of the altar and gently caressed the cross on the wall with his glowing hand before looking upward and slowly disappearing from sight. All the archangels were gone. The sweet smell of roses was all that was left to remind those present of what had just occurred. They had blessed and sanctified the chapel, thus keeping the Devil's Bible forever beyond his reach. Leo knew in his heart that, even though he could not see them, the angels would always be close-by and that he could still talk to them in his prayers.

Cardinal Lundahl knelt down and retrieved the Devil's Bible from the floor, holding it at arm's length like a venomous snake that could strike him at any moment. He glanced back at Leo and Morelli, and with a grim look of determination, he turned to face the altar and began walking forward with the book. The cardinal walked slowly, his scarlet robes brushing the still-warm stone floor of the ancient chapel. When he had reached the end of the room, he gingerly placed the book on the altar below the carved cross on the wall and backed away.

The smell of rotting flesh again filled the room as the book smoldered and then erupted in flames. Blue, yellow, and red fire burned brightly on the altar until only ashes remained. For a brief moment, Leo saw the golden sword of Saint Michael hanging in the air before it slowly faded from sight and the smell of roses once again dominated the chapel.

They had all just seen a miracle. Even if no one ever believed them, everyone present knew that what they had just witnessed was evidence of God's presence in the world. What they had seen with their own eyes would remain in their hearts and affect the rest of their lives forever.

* * *

The skies above the city had cleared, and the demonic wind was gone. The people of Rome peered out from the protection of their shops, restaurants, and homes. The sudden vicious storm had been accompanied by howls heard throughout the city, filling thousands with the certainty that the end of the world was at hand. Many had suffered from a form of demonic possession, falling to the ground in twisted shapes, growling and speaking in ancient languages they had no knowledge of. As the darkness lifted, the people affected by the presence of the demons found themselves wandering aimlessly through the streets in a daze with no memory of what had happened to them. It was as if they had just awakened from a very bad dream, but when they tried to remember, the details were too horrible for their subconscious to recall.

Inside the Basilica, the throngs of people who had crowded together to be closer to God had felt his presence in the face of a terrible storm, the likes of which no one in Rome had ever seen before. They had fallen to their knees and prayed aloud behind the massive doors protecting them from the wind and flying debris outside. The pope himself had rushed from his quarters to the altar in Saint Peter's, where he had prayed for the salvation of mankind.

The drama of the miracle below Saint Peter's Basilica was still unknown to the rest of the world. None of Rome's citizens knew why the mysterious events that had occurred in and around the city ended as suddenly as they had begun. With the sun setting over the Eternal City, the bewildered mass of people who had gathered inside the colossal church began to flow outside into the square. Together, they walked out into the piazza toward the obelisk in the center, their eyes filled with wonder at the damage caused by the storm. Broken statues, glass, chairs, and other debris littered the ground around them, but despite the terror and damage caused by the storm, an unexplained sense of peace had settled over the city.

CHAPTER 49

Cardinal Lundahl staggered from the ancient chapel and collapsed into the outstretched arms of the priests and cardinals in the tunnel. His skin was pale—his breathing rapid and shallow.

"Shouldn't we be getting him to a hospital?" Leo asked.

"No," Morelli said. "He's totally exhausted. I've seen this before after exorcisms. We will take him to his apartment and let the Vatican doctor look after him. He needs spiritual as well as physical healing now."

"What about you, Father?" John said. "You took a pretty good hit on the head."

Morelli smiled and pointed to his head for the others to see. The gash was gone. It had disappeared when he was translating what the archangels were saying. With evidence of miracles all around them, they realized that God was now working openly among modern man to show his presence in the world, and only fools or those hopelessly lost to his words would fail to heed his message of love.

Alon and John helped the priests carry the cardinal's limp figure, snaking their way through the tunnel until they reached some ancient hand-hewn steps leading out of the catacombs to the grotto above.

John suddenly remembered the radio transmission they had received earlier from the yacht. "Do you think the rocket hit Jerusalem, Father Leo?"

"After what we just saw in the chapel, any miracle is possible, John."

Everyone was still in a state of detachment following the supernatural events of the past hour. Their expressions were vacant. The physical world around them was slowly coming back into focus as they concentrated on going through the motions of living. They were functioning in the present, but their minds were still filled with the angelic vision they had just witnessed. *Angels really did exist.*

They continued upward through a doorway and out of the dank necropolis into the fresh air of the grotto beneath the basilica. The Swiss Guards loyal to the cardinal were everywhere as Francois guided Leo and the others through the doorway. A crew of paramedics and security officers carefully lifted the cardinal and placed him on a stretcher. Surrounded now by the light and splendor of the marble crypt, Lundahl opened his eyes and looked at Morelli as if he had just awakened from a dream. "Did we succeed, Father?"

Morelli took his hand. "Yes, Your Eminence, you placed the unholy book on the altar, and it was destroyed. Nothing remains but ashes now."

"Good ... good. Has anything else happened in the world since we were down in the chapel?"

Leo glanced at Morelli but was met by a look that indicated the cardinal shouldn't be burdened with any further news at the moment. Paramedics lifted the stretcher and headed off toward the cardinal's apartment followed by an entourage of priests and other cardinals. The Vatican's chief of security trotted along, never leaving the cardinal's side, while Leo and the others struggled as they climbed the final series of polished steps into the Basilica.

The enormous open doors of the Basilica and the fresh breeze from outside beckoned the group toward the entrance. Their walk turned to a jog before they noticed the bronze pillars surrounding the main altar, causing them to stop with the knowledge that they could never leave this church without offering a prayer of thanks to God for His intervention in the chapel.

When they were finished with their prayers, everyone turned and ran outside where they breathed in the exquisite Roman air tinged with the aroma of spring flowers that bloomed in the Vatican gardens. Especially the roses.

Lev looked up into the fading sky and marveled at the stars that seemed to be switching on one by one in the growing darkness. "I have a strong feeling that Jerusalem is still intact and that somehow the rocket was stopped."

Leo shot John a glance. He then turned to the newly resurrected Father Morelli. "Is there somewhere we can find a television set and tune in to the news?"

Morelli was about to speak when Alon's radio crackled to life. "Alon, come in. This is the Carmela. Do you read us?" Alon grabbed the mike and keyed it. "Yes, Carmela, come in. We read you."

"Where are you?" It was Alex. "Is everyone alright? Did you complete your mission?"

Alon smiled at the others. "Yes, we're OK. Our mission was a success. Have you heard any news from Jerusalem?"

There was silence. Standing in the middle of Saint Peter's Square, they looked down at the ground in the gathering twilight listening for words to return through the air over the still radio. The tension was palpable—they all wondered if their worst fears had been realized. The sound of Alex's voice broke the stillness. "There's been a miracle in the Holy Land. The missile headed for Jerusalem disappeared over the city about half an hour ago."

Leo exhaled. Exactly the same time as the Devil's Bible burst into flames.

Shouts of relief filled the air as they all embraced one another. Alon broke into a huge grin and physically lifted John off the pavement, causing Ariella to shriek with laughter. People around them looked on in amusement as the group danced around, hugging and clapping each other on the back.

Alex's voice came back over the radio. "Gabriella was flying over the city when it happened. Her unit was scrambled from their base in Tel Aviv, and when their helicopters arrived on the outskirts of Jerusalem, the incoming warhead just vanished in midair. They all saw the image of a giant golden sword appear in the sky overhead ... it lit up the whole city before it slowly faded away."

The group was hushed as they realized that two miracles had occurred on this day. It was a jubilant moment worthy of celebration. The Devil's Bible had finally been destroyed, and Jerusalem had been spared a nuclear holocaust.

Houston hadn't been so lucky. If they had been looking at a giant celestial scoreboard, it would have read God 3, Satan 1. Leo thought about the message that had been delivered to him by Gabriel. Men were still in possession of weapons of immense power, and he was not naïve enough to think that, in the realm of geopolitical affairs, the attack on Houston would go unanswered.

He knew that, even now, plans were being made by some in the United States to exact revenge on those they believed not only planned and committed the act, but also on those who sponsored it. That could mean a mindless nuclear attack on a city filled with people who did not share the vision of radical Islam and had no knowledge of what the evil attackers had planned. God had protected His holy city, but the world was still at risk.

Leo looked around at the other members of the team. They had been through so much together since they all met, and he feared they would face even darker days ahead. He looked forward to the day when man would not have to keep score between good and evil and wondered if mankind was truly living in a time when only God's intervention could save the world. Globally, people would have to someday throw off the shackles of nationalism and religious radicalism. They would have to come together without the presence of misguided super elders telling them what to do and who to hate.

Morelli broke the silence. "We need to get something to eat and drink. In my case, the drink comes first."

Leo had already forgiven Morelli for making him believe he was dead, but he couldn't resist one final jab at him now as he put his arm around the shoulder of his old, dear friend. "You've read my mind, Anthony. But since you died and left all your money to me, I'll buy dinner tonight."

The others roared with laughter as Morelli stood there speechless, his eyes squinting at Leo. Their laughter had barely died down when Morelli's red BMW sped up beside them. "My car!"

"No, my car," Leo said, enjoying the moment.

Morelli peered into the car after it screeched to a stop. "Is that you, Moshe?"

"Father Morelli? I thought you were—"

"It's a long story. What are you doing here with my car?"

"I've got to get back to the yacht. Our van was damaged in the storm, so Arnolfo told me to take this car and leave it at the dock. I didn't know it was yours."

"That's OK. It's all for a good cause. I'll pick it up later."

Lev rushed over to the passenger side and jumped in. "I'm coming with you. I need to get back to the boat and call home to see if everything is alright at the villa." Lev looked over the group. "When will you all be coming back to the yacht?"

"As soon as we have a few drinks and a bite to eat," Leo said. "Don't worry, we'll keep an eye on Ariella and make sure she gets home on time."

Lev laughed out loud. "Good luck with that."

Ariella threw her head forward and blew her father a kiss. "Bye, Daddy." With a wave from Moshe, the car sped off into the streets of Rome, headed for the harbor. The group turned and walked together out of the piazza through Bernini's columns onto the *Via della Conciliazione*. They strolled along the wide street to the *Castel Sant' Angelo*, where they stopped and stood for a moment, gazing up at the lighted statue of Michael the Archangel. They marveled at how they had actually seen this very real angel just a short time ago. It was surreal.

They continued to gaze up at the statue as small groups of people strolled by, going about their daily lives and not really understanding the mystical power that surrounded them. Leo pondered the miracle he had witnessed this day, knowing that sometime in the future, he would have to reach deep within himself to discover why he had been chosen to be a part of it.

Fittingly, they crossed the river Tiber over the *Ponte Sant' Angelo*, the bridge created by Bernini in the seventeenth century and lined with spectacular statues of angels sculpted by him. Leo never wanted to leave this wonderful city again. *Maybe he would transfer here someday.*

They headed down the *Via del Banco de Santo Spirto* to the piazza of the same name. It seemed like the entire populace of Rome was out in the streets, some cleaning and sweeping away the debris from the storm, while others simply walked about breathing in the warm air, their senses heightened to the fact that the scent of flowers was stronger than usual.

They found an open *trattoria* and sat together outside. Soon the waiter left a bottle of wine at their table and they were inhaling the aroma from their glasses as they took the first sips of their much-needed reward. Leo thought about making plans to return to the yacht, but the stillness and lack of motion at the moment was like a long, luxurious bath. The tension in their bodies slowly began to ebb as the wine took hold, and a warm glow descended over the group.

John and Ariella were busy talking a mile a minute to Morelli, regaling him with stories of their adventures in the Negev Desert.

"Amazing!" was all Father Anthony seemed capable of saying when hearing the details of Satan's underground cathedral and their escape from it.

Leo took a sip of his wine and eyed Morelli across the table. "Anthony, I need to know if you can answer a question about where the book was located in the cavern. Did you know it was encased under solid stone?"

"You were wondering how Father Bianchi was able to replace it there."

"Well, yes, we all were."

"Before he died, he told me that when he returned to Satan's cathedral under the desert, he placed the book on the translucent floor in the center of the room. He said the floor under the book immediately turned to blood and that the book sank from sight before the floor hardened again into a clear, black, gem-like surface, encasing the book several feet below. He knew this was Satan's way of protecting his Bible and felt that no one would be able to remove it again until either Satan or God allowed it to leave that place."

Ariella felt chills down her spine when he told them how the floor had turned to blood. "I still can't believe we were down in that horrible place, much less lived to tell about it."

John squeezed her hand and looked around the table. "I think the fact that we were singled out to be a part of all of this makes us the luckiest people on the planet right now."

Ariella smiled across the table. "Not lucky, John ... I think *blessed* would be a better choice of words. I guess we'll never know why we were chosen, but God definitely has something in mind for us in the future. Our lives have a clearly defined purpose now."

As the waiter approached the table to take their dinner order, Leo noticed the familiar face of the older security man as he materialized from the darkness of the piazza and headed straight for them

Arriving at their table, he nervously scanned the area around the restaurant before speaking. "Hello, Fathers. May I have a word with you?"

"Of course, Francois," Morelli said. "Pull up a chair and have some wine with us. Leo, meet Francois, the Vatican's chief of security and one of my best friends."

Leo had never known the name of this individual—he had always just thought of him as 'the older security man'. Father Leo had been slightly suspicious of this character, especially earlier when he had first met him standing next to the cardinal at Morelli's apartment, the same day he thought that his friend had died. Leo was relieved to see that this high-ranking officer in the Vatican Guard was in fact one of Morelli and Lundahl's closest allies.

Francois remained standing. "Thank you, Father. I don't have much time, and I'm afraid you don't either." This last sentence caught the group off guard and sent their nerves back on high alert.

Morelli sipped his wine as he looked up at the security chief. "What's going on, Francois?"

"Emilio has escaped our surveillance, and we don't know where he and some of his friends are now."

Leo and the others had completely forgotten about the evil little priest who grabbed the backpack in the tunnel while he was conspiring to have them all killed before they could reach the chapel.

Francois placed his hands on the back of an empty chair and looked around the table. "Until we have them in custody, I think it would be wise for all of you to leave Rome as soon as possible until we round them all up."

Leo looked down and smoothed the white tablecloth with his free hand. "Who are these people, Francois, and why would they still be interested in us?"

Morelli noticed Francois nervously eyeing the group. "Go ahead, Francois, you can tell them what we know about Emilio. They are certainly a part of all this now."

Francois relaxed slightly before speaking. "In short, gentlemen, Emilio and his followers are the evil ones we've been watching for some time."

"What exactly do you mean by the term *evil ones*?" Alon asked. "I mean … are they some kind of demonically possessed beings or something?"

"No, my friend, they're quite human. We've known for some time that the Church has been infiltrated by those who worship Satan instead of God. They've caused great harm to the Catholic Church. We've been gathering intelligence on them in an effort to see just how deeply they're embedded and who their leaders are."

"Are these the same people who've been working so hard to discredit the clergy in an effort to bring down the Church?" Leo asked.

Francois shook his head in agreement. "Exactly. We believe they were also tasked with obtaining the Devil's Bible and handing it over to the Antichrist when he makes his appearance as foretold in Revelation. They are his earthly soldiers and are committed to furthering his rise to power. We think they still believe you have the book and will stop at nothing until they have it in their possession. I'm afraid that, until they've been captured, you are all still in danger."

Ariella lifted her head from John's shoulder. "But the book burned to ashes on the altar in the chapel."

"We don't know for sure if they realize that yet, Miss. Emilio escaped, but we captured one of the men who was with him when he tried to flee the catacombs. Apparently, Emilio believes the book still exists. When he found that the backpack he grabbed from John was empty, he thought you were all making a trial run without it to see if you would be stopped. He thinks the book is in a different location with another member of your group and has gathered his men to search for it. The safest thing for now is to let me have some of my men drive all of you to your yacht so you can leave the country until we have them in custody."

Alon rolled his eyes at Francois. "These guys are all over the place. They aren't just here in Rome. They were spying on us at the villa in Israel, and they shot at us on the highway when we were driving to the harbor at Caesarea."

"That's why the safest place you can be right now is out at sea on your yacht. We've also been in contact with an Israeli warship off the coast in international waters ready to escort your boat back to Israel."

Alon stared at Francois with a newfound respect. The real Swiss security men really knew their stuff.

While they were still talking, a large black SUV pulled up alongside their table in the piazza, causing Alon to move his hand toward the gun under his shirt. Francois's policeman's mind immediately read his body language and quickly assured the group that the vehicle contained some of his men who would be transporting them to the yacht.

John stroked Ariella's hair before sitting up in his chair. "So much for a quiet drink and dinner." The exhausted group nodded their understanding and slowly rose from the table. John approached the SUV with Ariella and looked back at the others with a playful grin. "We call shotgun." Opening the front passenger door, he realized that the man already sitting there actually had a shotgun and was glaring back at him. John quickly gave him a sheepish look and closed the door.

Leo and the others piled into the SUV and looked out at Morelli, who was standing by the table as if he was the last one to be picked to play a game of kickball. "Aren't you coming, Anthony?"

Morelli walked over and took Leo by the arm. "I'm afraid not, Leo. My place is here. I'll be fine. Francois and his men are watching over all of us."

Right on cue, a second black SUV pulled up behind the first. Morelli hesitated. "We'll join up again after we get control of the situation. Besides, I need to go pick up my car."

"You mean *my* car." Leo was relentless. Morelli laughed knowing that this would be an ongoing thing for years to come. He grabbed a bottle of wine off the linen tablecloth and tossed the waiter some Euros before climbing into the backseat of the second SUV with Francois. Within minutes, the two vehicles were speeding off into the dark streets, one headed for the harbor, the other for the Vatican.

The SUV holding Leo's group raced out from the city center toward the harbor on the *Autostrada Roma Fiumicino*. Everyone except for the security men leaned back in their seats and began to relax when Lev's voice crackled over Alon's radio.

"Alon, do you read me? What's your location?"

"We're on our way, Lev. We should be there in less than thirty minutes."

"Change of plans. Right after we came onboard the yacht, a bunch of vehicles with guys in suits armed with guns drove up to the dock alongside the yacht. We're pulling away from the dock and out into the harbor as we speak."

Alon shouted to the driver of the SUV. "Are those your men?"

The driver appeared horrified. "We were trying to keep a low profile. They're not ours."

CHAPTER 50

The SUV increased its speed. Alon wanted to take the battle to the men on the dock who were now menacing his friends on the yacht. "Call for backup. We can take those guys out. No problem."

The driver was already on his cell phone, calling the headquarters of the Swiss Guard at Vatican City. He looked back over his shoulder at an agitated Alon. "Don't worry, sir. We have a team on the way along with the *carabinieri*." The *carabinieri* were the Italian military police distinguished by the bright red stripes running down the side of their trousers. They dealt with everything from major crime to speeding offenses.

Alon sat back in his seat, wishing he was more in control of the situation. He jumped as a frantic call blared into his earpiece. It was Daniel calling from Morelli's house south of the city. "Alon, do you read me? We're in trouble." Alon quickly hit the speak button and answered. "What is it Daniel?"

A chilling reply came back to him. "We're surrounded by Vatican security men with guns."

Alon's face took on a look of helpless panic as he yelled at the men in front. "Your men?"

"No, sir. We don't have anyone at that location."

From the backseat of the SUV, Alon glanced up and met the eyes of the driver in the mirror. He twirled his finger above his head as an indication to turn around and shouted for the driver to head south in the direction of Morelli's estate in the country. Alon keyed the mike. "They're not from the Vatican, Daniel. Stay put, and don't do anything unless you have to. You and Sarah hide somewhere until we get there, and stay off the radio unless it's an emergency."

Leo leaned over the front seat and spoke to the driver. "Do you know where Father Morelli's estate is?"

"Yes, sir. We do security sweeps of the property on a regular basis."

"How far is it from where we are now?"

The driver thought for a second. "It's about forty miles, Father. It will probably take about forty-five minutes to get there through this traffic and the narrow winding roads leading to the village."

Forty-five minutes was an eternity. Daniel and Sarah were surrounded by men with guns. Leo knew what these people were capable of if they found them. His leonine nature was expressing itself as he began to take charge. "Alon, let me speak to Lev on the yacht."

Alon immediately handed him the microphone.

Leo thought for a moment before he pushed the *talk* button. "Lev, come in. This is Leo."

"Go ahead, Leo," the reply came back. "We read you."

"Are you in open waters now?"

Lev and Alex traded looks on the bridge. "We're just passing the jetty into open water. What's on your mind?"

"Did you hear the call for help from Daniel?"

"Yes. Are you en route to them?"

"We're on the way, but it will take us some time to get there. It's located next to a small village through twisting, narrow mountain roads."

Lev looked back toward the harbor through the windows on the bridge. "I'll give the Italian police a call, but I doubt they have anyone in that area. It looks like they got the ones who came after us at the dock. The whole area is lit up with blue flashing lights."

Leo pressed his face against the side window of the speeding SUV, wondering what he could do. "Francois said there is an Israeli warship in the area. Can you give them a call?"

Lev instantly caught his meaning. "We understand, Leo. Give us the coordinates of Morelli's house." The Vatican security man in the front passenger seat overheard and immediately began retrieving data from their onboard GPS.

"Lev, are you ready for the numbers?"

"Go ahead. I'm ready."

Leo began reading off the GPS coordinates of the country estate as the SUV left the city behind and began to encounter thinner traffic. Determined to cut their drive time in half, the driver pegged the speedometer at one hundred ten miles per hour as the lights of Rome faded in their rearview mirrors.

CHAPTER 51

In the darkness of Morelli's enormous house, Daniel and Sarah had taken refuge in the twelfth-century medieval tower. Sarah had seen the cars coming from the highway before they turned up the long tree-lined driveway and came to a stop in front of the house next to the fountain.

She had called Daniel on the radio, alerting him to rush to the room at the top of the tower where they had an unobstructed view of the surrounding countryside. They had wisely chosen it as the perfect place to fend off armed intruders. The only entrance to the room was the small wooden trapdoor located on the floor in a corner.

The caretakers had left for the day, and no one else was around except for the men in suits now scouring the grounds with flashlights. Several of the men had entered the house and were going through it room by room, while others had fanned out and were looking around outside the house. Their search was hampered by Daniel's quick thinking. He had jammed a screwdriver into the main circuit breaker on his way to the tower and shorted out the ancient electrical system, throwing the palazzo-like residence into darkness.

Daniel grabbed his two radios and turned the volume down so as not to give away their position. Did these men even know they were here? If they weren't sure, they would know in time when they found the sabotaged electrical system. Daniel and Sarah had two automatic pistols, an Uzi submachine gun, and a shotgun. Anyone coming up through the trapdoor was in for a surprise.

Sarah peeped through the medieval slit in the thick wall. She had counted four small cars holding four men each. Sixteen against two. *What did they want?* She saw a short priest in the glare of one of the car's headlights as he stood in the circular driveway. He seemed to be giving orders to the other men as they spread out across the property. Within minutes, the search reached the bottom of the stairwell in the tower.

Sarah felt strangely disassociated from the scene below them. She had taken time off that afternoon and walked through the abandoned medieval village that had been turned into gardens by the Caetani family in 1921. The stone ruins were covered in vines and surrounded by lush vegetation and hundreds of flowers. A shallow, wide stream filled with slowly moving mountain water flowed through the remains of the village, and the rocks on the bottom were covered with moss, giving the crystal clear water a green background.

Sarah had wandered among the ruins and daydreamed as she sat by the stream, where she removed her shoes and dangled her feet in the cool water. This was truly a magical place, and images of living here forever had become imprinted in her mind.

The sound of voices below them shook her back to the reality of their situation. They could clearly hear the footsteps and low voices of men below moving upward through the tower. Daniel glanced out through the slit in the wall and was immediately struck with the beam of a bright light. *Did they see him?*

The sound of voices grew louder as the footsteps increased in speed on the stairs leading to the trap door. Sarah involuntarily moved away from the door as Daniel pointed the Uzi in that direction. *Trapped.* Sarah grabbed the shotgun and stood beside him, waiting for the inevitable. *Then silence.*

They listened for a moment, not daring to move. *No voices. No footsteps.* Had they given up and left? Daniel sided up to the slit in the wall and peered out. He could still make out all the cars in the driveway in the bright moonlight but could not see any of the men. He motioned for Sarah to stay where she was and slowly moved toward the trapdoor. Kneeling down, he placed his ear to the wooden floor. *Nothing.* It was eerily quiet. They had to be right below him, planning their next move.

Daniel backed away and stood next to Sarah. If they were going to make a move, it would be now. They were alone with no witnesses around and nothing to stop these men from getting to them. He knew they could defend themselves for a while, but the odds were not in their favor.

As if they had read his mind, a loud explosion rocked the tower as the trap door flew upward and shattered against one of the heavy wooden beams above. In a flash, a man jumped through the hole in the floor. Daniel fired a burst from the Uzi, knocking the man back against the wall. A second man was halfway through the opening when Sarah fired the shotgun. The man seemed to freeze for a moment before dropping back through the hole. Daniel threw another clip into the Uzi and aggressively advanced toward the hole while firing short bursts until he was directly overhead, looking down into the stairwell. A burst of automatic weapons fire spewed up from below, forcing him to retreat back against the wall with Sarah.

Bullets came ripping through the wooden floor, barely missing them as they crouched against the wall. It was only a matter of time now.

CHAPTER 52

A young Italian couple sat on an ancient stone wall overlooking the coast. They had driven their car to a scenic observation point overlooking the sea and were watching the surf crash below. The moon was full and reflected off two dots in the distance that grew in size and captured the young couple's attention. The moving dots continued to grow in size until two large gray helicopters loomed right in front of them and passed overhead, almost blowing them off the wall.

The helicopters hugged the treetops, racing inland toward preprogrammed GPS coordinates. The men inside wore night-vision goggles that made the hilly terrain of the countryside below appear painted in an iridescent green light.

Down on the highway leading to the isolated village, Leo and the others were speeding along the tight, narrow road in the black SUV en route to Morelli's house. They were still about ten minutes away when the two choppers passed overhead. Leo said a silent prayer. *Please let us be in time.* Off in the distance, they could see the glow of a fire. The men in the SUV exchanged glances. *Oh, God, they were too late.*

* * *

Daniel and Sarah had taken a bold step. They had known from the beginning that they were decoys. The only thing these men could be after was the backpack they had carried to throw off anyone trying to follow Leo and John to the Vatican. Luckily, Daniel had used the backpack to carry his radio gear into the tower, and it now rested in the corner beside them. He picked up two pieces of wood from the blasted trap door and placed them inside. They were about to play their trump card.

Bullets continued to fly up through the floor as he took a deep breath and ran forward in a zigzag pattern across the floor and threw the backpack down into the stairwell below.

Suddenly, the firing stopped. They could hear excited voices and footsteps running down the stairway inside the tower. Daniel pushed his eye against the slit in the stone wall, while Sarah kept the shotgun pointed directly at the hole in the floor. He saw the men standing in the circular driveway surrounding the short priest who now held the backpack.

The priest opened it and pulled out the pieces of wood before throwing it to the ground and glaring up at the tower. As he stood there, shaking with anger, his cell phone rang. Reluctantly, he answered it and began talking with someone. He clinched his fist and snapped the phone shut while screaming in fury and shouting orders to the men. Three of the men in suits grabbed something out of the trunk of one of the cars and ran toward the tower. *Now what?* Daniel wondered.

Within moments, he had his answer. The smell of gasoline preceded the smoke that began to drift up from below. The men hadn't gotten what they wanted and were now taking their revenge. He ran to the opening in the floor and stared in horror as flames enveloped the bottom of the tower and began to climb the wooden stairway. There was no way out. They were trapped in the top of a chimney.

The smoke grew thicker as Daniel peered out through the narrow slit. The men weren't leaving. They were standing in the driveway, watching the fire. *They wanted to watch them burn!*

Daniel had to think. The fire was raging closer, and the only way out was up. He searched the beams below the wooden roof and turned to face Sarah. "Lock your hands together, and give me a boost."

She understood immediately as he stepped into her intertwined fingers and pulled himself up into the rafters.

"Hand me the shotgun," he shouted through the smoke. She grabbed it and passed it up to him before he reached down with one strong arm and pulled her up beside him. Without waiting, he fired the shotgun into the old wooden shingles, blowing a hole in the roof.

Sarah looked into his eyes. "I'm afraid we're only delaying the inevitable." He paused to look at her. This was one brave girl. She hadn't flinched throughout this whole ordeal. "As long as we're alive, there's always hope. Maybe there's a pile of hay or something we can jump down into."

She smiled back at him as they climbed through the hole onto the sloping roof. Smoke poured from the opening beside them as they peered over the edge. The men below were watching. They were smiling. A rage boiled up in Daniel as he searched for a way out.

Suddenly, a loud noise filled the air as a fierce wind almost knocked them from their perch. A large gray helicopter with a blue Star of David on its side sped overhead and began circling above, while another flew in low and hovered over the circular driveway. The once-smiling men below began running in panic as ropes descended from the helicopter over the driveway and a team of Israeli commandos slid down to the ground while firing in all directions.

The fire was now flicking out of the hole in the roof and the smoke was burning their lungs. Above them, a line with two harnesses attached had been lowered from the first helicopter and was now dangling before them. Daniel strapped Sarah in and grabbed on before signaling the pilot. The helicopter lifted skyward as the roof of the tower became fully engulfed in flames and began to collapse. Daniel and Sarah held each other tightly as they flew over the treetops in the moonlight before finally being winched onboard.

Racing up the highway, the SUV containing Leo and the others turned into the driveway just in time to see the Israeli commandos chasing the men into the forest surrounding the house. Several of the men had made the mistake of trying to take on the Israelis and had opened fire on them with their automatic weapons before they were instantly dropped by three commandos.

Leo and the others leapt from their vehicle and ran to the clearing where the second helicopter was landing. Daniel and Sarah stepped out of the open door of the aircraft and were immediately embraced by their friends. They turned back to look at the burning tower and watched with sadness at the loss of such a historic structure and their former place of refuge. It had offered protection to men hundreds of years ago and had protected them tonight.

Luckily, with most of the wood inside the tower already burned, the fire had begun to die out, and the thick stone walls kept it from spreading to the rest of the house. A half-dozen commandos surrounded Leo and the others, while the security men who had survived were rounded up and herded back to the house to be handed over to the Italian police. Not wanting to explain their presence in Italy, or the six bodies on the ground, the Israelis handcuffed the remaining men together below the statue of the angel and headed for their chopper.

Daniel noticed that the short priest was not among them, but they had no time to search for him. In the distance, they heard the sound of sirens and saw a line of flashing blue lights coming up the narrow country road. The Israeli commander began motioning for the Bible Code Team to get onboard one of the helicopters, and after a few more high-fives, everyone jumped onboard and strapped themselves in. Both choppers then filled with grinning commandos before finally lifting off in the direction of the sea, while the Swiss Guard security men in the SUV stood guard over the men shackled together in the fountain under the angel and waited for the Italian police.

* * *

A mile up the road, a black limousine pulled to a stop. Within minutes, a short priest emerged from the brush and opened the door. Inside the limo, a young, handsome dark-haired man sat bathed in the blue glow from the screen of his laptop computer. He was impeccably dressed, as befitted one of the richest and most powerful men in Italy. He motioned for the priest to get in, and they slowly drove off into the night.

The priest looked nervously at the silent man next to him. "I'm sorry about the book, sir."

The normally warm and charismatic demeanor of the man changed. He looked up from his computer and stared at the priest with cold black eyes. The priest involuntarily recoiled and wondered if he should continue to speak. This was no ordinary man he was sitting next to, but someone chosen by Satan himself to protect his secrets here on earth.

"I didn't know until your phone call a few minutes ago that the book had been destroyed in the chapel," Emilio said. "When I discovered that the backpack I took from them in the catacombs was empty, I figured they had taken the real one containing the book to Morelli's house in the country."

The man continued to stare at him silently, totally unnerving the priest.

"Obviously, I was wrong. Is there anything else you wish me to do for you tonight, sir?"

The man switched his gaze back to his computer screen, giving the priest a reprieve from the otherworldly stare he had endured for the past few moments.

"Don't worry, Emilio. No harm has been done." He continued to gaze into the blue light emanating from his laptop.

The priest was taken by surprise. "But, sir, the book. There's nothing left of it but ashes now."

The man turned and gave the priest a sinister smile that was just as frightening as his most menacing glare. "I always have a backup plan." He hit a key on the keyboard, and a series of pages began running across the screen. Emilio stared at it in wonder. The writing and language were foreign to him.

"What is it, sir?"

"It's our Bible. Satan's book for the end of days. That Jesuit priest had it copied into a computer in Israel in case anything happened to it. I simply hacked into their database and retrieved it. We no longer have the power of the book itself, so let them have their rapture when the time comes. At least we still have the words, and they will remain safe with me until the time comes when our master arrives and we rule the world in Satan's name."

EPILOGUE

SIX MONTHS LATER

Lev and John relaxed on the rear deck of the Carmela while Ariella napped on the sofa in the rear salon. The yacht was tied up alongside its dock in Caesarea as the crew went about the daily ritual of scrubbing away the corrosive effects of the salt from the sea. On the flat-screen TV over the bar, the men watched the limited clean-up efforts that continued in and around Houston. The city was a shell of its former self, and the daily pictures that bounced off satellites to TV's around the globe showed that it had been reduced to a frontier-like existence.

Radioactivity was still high and would remain at lethal levels for years to come before rebuilding could safely begin. In Rome, the news of the pope's sudden death had stunned the world, and Catholics in every city on earth kept a close eye on the Vatican as the conclave of cardinals cast their votes for the next pontiff.

Lev lit a cigar and laid back in his deck chair. "Are you ready for the big day?"

John smiled back at his future father-in-law. "I'm as ready as I ever will be. I never knew so much planning could go into a wedding. Ariella is really excited."

Lev peered into the salon at the sleeping form of his daughter on one of the couches with Camp curled up at her feet. "She doesn't seem too excited right now."

"She's exhausted. I think she's been on the phone for two solid days now. All her friends here in Israel are coming, along with my family and friends from America. She wants to have the ceremony on the beach next to the villa."

"I thought she would choose the beach. Her mother and I were married there, and Ariella said it was one of your favorite places."

"I can't think of a more beautiful spot. By the way, Lev, thanks for the wedding gift."

Lev glanced sideways at John with a look of mock surprise. "What gift?"

"Ariella told me about it yesterday. I hear you're giving us a house."

"It's the house Ariella was raised in. We had just moved into the villa when her mother died, so most of her childhood memories of us as a family are in that little house. My wife designed it, you know. That's probably another reason Ariella has always held a special place in her heart for it. It's in a great location close to the sea and has the most beautiful garden on the property. I can't imagine anyone else ever living there. I hope you and Ariella will be as happy there as Carmela and I were." Lev looked over at John and winked. "It will be a great place to raise my grandchildren."

Laughter erupted above them as Father's Leo and Morelli came bouncing down the stairs from the top deck. Morelli flopped down in a deck chair, while Leo stood and looked out over the ancient harbor. The harbor at Caesarea had been built by Herod the Great at the site of an old Phoenician port in 22 BC and was dedicated to Caesar Augustus.

Leo and Morelli were in Israel for John and Ariella's wedding. They had both been hard at work beneath the Vatican for the past six months overseeing the construction of a new underground center surrounding the ancient chapel. The mysterious chapel was now considered one of the most holy places in the world.

In addition to spending time at the chapel, Leo had also been sifting through ancient scrolls in the Vatican library for hints of any ancient Christian sects who had once lived in Rome and who might have been led by a prophet. He believed that the people who constructed the ancient chapel and painted the images depicting future events must have been Christians inspired by God, and Leo hoped that someday the code would reveal their secret.

Sarah had returned to America and she and Daniel e-mailed daily. They would be seeing each other again for the first time in months at John and

Ariella's wedding. The wedding would be the perfect backdrop for a reunion of everyone who had participated in finding the Devil's Bible and delivering it to the chapel where the miracle of the angels had occurred.

Water continued to pour forth from the Negev Desert, and families were moving there from all over Israel to start farms as the government worked to harness the power of the water. Oil companies from around the globe were drilling for oil under contract from the Israeli government, and the country was now as rich as Saudi Arabia.

Moshe's wife, Hadar, called the men on the back deck to lunch, and soon, they were consuming turkey club sandwiches and drinking Cokes under the shade of the blue and white awning. The image of Saint Peter's Square filled the flat screen TV over the bar as the camera zoomed across the crowd and focused on the small, thin smokestack above the Sistine Chapel. The whole world watched in anticipation as white smoke began to pour into the crisp morning air. A new pope had been chosen.

The men watched intently as Saint Peter's Basilica came into view and the camera panned across the square showing thousands of Catholics standing in front of the huge church anxiously awaiting their first sight of the new Pope. The newscasters continued to debate which cardinal had been chosen—their cameras now focused on the polished wooden doors that opened out onto a balcony at the front of the church facing Saint Peter's Square. The doors opened, and after a brief pause, a cardinal dressed in red stepped out and looked over the crowd.

He adjusted his glasses and read from a sheet of paper. Speaking in Italian, he addressed the throng below with the news that a new pope had been named. Since the eleventh century, almost all newly elected popes had chosen to voluntarily give up their baptismal names and pick a new name. The crowd waited breathlessly. Their long wait was rewarded when a tall figure dressed in white and wearing the signature white skull cap of the pope walked through the doors and out onto the balcony. He blessed the crowd as the cardinal beside him announced his new name to the world. Cardinal Marcus Lundahl was now Pope Michael in honor of the archangel who had come to his aid in the fight against Satan.

A crewmember approached Father Morelli with a cell phone. "It's for you, Father."

After a brief exchange, a wide smile crossed Morelli's face as he thanked the caller and snapped the phone shut. Leo was still watching the proceedings at the Vatican on TV when Morelli tapped him on the shoulder.

Leo cast a casual look at Morelli and took a sip of his Coke. "What is it, Anthony? Don't you want to hear what Marcus … I mean, Pope Michael is about to say?"

"I'm glad you're sitting down, Father, because I have some news for you."

"For me? What is it?"

"That was Pope Michael's secretary on the phone. He wanted you to know that the new Pope's first official act was to name you as a Prince of the Church. You are now Cardinal Leopold Amodeo."

Leo was stunned. His hearing seemed to disappear momentarily while his friends congratulated him with hugs of joy. Lev took the Coke from Leo's hand and replaced it with a flute of the Carmela's finest champagne. Ariella sat up and yawned before noticing all the excitement and walked over to join John on the deck. When she heard the news, she threw her arms around Leo and told him how proud she was of him. She had gained a deep respect for this man, and over the past few months, he had become like a second father to her.

Leo paused and looked at Morelli. "But what about you, Anthony? All your work …"

"I was waiting for you to ask. I'm now a bishop and the new pope's personal assistant."

Leo tilted his glass in Morelli's direction. "Congratulations, my friend. You deserve even more."

A big grin crossed John's face. "Just think. A cardinal and a bishop at our wedding … what Catholic could wish for more?"

Ariella pinched him on the arm and reminded them that the new pope was about to speak on TV. They all gathered around the large screen and listened as Pope Michael looked out over the crowd and held his hands in the air. The multitude in the square grew silent with anticipation. Slowly and deliberately, the new pope began to speak.

"Today, we begin a new era of the Church. I have started by appointing several new cardinals and bishops who will lead us in the years to come in the fight against evil in the world. We will be meeting in the next few weeks to discuss what can be done in the face of a worsening world crisis. I have complete confidence that we, together with God's help, can convince leaders of other religions and nations to arrive at solutions that heretofore have not been considered by men in a world on the brink of some very dark days if we fail to act, and act swiftly. These are days that require men of action in the Church, and the soldiers of Christ will be called back to the field of battle. May God bless you and keep you safe in the days ahead."

With that short speech, the pope waved at the crowd below, and loud cheers went up in Saint Peter's Square. Leo turned away from the screen and took a long sip from his glass before he and Morelli exchanged looks. Both realized that they were the soldiers the pope had just referred to.

"This has been a day blessed in heaven," Leo said, "and I pray we'll have many more days ahead together. Here with all of you today, I feel like I'm with my true family."

Everyone raised their glasses in a toast as they let the meaning of the moment sink in. The true greatness of the occasion was not lost on anyone present.

Leo felt that he had to be alone for a moment and excused himself. Walking to the railing of the yacht, he felt the outline of the large golden cross under his shirt. At least now, as a cardinal, he could wear it proudly out in the open. The joy he felt on this day, along with the miracles he had witnessed months ago, had lifted his faith to new heights. His eyes narrowed as he scanned the Holy Land beyond the ancient harbor. The copy of the Devil's Bible on Daniel's computer had yet to be completely translated, and it would probably take years to discover what dark messages it might hold for the world. For now, that part of it would remain a mystery.

The Bible code was still their greatest source of information, and they would continue to study it for messages from God. It had led them to the Devil's Bible in the desert and the holy chapel under the Vatican where they encountered the archangels. Nothing would ever convince Cardinal Leo Amodeo that the code was anything other than the work of God.

The new cardinal inhaled the crisp fall air of the Holy Land. He knew that evil still flowed through the world like a river with many branches, and Gabriel's words echoed in his mind—words he had shared with Cardinal Lundahl before he and Morelli had left for Israel. The time would come when God would withhold his miracles until humans put aside their petty differences and came together. He sensed that the Antichrist would soon be in the world of men. The feeling was strong within him. Humanity had created fertile soil for the evil one to plant his seed, and time was running out.

Leo felt a hand on his shoulder and turned to see Lev standing behind him. "Care to take a little flight on my helicopter, Cardinal?"

"Where to?"

"I thought we'd hop over to Jerusalem for a while. There's something I want to show you."

"Why not. We have time. Let's go."

The two men ascended the steps to the yacht's helipad, where Nava was warming up the aircraft. They strapped themselves in and were soon skimming across the varied landscape of the Holy Land. After a brief flight, they found themselves at treetop level, hovering over a park in the center of Jerusalem. Nava circled once before bringing the small helicopter down in the middle of a wide green space.

Leo and Lev stepped out onto the grass and walked over to a beautiful fountain surrounded by sculptures of enormous bronze lions of different shapes and sizes, standing and lying around the perimeter of the pool.

"Where exactly are we?" Leo asked.

"We're in the middle of the historic Yemin Moshe district of Jerusalem, in Bloomfield Gardens. This is what I wanted to show you. It's the famous Lion Fountain. I thought you should see it before you return to Rome. To me, I think this fountain is a symbol of our group. The bronze lions here remind me of the Bible Code Team. God called his lions together for a reason, and we must stay united no matter where we are. There are other lions out there, you know. They are chosen ones too, and just like Sarah, they will find us."

A cool breeze ruffled the fading colored leaves that began to fall from the trees as Leo and Lev gazed up at the gigantic bronze lions. Just like the sculptures, they were frozen in action for now, but Leo knew that Lev was right and that, someday, God would call on them again. He would summon all of His lions.

Made in the USA
Lexington, KY
16 August 2012